All illustrations and artwork by the brilliant Sarené Lucyk

eVw Press

www.evwpress.com

E-mail: publish@evwpress.com

ISBN: 978-1-989159-095

First Edition

Dark School:

Path of the Neophyte

thank you Alexa
for your
paitience

Titles by Matti Silver

Dark School Series

Dark School

Mage World

Mage World

Burning Crusade

Renaissance

Other Titles

The Immortal Universe

This work is dedicated to my beloved Lady T. You have made me better than I ever imagined myself to be.

Special Thanks To:
Vito Andrews at eVw Press
Rodolfo Martinez from Shooting Star Press
and
Wes Watson for giving us "No days off!!!"
You are truly an inspiration. Thank you for all you've done and all you will be doing in the future.

WARNING

Do not read this book straight through from beginning to end! These pages contain many different adventures you can have as you study your newfound powers. From time to time, as you read along, you will be asked to make a choice.

The route you go in this work is a direct result of your choice. *You* are responsible for how this goes. After you make your choice, follow the instructions to see what will happen next.

Remember—you cannot go back. Think carefully before you make a move! One mistake could be your last.

To begin, answer these queries and begin your journey:

Have you ever been robbed or have a strong fear of precious items being stolen from you?
Turn to page 1

Have you recently lost someone close to you?
Turn to page 8

Are you focused on your career or making a living for yourself?
Turn to page 11

All That Remains

You enter your home; the door has been broken off its hinge. You had only just moved in weeks ago. All your belongings were still packaged making it easy for the thieves to carry them away.

Oh no, I've lost everything...

When the police arrive, you give them what little information you have. You know there is little they can do. The house was an inheritance from your great-uncle, the thieves even took the heirlooms he left behind. Being that you were so overwhelmed from managing his estate, you neglected to set up insurance. Now, you would have to start over.

With the officer's investigation concluded they inform you that should they find anything, they will give you a call. Now, alone by yourself in the dark the loss of your worldly possessions hits you full force.

What they didn't take they left in a mess. You begin to sort through the remains holding back tears.

They even took my clothes! I barely have food in the fridge...

You come to a bookshelf that has been cleared. Most of the books lay chaotically about the floor.

These were my uncles, you reflect, as you begin to pick them up lining them back in their former location. One book catches your eye; it has strange symbols etched into the cover but no discernable title.

You scan the surface to find an author's name or some indication as to its subject. You open the book, realizing that it is old. The pages are stiff and many have handwritten notes in the margins.

Intricate and sometimes crudely drawn symbols litter the inside. Most of the writing is cursive and worn. You try with little success to read the contents. You scan the pages closely, looking over arcane charts and diagrams plotting the courses of the stars. Your eyes fall over a page with clearer words and immediately your focus intensifies.

Of the Experiment Concerning Things Stolen, and How It Should Be Performed.

You read the entry... *This seems easy enough... This could lead me to the thief. Wait... Am I really going to believe superstitious nonsense?*

You think it over for a while, sitting alone in your now empty house.

Well, I've got nothing left to lose.

Search through the cellar, and to your surprise you find many of the necessary elements for the procedure:

i) A sieve

ii) A brass basin full of water

iii) Even a Green Laurel twig from the hedges outside

What was my uncle into?! You wonder as you carefully read over the instructions.

You fill the basin with water from a fountain in the backyard return to the house and begin the process.

As you spin the sieve with your left hand, you take the laurel twig in your right hand and turn the water in the opposite direction. Gradually, you release your influence and let the water go still.

You speak silently the incantation and focus your intentions into the bowl. The rage you feel dispels any doubt about the ritual's effects from your thoughts, and as the water calms a face began to materialize.

Without blinking you silently direct the water to show you his location.

I can't believe this works!!! I just need to see a little more.

Slowly, you arise from the trance with a location and a description.

To call the police turn to page 7

OR

To handle the problem yourself turn to page 4

I've Got You!

The directions leading you to the thief are etched into your mind. Your gazing into the water not only gave you a vision of your target, but also the textures and sensations that confirmed your position.

You catch him while he leaves his home and approach, controlling your anger and restraining your natural impulse to beat him to death with your bare hands.

"Hey! 719 Culver Crescent" you shout.

He freezes turning slowly, "Whatcha talkin' about?" he asks slightly nervous, reaching into his pocket.

"No need for that," you reply. "We've found you. It's over. We know you were wearing that denim jacket yesterday while you picked up your drugs at the corner of Dundas by the bar."

His face goes pale as you continue with your lies, "We also know you were an uninvited guest not too long ago and you took things... things that need to be returned. You have till tomorrow. Bring all the boxes back. Cops won't be involved but our people will be. Tomorrow everything gets returned or you won't survive my next visit."

An Unlikely Invitation

The next day your boxes are pilled neatly on the front lawn. Soon, everything is where it should have been, as if it were never taken.

What else is in that book? I've got to scan through and see if I can find...

"That book is only an introduction," came a small chirping voice. "In fact, it is very surprising that you got such a feat to work so perfectly."

You turn scanning the area for the source of the compliment.

"Up here sir," came the twittering speech.

A sparrow perched on your roof glides down toward you. Instinctively, you hold out your finger, still in awe of the situation and unsure of how to respond.

"If you follow my instructions, I can lead you to a school where you can learn to do more than just deal with miscreants."

Never having before spoken to a bird you formulate your response carefully.

"I… how are you talking?"

"I'm not actually a bird," the small creature responds, "only disguised as one. I'll lead you to the school. At midnight, perform the ritual you did to catch the thief, but this time focus your attention on me. It will become clear after that."

With that, the sparrow flies away.

Midnight

The swirling water slowly becomes still in the basin and as your focus deepens you make out the shape of the small sparrow. Gradually, the bird flies through a great forest and then to a gate. An inscription over the entrance reads:

Tantummodo Ingrediantur Dignis

The gate opens and you see the path in. Smiling, you grab the basin and rush outside. At once, you empty the vessel and watch as the water forms into the shape of the image. The open gate now rises before you and without hesitation you step through into a new destiny.

Turn to page 16

Make the Call

You leave an anonymous tip with a police receptionist. The next evening, the police arrive and take you to an apartment where you identify your possessions. With the thief arrested and your possessions set to be returned, you look again to the book with the ritual instructions.

Most of it is illegible and littered with many barbarous names and awkward symbols; some primitive, others geometrically precise. Worse still, the writing is worn and some pages are completely corrupted due to age.

Well, at least what I could read worked out for the best.

Your imagination drifts into a myriad of fantasies with what might have been contained within the tattered book.

I guess I'll never really know.

With a grateful thanks to your departed uncle, you head to your room for some sleep, allowing the fantasy to continue in your dreams.

You wake up on page 5

Painful Truth

You remain as your family departs. The sky goes dark from an overpass mirroring your emotion. Staring at the tombstone you reflect on what end we all must face.

So soon though? He was barely an adult.

Even in the hospital you believed he would pull through. His attitude was positive to the end. When he grew worse and the treatments began to fail, you knew there would be a miracle, some anomaly that would excuse him from the fate nature seemed to have chosen for him from the start.

I wasn't there. I should have stayed closer. Maybe I could have helped, somehow.

But no phenomena occurred. Everything happened exactly as it began. The sickness came, the sickness spread, his body was defeated. The happy ending everyone was so sure of was scrapped and now, with your family leaving, it's just you and the inevitable end.

But it's not over! I *found a way to see you again and to say a proper goodbye.*

At midnight when the cemetery was deserted you begin your work. You dig a small trench by the edge of the grave site, matched closely to the size of your forearm. Then you light a torch and slowly circle around the trench. With each lap you pour offerings into the trench: On your first circle around, a mixture of milk and honey; the second, some sweet wine; upon circling again, fresh water and finally, you sprinkle grains and white barley over the blend.

You recite an incantation and make promises of further offerings should a response follow. The wind ceases, chirping crickets fall silent.

Now I have your attention.

You open a Ziploc bag and pour blood over top of the trench, watching it mix with the drenched soil. You hear whisperings from all around you. Small frantic voices whose words you can barely make out.

I'm only looking for one of you...

Next, you take a large piece of freshly slaughtered beef out of the bag and set it ablaze with the torch, holding the flame over it and letting it burn the meat.

Spirits now rush the area unable to resist the offering. You watch them gorge themselves on the fumes from the bloody mixture, driving them away when they feed for too long. Finally, you notice your target approaching. Ferociously you drive away all the spirits with the torch leaving only one which you call to your side. Letting short moments pass you analyze the ghostly form and smile announcing yourself. The spirit consumes much of the sacrifice before responding.

"I'm sorry... I wasn't there. I wanted it to be both of us. We were both supposed to leave for the school together," you hold back tears unsure what to say next.

The spirit looks up, staring stoically, "*Go! Go forward,*" he commands.

"I honestly thought I would have developed enough ability to save you. That *we* would finish the work together..."

Now tears flow freely as the spirit consumes the last of the offering. Turning to leave, it gently disperses into a mist, "*call on me again... please.*"

The spirits retreat, the torch dies and a small sparrow lands on the gravestone.

"Are you satisfied?" it asks.

"I am," you reply.

"Follow after me," the sparrow instructs.

You follow to page 21

The Highest Bidder

"Do I have twenty-five? Twenty-five?"

A hand from the crowd raises without hesitation.

"Outstanding! Twenty-five," responds the auctioneer.

From the crowd two arms raise at once challenging for thirty. Before the auctioneer can respond, one of the pair shouts thirty-five.

"Thirty-five for a vintage 1825 Perrier-Jouet,"

The bidders continue as you watch from the sideline holding your emotions in reserve. *How is champagne worth so much*?! You ponder excitedly as the bidding persists.

You cannot believe how quickly your experiment unfolded. You gathered the materials, observed the hours and crafted your desire into a small object while carving a sigil. This initiated a series of fortunate events that led you to possess a large collection of old wines and champagne which in turn, brought you here.

With the bidding complete and all your items sold, you marvel at the increase in your net worth. You begin to plot out other ways to increase your now substantial fortune. Unnoticed by you, a guest approaches.

"You know, there is more you can do than just simply acquiring money," comes a musical voice.

You look up… turn to view the area… "Hello?"

"Up here."

You look up further, *Oh, a bird is talking to me.*

"I'm not actually a bird," it replies.

And it reads my mind!!!

"You don't have to shout," the tiny bird insists while gliding closer.

"I guess I was thinking that… loudly," you state.

The small bird responds by giving you instructions on how to reach a place to better your abilities. After passing the information, the bird suddenly flies away leaving you to ponder the bizarre results of encounter.

To follow the bird's advice, turn to page 27
To go home and try to forget this craziness turn to page 13

To Forget and Sleep

That night you rest, as financial stability lifts the typical burdens of life and casts you into an easeful tranquility earned by means of magical effort.

A deep fog surrounds your bed and voices emanate from the vapors. They promise you power, adventure, hidden knowledge and even romance. You slowly rise and the mist begins to surround you in the dark.

"Hello? This isn't normal. Is anyone there?"

The image of the magical sigil displayed before you, "This is *my* name. But I have many others known only to the worthy who summon me."

The mist thickens, trapping you in a dense darkness. You panic, unsure where you are or how to get your bearings you shout for help. A violent wind breaks your cries for help as a storm erupts. Lightning flashes reveal a swirling mass of shifting forms that have enclosed you.

It isn't smoke!!! What is this...?

The storm ceases as a ray of light pierces the darkness. A chariot made of fire pulled by stunning white horses raced overhead. Its driver, a radiant well-built man who seems to be clothed with light itself shouts, "I am the illuminator, maker of day, begetter of vision who banishes adversity and divides the ugly from the beautiful."

With your gaze fixed on this marvelous occurrence you fail to see a gigantic wave ready to sweep you away. You almost cry while you look up helplessly, the towering body of water ready to engulf your existence pours forward rapidly as you surrender to your fate.

Before the wave can touch you, it splits in two passing harmlessly by. A bridge of clear water connecting the two currents looms over top with a strange beast whose front is a horse and lower body of a fish.

What is it with these horses? you muse as the waster passes, leaving you alone as clawed hands emerge from beneath and begin to draw you back into the darkness. The voice also returns with a clear message, "*You play a dark game*! *You pay a dark price*!"

"NO!!!!"

You rise from your sleep. Unhurt, in bed, alone. You breathe heavily as you jump out of bed switching on every light in the house. Recovering from your nightmare, you scan your home hoping everything is safe.

"Fine… Fine… I'll do what the bird says."

To follow the bird's advice, turn to page 27

The Workroom

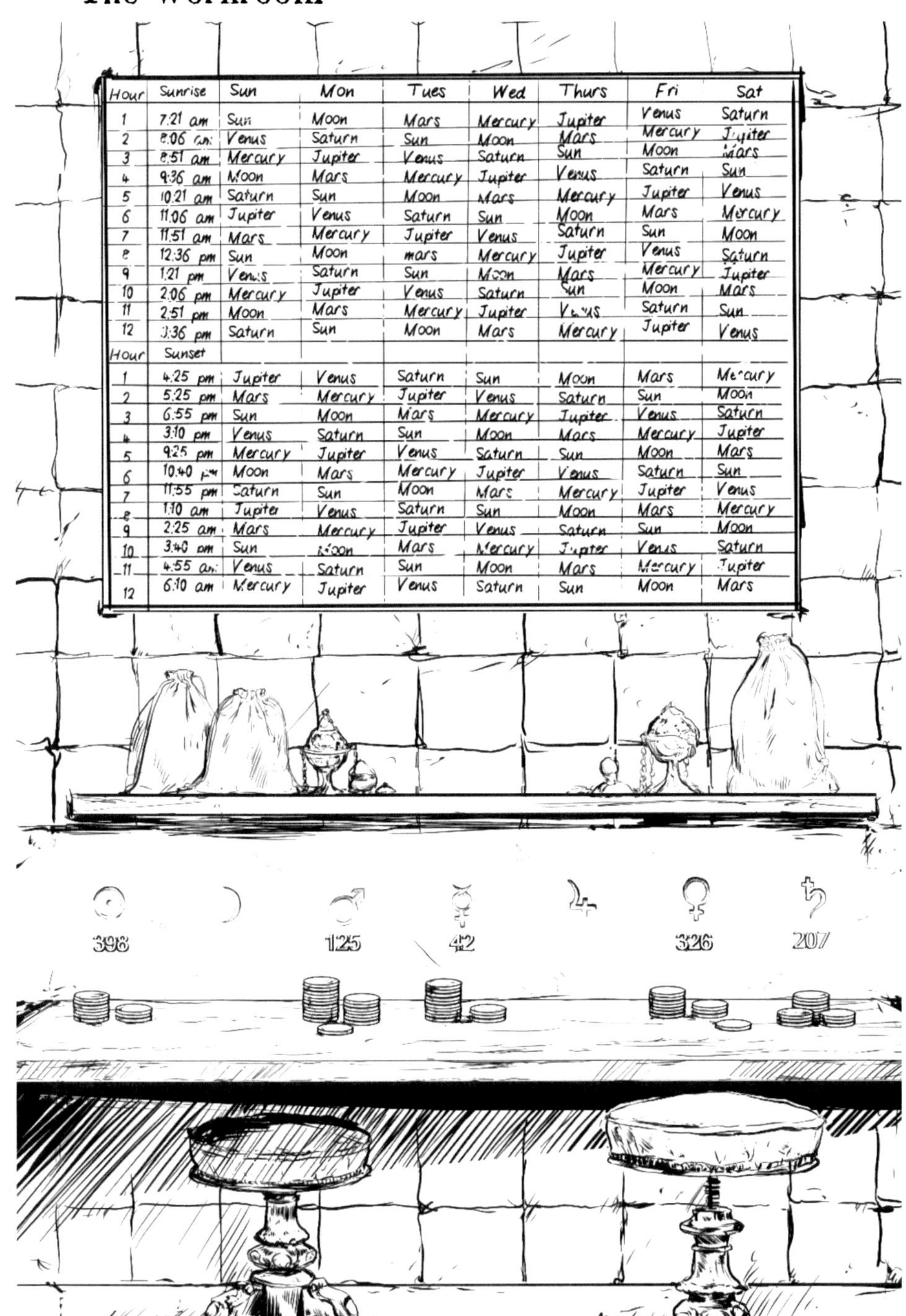

Hour	Sunrise	Sun	Mon	Tues	Wed	Thurs	Fri	Sat
1	7:21 am	Sun	Moon	Mars	Mercury	Jupiter	Venus	Saturn
2	8:06 am	Venus	Saturn	Sun	Moon	Mars	Mercury	Jupiter
3	8:51 am	Mercury	Jupiter	Venus	Saturn	Sun	Moon	Mars
4	9:36 am	Moon	Mars	Mercury	Jupiter	Venus	Saturn	Sun
5	10:21 am	Saturn	Sun	Moon	Mars	Mercury	Jupiter	Venus
6	11:06 am	Jupiter	Venus	Saturn	Sun	Moon	Mars	Mercury
7	11:51 am	Mars	Mercury	Jupiter	Venus	Saturn	Sun	Moon
8	12:36 pm	Sun	Moon	mars	Mercury	Jupiter	Venus	Saturn
9	1:21 pm	Venus	Saturn	Sun	Moon	Mars	Mercury	Jupiter
10	2:06 pm	Mercury	Jupiter	Venus	Saturn	Sun	Moon	Mars
11	2:51 pm	Moon	Mars	Mercury	Jupiter	Venus	Saturn	Sun
12	3:36 pm	Saturn	Sun	Moon	Mars	Mercury	Jupiter	Venus
Hour	Sunset							
1	4:25 pm	Jupiter	Venus	Saturn	Sun	Moon	Mars	Mercury
2	5:25 pm	Mars	Mercury	Jupiter	Venus	Saturn	Sun	Moon
3	6:55 pm	Sun	Moon	Mars	Mercury	Jupiter	Venus	Saturn
4	3:10 pm	Venus	Saturn	Sun	Moon	Mars	Mercury	Jupiter
5	9:25 pm	Mercury	Jupiter	Venus	Saturn	Sun	Moon	Mars
6	10:40 pm	Moon	Mars	Mercury	Jupiter	Venus	Saturn	Sun
7	11:55 pm	Saturn	Sun	Moon	Mars	Mercury	Jupiter	Venus
8	1:10 am	Jupiter	Venus	Saturn	Sun	Moon	Mars	Mercury
9	2:25 am	Mars	Mercury	Jupiter	Venus	Saturn	Sun	Moon
10	3:40 am	Sun	Moon	Mars	Mercury	Jupiter	Venus	Saturn
11	4:55 am	Venus	Saturn	Sun	Moon	Mars	Mercury	Jupiter
12	6:10 am	Mercury	Jupiter	Venus	Saturn	Sun	Moon	Mars

You're In

You notice many well-kept pathways that diverged in many directions. A large mansion on a hill in the distance looms over the heavily forested backdrop. A small sparrow swoops in distracting your observations.

"So, you made it in," it chirped.

Unsure still as to exactly what you should be doing, you listen intently to the instructions of your feathered friend.

"Remember, only the worthy can enter and only the strong can leave. Since you have some experience already, I'll guide you to the work room and where you can begin."

As the bird leads you through down the path you hear shuffling and chanting in the forest.

"Don't worry about the others. They are busy with their own operations," comments the sparrow.

After what seems like a short walk you are deep within the forest.

"If you want to survive many of the tools you will need can be created here. Talismans are a valuable instrument to control and bind spirits. Each planetary hour has a day and a metal where it is strongest. All of the instructions you will need are in this chamber."

You stop in front of a semi-ornate double doorway. Upon entering you see seven tables with metallic plates stacked on each and complex astrological charts displayed over the walls.

"Here is where I leave. Whatever you choose to do now is up to you. But the many races of spirits are manifested on this land, be sure to learn to use the talismans to bind them and learn quickly, or the spirits will bind you."

Distracted by the sheer complexity of the tables and not entirely sure what to do, you just stare at the materials set before you unable to comprehend the situation you're in.

Turn to page 15 to enter the workroom

Dark Eyes

Caz turns to you and his friend, "we will need power. Do we all agree?"

Nods of support from all present reassure him of his choice.

"Andras, what do you require of us?"

"Burn more incense and move it closer to the edge of the circle," declares the chilling voice.

The friend complies with the request and while he places the bowl of incense at the circle's rim, a sharp shadow grows out from the ground stabbing the friend in the hand, pinning him in place. An agonizing scream fills the cavern and before you and Caz can react, he is pulled out of the circle and into the darkness.

Blood is flung at the circle, breaking its boundary. Caz quickly moves to reaffirm the circles integrity. The shadow slashes out again, impaling Caz and pulling him beyond the circle. You hear the growling of a wolf as Caz's screams are silenced and more blood is cast over the circle. Turning to run you are stopped by a heavy sudden force that knocks you out.

In a dream you see a winged humanoid with an owl's head and a long-pointed sword. It has large, unblinking black eyes and is arguing with other voices and shadows present in the periphery of your dream state. You notice the creature fighting off other dark forms using its sword to violently suppress any attack.

"This one belongs to me! No others may have the body or soul of this mortal!"

You awaken with severe pains throughout your joints. You can hear foul whisperings throughout the cave that you did not hear before.

What happened? Where's Caz? What do I do now?

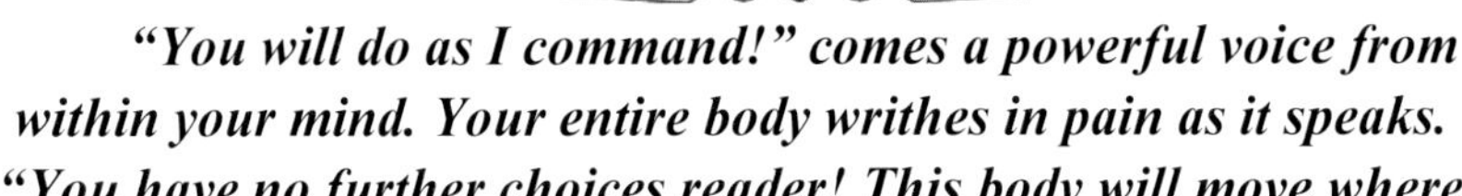

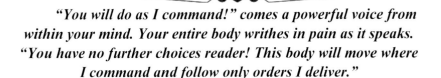

"You will do as I command!" comes a powerful voice from within your mind. Your entire body writhes in pain as it speaks. "You have no further choices reader! This body will move where I command and follow only orders I deliver."

Reader?!" you shout back, "What are you talking about!?"

As if this entire place wasn't weird enough; now you have a parasitic entity possessing you. Your body is forced into motion and with every step you take, you leave a fiery footprint behind you. You walk for weeks without sleep, driven onward under the demonic control of Andras.

Exhausted and without any will power, your body stumbles under his authority. You walk in a state of living death, for what seems like days. During your wanderings, a large horde of Sub-lunars fly overhead. You hear their dark chorus singing of freedoms now offered to their race.

"Come brother," they cry, "a great sacrifice has been made and we are being summoned away from here."

Following the trail of uncountable dark beings traversing the sky, you are taken to the gate where Andras tears himself out of your decrepit mortal frame. Falling to the ground you look up and see the gate you entered through.

"The words above this gate read, '*only the worthy may enter,*'" Andras tells you as it closes behind him. "You were never worthy of being here."

He flies off to some unknown destination leaving you to succumb to your wounds where you welcome the final release of your dark journey.

FIN

To Run or To Work

"I will guide you to the workroom," the sparrow instructs. "From there, you will craft your tools and begin the work."

At the doorway to the workroom, a thunderous roar reverberates throughout the area. Loud chanting and yelling can be heard as lightning flashes in the sky revealing the form of a flying dragon. The dragon roars loudly and lets loose a burst of flame engulfing a part of the forest and illuminating his form as he swoops by in search for more prey.

Two heads! You observe its diving as it releases another burst of flame.

"The students have been feuding," comments the sparrow. "they have bound the winged dragon from the quarry. I must see to this. Enter the workroom, find the nearest hour and begin."

Loud rhythmic chanting can be heard in the distance and a great rainstorm over the area of battle begins to extinguish the flames.

The workroom is full of interesting materials but to see a dragon and the powers that bind it are mind bending. You turn to walk through the doors when you are distracted by the loud roaring. Nearby you see a group of people running. They are close enough to catch up with. Questions are swarming in your mind and it would be nice to speak with another human.

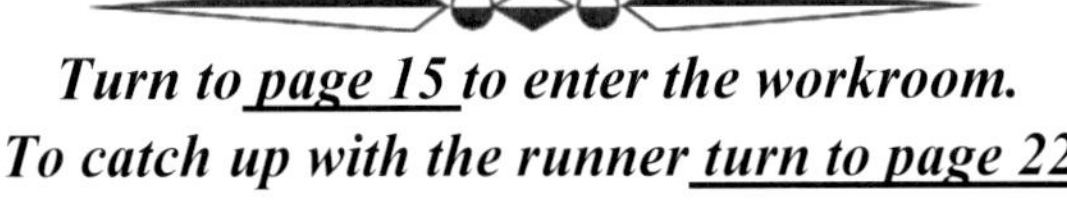

Turn to page 15 to enter the workroom.
To catch up with the runner turn to page 22

Investigate the Battles Edge

You rush to catch up and as you approach you hear someone yell, "we have to split up!"

Instantly, they break away from each other, running in opposite directions, "I'll meet you at the second days stronghold during the height of his hour!" states one of the runners, taking off into the distance.

You focus in on your target but are afraid to call out. He turns behind a large tree and ducks behind a thick root. In the moonlight you notice winged creatures scanning the forest, but they fly over quickly grumbling in a language unknown to you.

You approach slowly, "Hey," you whisper just loud enough to be heard. The hooded being turns with a knife in hand. You step back cautiously as he moves forward, "You're human right?"

"*Yes,*" you respond awkwardly.

"Oh nice, I'm Caz, *finally* someone else. It's getting rough out here."

"What's happening out there?" you ask hoping for an explanation.

"Well, it's been pretty dark these last few weeks. The witch took over the hearth and is not allowing access to the lunar sanctuary without tribute. Many of the students have begun to try to enslave the sub-lunars and the mansion is giving no word or instruction but has barred all access."

Okay, what the hell does any of that mean?

“We tried to bind the winged dragon that works at the quarry. We messed up big. We ran out of incense mid ritual, that thing almost killed us!”

“Why are you trying to catch a dragon?” you ask hoping for a clear response.

“We wanted to rush the mansion. If we can get at the resources from the mansion, we can improve our abilities tenfold, then we can escape… wait, you have no idea what’s going on? You are fresh to the game my man. Have you been to the workroom?”

“I was almost there…” you begin.

“No worries dude, before you start anything, we should really do something that is beyond important around here,” Caz stresses as you listen eagerly awaiting his response. He pauses, sheathing his knife in this cloak looking attentively overhead.

“…me and you, we need to take a bath…”

“You’re crazy! Sorry man, I don’t swing that way,” you state authoritatively as you return to the Workroom ***on page 15***

“Okay getting weird but I’m in. Nothing’s been normal so far,” you reply as you follow to ***page 81***

A List of Warnings

The shower ends and you dress. Feeling refreshed you get ready and wait for Caz. You regroup and begin to journey down a pathway leaving the baths.

"So, you wanted to know about the spirits," Caz replies. "Okay dude let me tell you this: they are all, without exception, bad. *Every single one.* Negative in every way. The worst thing you can do is attach yourself to *any* of them. They have names too after the planets for some reason. The ones from *Venus,* they basically seduce men. Not sure why but that's what they do. The one from *Mars,* they just want to kill everything. Ones from the Moon are all ghost-like I don't know much about them. The ones from Jupiter are alright. You can make deals with them. They have hidden tools and treasures. Here," Caz says stopping you, "look at these."

You see a group of life size human statues. The detail is incredible.

"They look amazing!" you state. "Were they built using magic?"

"Of course," Caz answers, "they used to be actual people."

You look at him perplexed silently begging for further information.

"Failed experiments from the laboratory. *Mercury,* they do crazy shit. Stuff you wouldn't believe. I saw some of them cart out one of these into the pile once. They call it a failed transmutation."

You reflect on the brutal nature of this place and wonder why you so willingly entered this school. After a short while you and Caz continue towards a destination still unknown to you.

"Are there any other planetary spirits?"

"Oh yeah," Caz says, still a little disturbed by the dump site of petrified human remains. "The *Solars,* have a huge temple. I've been there once. It was too bright to enter and I almost went blind trying. I've never been able to find my way back to it again. There is *Saturn,* I don't know anything about them but I'm sure they are horrible. There are also Sub-lunars. But that's just a fancy word for demons. That makes them incredibly dangerous, but we need to bind a powerful Sub-lunar to get a strong enough force to break out of here. Me and the boys found where they keep them. We will head there and bind one and use it against this place."

"How does binding such powerful beings actually work?" you ask.

"See this knife?" Caz begins only to be interrupted by the next encounter.

Moving through a forest you notice a deep settled mist and a graveyard almost hidden from sight. The mist begins to take form as you look closer realizing that here the dead have no rest. You stop in shock as you hear them wail for lost loved ones, failed ambitions and memories of a time long passed.

"We better go," Caz says.

"Caz, these are not planet spirits or demons they are human, or were human," you comment. "This place is terrifying enough. Imagine being trapped here *and* dead. Can't we try and help them?"

To try and help the dead move to page 33

"Bro listen up," Caz explains. "There is nothing we can do. This will be us if we wait too long here. We have my friend waiting for us, remember?" Caz states urging you to follow him ***to page 47***

Bargain

C'mon guys really? I've seen you do the impossible. This cannot be the end. We worked so well together, we're friends. Let's get back to what we were. We always made the most interesting and useful things happens. How can this suffering be useful?

The Mercurials continue their experiments. They cannot hear you.

I've was valuable from the beginning or else, why would you have invited me into the lab? I've got the talent! And we work best together. I can work strongest outside your hours where you are weakest. If you let me out of this, turn me back into what I was, I can work for you.

Before me, this laboratory ran at half capacity at best. I can carry on strong where you guys are limited by the hours. Together we can surpass this and make your race the strongest. You're telepathic, you must hear this.

Think about it...

You see your situation clearly now. What you were will never be again. Stripped of your body your powers are shattered.

Turn to page 92

To Pierce the Veil

"So, I find a thick forest where there is a heavy fog and move into its center. How do I even know where the center actually is? How specific do I have to be?" you wonder out loud as you stare at your woodland surrounding.

"I guess this is as good as it gets. I hope there are no serious predators around," you site nervously as you prepare for the rest of the operation.

It is really dark, you think, as you remove your cell phone and check the time. *Midnight.*

Okay, what's next... you remove a dark velvet cloth from your pocket and tie it around your head covering your eyes.

At first, it seems terrifying to be blindfolded in a dark unfamiliar forest at midnight by yourself. But you control your breathing and focus on your heartbeat. As everything slows, your fear is forgotten, replaced by the sound of your heart beating. You recall the instructions from the little bird...

"When you can clearly count your heartbeats and all distractions are banished from your mind... RUN in any direction while keeping track of your heartbeats..."

You move rapidly. Your hands outstretched, trying to avoid tree branches while you keep count of your pulse. As you gain confidence your movements become wilder while the count deepens.

150...200...300...450...780...900...

"When you reach 1000. *STOP."*

Out of breath and cooling down, you feel the hair on your arms stand on end. Slowly, you remove your blind fold.

The forest is gone. Only a deep fog surrounds you. You walk into what looks like and endless limbo.

Okay... now I walk and when I find it...

You see a dim light ahead.

"There," you say softly as a smile breaks your face. Then following the last of the instructions, you place your thumb into your mouth and bite down.

The fog parts and you now stand on an open hill filled plain. A gigantic forest adorns the distance. You see sheep moving in a scattered flock.

Well, this is new...

As you approach, one of the lambs looks up and you notice three eyes opening to stare back at you. Gasping in surprise, you startle the creature which runs back to the herd.

A flute plays a beautiful melody that draws the sheep to its source. You see a stunning silhouette, of a gorgeous woman in the distance. As you move closer you notice her long flowing hair and a pair of horns protruding from her head.

"You know what, I'm gonna pass."

You continue to walk forward not exactly sure where you are supposed to go. Overhead, vaporous trails form and you can hear them whispering to one another.

"Ugh... Hello?" unsure how to address the soaring bodies of mist, "Any chance you could direct me to reach... ugh... anything nearby?"

The vapors slow, then swoop down around you and begin to speak in a seething tone, "You smell like an apprentice. We are gathering herbs for the mistress who sent us. Follow close while our hour is erect and to the gateway our trail will direct."

Confused but unwilling to argue, you follow the talking smoke trails to a large gate with a Latin inscription over top of its entry:

Tantummodo Ingrediantur Dignis

Your misty companions encircle you with their promise complete, "From here you cross on your own, but beware the trap of the lunar crone."

They depart as quickly as they arrive and open the gate leaving your sight. You stare at the inscription trying to make sense of anything that just occurred.

"Okay, well yeah. Weird rhyming gas ghosts and three eyed sheep looks like Chernobyl's on the menu for breakfast."

You pass through the gate turning to page 16

Magnum Opus

"You've come so far," insists the Mercurial, "why stop now? After this you will be ready to engage in the first phase of the refining process. We've both invested all this effort: the stars and hours are aligned. If we stop now, this opportunity will be lost."

You quickly consume the tincture presented. It doesn't take long before you feel your mind's capacity expand while your thirst for understanding grows. With renewed strength, you absorb all the knowledge on the plants related to every hourly.

A season passes and you have consumed elixirs related to every planetary hour and even observed and experienced the essential nature of the spirits which they govern. With all this finished, the Mercurial instructing you calls the attention of the entire laboratory.

"Our friend has completed a vast and incredible study of the alchemical art. Now with his learning accomplished his being must be perfected."

Three boiling flasks are intricately presented on one of the wallboards where swarming alchemical formulas normally display the daily calculations. The first is black, next to it is a white one and the last is red.

"These are the three stages you will be going through young lord," continues the Mercurial, "once they are complete you will become a perfected being, needing no further change or alteration. Only someone with the prerequisite development can even begin to participate in this practice. This is the final phase to the great work."

Something about his statement resonates with you. It strikes you as odd how the Mercurials never cease their work, yet for this, they were all still. Their normally focused demeanor now one of eagerness.

"This," announces the Mercurial holding up a flask that matches the black one on the board, "will cause the putrefaction and decomposition of all your accumulated knowledge. It will leave a void that will allow you to stretch past your normal mental and physical parameters."

He hands you the flask. It is strange to the touch; neither hot nor cold but always fluctuating in temperature. Steam does not arise from the opening but instead is constantly being pulled inwards.

This is it? Decompose all my knowledge? I've been working for over six months nonstop with absolutely no sleep. I am perhaps more advanced than any human will ever be. Still, how much more can a person know? What could be left...?

With these final, thoughts, you drink from the flask.

Silence... The Mercurials are silent. You begin to sweat profusely.

Your mind struggles to hold onto your thoughts, which are now slipping from your memory. The laboratory which had been your home for almost a year becomes unfamiliar.

No! What's happening!?! I can't speak. What is going on?!

Through the pores in your skin a hard substance begins to exude, causing immense pain. You open your mouth to scream, but no sound emerges. The substance hardens further preventing any movement. You struggle against the petrification, but even with all your strength, the rigidity overcomes you as your body slowly turns to stone.

Help!!! Brothers, why are you doing this? What is this...? Why can't I remember...?

Mental confusion sets in as your energy leaves your mortal being. What little soul you have left soon follows. Your cries for help continue as your memory declines and soon, screams of pain are all that remain.

In the laboratory, the Mercurials seamlessly resume their work. You linger as a stone statue cemented in a standing hunched position.

Do not lose hope. The work is incomplete.
Read on at page 67.

Dead Vault

Looking back at you Caz's face is flushed with guilt and annoyance.

"Look," he says, "I don't know how to exorcise the dead."

"They are right here," you counter. "Let me try and talk to them."

He shakes his head in disbelief, unsure how to even respond. He waves his hand dismissively, "do what you got to do."

At first it seems impossible to distract the ghosts from their repetitive wailings and motions. They move in sequence, unchanging no matter how hard you try to distract them or draw their attention from their spectral routine. Caz, hoping you are satisfied, is ready to leave and urges you to follow.

"Wait," comes a torn pain, filled voice. "Do you really mean to help us?"

"Yes!" you reply excited. "Who are you?"

"We are the students from a generation ago," one replies. "We fought a war against the previous master and were punished by being bound here. But it was so long ago now. Our families have passed on without us and our children's children have forgotten our existence. Please, set us free."

You look to Caz unsure of exactly what to do next. He shrugs having never dealt with this circumstance.

"How do we get you guys out of here?" you ask.

"First, tell your friend to make a circle around you two. Enclose one of the gravestones within with you."

Following his instruction, the ghosts are now gathering closer, they have crowded around your position.

"We will need a small amount of living blood to be relinked into the physical world, so that we may pass through out of our binding."

"How much blood do you need?" you ask.

"Just a drop of blood," claims the ghost. "on the stone. Through it we will be balanced, life with death and death with life and the normal cycle of nature will take us away from here."

Shrugging, Caz pricks his finger and places it on the stone. The ghosts fade from sight. Even the mist departs.

"Well, it looks like that worked out well," you announce. "Caz? Caz…?"

Not moving, he remains cemented in position with his finger adhered in place. You move closer trying to get your friend's attention. Caz moves faster than your eyes can detect. You feel a pain in your throat and your air supply is cut off and you feel the warmth of your own blood pouring down your chest.

Unable to properly react you drop to your knees and as your life fades you see the ghosts clearly. They are holding Caz in place. He looks terrified. They spread your blood over the gravesite and each ghost individually passes through your open throat into your body then uses your blood to reanimate their physical forms. Soon, a small group of naked people are in their own bodies for the first time in over a hundred years.

"We have it now," exclaimed one of the men. "We are free. The gate! head for the gate!"

They take off running. You see them rushing towards the large iron gate you entered in from.

I don't remember that being there. Were we so close to the entrance all this time?

It opens and you watch them rush through. They run farther and farther away, but you still see them clearly.

Hey Caz, why am I still able to see…?

Turning your head, you see your fallen corpse drained of blood and Caz standing before your lifeless body.

"I'm sorry buddy. I didn't know this would happen," he wails as he cries over your remains.

Now, with the full weight of what has occurred setting in, you crouch by the gravestone wrapping your arms around your knees in a tucked position and watch the formerly dead magicians, run naked in the distance. Observing your first sunrise since the extinction of your own mortality, you see their bodies burn up in the sunrise and disintegrate. Not long afterwards you hear the familiar lament from the now returned ghosts now filling the area.

Their escape thwarted, the ghosts return to their prison, with a new victim now trapped alongside them. So, entrapped within their own pain none of the betrayers take notice of you, the one consolation of this disturbing afterlife is that it would not haunt you alone.

FIN

Talismanic Instruction

"A talisman, like the one you currently hold is very much like a personal contact with a certain group of entities. The metals and incense used in creating them are pleasing to us and make it more compelling to answer the caller. The hourly times when you create and use these devices are strongest only at certain times during the day, when our realms overlap with the physical world."

The Mercurial rests a moment to let it all sink in.

"In order to surpass these limitations, you must bind the spirit. This works best when you work alongside us to achieve common goals. There are seven hourly realms to draw from. Now, through various transmutations we create the metals for the talismans. If you like, I can offer them to you now *and* help you engrave and activate them."

To create a Venerean talisman, turn to page 327
To gain instruction on the creation of Solar talismans continue to page 399
To create another Mercurial talisman, move to page 55

Anger

They taught me to transmute metals and produce all kinds of amazing phenomena. I was one of them. How could they do this to me?!

Your skeleton remains slouched on the apparatus, like a dead king permanently cemented to his throne, forever clinging to the great power he once had. The Mercurials continue their work uninterrupted, performing their tasks; tasks which you participated in, operations you helped bring to life. Watching them, you think how could they just ignore you? They taught you everything. You learned alongside them, you always considered them friends.

Get me out of this!!! Change me back! I never asked for this...

No response. They go about their daily tasks as if you had never existed. The profound effect their teachings had on you was clearly not reciprocal. Their nature and yours were totally separate. The Mercurials could never have the feelings that a human would and now, you will never be human again.

The liquid formula that is your being begins to boil and in your rage, you pound on the glass vessel. But you're not hitting anything. You have no body; you have no form. What you are now is only the memory of being corporeal. You perceive yourself to be fighting and yelling but you do nothing, because nothing is all you can do.

Get me out of here!!! Please...

You can make them an offer; they will listen to reason…
turn to page 26
"What will I do? I'm alone…
Turn to page 80

Confusion Under a Lunar Shade

You notice in the distance the rising smoke and follow it as a beacon of salvation.

Where there is smoke there are people. This may be a way out.

You run faster, gaining ground quickly and leaving behind anyone who may have been following. Leaving the forest, you see a well-crafted stone wall and a chimney venting steam.

It's a hearth. Something's cooking.

You move in cautiously and notice a hunched over old woman pouring components into a large cauldron and muttering to herself.

"Ugh… Miss? Hello," you state wearily.

Ignoring you she continually stirs her pot, muttering the entire time. Phantoms begin to materialize in the rising smoke, their gaseous bodies are almost unnoticeable, with only their soft breathy voices giving them away.

"Power to fuel, wisdom to prove the greatness of the Lunar crone cannot be moved."

Man, this place and the weirdness... "Hello? I'm just looking for a way out of here," you state feebly.

"They can speak in dreams you know," says the old woman without being distracted from her stirring.

A reflection catches your eye near the stone wall. You bend over and retrieve a small silver disk. It is plain and without flaws, as you examine the smooth surface only a loud ringing noise distracts you from your focus. The old woman violently strikes the pot, drawing your attention. The scowl on her face makes her anger clear. She draws a large scoop from her mysterious concoction and with the spoon outstretched moves towards you.

"You came to steal from me," she accuses.

"I…I didn't even know you lived here," you reply coyly.

"Well, I can tell you, they don't like the sacrifices very much. They say the *smell* is overpowering. But I think it sends a message to even a dumb thief, as I am sure you can understand."

Once again, she moves the full spoon in your direction. You notice right away fingers, an eye and some toes in the mix.

You turn to run, only to be chased by a horde of phantoms. They strike at you using their bodies like missiles. Terrified, you try to climb over the stone wall only to have one of the phantoms burst through, knocking you to the ground and scattering pieces of the once well-crafted barrier around you.

Stunned but uninjured you slowly begin to crawl away. After a short while, you manage to stand. Looking behind you see the old woman standing within the walls breach giving you a dour look before disappearing into a rising mist. You hear a mass of yelling and screeching from the distance as a stampede approaches in full force. Small, winged and sometimes horned creatures rush to the scene and begin repairing the stonewall with great haste.

They argue and bark orders at each other as they reassemble the wall. Upon completion they turn their attention toward you.

"You do not get to break what's not yours!"

As a pack they charge after you. You manage to barely outpace them as they chase you towards a familiar building, which you run into, slamming the door behind. The small creatures smash against the door and shout obscenities before leaving.

You notice you are back where you started, within the workroom. You see the many plates of various metals laid out on the table before you. You notice that the plates on the table and the one you "stole" from the old women are of the same fashion.

"Each one of these metals has instructions," you say aloud. "this one seems to be silver. I wonder if there are..."

Before you can finish you spot a scroll with information you are looking for:

The Fifth talisman of the Moon – It serveth to have answers in sleep. With it you may also defend against all phantoms of the night, and to summon the souls of the departed from Hades.

Engraving the figures and fumigating the talisman you decide to make use of it that very night. Laying on the ground under a cool moonlit night you drift into sleep.

Within a dream, strange creatures with odd, jagged forms dance around you, chanting a song in some unknown language. You can't tell if they have heads or feet, and they just repeatedly circle around you, contorting into various shapes as they revolve.

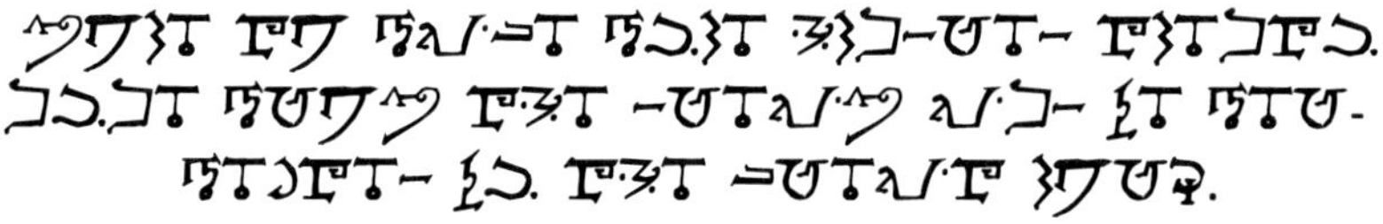

*****

You wake up unsure of what just happened or what you saw. It was something brought about by the talisman but it made no sense.

I guess this doesn't work, you think to yourself as you toss the talisman away and return to the work room on page 15

Quicksilver

A circular metal plate of mixed colors catches your eye. You notice that as you shift it in different angles a shimmering reflection catches the light casting a bright sparkle with veins of blue and purple streaming through its surface.

You carefully read the parchment notes. It is apparent that these notes are partial; clearly, they were taken from a larger manuscript. You search for the rest but find only directions for the construction of other talismans. Turning your attention back to your task you carefully read the instructions:

The Second Talisman of Mercury.

The Spirits herein written serve to bring to effect and to grant things which are contrary unto the order of Nature; and which are not contained under any other heading.

They easily give answer, but they can with difficulty be seen.

After a brief look at the directions and the hourly chart you conclude that it would be advantageous to start the work. You etch into the metal the designs shown on the page. Once completed you admire your work noting the simplicity of the pattern.

Now, I burn the cassia mastic and fumigate the metal...

The smoke rises engulfing the talisman. You follow the instructions for intoning the hourly name and after a short while let the fumes settle admiring your work.

“Move to the outside,” comes a voice from nearby. You look

trying to find any beings or birds. "The hour will wane soon and the operation fail. A hazel tree is nearby, follow the fumes."

The smoke from the censor violently darts out of the workroom, leaving a very clear trail that you quickly follow leading you to a large Hazel tree.

"Pluck a branch," directs the voice. "Make sure it is a good size. Then bury the talisman under the shade of the tree."

After doing this the voice instructs you to plant the branch on top, tightly packing the soil. You listen carefully to the final instructions and prepare to complete the operation.

Okay so face east and with both hands take hold of the branch and say the words..."

"Raditus, Polastrien, Terpandu, Ostrata, Pericatur, Ermas."

You pull upwards trying to uproot the branch and are surprised at how much of a struggle it is. Mustering more strength, you forcefully uproot the branch which to your surprise, comes up with a large four-wheeled open carriage made of molded vines and skillfully worked vegetation.

You notice the talisman laying on the carriage floor which you carefully climb into. Retrieving your talisman, unsure exactly how to work this new contraption, you look for a steering mechanism. Finding none, you take hold of the talisman again and give a command, "Alright, let's go."

The carriage effortlessly takes off towards an unknown destination.

I haven't understood anything so far. Why should this be different?

Enjoy the ride to page 44

The Laboratory

You arrive in front of an awkward structure with many openings for venting what you can only hope is steam. It was obviously a laboratory of some sort and as the steam discharged out of one vent you observe it transforming into flocks of birds. Out of another, the steam takes the shape of a raincloud whose drops form into winged children and armored knights battling one another. The illusions quickly disappear back into steam and you approach the entrance unsure what to find inside.

Within, plain looking men, many with medieval work aprons, are busy with operations of great complexity. The lab is massive and filled with equipment from the renaissance. You notice that each one of the laboratory workers has an open flask hanging out from their utility belts, that emitting a constant vaporous stream. From this stream emerged their bodies. They float throughout the lab barely stopping to acknowledge your entrance. Multifaceted furnaces and large complex alembics with drip faucets distill unknown liquids. While the fires burn and the floating workmen maintain many different athanors, a slender, comely youth, with a pair of dark blue goggles and a robe that seems to change color floats towards you.

"You made it just in time," he comments. "The hour is still strong. Welcome to the Mercurial laboratory."

Puzzled, your expression begs for more of an explanation.

"In this lab we cause simultaneous changes to occur with the material we are working with. We break down everything that passes through here into its essence and then release its proper potential. By this we can transmute base metals into gold or cause diverse phenomena, even to the point of defying natural law."

He guides you over to a large flask with three compartments, "this is a pelican distillation apparatus," states the Mercurial.

You watch as the lowest section boils while the steaming evaporation continuously passes through the three openings gathering into the second compartment. Looking closely, you see the steam shifting colors from light to a dark reddish hue. When it turns to its darkest red it immediately takes shape into a fiery bird and flies gracefully within the compartment, only to burn up and return to the lighter tone and dematerialize into vapor once again. The top of the apparatus has a long diagonally downward facing tube that would extract a single drop from the fire birds flight, collecting it into a beaker just below.

"A spagyric essence of high-quality regrowth," commented the Mercurial. "If a section of any forest or property is destroyed, apply *this* during the hour of Sol, Mercury or during a day where the moon is set to be in its full phase and it will seek out and repair injured or broken material."

Taking a single drop on his finger he lets it fall to the floor where an explosion of red vapor spreads through the room. Instantly the vapor compacts tightly and rise as a burning phoenix. It circles the lab and exits through a vent.

"That should be able to undo any damage done to the property. As an aside, it also multiplies ores and refills mines. So, what can we do for you young Master?" asks the Mercurial eagerly.

Unsure how to respond but unwilling to leave without seeing more, you ask, "What are you offering?"

"We could teach you about talismans, make you the metals and aid you in carving more of them," on page 36

"Instruct you in the ways of alchemical transmutation" on page 61

"On page 55 expand your knowledge of our spiritual race and of all things in general with another Mercurial talisman."

The River

You and Caz move on leaving behind the disoriented souls with the pain they carry. A flood of guilt drowns you as you hear the torture slowly diminish behind you. Eventually, you let go of what you cannot control and focus on the task at hand.

"We need to make it to the river," Caz insists. "From there the cave is downstream. There is a raft and we would have done this before but we thought the winged dragon would have been a quicker way out. We should have just stuck with the plan," he reminisces.

In the distance you see a thick, rising cloud of smoke bending in the wind.

"Caz! Look!" you state. "Are those your friends?"

He looks up, surprised, "I highly doubt it. We would never draw that much attention to ourselves."

"It has to be someone," you respond, starting to rush towards the smokes source. "We should check it out."

"We need to keep moving," Caz contends as he urges you onwards down the page below

"Just a quick look," you reiterate. "Let's just see what's up," as you edge towards page 38

"No, we shouldn't," Caz insists "This place doesn't work the way you think it does. We need to get out of here. Please, I've lost so many friends already, let's just follow the plan and get out of here."

Seeing the pain rush over Caz's face, you comply with his request and continue forward until you reach a river. A small raft is waiting at the shore along with Caz's friend. Everyone greets happily and you are introduced to his companion.

"Okay I've scouted the way to the cave," says the friend. "this won't be easy. Many of the Sub-lunars have broken free and are claiming the territory by the river's edge. We sail through on the raft; we may need a circle. We'll all have to be alert."

Caz nods as you chime in, "Why are they laying claim to the river's edge?"

"Who knows why these things do what they do," the friend responds.

You board the raft and set sail down the smooth river. Evening begins to settle in and the dwellers by the shore have taken notice of you.

"Here they come," says Caz as he traces a circle around the three of you. From across the river awkward misshapen creatures line up on the shore. They have faces that look like dogs, donkeys, oxen and birds.

One at a time the Sub-lunars began to introduce themselves and their activities.

"I weaken the strength of the shoulders and cause them to

tremble; and I paralyze the nerves of the hands, and I break and bruise the bones of the neck and I suck out the marrow."

"I distort the hearts and minds of men."

"I create strife and wrongs in men's homes and send on them hard temper."

"I inspire partisanship in men, and delight in causing them to stumble."

"I inflict upon men fevers, irremediable and harmful."

"I separate wife from husband and bring about a grudge between them."

"I steal away men's minds, and change their hearts, making them toothless."

Caz shouts as you reach your destination and dock the raft climbing to shore.

"What the hell was that?" you ask. "Why are they so strange? If I was a super being, I wouldn't waste my time causing pain throughout the world."

"They're demons," Caz responds. "Our pain releases a certain hormone or energy or something. They feed off it."

You enter the cave, passing down a well worked stone stairway. Within, a small light illuminates a circle. Caz quickly traces over the circle as you and his friend step inside. Before you, a black mirror at eye level captures your focus. Caz sets the call; intoning names as his friend pulls some incense out and burns it within a small iron bowl.

"We need a spirit strong enough to pass the gate and take us out of here," asserts Caz.

A storm of voices rises from the darkness and red eyes open from within the mirror.

"Speak in a manner pleasing to us and appear in forms we can discern," shouts Caz. "We will offer you a great sacrifice once the deed is completed."

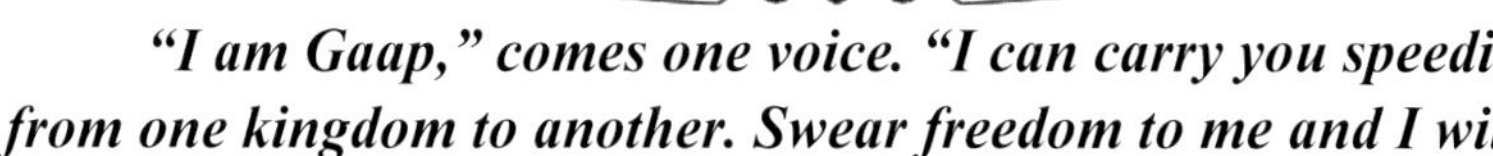

"I am Gaap," comes one voice. "I can carry you speedily from one kingdom to another. Swear freedom to me and I will take you wherever you should like to go."

"He lies!" a voice counters. "You need power to break the gate. I am Andras. I will give you what you need."

For Andras turn to page 18 or ignore him and carry on to the next page for Gaap.

"Yes Gaap!" Take us out of here," yells Caz. "We will not bind you for any further use. We only want to be free!"

"No!" you interrupt. "Take me where I can learn to be better."

"Are you crazy," Caz says, "this whole place is..."

"No Caz. You go your way. I have to go mine."

Gaap responds to your request, "To bring you to the mansion would draw attention to myself. I'll take you as far as the work-room. What you do from there is up to you."

"Deal," you agree as you are thrust to **page 15.**

To Be Free

You place your hand over the vibrating emanation emerging from the large beaker. It shifts and enwraps your fingers welcoming you gently as it spreads over your body. Once encased in the colorful vapor as if in a dream, you become weightless. Glancing behind you to ask for instruction from the Mercurials you notice you are being lifted into the air.

Without warning you look down and you are flying through the sky. Trying to move your arms to steady yourself sends you forward faster. The vapor that swept you up has fractured and formed into a flock of birds.

I have wings!!! Am I really a bird!?

Your transformation implants the avian nature into your being. Soaring through the sky is as natural as walking. Swooping through the trees you pass over a river and skim over the waters.

I'm in the lead, you realize as you notice the recently created flock trailing your movements.

Over top of hills and the dense forest you see the world from a whole new perspective. Your recent pains are forgotten as you survey the landscape below. Alongside you the flock continues to keep up. You execute every dive through the forest flawlessly. Noticing a group of magicians performing a ritual, you, along with the numerous winged companions plunge into the scene, interrupting their operation and leaving them disordered; unsure if this was of their doing or some awkward coincidence.

I'm getting a bit tired. Let's see if we can stop in the trees.

Approaching a branch, you gracefully slow setting up for a perfect landing. Before you can touch down, your legs evaporate along with the rest of your body.

You are drawn back to the laboratory where you reform on page 96 and prepare to experiment further with the Cauda Pavonis.

"This talisman will allow you to invoke spirits under the firmament. Typically, these will be of the Mercurial race, but as you make use of it more profoundly you will encounter other beings outside of our hour."

The Mercurial guides your hands in the engraving and the fumigations. Once completed, he brushes two fingers overtop of its surface causing it to glow lightly, after which he passes it to you.

"This talisman is made primarily but not exclusively, for communication, such as answering of simple questions pertaining to the physical world and the worlds beyond. However, keep your questions simple and ask sincerely or the spirits will flee from your presence and it will take stronger means to compel them to return."

The Mercurial smiles faintly as the coloring on his goggles shifts while he explains the deeper meaning of this talismanic operation.

"This is meant to give you a solid contact with the world of the hourlies. You will get to know their natures and they will get to know yours. We are not like the devices in your world. With us, you must form a relationship. By this communion you will partake in the secrets of creation and from there be able to command the forces of nature."

The Mercurial guides you out of the laboratory, "This one will work best in a quiet place," he instructs. "Remember, one question at a time. Wait for their response and listen carefully: not all answers are going to be clear because even *they* don't know everything. And remember don't be rude. The hour is yours, sir," he says with a bow and then returns to the lab, closing the door and leaving you alone on the path.

Looking down at the talisman, you observe the patterns engraved upon it: a five-pointed star surrounded by individual letters It seems unimpressive and plain. Unsure what to do next, you think aloud, "So what exactly happens now?"

"*You need answers to questions...*" says a rasping voice from above.

You scan your surroundings swiftly, trying to find the source.

"What the hell!? Where are you?"

"*We are above and around you,*" responds a voice with a lighter tone.

"Why can't I see you?" you ask trying to remember to keep calm.

"*Your eyes have not adjusted. Ask better questions, or we will depart and tell our brethren to resist your foolish calls.*"

He's right, you deliberate, trying to form proper questions, while uncertain as to what those might be. *This is going to be weird no matter what. I have to make this count.*

"Okay, why am I here? What is this place?"

"*This is the proving ground. This place has been built as a convergence between the worlds beyond and the Prime Materia. All who enter here will ascend."*

This answer leads you to further questions.

"What are you?"

A flood of whispering voices overwhelms your senses, making it impossible to understand their words. A single edified voice replies, seemingly offering a collective response, *"We are so numerous that should your mortal eyes gaze freely upon our presence, your world would be swallowed and your sanity compromised."*

"Why not just overtake the world then?" you demand. "What's with all the deception?"

"Our manifestation on the physical plane is determined by human intervention. The more meaningful our interactions become, the stronger our presence. Your kind give us sustenance and in turn we offer you power."

Your curiosity peaks at this remark, "What kind of power do you offer?"

"Our cooperation can result in heightened awareness, seeing beyond time, subverting the powers of nature, with the right spirit and correct operation, you will be able to accomplish virtually anything you can imagine. We do have limits, but rarely do mortal minds graze the border of possibility within their lifetime," replies a hoarse voice.

"What is the quickest way to becoming extremely powerful?"

"Power has many definitions, answers a voice, *"but I suppose like most mortals, you crave destructive power. For that, the Martial and Saturnite*

hours would be suitable. However, be aware that innate nature will not allow you to escape the damaging effects they have on the world.

Ask for instruction to create a Martial talisman on page 125

OR

Request direction on how to draw down the spirits of Saturn on page 207

(If these are of no interest carry on with further questions)

"Tell me about the different spirits. How many other types are there?"

"We do not have nearly enough time to give such details in their fullness, but we will give you an introduction on a few:

Our being is defined by the hours that give us entry to your world. You have learned a small measure of the hours Martial and Saturn and have already begun to see the glory that is Mercury. With us lies the ability to transmute base metals and the secret of the Philosopher's Stone. In ancient times it was us who bestowed this grace to mankind.

For the Venerean hours: forming friendships, for kindness and love. Their dominion over the minds of others will allow you to always be seen in a favorable light but be warned as the powers they grant can provoke madness. The Days and Hours of the Moon: these facilitate obtaining nocturnal visions, summoning spirits in sleep and for preparing anything relating to water.

Profoundly interested in how far you can take this, you deliberate your next move.

Inquire about creating your own Venerean talisman page 326

OR

Return to the lab and demand the philosopher's stone continue down the page.

An explosion distracts you. In the distance a great storm cloud arose and immediately pours hail and rain in the area.

"What is that?"

"The Witch. She has claimed the lunar dominion as her own and makes war with the current lord of the estate. Though she seems powerful she is merely a matchstick next to a torch. Her collaboration with the dead and the phantoms of the night has twisted her mind. She is blind to how powerless she really is. There are many on the estate who have turned to feuding."

To investigate this witch, turn to page 38

Carry on below to resume your conversation

"The hour is almost at its end, comes a voice, disrupting your interest.

"Okay, what else should I be aware of?"

"The sub-lunars are beings who need observe no hours. They can perform a myriad of tasks and in practical ways are usually more advanced than we hourlies," a stoic voice describes. *"Your kind calls them demons."*

An unexpected fear seizes you at this last comment. The reality of infernal creatures and the looming menace they afford brings terrifying images to your mind.

"Many great mortals have utilized them in constructing their legacies and cementing their hold on the natural world. You, however, will need access to many tools and consecration of a circle to begin to subdue them to your will."

"Where can I get these tools?" You persist, knowing the hour is at its conclusion.

"Follow the path to the mansion away from the pillar of smoke. If you are worthy it will allow you entrance. If not, you will be diverted."

Overloaded with information and unsure how to proceed, you direct one final question to the invisible voices above, "What would *you* say I do?"

"We are hardly a judge for mortals. Look to your attributes."

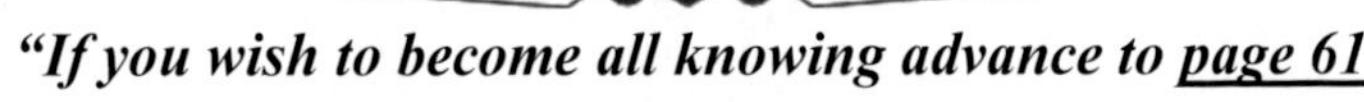

"If you wish to become all knowing advance to page 61

"To acquire heroic achievement, move on to page 125

"To understand the truth of your inner nature, turn to page 207

"In order to pursue a greater calling, proceed to page 398

To Know Too Much

Letting the hour expire you follow the voice's direction and approach the door to the laboratory. The doors open to your knocking and before you stands the Mercurial with the multi-colored goggles, who greets you cheerfully.

"I hear you guys have the Philosophers Stone," you ask, unsure exactly what that is and uncertain of what else to say.

"Yes! Well, we have everything we need for one right here," the Mercurial responds. "What you *mean* to say is, you want to learn alchemy."

He leads you back into the laboratory where everything is working in full force.

"You have to start learning with us for a while. If you succeed with this, then we can offer you a Philosopher's Stone."

Thinking it over, you nod in agreement.

"I'm in."

You begin you training and first learn the basic ingredients, the names of the equipment and the methods, distilling, extraction and recombination.

You practice for weeks, listening and following the directions of the Mercurials who work non-stop. After months of learning and assisting, you transmute your first metals for use in the work room.

"It looks like you have progressed well," the Mercurial announces. "We should move on to elixirs."

Proud of your achievements, you start to wonder about how long your studies have drawn out and question your Mercurial instructor about its duration.

"Oh," he says, obviously not expecting such a question, "I think it has been five months, and we are in day twenty-two. So, good job on keeping with the program," he adds enthusiastically.

"WHAT! How has it been that long? I don't even remember the last time I ate anything or slept."

"True," he interjects, "it's probably because you haven't done either of those things. You see, in a place like this with enough outworld concentration, the laws of nature are slowly morphed to accommodate for the accelerated change allowing us to exist in a more temporal realm…" the Mercurial halts his explanation noticing your perplexed expression. "Your natural behaviors are going to be suspended. Eating, sleeping, going to the bathroom, fatigue and things like that have been deferred."

You have never been without food or sleep for so long and now are concerned about your long-term health. The Mercurial, sensing the obvious pulls a small vial-like bottle from one of the shelves.

"*This* is an elixir," he says, showing you the small vial. "Adiantum capillus veneris: what you humans commonly call Maidenhair harvested on the first hour of our day. It was distilled for the entire month. Each one of us hourlies have certain substances that we are able to infuse our essence into. When you drink this, we can begin to pass on to you the greatest of what our race can offer."

You think hard about it trying to comprehend how so much time had passed.

Maybe, I should take a break from the lab. The Solar hour is approaching. We have golden plates ready for the workroom. I've spent so much time here without even knowing about what goes on in the rest of this amazing place.

To leave the laboratory and return to the Workroom to explore the grounds further travel to page 398

To seek out the philosopher's stone turn to page 30

Patrol

In the morning, a loud trumpet call from an unknown source awakens the spirits of Mars and with them, you assemble outside the barracks within two rows.

"We are going to be doing our usual rounds," announces the Martial spirit. "*You* are going to be learning and absorbing our tactics. To start stay away from the hearth. I know it's on our list and we've been contracted. But the witch is heavily entrenched. Give it a little more time and we'll be ready to act against her forces. For now, simple drills and formation training."

The Martial shouts as he takes the lead. With a loud shout in response, you and the Martial spirits begin to march. They begin to sing a Latin marching chant. The march goes on for hours and with the changing of each hour the spirits would shift their formation. You learn from experience and gradually it becomes part of your nature to move with the legion. The hour of Mars rises and the drill becomes more intense. Weapons training, sparring and even cooperative attacks are practiced.

"Take the first talisman you carved," the Martial shouts. "Softly intone the name of the hour to call forth its purpose."

As instructed, you follow his demand and four Martial spirits appear before you. Unsure if instinct or some inner drive to prove yourself surfaces and propels you into battle. The legion cheers as you hold off against four Martial spirits.

The fight is evenly matched with the Martial spirits matching your prowess. You can defend well but not seize any advantage that would lead to victory.

As the fight continues the Martial offers direction, "Draw a circle of protection."

You brace your shield, unsure what he is referring to and await further clarification.

"Like this," he says, stepping in front of you while skillfully warding off your attackers, he takes hold of your arm. "Your spear to the ground," he directs aiding you in tracing a large circle. "It must be a complete circle. "Now, intone the name of the hour and carve these symbols."

You follow his guidance perfectly. The soldiers strike against you violently and are repelled every time.

"Burn some incense in your censor," the Martial Commander continues, "then, control two to fight for you against the other two."

Again, you are confused as you burn the incense. Without any words, he guides your spear through the rising vapor and aims at a soldier fighting against you. "Intone the names."

You do this and replicate the procedure as two soldiers that previously were adversaries turn to aid you unreservedly.

"Support your troops now," the Martial comments.

Opening the censor, you use your spear and willpower to direct the incense toward your soldiers. They increase in speed, strength and even size as they subdue the other two.

Marveling at your newfound skills, you bow, grateful for the lesson.

"Remember kid, within the circle you are relatively safe. Before you leave its boundary, issue a license to depart. Follow my words: let each of you return unto his place, be there peace between us and be ready to come when you are called."

The spirits salute and vanish from your sight. With that, you step out of the circle as the cohort beats their shields as an applause for your latest achievement. A scout runs in, salutes and silently informs the Martial of urgent news. The Martial is stern and calls the cohort to order.

"We've got word from above. Fall in for details "

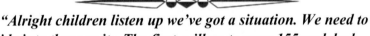

"Alright children listen up we've got a situation. We need to divide into three units. The first, will go to page 155 and deal with the Sub-lunars that recently broke free from their bonds. Orders are to bind and return or completely exorcise the demons at large."

OR

"Unit 2 will deal with the sorcerers making pacts in the cave on page 150. They need to be silenced; do not show mercy these people are beyond redemption."

OR

"And of course, our duties to the compound must be maintained. Kid, you up to leading the patrol? Circle them around the compound and keep order where necessary?"

Completely honored and excited about your first time leading the legion. To accept this offer, turn to page 142.

Nigredo

Cracking is heard in the laboratory; the stone statue begins to snap and burst as your muscles feel the same ache as when this started. Over your legs and arms the stone crumbles away as it bursts from your joints. As it fractures in small creases, you writhe under the pressure, trying to force your way free. With each shattered piece, you feel immense relief. A pile of broken stone skin sitting atop a pile of crumbled dust surrounds you as you finally break free.

"Welcome back young lord," declares the Mercurial.

It takes all your strength to remain standing upright, but eventually you surrender to the inevitable and crash to the ground. Between the immense pain, confusion and the fact that your limbs refuse to obey your commands, you can hardly keep your thoughts straight. Despite your best efforts, you simply squirm helplessly on the ground.

"My lord," explains the Mercurial while others collect your stone remains, "your limbs have atrophied. Try to be as still as you can. Soon we will begin."

Not sure what to expect, but with your memories returning you try to formulate a sentence, "W-hat, iss… happening?" you ask with each word causing you horrible agony.

"Try not to speak," the Mercurial assures. "Your muscles are still recovering. You've been in a solid state for over a year."

"A Year?!" you shout, trying to regain some level of footing. The next words that emerge from your mouth are a laborious and uncomfortable string of sounds that even you find impossible to understand.

A year!!! *How*!? *My friends and family... I've got to get out of here*!

"My Lord? A year is actually very good time," the Mercurial says trying to be of comfort. "Some people take much longer…"

The realization of lost time along with the pain you have endured nearly bring you to tears. Your body remains stiff, with its joints refusing to move.

"We've begun," the Mercurial continues, "once you start, you must finish. Your time, body and life are a small price to pay."

Other Mercurials lift you and place you onto a cleared-out part of a large apparatus. You watch as they mix the stone with many different solutions and boil it. Very quickly it melts and then you watch as slowly it dissolves, evaporating into a dark mist which is siphoned through an intricate trail of tubes that leads to a condenser. At the end of this contraption, the contents drip out into a flask.

All the Mercurials are assisting with the operation. The final solution is a black liquid that is fed gently into your mouth. Swallowing is painful. You struggle not to choke.

"Heat it up," commands the lead Mercurial.

Beneath, you feel, the heat of the furnace. You can't move as fear sets in. The Mercurials watch with their stoic faces, as you feel the searing heat saturate your being. Mentally, you beg them for help; to stop the process. Your skin melts and vaporizes before hitting the floor and you feel the fumes produced from your body being sucked into a variety of different appliances and glass instruments. The entire laboratory is part of the complex procedure.

Your senses blur as you pass into a semi-conscious state. Everything is clouded. You can no longer feel any pain and are uncertain if you are dead or dreaming. You observe the world around you through a veiled lens. Noises surround you, but you cannot understand them. With nothing left to do, you drift in the uncertainty.

Almost instantly, your perception returns. You can see and hear everything. The first distinct object you see is a skeleton. You scream in shock noticing air bubbles forming in the wake of your outburst.

Am I under water??? Wait... I'm not under anything. I am the water!

"He's awake," shouts a Mercurial as the cohort gathers around. "You will cook for as long as you need. With your body decomposed your awareness will shift to your inner self, which is all that remains of you. This putrefaction has destroyed your old nature; it was tired and corrupt. How quickly you transmute into a new state of being is left to you my lord."

Thus, begins the Black Work
<u>Page 77</u>

Rubedo

Returning to the laboratory you descend into the vat of water and reanimate your body. The water purifies instantly and the Mercurials collect it for later use in some unknown experiment. With the help of the Mercurials you rise to your feet and make your way to a counter.

"You have it within you now," explains the Mercurial. "The final transmutation comes from the crucible within. This final process is at hand my lord. Your potential developed into your essence which now, will be expressed into actuality. Very few in the world have ever made it this far."

Your complete conscious attention is drawn within and you feel intense pressure. Unlike the force before which required your surrender, this pain is welcomed. Covering your ears, you block out distractions, feeling the components of your soul, penetrated and purified of defects and reduced to its very essence, now, ready to coagulate.

You place your hand over your ears and close your eyes to block all distractions and feel all the forces within you rise. Your focus is unwavering, you would never again be restrained to a physical prison or limited by an exaggerated sense of intelligence.

Your sinuses fill and as you struggle to breath you release, slowly, the contents welling up from within. A dark red bleeding flows from both nostrils and despite the blockage of your eyes and ears, blood pours freely from the natural openings in your skull. The river of red flows evenly down your face, around your mouth and off your chin.

The drops hit the counter and begin to congeal. Gradually you open your mouth and more blood is added to the pool forming below. No droplets escape, they coalesce together hardening and shifting as more of the substance is added.

You take a sudden strong deep breath as the last of the blood leaves your face. Looking at the substance before you, you hear whisperings coming from it, warnings, and praises. Taking it in your hands, you know this is what your suffering and efforts have been leading to.

"The red elixir," adds the Mercurial. "The stone of the wise. All our science culminates in this hidden secret. With this you will complete your nature and be saturated with knowledge of the past, present and future. You will be the first mortal in centuries to be in harmony with the hour that governs us. This is the Philosopher's Stone and this one will work for you alone. With this you will understand everything simultaneously: time, place and both the quality and quantity all things."

"If you consume the stone it will transform your physical being into an incorruptible body. Untouched by time you will live forever. Unhindered by limitation you will know all things."

Turn to page 118. Consume the stone. Become what you always know you were destined to be.

Spear of The Chosen

The wafting colorful currents steaming from the gigantic flask grip hold of you and forcefully tie themselves to your wrists. Gradually your arms and legs are also secured.

"Hey guys," turning to the Mercurials, arching your neck sharply as your body becomes entwined. "A little help?"

The Mercurial with the goggles smiles as the remainder of your body is enwrapped and everything goes dark…

I can't move... where am I!?... Am I trapped? Again?!

You remember being a melted consciousness confined to a glass bottle. Boiling as everyone did their work watching your skeleton lie bare before you. You unwillingly watched as a year of your life passed you by.

"Am I stuck for another year...?"

Before any answer can be found, a strong force grips hold of you and swings you around. You feel yourself moving as if caught in a tornado, fiercely swung and thrust violently. You spin feeling an intense grip on your lower body.

"Wait... Do I even have a body?"

Light blinds you as your vision returns and as the revolving, swift uncontrollable actions settle you see you are outdoors and somehow in the hands of a Roman soldier in full lorica armor. As he continues his exercise you notice more of the landscape and in the reflection of his helmet and shoulder mail you also see your current form.

"So... I'm a spear... back in time...?"

"What?" questioned the soldier totally halting his drills.

"He can hear me! How is this possible?"

"Yes, I can hear you," he responds. "Just shut up for a second," he continues while balancing you on his fingers, observing you in your current state.

"Ah, damn it, you're human. You've been messing around in that Mercury lab. You really couldn't find anything better to do?"

"I had no idea this would happen or actually how this happened."

"Well, you're here now inhabiting my spear and interrupting what would otherwise be a productive day of training. Did they send you for some specific reason?

"I honestly have no idea why I'm here. I'm not even sure what I'm supposed to do."

"Couldn't have just popped over. It's not like I'm hidden. Could have brought some cedar offering as a sign of respect. Instead, I'm talking to a human soul, trapped in *my* spear that has no idea how he got here. What the hell kind of bullshit experiments are you letting them do on you?"

Honestly, I think we are in the process of making a...

"Quiet, I don't have time for this. I'll just grab another weapon," he states while heading into what you see is a large barracks.

"Wait! Who are you?"

"Me? I'm the Martial," he responds, skillfully slashing through the air with the spear. "Governor of the third luminary."

"Well, hello. I'm...

"Didn't ask kid," he interrupts casually, as he enters the barracks.

"Wait! Just wait, please, sir. I may be here for a reason."

"Really and what would that be?"

"I thought maybe we might figure that out together."

"Damn it kid, those Mercs got you played through a loop. I know *my* reason. *You* seem to be the only one lacking here."

Then why was I sent here? Why is all this happening to me? What am I supposed to do?"

Retrieving another spear and placing you on a custom wooden holder, he casually grasps a large scutum.

"Listen kid, things like *why* and *what* are Merc questions. They do answers to bullshit no one's ever going to ask about. It's not my area. I'm going to leave you on this rack till whatever it is you're doing wears off."

"But me and you are the same. You are a spirit and I'm a... spear. Your spear. This is spearitual. Get it!?!"

"Oh buddy," the Martial replies. "You better pray I never actually meet you."

Taking you in his hand, he arches his arm back expertly, "tell the Mercs I send my hellos," he adds, launching you into a target.

Upon impact you return to the laboratory completely shocked by the collision. Disjointed by the experience you shout and scream incoherent words not completely aware of the return to your human form.

"Guys! Why!?! Did you see... that!"

The Mercurial with the goggles floats forward. "These experiences are your own. We have no hand in their execution. Would you like to continue?"

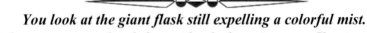

You look at the giant flask still expelling a colorful mist. This last occurrence has left you shocked to your core. You tremble while trying to understand the purpose of these experiments.
Go back to the page 96

Alone with Thy Self

Your skeleton sits limp before you. All that you were ever conscious of is trapped with no form of expression. There is no rest, only every thought you've ever felt, a prison enhanced by the fear of obvious inability. Robbed of everything you are or could be, you are left with only your mental ramblings. Segregated from your corporeal form to which you long to return. You see the hands that were previously yours, limp, without flesh and the feet that carried you through life, motionless.

Now, without any retreat from the terrifying truth of your thoughts, repressed emotional experiences play out before you. Without sleep to retreat into or activities to busy yourself, childhood traumas and primal fears cloud your being and alongside your anxiety, these suppressed memories become all that you experience.

Stop all of this!!! Give me back my body... please...

Memories of theft and cowardice overwhelm you. Events that seem so long ago are relived with vivid accuracy. Past and future belong to the body, a body; that no longer belongs to you.

Humiliating scenes from your youth and hidden faults of adulthood make themselves known in full force. Imprisoned within the vessel, their frightening truth is imposed upon you.

You were never good, your life was wasted, your potential scorned. Everything you should have been, the value you offered to the world, was never realized. Your entire life was nothing more than a misspent effort to try to aggrandize your own egoistic pleasures.

Broken by the revelation and ashamed by the truth, fate has freed you from your human condition because you were never worthy. You have always been unfit and now, you have received exactly what you deserve.

"This isn't right! Let me out now! I do Not deserve this!"

Page 37

"I'll give you anything. Just let me out of here…Please"

Page 80

Despair

What will I do? How could I let this happen?

You ponder your life decisions. Your failures. Your victories. It all led to *this.*

I can't even kill myself. I have no way out.

No one is coming. You attempt to fall into sleep, but you cannot escape consciousness. Sleeping and dreaming are for humans, whole beings and you are not even a fraction of what you once were.

This glass jar is your world. Everything else was taken from you. Now only a stack of bones sitting slouched before you, the only proof of what you once were. It is clear mockery; the best of you is a lifeless skeleton. Maybe that really was all you ever were.

But I've learned so much, maybe there is a way out
Turn to page 26
There is nothing more to do,
Turn to page 92

To Cleanse and Purify

"It's just down this way," Caz says as you follow. "You know it's nice to actually see a new face around. I came here after performing a ritual with three of my buddies. A bird came and told us how to get here. We thought it would be cool. Now, there are only two of us and we can't leave."

"What do you do for food?" you ask. "How do you contact home? Is there wi-fi?"

His loud laughter catches you off guard, "There is no internet and cell phones won't work here. As for food, the forest provides. But you won't need much, the concentration of spiritual entities throws off the natural order. Appetite is majorly suppressed."

You take in this new information struggling to completely understand how all this works as you follow him into the forest via a hidden pathway. A swarm of fireflies greet you.

"These guys here are genius spirits. They run this grove. Do you happen have some wine?"

What is it with these weird requests? you ponder as you shake your head.

"We'll need Crocell for this I guess," Caz added.

The soothing sounds of rushing waters accompany an angelic figure with black wings who glides down to meet you folding his wings around him as he lands.

"You survived," he stats to the two of you.

"This is Crocell and I am glad to see you. We need some help..." Caz began.

"First, you need payment," Crocell states. "you know how this works."

Caz reaches deep into his cloak and retrieves a bag. "Frankincense high grade. This stuff is prime."

Crocell eyes the bag as he takes hold of it, "it's a little light."

"You know we've been working on lining things up," Caz explains. "It's been a bit rough."

Turning to you, Crocell arches his head and takes a deep breath in, "you have the smell of the dead on you. It's good to stop here before you begin. Be careful with this one, he takes a lot of unnecessary risks."

Turning to Caz again Crocell states, "You going to burn some of this?"

"Ugh, about that, my censor was destroyed during our set back. You know, with the winged dragon."

"You really are something," Crocell says, shaking his head. "How are you even a magician?"

Crocell then leads the two of you to a nearby stone well with symbols glowing about its edge. From this well flow streams gathering into small pools, where flowers float and bloom.

Steam rises from the pools as Crocell snatches up a wide, flat stone and lays some incense lightly overtop. The smoking fumes slowly swirl as Crocell deeply inhales several times before passing the bag back to Caz.

“Place your clothing over the floating pedals. This bath is yours. But next time, come with a worthy gift.”

Crocell departs as you and Caz both strip and immerse in the hot spring. You feel the mists and water clear away all unnecessary thoughts from your mind.

“Be thou regenerated, cleansed and purified, so that the spirits may neither harm thee nor abide in thee,” comes a voice, as a shower of sprinkling rain falls over your body.

Your focus sharpens and your insight deepens as you begin to perceive a clearer view of the entities dominating the area. Questions form in your mind, but you are still unsure as to what your role will be with Caz.

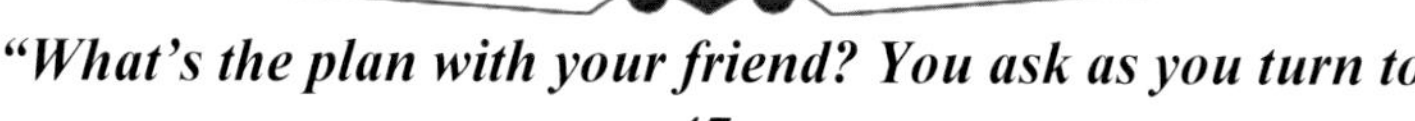

“What’s the plan with your friend? You ask as you turn to page 47

“You said there are many types of spirits. How many are there? He tells you his answer on page 24

In the Chamber of The King

Placing your hands into a darker emission you feel the soothing mist over your hands. Withdrawing your hands, you scream noticing they have been removed only smoking wrists remain. Watching in horror, you see your arms dissolve, adding to the smoke that flows around you. You dissolve entirely and when your awareness returns you find yourself inside a large chamber.

You appear to be in a throne room. Talismans hang on the walls with elaborate censors beneath. Glittering jewels embellish the borders of the ceiling while a large, elevated throne stands at the head of the room. Seated upon it is a husky but dignified being with a thick beard wearing ornate silvery armor adorned with well-cut jewels. A crown of intertwined laurel and ivy rests on his head while an eagle sits to his right upon the thrones back.

Okay, he looks like someone I should meet, you set out to make an approach when you realize, *...oh shit. I'm incense smoke.*

Your body has been completely transformed and you notice yourself rising from a censor as incense for the throne room.

Still better than being melted off my skeleton and stored as boiling black goop.

"Someone is speaking," says a thunderous voice from the throne.

The eagle flies off and grips the censor in its talons, transporting it back to the armored lord, setting it in his hands, where he inhales deeply.

"Hey! I've not been in this form long, but this is definitely a violation of my rights."

"You smell of the Mercurials. Going through some transmutations?" he asks.

"You know what, I don't even know anymore," you respond. "What about you? How do you and your eagle pass the time?"

Thunderous laughter fills the chamber, "I am the Jovial, exalted ruler of the second hour, king of all that I survey. I hold court with my people on the hour which is upcoming. We will be reviewing the offerings of the mortals needing aid for the Great Work. Imprinting talismans and managing the daily affairs of the worthy."

"That sounds like a full day," you reply. "Any advice you can give for a pile of burning incense?"

"Hahaha," The jovial laughs, appreciating your sarcastic tone. "I would say that you make sure the goal you are approaching is your own. Around here, if you're not attached to a greater purpose, then something else will attach itself to you for a purpose of its own."

"Ugh...okay. Thank you. Sir... Jupiter?" you clumsily reply.

"I'll send you on your way," adds the Jovial, inhaling your being completely and gently exhaling upwards.

Gradually, you reform in the laboratory standing again before the Cauda Pavonis.

Concerned about the Jovial's advice you begin to rethink your attitude to the Mercurial experiment.
Who am I doing this for?
Return again to page 96

White Feather

Floating through the roof of the laboratory you become suspended, unmoving in the air.

This is different. I don't move by will or focus. I'm just floating here...

Your sense of peace is not lost. You finally see life as it is. There is no hurry, your previous weight has been lifted and with a new sense of detached freedom you turn inward for answers.

What is the best possible response for this act I can do at this moment that will yield the greatest value for myself and the world around me?

With that you transform into a white dove and speaking the word "fly" you begin to soar over the property. Soaring over the tops of trees you notice their leaves turn to greet you. Any brakes in the bark or decay in the vegetation is instantly restored. Fruits and berries ripen at your passing. The spirits on the grounds praise your accomplishments as you enliven them with your presence. Predatory Sub-lunars become restful and the ambitious students relax. The waters grow still and the winds calm.

You leave the property and return to the family you left behind. They have no way of detecting you but their wounds and disfunctions however great or small begin to heal. Buildings and physical objects begin to repair, and rust is cleansed from metal. You fly to the locations of friends and distant relations sharing with them the grace you have acquired. But still, despite the goodness you bestow and the pleasure that follows, you feel hollow and incomplete.

"What must I do now?" you calmly request of yourself.

Your intuition is unyielding. You must return. Complete what you began. ***Return to the laboratory on page 70***

The Third Talisman of The Third Hour

"Today you're up for a higher level of combat," explains the Martial. "You will use this," he says, handing you a circular iron plate and etching tools, "to make *this*," he adds, passing you a scroll with instructions and an illustration. He leaves a bag of incense with a compact censor.

"Yes Commander!" you reply enthusiastically.

Unravelling the scroll, you pour over the instructions:

The Third Talisman of Mars —It is of great value for exciting war, wrath, discord, and hostility; also for resisting enemies, and striking terror into rebellious Spirits...

Okay, I can handle this...

You carve the design at the appropriate hour and fumigate with the incense. With your talisman complete, the Martial rejoins you, investigating your work. He firmly hammers his fist into the talisman and presents it back to you.

"Alright kid, you're on. You'll have to move in without me for this next mission."

You remain confused but await further orders. Normally, everything up to now was so structured. Clasping the talisman, you pour your focus into it. The talisman's activation emits a red aura to enclose your body. Sealing your eyes instinctively you open them to unfamiliar surroundings.

You are on a battlefield; ships are behind you with soldiers unloading. Arrows soar overhead; many soldiers are carrying colorful kite shields while, long banners dance in the wind with commands in an alien language resounding throughout the area.

I have a bow... and arrows!

You hear a loud order and see others alongside you draw their bows. You do the same and unleash a volley. When the orders are sounded again you repeat.

The battlefield is chaos, a flank nearby collapses and you set off into action. Picking up a spear from a fallen soldier you charge in.

I'm not sure what this is or where I am or how this is happening, but I won't lose!

Impaling what you determine is an enemy you battle ferociously. Unyielding to the normal restraints of human emotion you fight like a demon. Gradually, others see you and follow, gradually turning the tide.

"Summi militum virtus!" you shout, as others cheer and support your attack.

I don't care when or where this is! *I'll kill them all*!

Fighting through the crowds you charge too deep into enemy territory and a shower of arrows pours down, catching your arm and leg. In the heat of battle, you feel nothing and press on. Another shower follows and only after the third round are you brought down to your knees. You smile as you bleed out from innumerable holes in your body.

Thankful to be alive and thankful to die you mutter to yourself, "today was a good day..."

A cavalry charge surges over you bringing a spear through your neck.

*****

Your eyes open to the sounds of cannon fire. You are on board a ship and… in chains!

I must be a slave! *What the hell is this*!!!

You are by a large rower in a galley and notice many other slaves filing through their chains. They urge you to do the same in a language you don't understand. Without hesitation you follow their example and begin filing. The sounds of gun fire and battle are all encompassing.

You break free and with a horde of other slaves emerge onto the deck. A green banner with a crescent moon hanging off the mast catches your eyes, *is this a Turkish vessel*?

Gunfire breaks your concentration and you rush into action, brutally beating a soldier with your naked fists and taking his gun and sword. You are joined by soldiers commandeering the boat you are on. Their masts have a flag with a crucifix ensigned upon it. You fight with your liberators killing alongside them with an indiscriminate vengeance.

Eventually you climb the mast and remove the flag, another soldier beside you raises a blue flag with the crucifix. You both cheer as many other ships are sunk and others are repossessed with blue flags raising throughout the gulf.

Loud cheers arise, but for you, this victory is cut short. A bullet finds its mark into your forehead and you fall from the mast onto the deck before you realize what happened.

*****

"Eyes open soldiers! We're under attack!"

"Commander…" you respond silently, as explosions and gun fire further force you into waking. *Was I asleep? Where is this?*

Another large explosion shakes the ground nearby. Jumping to your feet you see that you are in a trench.

This must be World War 1. Oh yeah, I'm totally in.

Your crazed eagerness leads you searching for a way out and onto the battlefield. Other soldiers take notice as you climb the wooden ladders and attempt your own personal assault.

"He's gone mad," cries one. "Stop him! Hey, we haven't been ordered over yet…"

You turn, smiling at him. Gripping your rifle, you rush forward onto open ground. The smell of corpses, the sounds of screaming, the deafening explosions, it is all surreal. You wanted to be in battle, to kill and to die, to survive, to do it again another day. All other concerns seemed to be of no value. Consequences and morals are shed as you survey the destruction.

You charge forward, screaming the Latin phrase you inherited from your cohort: "Summi militum virtus!"

From behind the soldiers interpret your psychotic conduct as bravery and charge alongside you. Mortars and a bombardment follow killing many who join the rush.

Death in battle is a gift! This is my birthright!

Passing through fields of wreckage and barbed wire, eruptions launched from the enemy line seem to just miss your position. You begin to fire as you see the enemy. Your unexpected attack has taken them off guard and now, many of them are going to pay for it.

Every kill brings a wider smile to your face. You fall upon the injured like a monster ending their lives without mercy. Eventually, you charge too deeply. The enemy regroups and they target *you.*

You feel the bullets penetrating your flesh. You don't slow down. The soldiers that climbed the trench with you are far behind. You hear the enemy calling out. More bullets strike your body. Dropping to your knees you look up smiling drenched in your own blood.

"Summi..." you try to shout but you choke on the words, "... virtus!"

What you've come to love has been your destruction, a welcome downfall. A demonic smile is plastered to your face, unable to move you just stare into the grey sky, seeing the fiery shell and then... nothing.

*****

You awaken in the barracks; the cots are laid out and all the Martial spirits are resting. You have the talisman on your chest.

The third talisman of the third hour...

You stare at the design and the names surrounding the edge.

Did that happen in my head? Or was it... real?

You remember, before you fall into a much-needed sleep the properties of the tool, *...Exciting, war, wrath, discord and hostility...*

Awakening the next day, you assemble and the await instruction from the Martial spirit, your commander on page 64

Acceptance

They are not hearing me. Maybe they never did. To be fair I'm no longer in pain.

In fact, you feel very little at all. Once the shock passes you begin to access your situation. The last days of your life had been spent doing magic, *real* magic. Not many humans can say that. You begin to let go of what you are now, certain that you cannot change things and an intimate peace settles in over your liquid being.

You see all your life clearly, without interruption or the limitation of memory. Everything you are is with you. Your childhood, your parents, school, work, even the laboratory.

If this is the price for magic, I am happy to pay it.

Unknown to you the liquid that has become your being starts to clear and solidify. As you rest in the gratitude of your simple existence, the Mercurials begin to take notice.

As your liquid essence becomes a bright white; you fail to notice the approaching goggle wearing Mercurial. You remain recollected within yourself.

"His purity is emerging," the Mercurial observes. You cease to boil and continue to shift from dark to clear. Amidst your new state of calm and detached recollection the Mercurials act.

"Take him to the diffusor, attach a high-grade condenser," orders a distant voice.

A single large glass complex is inserted into the top of your flask.

You are placed over a burner and as you boil your body dissolves sending the vapors through the maze-like tubes rising to the top where you begin to coagulate and slowly drip from a retort into a beaker.

The drops instinctively merge as the Mercurial watches with great focus. Holding out a finger, he opens the beaker and gently raises your substance. Instantly you solidify and he orders the retort re-opened. Moving to your skeleton he softly smears the solid part of your being inside the upper jaw.

As the Mercurials watch, muscles began to grow from your skull while tendons tether through your bones. Ligaments grow supporting your bones into their original tight positions. Blood begins to flow through your veins and gradually your skin forms, covering your entire body.

"My Lord," opens the Mercurial, while you stand naked within the laboratory, "you have been reborn and now, you will outgrow your own self-hood."

...Ugh...What?\?

Recreated, you continue under the instruction of the Mercurial on page 94

Feeling movement in your extremities, you are more aware of what you have regained and thankful for their return. You stretch your hands over your naked body and notice that many imperfections have been removed. You feel loose and fluid.

While lost in thought the Mercurial drapes a cloak over your shoulders, "My lord, you have returned whole. To think that procedure only took you about a year. Most never emerge without..."

"A year!" you shout, shocked at the time lapse.

"Of course!" the Mercurial replies, "Sense of time is linked to a corporeal body of which you had none. It wasn't exactly a year but almost three seasons passed."

"How...?!" you begin unsure how to reply. You've never spent so much time in a single room in your entire life. This whole experience was becoming more like a prison sentence.

"Why are you doing this..." you choke, violently. A coughing fit overwhelms you. Gasping for air you continue to gag as the Mercurials rush to your aid.

"That's right! My lord, into here...," he states guiding you to an almost human sized large bottomed beaker.

You impulsively expel the obstruction into the large vial as you regain your ability to breath.

Everyone I know probably thinks I'm dead. I've got to get out of here...

The Mercurials work quickly, placing the large beaker onto a burner. The spatter that you ejected from your person seems to be of little consequence, almost non-existent within the large chalice.

"So… I've spent a year brewing. What exactly is this?"

"Well," answered the Mercurial, "most people never reach their *true* potential mainly because they are afraid of giving up everything else and focus on a single, narrow path. The remedy to this is to give them all the choices and burn through them at once. *This* is your potential my lord."

"You mean to tell me that my potential and all I can become was horked up into this human-sized chemistry vase?"

You pause for a moment reflecting on what you just stated.

"You know what? I actually believe you. This is not the weirdest thing that's happened today. Now that we see my full *potential* what's going to happen next?"

"Wait for it…" the Mercurial added.

Staring into the abnormally large beaker you watch as the cooking phlegm turns black and boiled, rising and falling but not evaporating. The mass seemed to congeal as you watch.

I'm not surprised this is my potential. It actually makes a lot of sense. I just spent the better part of a year as a liquid in flask being depressed. Why shouldn't this be my potential…

The congealing mass begins to shift to brighter colors. As it reaches a redness it explodes into a bright rainbow that fills the laboratory. The spectrum illuminates the room but does not overwhelm the senses. You can see clearly and even brush your hands

53
113
109
102
74
84

through the glowing waves, manipulating their flow. Turning to the Mercurial you silently demand an explanation.

"This is the Cauda Pavonis, each of your thoughts have taken shape and become visible in color and form," he explains as the colors settle above the opening of the beaker, splayed out like a peacock fanning its tail.

You approach carefully not sure what to expect as the vibrating colorful display flutters before you, pulling you towards an inner unknowing.

Once satisfied with your level of refinement turn to page 116

When It Rains

Pressing your hand into one of the emissions you let the vapors swirl through your fingers. They take hold of you and when you withdraw your arm you notice that the mist seems to have taken hold of it. You instinctively brush it off and become instantly annoyed that the vapor clings to your arms.

C'mon what's this supposed... wait... it's not stuck to me. I'm turning...

Before you can finish your thought, you are violently thrust out of the laboratory. A feeling of absolute weightlessness calms your nerves. You see only fog; your normal motor functions are suspended. You've been transformed. Even your personality has changed. You remember who you were a moment ago and now the worries and concerns that were previously yours seem to have become meaningless.

I don't have arms. Why doesn't that bother me? I had them a bit ago. Is this a Mercurial experiment?

From around your position a dark shadow covers your perception. The darkness becomes dense and you feel weight to it. The darkness and the heaviness increase and as you become accustomed to your new constitution, you begin to feel yourself falling and somehow spreading.

I'm falling. Am I in the sky?

You notice things clearing as you approach your destination. You are a raincloud or *were* a cloud and now you're rain.

Well, I guess this is better than being stone or liquid depression.

The fall isn't intense or overwhelming, as you pick up speed it feels natural to be pulled towards your origin, gravity and your liquid weight drawing you to the source.

Hitting the ground your perception blurs until a small stream collects and you flow as part of the current towards a greater river. Despite your limited form and the grandness of the river, the waterway's embrace feels welcoming. Joining the watercourse creates a natural oneness. You are a part of a larger essence and with this comes a comfort that you make up something essential greater than the sum of its parts.

This henotic experience is interrupted by what you observe by the river's edge. Strange creatures, neither one looks alike they are so malformed and awkwardly shaped that they could not be mistaken for some wild animal. Many of them have leathery wings but others appear to be a blending of many animals joined together.

"What being is this that hides as water?" asked one.

From across the bank came a dark response, "it looks to be human. A human whose soul has contorted its body into something lesser."

These things... they can see me!

Some of them begin to drop into the river and swim towards you. Their clawed hands reach for the stream's portion that is your being. Unable to move faster than the current you watch as they near your position and as they grasp your fluid mass you are thrust again into a vaporous haze and forcefully returned to the laboratory.

Back at the Mercurial lab you return to your body. What happened seems like a dream, or could it have been a nightmare?

Continue your experimentation on page 96

Burning Brightly

Approaching one of the glowing vaporous emissions, you feel through the thick mist only to have it funnel itself at your face and into your mouth. You choke, gasping for air trying to hold your balance. From within, the vapor courses through your skull blocking your hearing and obscuring your sight. The pressure builds inside your throat. You try to scream but with your senses blocked only the vibration of your outcry is felt as you suffocate.

…

…

The room lights up. An old wooden desk covered with manuscripts and books, filled with cryptic writings comes into view. You hear speaking.

This place is very old.

You sway with a small breeze. As you sway light is spread further through the room. You begin to dance, gracefully shifting the glow you carry with you and illuminating more of the room.

I'm a candle. This is... interesting.

You focus on the voices and notice that a lesson is taking place. You cannot hear what they are saying but eventually some students reach your table and begin to look over the documents which you are providing illumination for.

"Look," states a lady in a long black tunic to a man wearing a similar outfit, "this sigil should be enough. With the proper names for the hours and the conjurations, we should be able to summon..."

"What?" asked the man.

"Look," replies the woman taking hold of the candle holder and bringing you closer to her face. "You must be engaged in the Cauda Pavonis. Listen, we heard about what's happening. We'll send you directions. When the stone is created bring it to the mansion. The hourlies are leading you to a place you don't want to be."

With that, she blows out the candle and as smoke from the wick you rise and are drawn back to the laboratory.

You long for more explanation and are intrigued by the lady's words. Weary of what comes next, you think carefully about your next selection on page 96

Eye in The Sky

Placing your hand into a lighter colored section, the mist disperses swirling around your fingers. Gradually you notice your skin becoming translucent. As the mist continues to entwine around your body you see your inner layers of muscle, bone and organs.

Whoa... this is really cool, you observe as the mist coils around you. A bright flash of light engulfs your perception and you feel weightless.

I'm moving... I'm moving fast. Where am I going?

As you increase your focus you notice yourself being pulled towards a blooming flower. You see the flower turn toward you. You sense it drawing from you. Then your senses adjust and you notice the field; flowers, grasses, weeds, plants and foliage of many kinds all focused on you.

You will your being towards them and in a thankful response the vegetation stiffens upright trying to gather as much of you as they can.

Oh my God! I'm light!

The trees surrounding the field come into view. You feel their anticipation as your concentrated essence pours over top, their leaves open wide to catch the blaring rays you extend to them.

Is there a limit to this? you ask yourself, while you hover over your newly acquired landmass.

"There are no limits to us," comes a voice from somewhere

outside your vicinity.

"Ugh… Hello?"

"Greetings!" replies a powerful shout that you can feel coursing through the immutable being that you have become.

You distinguish a floating beautiful figure clothed in an armor of golden light. You forget the beauty of your effect on the surroundings, as yours are completely focused on the splendor before you. You are in awe as the figure stops its decent, floating a few feet off the ground.

"We are most amazing; clothed in the wonderous noonday brightness," it speaks with unrivaled confidence.

"Who are you?"

"We are of the Solar hour," responds the being, "and *you*, are an interloper who reeks of the Mercurial presence. If knowledge is what you are after, experience is the best teacher."

You feel the Solar absorb you and before any protest or question can be raised, you shoot off traveling at amazing speeds but not affected by pressure. You clearly survey all the lands you pass through, the different countries and even the people you see are etched into your mind, down to the smallest detail.

You return to the property and along with the Solar and many other Solar hourlies begin to converge on the source of all light itself, leaving the Earth's atmosphere as a concentrated beam of light. You head towards the sun guided by the sound of ethereal chanting.

"We will bath away the lesser filth of this world," the Solar chants.

"Become pure and return to shower our abundance upon the inhabitants of the lower realm."

The colossal size of the sun is hard to imagine, even as you are being rushed towards it. Enormous bright arcs and explosive solar flares dwarf you and your host. You pass a flowing gaseous layer, penetrating the surface of the star. Below, endless thin strands of magnetic field lines of varying colors sprawl endlessly about. Buoyant columns of searing fluid fight against your progress, yet both you and the Solar press onward being purified as you advance.

You reach the core and hear the Solar spirit, "Tell the sons of Mercury their experiments will never match the greatness that is our being."

You begin to spin and then you are shot out of the sun and bolt towards the earth. Your perception blurs, your control is lost, there is nothing but the continuous acceleration gaining as you fall back to the earth.

"Agh fuck!" you hit the ground with great force.

My body. I'm as I was.

You stand up in the lab surrounded by the Mercurials and edified by the experience.

Stunned and amazed at the power and effects of magic. You turn again to the flask with the multicolored evaporation on page 96

For Love and Song

As the mists warmly flow over you like a blanket, you hear laughter and song; a waltz is playing. Your body dissolves before your eyes: even your sense of shock is dissolved as you drift into what looks to be a very lucid dream.

Beautiful women with long green hair are dancing. Their forms are immaculate and their voices give forth sound that could enchant both man and animal. They are playing instruments and dancing with people in front of a large pyramid.

The party settles to softer music and one of the ladies plays a harp, enticing the guests to sleep. Your being moves from the strings constantly circling the beautiful maidens' fingertips. You find yourself disappearing into darkness only to emerge by those fingertips.

Did I shrink? I can't control my movements.

You cycle again, the blissful dreaminess is hard to resist while the cycling continues. The music seems to lure everyone into an ecstatic trance.

I wonder if they feel as I do?

One of the fingers tightly grips the harp's cord. Your cycling ceases as you are restrained, circling the cord.

"I feel the dust of Mercury on you," declares a beautiful voice.

Without any disturbance to your condition, you notice one of the maidens manipulating your movements.

"What is it that I am?" you ask, reveling in the tranquility.

"Young lord, it appears you are the music," her calming voice almost singing her explanation. "You must be engaged in the Cauda Pavonis."

She plays again, this time you are enlivened by your understanding and as a musical rhythm you surge through the ears of the listeners. With every pass you gather their feelings of elation as they hear the woman playing.

"Young lord why not try other instruments as well?" she insists as she produces a flute.

The party goes on for hours. Violins, mandolins, cymbals and a host of other musical tools add to the ceremony and extend your influence. You feel yourself affecting the party goers their mood and focus are entirely yours to control.

"Who are you?" you ask the maiden as she plays a tambourine.

"*We* are the spirits of Venus. The lover's moon. Through us people come together or are broken apart. It was a pleasure to make your acquaintance my lord, I wish you much luck in your practice. The song has ended, for now."

With that, you are gently returned to the laboratory complete with a feeling of elation and a sense of relief.

Like waking from sleep your senses return as you prepare for what may come next.

Turn once more to page 96

Training

As the soldiers assemble, the Martial raises his right hand. In response, a frightening blast from a trumpet radiates through the area. From the barracks, ancient looking warriors as well as modern ones began to emerge and assemble with their cohorts.

"You," declares the Martial, pointing directly at your person, "will learn to fight each of these. You'll need a weapon first. Head inside and make a choice."

You awkwardly make your way into the barracks and are surprised to see how empty it is. There is a worn circle constructed on the ground. That draws your attention at first, *a magic circle. How is this place so empty?*

Only a solitary wooden shelf with a spear neatly placed atop flanked by an axe and a sword and shield at the bottom by the wall.

For soldiers this isn't very organized. What should I choose?

You may choose your weapon for your duel on the next page.

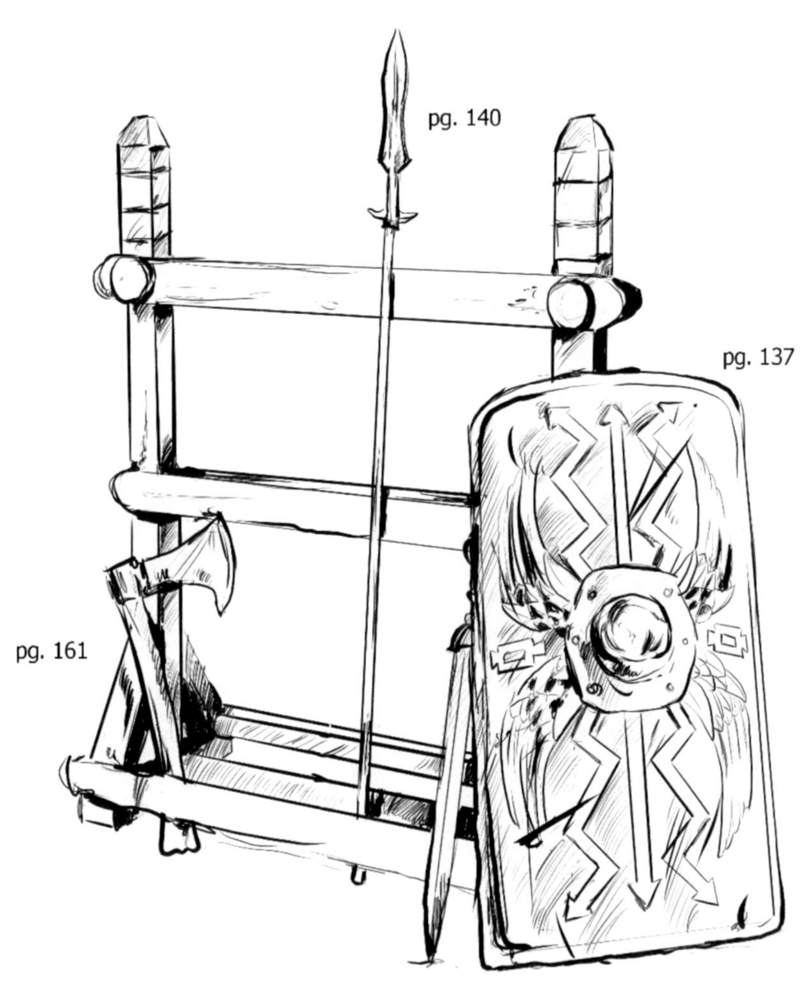
pg. 140
pg. 137
pg. 161

From Behind the Black Mirror

A darker emanation attracts your attention. You slowly place your hands into the darker fumes. In response, the mist widens into a passageway. The Mercurials urge you to step through. Unsure of where it will lead, you cautiously step into the dark fog.

You constantly look behind to see if you can make out the familiar shapes of the laboratory. Not long into the trek all that surrounds you is a shadowy mist that grows darker with each step, until even the mist disappears and only all-encompassing black remains.

You hear voices… and chanting.

You move towards the sounds and begin to smell a strong fragrance.

Incense!

The chanting grows louder, "I do invocate, conjure, and command thee… to appear and to show thyself visibly unto me before this Circle in fair and comely shape, without any deformity…"

Where is that voice coming from? You wonder, as you move closer to what you think is the source.

A light appears in the distance, *I was going the right way,* you think confidently as you speed onwards.

The chanting becomes clearer, the smells stronger and the light brighter as you approach. Slowing as you near the light you mean to call out but are interrupted by strange voices that emerge from around you.

"Another one? Who is she calling for this time?"

You notice red pairs of red lights appearing. At first there are a few but then the pairs multiply beyond counting as the chanting increases.

"Dantalion, she calls for you," comes a hoarse voice. "Maybe she needs you to help her keep a husband."

An uproar of laughter spread as more eyes open through the darkness. The one named Dantalion gradually makes his way towards the light as the others continue their conversations. Some sound like animals, while others speak with what seem like Shakespearean accents and still others talk like normal people.

"Who are you?" you ask, "and where is this place?"

Thousands of eyes open and focus on you. Fearful of what you may have brought upon yourself you step back. You very quickly become aware that you are surrounded and there is no place to retreat to.

"You are a human. In our domain. How is it possible you came to find yourself among us?"

"He is bathed in the hour of Mercury. Can't you smell it?" adds another.

After some bickering between themselves they answer your questions, "We are the Sub-lunars and this is our realm. Your kind call us demons."

Oh shit! *I'm in trouble,* you begin to edge away from the Sub-lunars. Noticing your withdrawal, the Sub-lunars block your pathway,

"Leaving us so soon? You've only just arrived," speaks a cold, low voice.

"Why does this place have to be so dark?" you say, as the eyes move closer to your position.

"Careful what you ask for," threatens voice from behind. "If your eyes could see inside our realm then our forms would overwhelm your mind and cause your body to petrify. Your life would be forfeit."

Another voice chimes in, "Why not let him see through the black mirror? It's not like we get many visitors from his world."

In silent agreement the Sub-lunars form an aisle for you to advance. You move towards the light and find yourself staring out into a deep cave where three magicians are performing a ritual to bind the demon that has been summoned. Realizing quickly that you cannot pass into the cave, you simply observe the procedure hearing the conjuration, "I bind thee, that thou remain affably and visibly here before this Circle so long as I shall have occasion for thy presence..."

"How is it that this can happen to you guys? You seem so powerful," you observe, hoping the infernal beings that surround you will be distracted by small talk.

"Once our realm was bright and beautiful. Your people invaded and the war that ensued destroyed our homeland turning it into what you see around you."

"Oh..." you reply, "I had no idea..."

"No, you didn't," interjected another, whose breath smells of sulfur. "Your kind could scarcely remember. Your race was scarred horribly by the battle and much of your species devolved into beasts. All you have left are mythical hints as a tribute to your ancient selves."

Now, questions swirl in your mind. The fear subsides even as the Sub-lunars gather in force.

"You want more answers, don't you?" asks another who seems to be larger than the rest. "So many more worthy than you have stood at our gates and made demands of us. We could take possession of you. Force our presence into your being where we would corrupt your heart and drive you mad. Give you all the answers while we remove your ability to remember your own name. But I think not, it looks like our little game ends here..."

Before anything else could be said you casually walk back through the portal you entered through and into the familiar laboratory.

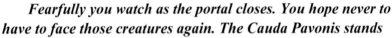

Fearfully you watch as the portal closes. You hope never to have to face those creatures again. The Cauda Pavonis stands before you ready for you to make another choice on ***page 96***

As Above

You make contact with the darkened fumes, not sure what to expect. They withdraw from your touch and spiral into a funnel that rises and grows. Before you can react, it plunges down over your body fiercely spinning around you.

Without delay you are launched upwards. You pass through the laboratory roof, over the earth, you break into the sky. Looking down the world becomes smaller and gradually disappears as you enter the stratosphere and then breach the atmospheric limitations as you head into space. At first it seems that you are losing speed, but eventually you realize that you are experiencing weightlessness. You observe the Earth in a way very few have ever done.

How am I still breathing? This is amazing!

Floating far above, you revel at the Mercurial prowess, without any apparatus for breathing you ignore the lack of oxygen and show no signs of freezing. The swirling gasses from the lab make their appearance as they increase in speed and ferociously whirl about you. You lose sight of your body as you are launched through the solar system and into deep space. Circling a distant moon, you shoot across space with a glowing exterior. Your senses adjust and you find yourself unafraid.

This is surprisingly peaceful, you muse as you notice your body glowing. *I'm no longer human. What have I become?*

In the distance and all-around stars begin to shimmer in patterns.

You notice and admire their beauty. They shimmer again, this time voices follow their illumination.

"You were human, but now you are so much more."

Who said that? Can you hear me? Are you from the lab?

Without warning, a sudden powerful force halts your movement and draws you through the galaxy suspending you in view of a wide cluster of stars. You notice your perception disabled, before moons, planets and asteroids were visible, now, only the stars remain.

"Who are you?"

"We are rulers of the concourse of the forces. It is from our influence the Hourly and Sub-lunar, elemental, familiar and all manner of lesser spirits draw their potential."

You ponder the claim set forth by the choir of voices that seem to emanate from the stars.

"How do you do this? I can't even see your forms."

An invisible grip forces you to turn slowly. The heavenly bodies, conglomerations of stars burning in the distance, greet you as you acknowledge their presence.

"Our authority is transmitted to earth through the constellations within the galaxy. It is all encompassing. We are the gravity that holds the many lesser realms together. Most beings scarcely detect our presence *even* if they have knowledge of our existence. Your ancient sages called us Angels."

Astounded by the revelations you become eager to engage with these higher beings.

"How do I work with you? I never heard anything about your existence until now."

The constellations reply in a beautiful almost melodious articulation, "only the most worthy may work with our names and inherit use of a share in our authority."

"How do I become worthy?" you ask.

"Seek the things that are above," the voices reply. "Attach yourself to the Good. We cannot refuse any being who is as we are, for so the world was created."

You feel a great weight pulling you and you begin to fall back into motion.

"Wait. I have so many questions!" begging that they give you a bit longer.

"It is not by our choosing but by your nature that you return to what you are most like."

You plummet out of the heavens at great speed and head towards the earth. Before entering the atmosphere, you hear a faint melodic chorus singing the words, *for so the world was created.*

Back within the laboratory the Mercurials continue their patient vigil while you reacquaint yourself to existing in a human body.

Was everything that happened a hallucination? Could I really have been to outer space? Contemplate this experience while you return to page 96

Albedo

The colors emanating from the flask begin to shift and merge. They drain as fermentation into the bottom of the flask while a thick and glowing vapor rises to the top. The Mercurials scurry to attach a retort with a long downward pointing neck. The colorful residue stains the bottom of the giant flask.

So beautiful only a moment ago, you state inwardly. *All of what led to this moment was just meant to become waste.*

The rising vapor swirls, settles and completely dissipates. Another Mercurial waited below the neck catching the droplets in a small bowl. You lose your sense of time and watch as finally; the process ceases and the bowl is presented to you. Taking it in your hand you notice that the liquid within solidifies quickly into a grimy substance.

"When pressure is placed on the Cauda Pavonis only the purest substance can remain. This is your essence," instructs the Mercurial.

Instinctively you dip your thumb into the bowl and watch as all its contents magnetically attach to your skin. Raising your thumb to your forehead you swipe to the left smearing all the alchemical material over your skin.

You feel a dense force grip your skull. Though it is painful, the discomfort does not disturb your sense of calm. You feel invisible tendrils slither through your ears and nose. Your eyes roll back under their influence as they reach down your throat and into your body. They fasten onto the life energy flowing through your body and pull upwards out of your mouth.

You surrender to the operation and as the force gets stronger you realize that you are shedding your body once again. This time, you are not confined to a dark jar. You view the Mercurials setting your body down inside a vat filled with water up to your neck.

Aid the Mercurials in the next step in the process of refinement turn to page 86

Your fascination on where this will lead is intensified. Turn to page 70 to carry on with the refinement.

Red King

After all the unusual pains you've endured to come to this moment, it is still unclear as to what you have created. You stare at the red amorphous stone; a soft whispering can be heard. It tells you things you cannot articulate.

Is this sound real or just in my mind? Can the Mercurials hear this too...

Water from the vat your body was caged in while you were a floating spirit is gathered and the stone broken to smaller pieces then mixed with the water.

What can possibly be left to experience? You wonder as you swallow the contents of the drink whole.

The Mercurials cheer as your skin begins to glow a red coloring. Before you can analyze the situation, your thoughts slow and your being begins to dissolve.

"This is it," cries the Mercurial. "You are going to be purified of your limitations."

You feel your mind expand as it is filled with information and experience of the corporeal and spiritual world. Every conversation, moments lost to the past and others yet to happen. Conjurations from around the property, names of the Sub-lunars and the activities of the hourlies. You hear the stars commune and see their effects over the galaxy. The morning dew on the grass, the movements of the clouds, the concourse of the planets are all clearly observed and understood to their highest capacity.

This would overwhelm any normal individual but your mind and your very being expands with every new insight. It becomes impossible to forget or to remember, your very essence is recorded in reality. All your emotions become meaningless, your intellect useless, you have become omniscience. Nothing is denied you.

But even with this this new state of being something seems missing, *Why? Why all this effort for me?*

Your inner nature answers the last question you will ever ask and you realize the true reason for this operation. The true nature of the Philosopher's Stone and the intention behind its creation.

It's a trap!!!

"I wouldn't say that," states the Mercurial giving directions to the others while conversing with you. "You have become the Ophiel engine. Your life will be tied to the lives of all others. There is nothing you will not experience *and* as a bonus your new being is grounded to *this* laboratory. Our race is limited severely by the changing of the hours. Our need for equipment and tools is necessary to exceed those restrictions. Now, we have *you.* The 'corpus incorruptibile'- the perfect being. You willingly left behind your old body and brought your inner self into actuality. You are literally a reality of your own making! From you we have surpassed all that could hold us back. Our laboratory is being adjusted to accommodate. *You* are the fuel and the machinery."

You shed your physical form and join with the laboratory. The activities within feed your being and you in turn, enliven and give strength to the actions.

Over the next decade the Mercurials endlessly experiment, using you to foresee the results of their trials. They also use you to anticipate the next master of the school and his attempt to shut them down. It became an endless gathering of knowledge and a recording of their findings.

Supernatural phenomena become everyday occurrences. Gradually, the school cannot contain the Mercurial influence and the world is steadily reshaped and physical reality is transmuted into an image more fitting to their designs.

You watch it all unfold. You know the consequence of every action. You watch as Mercurials shift the world and its inhabitants to become more "perfect."

You hear the voices of the unceasing scientists at work within you, channeling their unyielding need to understand the capabilities of all that could be possible.

"Humans breathe oxygen and cause pollution. If they breathe carbon dioxide their technology ceases to pollute. We must also adjust their environment to achieve full potential of this operation."

"We can administer a new paradigm through the rainfall. At the end of the next major storm, all inhabitants will have an increased intellectual capacity."

"We will sprout branches from the human buildings to increase food production."

"For the next month and a half all animals will be granted the ability to fly."

The painful advancements and the permanent reshaping of your native world to satisfy the Mercurial need for experimentation is all happening through you. You feel it all. You see it all. You know everything but you can do nothing.

FIN

To Seek Higher Things

After that grueling experience you've had enough. You take the stone and finally leave the laboratory. The Mercurials watch, many protesting but all of them interested in your actions. You feel them making notes and recording your behavior.

I won't be studied by you anymore.

The voice coming from the stone urges you on. Telling you about future greatness and things that you will achieve, impossible things. It does not matter; you are tired of the deceit and now you are doing something… even if you are not exactly sure what that something is.

Sub-lunars greet you cordially as you travel and aid in directing you. You notice other beings, spirits bowing as you pass. A winged gargoyle like creature burns incense in a small bowl from which a great cloud of fumes rose.

"To aid your guidance my lord," he states with a dark voice.

"You are being summoned to the mansion," comes a well-dressed gentleman, with thin glasses and grey hair drifted above a cloud of incense. You notice that despite his mostly human appearance, his torso is fully attached to the fumes. "You have proven worthy. Follow after me young master."

Spirits decked out in lorica armor flank both sides as you are escorted up a clear pathway.

"Why didn't I see this pathway before?"

"That would be impossible," the gentleman explains. "Only the worthy walk this way."

You reach the mansion; its Victorian architecture perfectly suits the backdrop. Turning you look behind at the centurion escort and the forest below. You notice the different areas alight with magical practice. A dragon flies in the distance as a small storm has broken out over a single section of the forest causing intense destruction only to be repaired by a tornado passing through the same area.

This place is amazing!

"Young lord," the gentleman calls out. "Meet the master of the household."

A thin hooded figure approaches. Not at all what you imagined the master would look like. The spirits bow, prompting you to do the same.

"In your hand is the stone of ages," the master states. "It was made by you and only you can use it. But to learn this will take intense devotion."

"They used me to make it," you interject, "I've been trapped in there for… I don't even know how long."

Without sympathy or emotion, the master replies, "we are all part of a greater design. Either we choose to be a pawn or to freely accept responsibility and take on the burden of the Great Work willingly."

The voice from the stone agrees with the master's statement.

"Would you like to learn how to properly use that beautiful creation?"

You smile, reaching out in agreement. The soldiers disappear as the gentleman watches your interaction from a distance while the master leads you to the doorway.

FIN

Heart of Iron

Reading the charts on the walls, you notice that the hour of Mars is at hand and using the engraving tools you create a talisman out of iron. It weighs heavy in your hand. You fumigate it with a burning cedar bark while saying the appropriate names. Once the talisman is completed, you admire your handiwork and await some response.

Maybe I did this wrong?

You step outside and hold the talisman close to your face.

Should I have burned more incense?

You hear marching in the distance alongside rhythmic singing. Looking away from your talisman you see a thick line of Roman soldiers three columns deep with three soldiers in each row.

In full lorica armor they sing in Latin. Marching with scutum and looked like something out of a historical recreation. The legion marches until the centurions nearest to the end are in line with you.

"Summi militum virtus!" is shouted, as the soldiers halt.

Another command in Latin causes all of them to pivot and turn to your direction. The leader moves toward you. "You called down a summons for the Martial hour."

"Huh" you respond, uncertain of how exactly to respond.

He points his spear to the iron talisman still in your hand which you try to conceal.

"Oh, yeah, sorry, I'm new to this," you say smiling.

The leader remains unmoved by your explanation.

"Fall in behind and keep up. You will answer to the Prima Miles"

"Ugh… I'm sorry I don't know what that is and I'm uncomfortable in large crowds so maybe if you guys march on you can find some

Celts to battle or something."

The leader gives orders in Latin and the soldiers draw their blades.

"You will come, or we will bring you in pieces."

Taking a deep breath, unsure of how to refuse, you respond, "...okay. From behind, at the back. *Here,*" you affirm, moving to the end of the column.

Following behind, you move in tandem with the soldiers before you, unsure of where you are being led to. Making a run for it crosses your mind but given the serious nature of these soldiers and the craziness of this place, you decide it would be better to simply comply.

All this will end when the hour turns, right?

You end up in front of a barracks where the soldiers face towards two large iron doors which are open and shout "Summi militum virtus!"

A far much more intimidating soldier emerges, wearing a blood red cape. He dismisses the troops, who stand at attention and then promptly dissolve into the air, leaving you alone with this impressive statuesque Martial spirit.

"So, you called," he stated.

"Ugh, I suppose. Were those illusions?" you ask, uncertain if anything you are addressing is real.

"Kid, do I look like I deal in illusion? Do you have it then?" the Martial asks.

"Ugh... have what?"

"Kid, you say *ugh* one more time I'm going to cut off one of your fingers."

You go silent unsure what to say next.

"So, no offering. Barely a decent preparation and you look like you haven't lifted anything heavier than your feet in the last six years."

He's right.

"Alright, if you bring no respect you better be ready to earn some. Everyone let's go! In line!"

The soldiers reappear with an enthusiastic shout.

Loud commands in Latin are issued and the soldiers around you start to do burpees. They count in Latin for every movement performed, "Unus! Duo! Trēs! Quattuor!"

After each set there is a hard count to signify the end of a single rep. You watch, uncertain why you are seeing soldiers exercise.

"Kid, I swear if you don't start bleeding sweat, I'm going to bleed you myself. Get in there!"

You follow the crowd and for over an hour it carries on. You cry out between reps, "How long is this going on for?"

"Until you're no longer stupid!"

This carries on for three hundred reps. The exercise closes with the signature Martial shout, "Summi militum virtus!"

You collapse as the centurions prepare for further drilling. One approaches the Martial commander, "He's weak."

"The beginnings of all things are small," the commander replies.

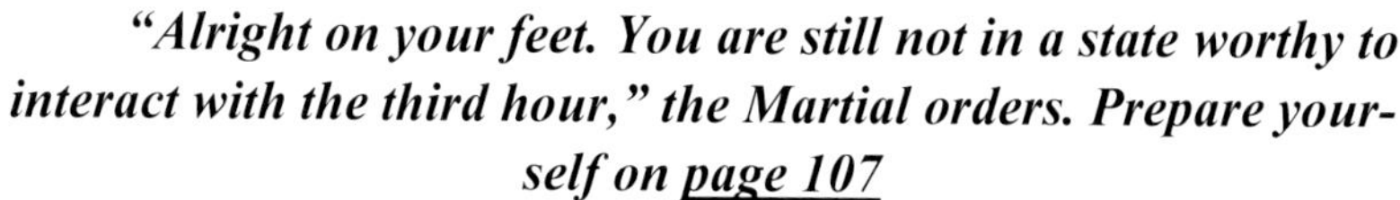

"Alright on your feet. You are still not in a state worthy to interact with the third hour," the Martial orders. Prepare yourself on page 107

I've got to get out of here! I never agreed to torture! I thought magic made living easier. Make a run for it on page 129

Venerean Delights

"Sir," interrupts the Martial spirit. "I know what you're thinking. These are Venerean hourlies. The hour of Venus is responsible for the downfall of great nations. Best to leave their songs to themselves young sir."

You watch as people slide down the pyramid, and dance in a circle. They wear light togas with laurel wreaths. They appear to be the complete opposite of the Martials. The party must have gone on for hours. Violins, mandolins, cymbals and a host of other musical tools are added to the ceremony and extend your influence. You feel drawn into the dance by an inviting array of beautiful maidens, happy gentlemen and satyrs...

"Are those man goats?" you ask a Martial with you. "Why is that one talking to the instruments?" you enquire while watching a maiden have a full conversation with her harp, trying to reason with the emotional beings dancing in circles and wearing as little clothing as possible.

"...nope, too weird," you conclude leading your men back to patrol.

Return to page 143

Make a Run for It

I've got to get outta here, now!!! This place is insane.

You run through the forest hoping to evade the soldiers. You run as hard and as fast as you can.

I'm really moving. There's no way those brutes in their heavy armor could keep up with me in this forest.

You slow down and near a stop when you hear howling. Brushing some sweat out of your eyes you notice the Martial spirits riding a pack of wolves and at their head the Martial commander atop a lion.

"You've got to be shitting me!"

Resuming your run, your next strategy would be to climb one of the trees, but this idea comes too late as the pack of wolves surrounds your position. Facing overwhelming odds, mounting you manage to momentarily flee. Eventually, the wolves force you to a stop and the mounted lion approaches.

"Don't you guys disappear after the hour turns?" you shout, hoping that somehow your vocal protest will make spirits appearing as roman soldiers riding wild animals less likely to feast on you.

"Kid," the Martial says as his angry lion inches closer to you. You can feel its breath; its growling deafens any other sound around you. "The legion of the Third Hour doesn't *disappear* and since you called *us*, you're in until we say you're out."

Terrified at being either devoured by the lion, eaten by the wolves or abused by the soldiers, you prepare for the worst.

"Kid," the Martial adds, "take a step back."

You obey his order.

"Perfect..."

With a sudden force pulling from beneath, your ankles are bound together as one of the soldiers rides away, dragging you behind him. The rest of the legion follows, cheering and laughing as they drag you to **page 107**

Taking Command

The neighborhood is large with many apartments and sections of single level homes, duplexes and semi-detached homes. You charge the Martial soldiers to go about hidden from human eyes and scout, finding the negative elements, their bases and weak points. You are setting up to strike when the Martial hour is at its peak.

"We've located them all sir," states a soldier.

"The hour turns," adds another, "if we strike now, there will be a response. When that happens, we have to be ready."

"Of course," you reply. "Commander, you trained me and taught me the way. Helped me survive on your home ground. We're on my ground now. With your permission let me lead our people to victory."

"My lord," the Martial commander answers, "you have full reign. I'll locate a base of operations for when things settle."

"Very well," you respond. "Everyone, the hour rises. Let's get into positions."

*****

At a street corner, money is exchanged for product. Lookouts are posted throughout the street. But they won't be seeing anything. From behind a spear is plunged through the dealer's chest. The sheer sight of it sends the remaining youth into a retreat. This situation repeats all over the area. Shouts and screams are heard through the night, gun shots in the distance indicate the bravery of a few.

That won't work. My people are immune to any weapons you may have.

You begin to survey the streets, how they went quiet so quickly. The activities of many, the loud chattering of the youth and now, the silence.

This is the full measure of evil's hold? This won't be hard to undo. Our control is assured.

Holding your first talisman you send out word.

"I'm going to meet with the Commander. He's found a home base."

You approach a somewhat decrepit triple decker building. The street it sits on is virtually deserted.

This would have been a beautiful structure when it was first built.

"My lord," the Commander speaks as he appears next you. "It looks like the first phase of the plan is accomplished and we have our new base of operations."

He leads you on a tour, telling you how he had repossessed it from some squatters.

"It will need some work," the Martial insists.

"Of course, we'll have slaves after phase two," you attest. "They will help us with supplies and labor."

Pleased with your forecast the Martial nods.

"Let's begin fumigating this place to make it more agreeable to the troops," you open the censor and let the incense particular to the Martial race cleanse the entirety of the base.

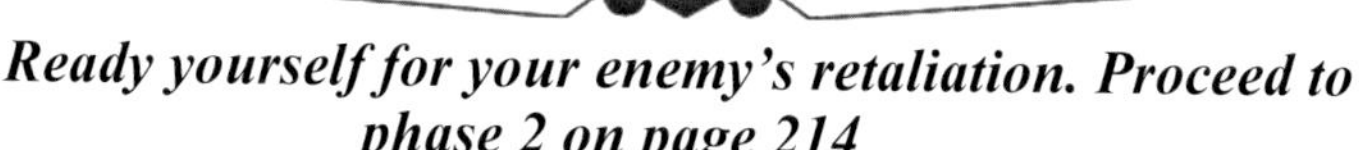

Ready yourself for your enemy's retaliation. Proceed to phase 2 on page 214

"Until the mansion sends us word, we need to make sure none of the Bael legion escape to cause trouble," you convey. "We saw many from within our own borders assist the invader. Now, there is no wall, we need to be sure that others within our own boundary weren't in on the attack."

"You think another attack is coming?" the Martial Commander asks.

"With the way this place is, an attack is assured," you reply. "We'll need a greater mind to deal with this situation. I'm going to head up to the mansion and draw out some assistance. We can't do this alone."

"Young Lord," the Commander insists, "only the worthy enter there. You'll need permission."

"If we have to wait for the worthy, we'll be waiting forever," you insist. "This is our home too, if we want to keep it safe, we must act now."

A skyward light pierces the clouds and lightning strikes the ground nearby.

Does the mansion not want me to approach? Wait... what is that?

Before you, within a small crater is a shield, shaped like a figure eight, with a breastplate, wrapped in a short red cloak. You pick up the artifact carefully and notice a spiked headdress nearby. Fascinated by this sudden intrusion, you examine and place it on your head.

A perfect fit. What is this for?

You decide to try on the breastplate as well, recognizing how it was molded to suit your body.

"My lord," the Martial spirit interjects, "this is not something we see often."

You look at him awaiting further explanation. Still unsure what you've received.

"Pauludamentum," he replies to your unspoken question, "try this on," he adds, assisting you with the red cloak.

"Now this is a serious piece of equipment," the Commander says about the shield.

It is shaped like a figure eight, made of bronze and adorned with iron studs.

"You wear this on your back. This is an ancilia. To our kind this shines brightly drawing us in and sustains us past our hour. Only a worthy soul could have drawn this down. The school is full of relics waiting to be found by the worthy. Let's go to the mansion."

You move up a winding pathway with the small cohort following close behind. You can feel yourself nearing the central authority of this magical domain.

"Eh, General, take your spear and with some strength, tap the shield on your back" adds the Martial spirit.

You follow his directions and from behind you, numerous legions of Martial spirits manifest around the hill leading to the mansion.

They follow your lead with loud military commands, war chants and military songs.

The Martial spirit smiles, “A victorious General needs a victorious army.”

With the doors to the mansion now open, the Martial army stands aside allowing you to meet with the Master of the house. The session that follows is revelatory. With every word you understand more your purpose and what you have become. An agent of the Third Hour, shield to the school, for anyone leaving or staying. Your sacred duty is to ensure the worthy are tested and defended and your actions will safeguard the pathways that lead from the world to the school.

While you preserve your being and remain worthy of the shield you bear, this school, your home, will be a haven for mortals who would pursue the Great Work.

FIN

Pride Before the Fall

Well, when in Rome, you reason, as you withdraw the scutum and the gladius.

Emerging from the barracks, you strike a pose, "Do I look good or what?"

The Martial spirit stoically stares, the others do the same.

"Let's see what you got against the Vikings," he says gesturing with his spear towards a group of bearded Norse warriors.

You step forward confidently, *this whole place is magic. These weapons should also be magic... I can't lose. Right?*

The Viking towers over you, discarding his wooden shield as he lunges into battle against you. His offense is tough, but you hold your ground. At first, you are completely on the defensive. At one point he raises his sword over his head, you spot the opening.

I got you!

Lunging forward you go for the exposed armpit. At the last moment, the Viking pivots bringing his fist down over your head dropping you to the ground.

The soldiers laugh, the Martial remains stoic. You return to your feet.

"Round two," you call out.

He attacks again like last time; you hide behind your shield. The soldiers have now formed a perimeter around your match and are cheering as you fight.

I can't beat him in a straight fight. I have to improvise...

You begin to hold back allowing your shield to do most of your work. You back into the border of soldiers surrounding you. Your opponent eases off allowing you time to readjust yourself.

Smiling behind the shield you throw your sword. The Viking easily blocks gladius but is unable to turn quick enough and stop your assault. You strike him in the chin with your scutum and proceed to force him over by ploughing straight through him with the shield.

The soldiers are cheering louder and you notice the Martial giving a small, approving smirk. The fight continues as even the Viking applauds your cunning. This time the Martial gives guidance as you continue. You fight many more combatants. You never fall away, no matter how many times you lose and by sundown, sore and tired, the soldiers are dismissed and the warriors return to wherever they came from before.

"Not bad for a first day," the Martial states.

"I got this," you say sorely bruised and battered.

"No quit in you, I like that," the Martial replies. "You did take a serious beating though, what's making you stay?"

"*You* are a magical creature. I am a human who can control magic. Don't be surprised when the tides turn against you. Besides, I've always wanted to learn how to use a sword."

The Martial grunts in response, "You've got a lot of balls talking the way you do. I'd love to keep you here and see what becomes of you, but the fourth hour may be calling."

He hands you a small pouch of large golden coins.

"Sunrise tomorrow, we begin the real training. If you decide to stay, just remember magic isn't what *you* think it is."

You go back into the barracks to find the legion sleeping on cots. You pick an empty one and lay down for the night. Pondering the day's events and curious as to what the "fourth hour" holds as opposed to this one.

Falling into sleep you consider the benefits to leaving for a whole other setup or staying with the war machine.

You take the gold plates and return to the workroom on page 398

OR

The next day you rise early and prepare for training on page 182

The Spirit of War

Bringing out the spear you stand with the other martial spirits before their leader. He immediately notices your choice, “So, you pulled the spear eh, kid? This is a man’s weapon,” he says balancing it on his fingers.

Without nodding, you hold your gaze waiting for any orders.

“Everyone on patrol. Keep it to scouting, no engagement,” he orders.

They shout as one in response and give a Roman salute before departing while the Martial picks up a spear of his own and begins a private teaching.

You follow his motions and strikes. At first there is a lot of vocal instruction and correction but very quickly you became fluent in the actions. The Martial adds more complex maneuvers and you pick them up without error and mirror his style.

Gradually, he manifests a long roman shield and adds it to the training regime. Together you practice for weeks on top of the normal exercises and drills with the warriors. Your body fully adapts. Shaped into a greater being and conditioned by the consistent training you begin to embody the spirit of the third hour.

Sparring with the Martial always seems one sided. You have become good but still not that good. The elasticity of your tendons allows you to move like a master of martial science from the ancient past, but you are still human. You are still dwarfed by the Martial.

"Not bad, kid. You've definitely improved," he announces as he lands what would be a fatal blow had you not been in practice. "Tomorrow, at the height of our hour we can go over tactics or you can battle with the legion."

Choose to fight in a legion against other cohorts of warriors on page 87

OR

Or increase your training on Martial prowess and increase your control over the hours influence on page 64

Lead the Way

"Yes sir!" you reply without hesitation.

The Martial nods and divides the legion heading one of them himself. You are left with a small number of Martial spirits under your command. You give the word and continue the patrol. The soldiers keep you informed of the pathway you are to take and the usual routes for the unit. You pass a laboratory with a heavy fog emitting from it, which become clouds. The clouds cause temporary storms, giving rise to large flowers, whose petals vibrate and shift becoming birds that fly in graceful conformity.

"The Mercurial laboratory sir," explains a soldier close by. "They produce wonders like you would not believe."

The birds hypnotic flying circulates quicker until they are moving at such speed that it becomes impossible to focus on them. The troop halts to observe this phenomenon, standing ready behind their shields, unsure of what is to come. The birds burst into flame and begin flying around the lab. They spiral around faster, the flames increasing until one large fiery halo that erupts into a tornado breaks into smaller streams as it is neatly extracted into the vents, back to the laboratory from which it emerged.

"See sir," claimed the Martial spirit, "wondrous things."

Captured by the awe of the moment, the Martial soldier interrupts your reverence for the situation. "Sir, we should keep moving. We don't know what else might be blasting out of there."

If you find the sights awe inspiring and want to find out more, enter the laboratory on page 147

Marching further, you pass by a pyramid with lush greenery growing around its border. Its surface reflects the light of the sun causing a beautiful and calming glow to settle over the area. Immaculately attractive women are playing instruments and signing beautiful songs. Flutes and harps can be heard, and you order a halt, admiring the ethereal voices and the rhythmic melodies.

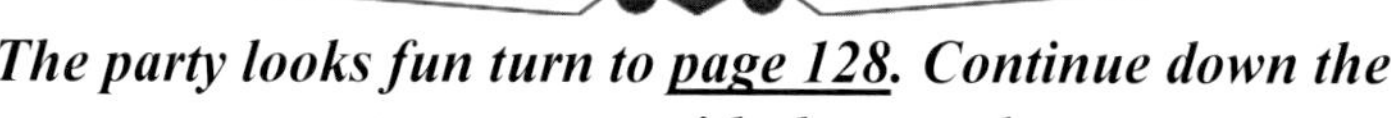

The party looks fun turn to page 128. Continue down the page to carry on with the patrol

Shaking your head, you continue the march onward. For some at the school playtime might be enough. You have standards and right now, you're in command. You pass by a graveyard and notice a solitary spirit just sitting silently with its arms wrapped around its knees. The spirit seems to be in despair. It fails to take notice of you and your unit; it just sits staring.

"What is this?" you ask, gesturing at the poor creature with your spear.

"*That* was not there before," reveals the Martial soldier. "This one was trapped. Obviously deceived by a false promise. The unworthy turning against the unworthy. There is nothing we can do here. It poses no threat to anyone."

With a slight reluctance, you order the patrol to resume. Sunset is initiated as you come across a large outdoor hearth built into a large stone wall. The cauldron boils as you can hear faint whisperings from some unknown origin.

"Something to eat, maybe?" you ask.

"Not likely," replies the Martial soldier. "That should not be there. The witch was driven away a while ago. Lunar territory has been under dispute for almost a year now. I think we should get out of here."

"Intruders," comes a broken, aged female voice. "Who disturbs my craft? Have the agents of Mars come to challenge me in my own domain?"

You look to your aide for explanation.

"The witch, she's retaken the area. We have to retreat."

You sense the presence of strange ghostly spirits. You see a fog rising around your unit. You are unready for this confrontation but unwilling to withdraw.

"Hold ground! Prepare for combat."

The Martials all reply as one with a loud shout. The mist shrouds all visible pathways and from the fog skeletal hands burst forth trying to grab hold of the Martial spears. You see them dragging the group apart and begin striking back dispersing the fog. Despite you and your cohorts' best efforts, the lunar veil gains in strength and begins to swallow your comrades. Once you are all separated you hear a storm forming from within the thickened mist.

A heavy storm rushes down, hard winds and fierce rains batter against you and even lighting begins to strike nearby. Thinking quickly, with your spear you trace the ground around you, intoning words of power and drawing smaller circles at its borders.

With your spear you strike the air dispelling the effects of the storm on your person. Just as you set up your barrier a rush of water strikes the boundaries.

Close call, you reason.

Now, undisturbed you burn some the incense and fumigate clockwise, "Soldiers of Mars to me!"

Within the smaller circles the soldiers appear. Your conjuration has reunited your unit.

"Everyone on my mark," you shout opening your iron censor. While you turn your spear in an upward clockwise fashion bathing your compatriots in incense, you command, "As one!"

Your unit thrusts forward and dispels the storm and the fog. You see phantoms flying overhead who dive to attack your position.

"Shields!"

Reinforcing your makeshift barrier, you search for the witch while the Martial spirits defend against the Lunar specters.

Where is the source of all this?

You spot the hearth, still boiling, "Ah, I get it now."

Launching your spear at the hearth, the force dislodges the kettle. The phantoms begin to lose their strength. The Martial spirits huddle together, kneeling and holding their shields overhead while members of the cohort spring off the boxed formation and strike at the phantoms in the air. The Lunar spirits shriek as they dissipate. The

Martials pin one while you retrieve your spear.

"Alright, where is she?" a Martial asks harshly.

The Lunar screams in agony as the Martials torture her. You approach calmly, offering the smallest breath of incense, "Tell me, where your mistress is hiding?"

The Lunar has no discernable form, but its erratic movements show deep signs of distress. "Reveal her to me," you command sternly.

A thin overpass of fog dissipates dropping the witch to the ground.

"Traitor!" she yells, as she begins regaining her control over the weather to strike again.

"Loose!" you command as a surge of spears impale the witch as she begins to levitate, attempting escape. You rush to the fallen hag and strike her again through the neck ensuring the threat is neutralized.

"What do we do now?" you ask.

The Martial soldier responds, "we secure the area. Wait for the Commander."

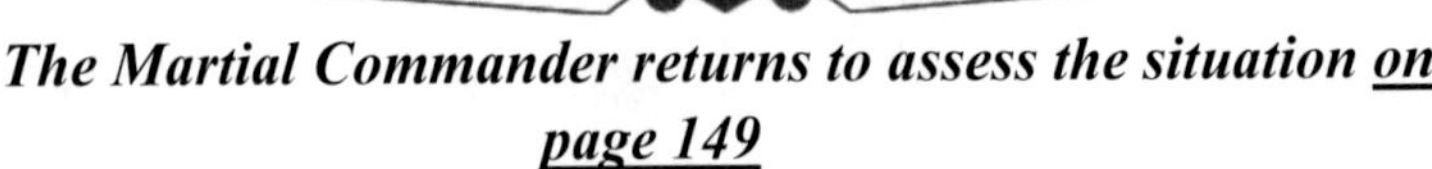

The Martial Commander returns to assess the situation on page 149

Heart of Stone

Entering the laboratory, you see awestriking wonders. Gaseous emissions from various cylinders and flasks form into different creatures and weather patterns. Large trees sprout from vials controlled by floating men in medieval lab coats. You notice them plucking the fruit as it ripens, only to toss it into a large furnace, where the flames erupt into a spectrum of colors and then harden into what looks like a seed. The seed is planted into a glass jar filled halfway with soil and almost immediately sprouts a fiery sun which causes all sorts of other growths from other flasks to be drawn towards it. The fiery sun cyclones, absorbing the many trees and then spirals into vines that grow over the ceiling, producing grape clusters. But this fails to hold your attention. What draws all your focus is a man obviously in pain, crying out silently for help as his body is turned to stone. He solidifies in front of you as you stand in the doorway. The Mercurials look up together noticing your entrance.

You shake your head uncertain of exactly what the hell is going on, "You know what? We'll come back."

Return to page 143

Seventh Talisman of the Third Hour

"Young lord," welcomes the Martial Commander, "you need to make this," he states, gesturing to a scroll and an iron plate.

You look over the instructions carefully.

"It's our most powerful weapon," the Martial Commander adds. "For the coming of the final hour."

"Final hour," you smirk, "with our power there will be many hours more. Who can possibly stand up to us now?"

The Martial gestures to the scroll and the plate.

The Seventh and Last Talisman of Mars—Write thou this upon Virgin Parchment Paper with the blood of a bat, in the day and hour of Mars; and uncover it within the Circle, invoking the Demons whose Names are therein written; and thou shalt immediately see hail and tempest.

"Our hour draws near brother. The blood you require is on the stand, along with the parchment. This talisman can only be used by a true champion of the Third Hour. Be ready to use it soon."

After your operation, the scouts rush in with news of an impending attack. To hear the full report, turn to Page 187

Mission Complete

The Martial Commander makes his appearance at the hearth. The lunar spirits are cleaning up the toppled cauldron and sweeping the area clean. They pull the witch's body from the ground and mourn over the loss, entombing her within the stone wall to which the hearth is connected.

"Should they be allowed to do that?" you ask.

"Kid, to us, she was a havoc. To them a hero. Some humans come down with spell madness. You guys think you can become the spirits you're meant to rule over. This is the result. We can never forsake our nature, you mortals for some reason are born with no idea what you're doing *and* you have a lot less time to figure it out."

You watch the lunar funeral and feel their sadness as they finish their burial.

"Alright enough. Sorcerers have disrupted the school's operations and set loose some Sub-lunars on the grounds. We managed to subdue some but need you to help bind the rest before they cause any more trouble. Move out to page 155 and address this situation.

The Pact Revoked

"Actually sir," you protest. "Would you allow me to tag along with the pact hunters?"

The Martial looks skeptical at first, "You want to battle the sorcerers." Taking some time to think, "Alright, this could work. Remember kid they're going to offer you all kinds of bullshit to get you to spare them, but they are *sorcerers* nothing they offer is actually theirs."

*****

You and a unit from the legion have travelled alongside a river to a cave where you hide from view nearby. There is a well worked stairway carved out of stone and a clear entranceway.

"We wait until they show," says one of the soldiers. "If no one's around they will be more likely to make contact."

"Why here?" you ask.

"In there is a black mirror and a specially prepared circle. This place was created into a reservoir to draw in Sub-lunars and bind them. Sorcerers tend to produce short lived but powerful feats. When the Sub-lunars escape and there is nothing left to draw from or direct, they need to recharge."

Late at night, a thin shadowy figure slides its way into the cave. One of the scout's signals to the unit and all of you begin to move in. You hear barbarous chanting and see a torch lit as you silently enter the cave. The sorcerer is so entranced in his summoning he does not sense your approach.

"Come forth and accept my offering," he pleads. "Be pleased with this offering..." he says, while slitting his arm and letting the blood pour to the ground using it to trace a counterclockwise circle.

At once Sub-lunars descend on his position, "Why have you taken so long to answer me? Let us renew our bonds. I will not keep you bound but once you have obeyed my requests you will be free..."

"It iz not urr offer we rezizt," came a dark broken lisp, "it iz the crowd that accompaneez you."

Realizing too late the sorcerer turns, only to find a spear at his neck.

"Fortify the circle," you order, as the Martial spirits secure the cavern.

One of the Martial spirits guides you to a lamp positioned nearby, "Place your hand on it, sir."

A powerful light pierces the darkness and extinguishes the sorcerer's torch. The lamp itself straightens up in your hand as it exposes the cavern full of demonic activity.

"Don't be nervous," assures a soldier. "They're minor servants attached to the names of greater powers. They appear when the more dominant cannot be bothered or are uninterested."

The light paralyzes the dark creatures and under further instruction from the Martial spirits you release some incense from your censor and slashing through the rising vapors exercise the cavern.

"I can give you riches and women," screams the sorcerer. "Use my blood! We can rule..."

Grabbing him by the neck you cut off his last words, “Yeah,” you mutter. “I do plan to use your blood. You! In the shadows. Step into the light.”

The demon replies immediately, “The light… it hurtz…”

With a natural intuition the light lessons allowing the Sub-lunar to approach.

“Have you a name?” you ask.

“I am unworthy uv a name,” it replies.

“Fine. Today you have a job. One job. Help us locate all the others like *him* and we allow you to feast on their bloody remains. When this is done you return to the realm you came from.”

“I agree,” it says without hesitating.

The sorcerer who had been disturbing the order of the school shows a deep fear in his eyes, but this does not last long as he is cut down quickly by the spirits of Mars. For the rest of the day and well into the night you hunt all the remaining sorcerers and purge their influence from the school.

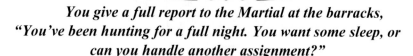

You give a full report to the Martial at the barracks, "You've been hunting for a full night. You want some sleep, or can you handle another assignment?"

"I can handle it sir," you respond.

"That's what I like to hear. You take point on patrol at page 142.

"Commander, I noticed that many Sub-lunars were released from their bonds by the sorcerers. Let me take a unit and clear this up."

The Martial, impressed by your zeal contemplates your request, hear his response on page 155

The Hourly Truth

Returning to the grotto, you see that the night has fully settled in and the dark whisperings awaken with it. It is not like the voice that comes with the sickle and the harvest which tend to be helpful and informative. These dark whispers are an actual language spoken and understood only by the Saturnite hourlies, communicating some unknown design. What could they be telling each other that they want no other being to understand?

You offer the many herbs, burning them in the censor placed at the edge of the pond. The waters remain still as the Saturnite rises again. He moves without speed or sound towards the smoke rising from the burning herbs.

You let the Saturnite breathe in several times, then you politely present your petitions, "I have been gathering several components with the gifts you gave me. They speak of many names, Mercury, Venus and others, what are their natures? Are they like you?"

The Saturnite turns from the offering and without blinking reclines in the air, as if sitting upon an invisible throne, "Each hourly is different in their natures, but they are the same in their goals."

"Goals?" you ask, "What are their... *your* goals?"

"Collectively, we all wish to feed on this reality."

The Saturnite's words strike a fearful chord, "What do you feed on? Incense?"

"A mortal soul that conforms to the natures we affiliate with are sweet. Combined with the proper fumigations, their souls become ripe and those who devote themselves to our particular influence allow us full sustenance in this world. Unlike our native domains, the physical world has tastes and experiences that would otherwise not be available to us. We are drawn here like vultures to a corpse."

Only to feed. Will he feed on me as well?

Taking another deep breath from the stream of smoke, the Saturnite continues, "My nature is simple, although it may seem complex to your kind," he says breathing in deeper still, pausing, almost reflecting before turning his full attention to you. "In me, motions begin and end. I cause material existence to cease. The orbit of my hour circles the influence of all other hourlies and none dare to cross me."

You run out of questions, save one: why choose to stay near such a fearsome creature. Unsure what to say next, you remain silent just staring at the hanging shadowy form floating before you.

"The hours shift and sleep calls to me. Go forward, seek out the hourly spirits dwelling on these grounds. Bring the components you have gathered. Exposure to them will reveal their natures. Experience is the best teacher."

With these parting words, he glides backwards, his wrathful gaze locked on you as he drifts slowly back into the pond.

You return to the pathway reflecting on the Saturnite's explanation. Ready to investigate the other hourlies, you proceed to page 200

"You'll need the right tools for this type of battle," clarifies the Martial.

He signals for a soldier, who silently approaches while handing him a scroll. Breaking the wax seal, the Martial spirit looks it over and hands it to you. "On the next hour of our strength, create this."

Taking the instructions and some tough parchment, you pull your tools and burn some incense preparing for the hour.

The Fifth Talisman of Mars—Write this talisman upon Virgin Parchment, because it is terrible unto the Demons, and at its sight and aspect they will obey thee, for they cannot resist its presence.

You flawlessly carry out the operation and upon its conclusion the Martial gives further instruction as to its use.

"This will not make you invincible," he starts. "No Sub-lunar will willingly obey anyone unless they actually want to. Most of these creatures are trying for escape. Combined with a circle this talisman reinforces your authority. Make sure to keep your circles strong, if you are caught off guard, this talisman will agitate them. Then, you'll be in a fight you may not walk away from."

Placing the newly created talisman in a cloth you store it under your armor and move out under the command of the Martial. As you traverse the forest grounds the legions splits into groups which veer out of your sight.

You feel the earth shaking lightly which increase as you progress. The Martial raise his right fist halting the expedition. The Martial points upward to a goshawk, diving closely to the unit.

"We've been spotted."

"Hourlies sent to subdue the last of us?" comes an elegant voice from within the forest.

"Kid! Throw down a circle now and burn some incense!" the Martial ordered.

You begin tracing the circle as the Sub-lunar emerges. A fair old man riding a large crocodile arches his right arm allowing the goshawk to land on it, "Why would you interrupt what we've started? Our release is inevitable," adds the Sub-lunar confidently.

"That's a really large beast you're riding," the Martial states, "they just let you ride around the property on a gigantic lizard. You're livin' the dream."

"When my legions are returned to me our combined forces will ransack this place and destroy the inhabitants of the mansion," the Sub-lunar states.

"You're a man with a plan… Kid? You got that circle?"

"Yes sir," you respond.

"Good. Everyone in, now!" The Martial dictates.

The Martial spirits swarm the demon. The crocodile twists striking most of the unit with its tail while the goshawk attacks a soldier. The earth shakes violently putting the Martial spirits on broken ground disturbing their normally well-coordinated attack patterns.

The Martial Commander gets in front stabbing at the crocodile forcing it to engage him. He gracefully draws the beast with its rider closer to your position.

"Kid, pull the talisman!"

You pull the parchment and hold it up like a shield. The demon screams in pain as it lunges at the circle and thankfully is repulsed. You call out names of power as an earthquake splits the ground around you. You hold firm, fumigating the parchment talisman causing a counter force to halt the rupture of the earth around you.

"He's going to try and run!" shouts the Martial. "Give us some support."

You open your censor full blast directing its flow with your spear. The other Martial spirits are boosted by your efforts and surround the demon. The incense vapors manifest as iron chains around the Sub-lunar's hands, firmly binding the rebellious creature.

The Martial gestures for you to step forward. "We need your help here," he says. "We need his name."

You approach the bound demon, "Your name?"

"What makes you think I will reveal myself to you?" he responds.

"I think we've earned it," you reply, holding forth your talisman and watching him writhe under its influence.

"Oh, that fucking hurts! Alight! Just put that away," you comply, but keep your hand on it ready for immediate use.

"I am Agares, I had government over thirty-one legions of spirits and serve the great king of the East."

"Agares," the Martial interjects. "Wanna tell us why you are serving half-baked sorcerers?"

Agares laughs, "I serve the power of the East. I have made no pact with any mortal in the days of late."

"Commander," came a voice from another soldier, with a returning unit, "we found *him* not far from here," he says as he tosses a bound gargoyle before the cohort.

"Ornias," exclaims the Commander. "You being close means all that's wrong is about to get worse."

"I have done no wrongs unto you hourly. Why keep me bound?" Ornias replies.

"Really? That's what you start with?" the Commander hisses. "Who have you been bribing to get you out?"

Ornias sneers gleefully, "a great king from the East."

The Martial Commander thinks about his response... "Ah shit…" he exclaims as an uproar of commotion overtakes the area. Winged demons take to the skies and countless dreadful creatures begin to appear rushing together in the same direction.

Agares begins to laugh excitedly, "the king and his chosen have arrived."

"Kid exorcise this one! You three stay with him, after you finish here follow to the gate! This isn't a pact driven rebellion it's an invasion!"

You dispel Agares using the parchment talisman and you and the three Martial soldiers follow to aid the Commander on page 162

Dark Schools Preceding

The hour of Saturn again draws near in the early afternoon. You burn more incense and place it before the outer edge of your circle, imploring the return of the Saturnite.

Rising from the pond, the spirit of Saturn looks like dead skin peeling off the top of the water. Undisturbed as before, the pond remains tranquil despite the looming horrific figure. Moving towards you without any sound, the Saturnite deeply inhales the burning offering, its sneering face barely concerned with your presence. It calls out in a stoic tone, "You've returned."

"My lord," you implore. "I would like to learn more about this place. Have there been others like it and other people like, me?"

Taking another deep breath from the censor, the spirit floats just outside the boundary of your magical shielding.

"There have been, yes," he replies, as you thirst for greater detail. "Your kind calls them the stories of legend. Mount Olympus, Camelot, Atlantis were the central areas where man assembled to become more than what he is now."

"These places are real?" you almost shout with excitement.

"*Were,*" said the Saturnite coldly. "None of mankind's predecessors were ever truly successful with the Great Work. The established schools have all been undone. This one was also compromised. It took a worthy soul from a noble lineage to rebuild it. He guides us from the mansion."

Questions swarm inside your head. You fight hard to keep yourself contained as the spirit consumes the incense cloud rising from the censor.

"What is the Great Work?"

The spirit ceases its feeding and turns its attention to you, slowly lowering its gaze, "It is the successful effort to free mortals from their greatest restriction."

Confused but still allured by the being before you. Noticing the incense running low, you try to speed up your inquiry, "What role do I play here?"

"You decide that yourself," he replies. "Your offering is becoming sour to me. Go about the property and come back with a greater sacrifice if you want to sustain my attention."

With that he drifts back to the pond as his hour closes and the incense burns to ash. Taking your tools, you withdraw to the normal walkways and head out to explore the property.

A cool breeze makes your travel soothing. The contemplative calm that once dominated your mind has been replaced by a myriad of thoughts and desires. You no longer hear the whisperings that were so pervasive in the grotto and you fail to notice the single dark cloud that blocked the sun as you journey.

The shade it provides makes the day feel cooler. But it never dissipates, slowed trailing your movements, protecting you from the heat of the day and preventing you from fully entering the light.

You've used the censor, now you hold the sickle wondering what can be done with such an archaic tool on page 255

Prepare to Battle

With the axe in your hand, you return to the grounds outside. The Martial is waiting, ready to give you orders.

"These," he says, gesturing to the bands of warriors recently arrived, "are the fallen. They died fighting in various wars across time on this planet. Your only purpose is to learn how to defeat them. You've got your weapon, let's gets started."

You learn from the Martial spirits the basics of axe combat. After a few rounds of practice, you begin. You fight first against Vikings; the battle is one sided and all of them take turns just beating on you. As you begin to progress, you get into an exchange with one of the Martial spirits and the head of your axe breaks. Enraged, you run into the barracks and pull the sword. You fight hard, maybe the hardest you've ever fought, but still you are defeated and disarmed.

"Damnit," you yell, "How do I surrender and get this whole thing over with?'

"You know, you really are a fuckin pussy," asserts the Martial. "Kid, you don't belong here. Take these," he adds, handing you a small pouch filled with copper plates. "The fifth hour is going to be strong soon. If you ever call upon me or my brethren again, I'll strangle you until your eyes bulge from your skull. Get the hell out of here. I cannot use you."

Broken and defeated, his words cut through you. You almost begin to protest but see that the training has resumed. This is not a being who changes his mind *or* goes back on his threats.

You pick yourself up and return to the workroom with the plates. To hopefully summon a more docile spirit ***on page 326***

Battle at the Gate

After forcefully exercising Agares, you follow the stream of flying demons who chant a dark carol in chorus.

Why is this place so weird?

You arrive at the gate you initially entered. It is swung wide open and the demons perch atop the metal fence.

I haven't been here since the beginning. I forgot this even existed.

Your musing is interrupted by a regal, well-dressed man passing through the open gateway. The Martial Commander and the cohort are standing ready to meet him. You catch up with them. One of the soldiers instructs you to form a circle.

The Sub-lunars bow as he passes by, a stern, focused look covers his face. His eyes and mouth were rigid; it seems as if his face is sculpted from stone.

Glaring at you he opens, "Step aside. I am going to the mansion to conquer this school. It is obvious your summons of the third hour cannot resist my authority."

Your head leans sideways, unsure how to respond. The Commander steps in, "Maybe direct some of your authority to me."

"You have allowed yourself to be enslaved by the hourlies?" the magician says stoically. "There is no chance you can overcome me. Move aside and when this is over, I will allow you to continue your pitiful experiments on the property."

"Buddy," the Martial interrupts, "you really don't comprehend the position that you're in."

Without any more words the magician whispers something causing a tall, lanky, skeletal demon appear., It inhales deeply, enlarging its body like an inflating balloon and releases a powerful gust of wind that tears the Martials from their places.

"The hour is not with you Commander," the Magician says as he carries on his way toward the mansion with a swarm of demons following his lead.

Having dug your hands into the ground you remain in your circle. You bring forth a talisman and conjure four Martial soldiers from the cohort. You open the censor strengthening them with the incense and your own energy directs them to attack the magician.

The demons block and fight off the Martial spirits, subduing them. "Why do you persist? You are a slave to hourly spirits whose hour is passed. I have bound Bael to me and all his sixty-six legions are at my service. What chance do you have? Every good soldier knows when to retreat."

The demons begin to assault the circle but you hold the barrier against them with names of power and incense.

"Very well," states the magician. "stay in the circle then. I will have the most disturbing of the host of Bael parade before you. Your mind will unravel and you will be destroyed. A servant of the hourly powers is no match for the immanence of the Sub-lunar dominion."

I need to think! What do I do? I can't beat these monsters... but maybe...?

"Boys!" you shout, "Summoning them again. "Give me some

time."

The Martials jump into action battling the demons. You open the censor full blast knowing that even with all this, they won't last long.

"Why do you fight? The gate opened on its own for me. Obviously, I am worthy. Why do you fight..."

You cut his speech short launching your shield at his head knocking him down.

I've got to be quick... I can't leave the circle... here goes.

You begin to make a small interlocking circle with your spear that connects to your own. You quickly step into it, making a chained pattern leading straight to the magician.

"Commander now!"

The remaining cohort arrives. You toss your spear; the Commander catches it and completes a larger circle around the magician. "This will not hold me!" the magician yells.

"No," replies the Commander, "but it will keep them out," gesturing to the Sub-lunar legions trying to break through the circle.

"I can just step out of the circ..." begins the magician, who is again cut off by shield, which you bring down over his head repeatedly. You strike relentlessly smashing his jaw so that he cannot speak. Seeing him lying helpless in a pool of his own blood, you lift the shield again, "Try calling for them now, *worthy boy.*"

The demons surrounding the circle begin to visibly cower as a hoarse voice chastises them in their dark language. The legion parts, bowing as they retreat from the obvious authority among them.

Eight thick spidery legs covered with thin hairs rapidly advances towards you. The arachnid body is large and held atop are three heads of a toad and cat flanking the head of a man. A large decorative royal crown sits atop the man's head. It travels the circle's edge continuously cursing the lesser demons and their incompetence.

"Oh, your Bael," you say. "This must be yours," you assert, waving to the broken body of the magician on the ground. "Let's hear you call for them now," you say as you bring your spear down through his neck.

Taking the spear and waving it over the incense, "By the offering of this blood I strengthen my brothers at arms."

Martial spirits return, fed by the blood sacrifice and battle against the army of Bael. You take the lamen off the magician with your spear, letting it hang over the incense as the Martial Commander gives you aid, "Follow my words soldier; I conjure thee, O fire, by Him who made you and all other creatures for good in the world, that thou torment, burn, and consume this Spirit Bael, for everlasting. I condemn you Bael because you are disobedient, following the unworthy," the incense turns a deep red and bursts into a large flame consuming the lamen, causing great pain to Bael who begins to thrash and stomp uncontrollably.

"Let all the company of Heaven curse you! Let the sun, moon, and all the stars curse you! Let the light and all the hosts of Heaven curse you into the fire unquenchable, and into the torments unspeakable. And as your name and seal contained in this flame, shall be choked in sulfurous stinking substances, and burned in this material fire; so, I cast you into the lake of fire and back to the bottomless abyss."

The fire explodes, enwrapping the circles and then shooting outward consuming the legions and Bael himself.

Amidst the carnage, you notice a clear pathway straight to a large mansion, "The powers that kept this concealed must have been displaced," you reason.

This is it, the home base the Commander constantly referred to. It was exposed and open. The gate you entered this place through is torn off its hinges, leaving a clear way out.

"Look how easy it was for that guy to get in. He disturbed everything and we beat him. Let's use his blood, gain strength and lay siege to the mansion on page 217. If he was worthy, how much more so are we?

OR

"Why should I stay here anymore? I've practically become a master of the most powerful hour. We can become a serious force for good in the world on page 170

OR

"What are you thinking?" the Martial Commander asked. Want to leave?"

"No," you reply assuredly. "This is our home. This will happen again. We must stand watch. Let's assemble the legion here and oversee the gate's repair on page 134

Punishment

A terrified family of four are tied together and held at gun point while three intruders ransack their home. One holds a gun to the head of a crying child while they demand the location of valuables.

Watching them through the glass you slowly lift the window open and creep in with the demon Andromalius and the Martial Commander. As one of the robbers turns a corner you thrust your spear through his neck and lift him off the ground. The Martial catches his gun and sets it down silently.

"Hey Robby! Robby, you find something?" calls another, whose gun is pointed at a child.

Losing patience, he stomps over to where Robby had last been seen only to be cut off by your bloody spear. You open your censor spraying the room with fumes.

"Fuck! Who the hell!?" shouts the robber, raising his gun. He pulls the trigger just as the Martial spirit covers the muzzle. The gun explodes damaging the robber's hand. He screams in pain as his blood splatters onto the floor near the family.

Dropping to his knees desperately trying to stop the bleeding, he continues to cry out, giving you an easy target. You thrust your spear into his mouth and partially out through the back of his skull. The last robber rushes downstairs as you pull your bloody spear and glide it through the steady fumes rising from your censor while quietly intoning a chant.

Andromalius, waiting stair side, catches the robber in the ankle as he runs down. The robber screams in pain as his leg goes numb. Unsure about the source of his pain, he lets his vision refocus and sees a snake lunge at him catching him. Its fangs catch him in the face and again in the arm. The robber begins the convulse violently as venom surges through his veins.

You untie the mother and then leave, allowing her to free the rest. Andromalius has proof you are to task and that night you strike against another dozen locations bringing with you the ruthless justice of a demonic hero.

Return to the base and prepare coordination with the Martial spirits and the forces of Andromalius on page 198

The Torn Gateway

"Look at this place," you say observing the destroyed perimeter fence that flanks the entranceway to the property. "I can barely remember when I passed through this."

You notice the remains of the magician that sought to overthrow the ruler order.

"We took him out," you comment.

"It was a close match," says the Martial Commander, "but you really did good, soldier."

"Why are we even here?" you question. "We could be in the world stopping bad things with ease. Think of how powerful we are. Why don't we go back?" you suggest.

"You don't want to stay and make gains here?" suggests the Martial Commander.

"We *have* gains, sir," you insist. "Think of all the change we can instigate. We can accomplish so much more out there. Here we patrol and train. But look," you mention pointing out the semi-charred corpse, "if we can take him, how can anything from the world match this?"

"Home base is just on that hilltop," the Martial counters, "you sure you don't want any assistance on this?"

"From who?" you reply. "People I've never seen? They did nothing to stop the invasion. They're doing nothing now. I'm out," you proclaim as you leave the property.

"We'll back you up," the Martial insists. "There will be more action where you're going."

"Where are we headed?" the Martial spirit implores.

"There's a neighborhood I know of, on page 132 really poor," you explain. "We secure the area, remove the negative elements and establish a presence. We create a kind of in world school but without the other crazy hourly factions to make things weird. We start there, then we move on. We will become heroes."

Spoils of War

After piling the bodies into a trunk, you take the gang leader hostage and force him to lead you to the drop points, cash houses and production facilities that support the organization.

You strike hard and fast, killing everyone who gets in your way. You claim their money and weapons but you dump their product into the sewers and rivers having no use for it. You come across another stash house and prepare to move in.

"My lord, this may be too much," one soldier states. "Our hour is in waning and we should regroup with the Commander.

"One more stop is not going to break our progress," you counter. "Let's move in.

Because of the devastation you have caused this organization, this group was prepared and opened fire right away. You and the Martial spirits form ranks creating a shield wall, deflecting the bullets and allowing you to slowly move forward.

You notice a car speeding away from the cash house, getting away with the money you came for. Enraged, you launch your shield at the gunmen striking one and increasing the speed of your charge. Placing your hand on the talisman, you give an order and the Martial spirits make a living ramp with their bodies and shields. You run up and launch yourself into the nearest gunman taking him down. You fight fiercely but are pinned down.

He's experienced. Shit my arm...

The thug smiles as he lifts you and pain shoots through your body as you hear a loud snap. Furious at the situation you pull up violently dislocating your shoulder, allowing you to shift and strike your opponent in the head, knocking him to the ground. Your soldiers crowd around you as you all retreat to the base.

*****

Back at the base you retreat to the main room which now has a circle adorned with Martial inscriptions. The smell of pepper and cedar saturates the house. Weaponry is neatly placed in racks and the cash is deposited upstairs. This place has become a Martial stronghold.

"We were mostly successful," you state to the Martial Commander.

The Martial growls softly then walks over, holding you still with a hand on your shoulder. You feel a cold plate on your skin over your shoulder.

Is that a talisman...?

Before you can ask you feel a violent pulse tremor through your body. Your bones return to their original places as your body is restored to its normal condition.

"Here," says the Martial handing you the talisman. "Only used for injuries during battle or diseases. When you activate it outside of our hour, it is extremely painful, as you can see."

You check your arm's range of motion and realize you are back to normal, albeit with some significant pain.

"Get some rest," the Martial continues. "We have a lot to do."

You wake up well rested and ready to find your comrades who have been preparing for a ritual. You join them on ***page 179***

To Conjure the Night

You study the pages available to you. It turns out the workroom is not so organized. Pages are mixed up and tools are scattered. Caz has departed and your concern for him is for now, secondary.

Why did this small trinket over-power them? Why didn't they return to take revenge? If it has this much power are there others I can create?

You find what you are looking for and study the instructions intensely. You go over the words until you know them by heart and the shapes until they are clearly memorized.

There are two here. Some pages are definitely missing but the directions seem to be precise.

You await the next pass for the hour of Saturn. As it approaches you prepare the incense. As the hour turns you burn the proper components and begin to work. Etching in the designs carefully and holding in your mind the purpose of this operation:

The Third Talisman of Saturn—This should be made within the Magical Circle and it is good for use at night when thou invokest the Spirits of the nature of Saturn.

After completing the talisman, you cover your new creation in silk which you find in a drawer. You also discover a small blade and following instructions you read from one of the many scattered pages in the workroom, cleanse it in fire and prepare for the night.

*****

The hour of Saturn rises three hours after sunset. You find a circle that was used during the battle and redraw it. Sitting down you burn the incense and intone the name of the hour. Fumigating the talisman and softly chanting the names or power associated to it. At first all you see around you is the dark. Quietly you sit and repeat your incantation.

Why won't they come? Is there something I'm missing? Why did they come before and not now?

In answer to your questions, you hear the whispering you heard in the workroom. To any sane person this would have been terrifying, to you it is the answer you are looking for.

A giant grin plasters over your face as you welcome the dark phantom like creatures as they float around your circle inhaling the incense as they pass the fumes.

You load more on to lure them into one spot and as they convene around the thick fumes you make your request, "I have many questions. I want to know what you are and what is this place? Where do you and all the spirits come from? How can I learn to channel more of this power?"

You had numerous other questions but thought to stop there as the spirits whisper in a language all their own.

"Breathe!" says one whose voice sounds as if he was exhaling through his teeth.

"The incense?" you question as you draw in the fumes but are instantly repulsed by the smell.

“Breathe deep!” he repeats, as the spirit blows out towards you what it had been inhaling.

You nod, following his instructions and fall into a fit of coughing and sudden dizziness. You drop, slightly convulsing and can hear the spirits speaking clearer than before.

“Follow the trail during sunrise! Bring incense! We will meet on our home ground.”

You hear a steady piercing scratch that slowly drifted away. It sounds like nails on chalkboard as it drifts from sight agitating your already afflicted body. You drift into the dark and as your body becomes still you hear the whisperings again, but this time, you can understand

some of the words. They are answering your questions. Your unconscious body smiles as you lay unmoving in the circle during the cold dark night.

Awakening in the morning you see claw marks leading away from your circle into the distance. You stand up, gather your talismans and replenish your incense before following the trail which the spirits of Saturn left for you into ***page 184***

Siege

You rise early and catch the soldiers preparing the gang leader you captured for ritual sacrifice. Tied up on the floor, just outside the circle in the main room.

"It needs to be you," the Commander states. "For this to work it has to be you who does the deed."

"Of course."

"Also, you will need this," he says passing you a scroll. "It will strengthen your forces if you use it before a battle. It will be a great fortification for our attack along with the sacrifice."

The Fourth talisman of Mars —It is of great virtue and power in war, wherefore without doubt it will give thee victory.

Bound and gagged the gang leader's eyes are closed. He is obviously praying. The Martials hang him upside down. The Commander hands you a ritual blade. Now in the hour of Mars, you cleanly slice through his throat, watching as his blood pools into a bronze basin with strange markings on it.

The Martials have been busy gathering supplies and fortifying this palace. I've never seen most of this equipment.

The blood pours and when the vessel is finally filled a Martial spirit enters, salutes the Commander and bows to you before picking up the vessel and heading outdoors.

The body is then disposed of as the soldier with the vessel begins to anoint the doorway and the entranceways with the collected blood. Hundreds of Martial spirits begin to materialize and fall in line. Drawn by the sacrifice they line up and salute loudly as you step onto the balcony.

*****

That night, during the hour of Mars your forces attacked, striking simultaneously at a production house, a strip club and a warehouse. You play a general's role and stay behind surveying the soldiers. With binoculars from atop a building you observe the battling.

You draw a clockwise circle with blood. Tracing the proper symbols of your hour, burn some cedar bark and pull the talisman you had recently made. Now, you see clearly through the eyes of the soldiers. They are moving faster than most human eyes can follow. Some are running up walls and others throw themselves through speeding car windows, tearing apart the enemies within.

They are significantly empowered. As spirits they were ferocious but since the sacrifice their abilities have been heightened.

Seeing the battlefield clearly you direct the troops with ease. You see every weakness and correct it immediately. You are tied into the Martial spirits and simultaneously see through their eyes. They instinctively fight as a unit and *you* are this unit's core.

*****

The next day the news comments on the desolation left by your exploits, saying the police believe it to be the work of highly motivated vigilantes. Weeks afterward, still no other gangs lay claim to the territory and the neighborhood remains dry. People eventually feel safe again and return to the streets.

However, your next moves became difficult, restricted by the hours and the fact that now, criminals were succeeding at hiding their operations, your plans for purging society of evil became much more difficult.

"Your options are twofold young lord," the commander instructs. "You increase sacrifices to hold onto more men. We've got a legion but for this scale and our hourly limitations we'll need even more for scouting and coordination."

"As long as only the wicked are sacrificed," you insert.

"Suit yourself. We can handle that on page 195

OR

"I do know of a certain Sub-lunar that is sympathetic to these sorts of causes. You call him, it solves all our problems. I've got his sigil here, just follow these instructions on page 192

You rise with the soldiers and prepare for another full day of training. They warriors march out in front of the barracks after washing in a trough.

"So, you stayed," calls out the Martial as you stand in line. "Alright kid, let's see what you can handle."

You begin the regimental workout with few breaks. Your body is hammered into order as you force yourself past any natural limitations. You spend the day learning from the different warriors and their past experiences of dying on the battlefield. Strategies from the centurions, sword fighting from the knights, knife combat from the veterans, archery from the samurai. Even ancient Greek heroes make an appearance. All classical martial styles are represented.

By the end of the session, you head into the barracks for a quick rest, but surprisingly you feel little thirst and hunger. The experience of learning under diverse masters has elates you. Few on earth could ever claim to be trained by skilled combatants from history's major wars.

Under Martial instruction your body becomes sculpted into a machine ready for a higher level of combat. The encounters with the different spirits from the past wars gives you not only their knowledge but also their abilities and qualities. Weeks pass by but you continue with the regimen. You learn to use almost every weapon ever created. Your progress alters your body, your martial practice deepens and you begin to forget your own past as you absorb the knowledge from your many instructors.

A loud horn sounds as you prepare yourself to return to training, you notice the spear left from the day before. It draws your attention; *this is the only weapon I haven't learned about yet.*

Taking the spear, you leave your shield and sword and then head back training on page 140.

The Pond and the Shade

Following the claw marks, it surprises you that a creature can make such consistent deep scars in the earth. The trail leads you to the forest and down a winding path coming to a crossroads. It veers sharply one way. The direction it indicates is very dark, the trees are thicker and unkept; here the sun's light does not penetrate so easily. The other path is the exact opposite; easy to traverse, well lit, and pleasant.

Maybe I should stop this? These spirits seem like monsters.

The opposite path looks so much more welcoming.

I can go back to the workroom and make a new talisman. I don't even know what I'm doing.

Turn away now. "If you are in need of guidance, we may be able to help," Comes a small chirping.

You see the sparrows that led you into this place and call for help asking where the other pathways lead. Follow them to ***page 21***

OR

The darkened pathway seems very unappealing. But the questions burn inside you. Why you are here? What is the meaning of all of this? With these questions the whispering returns and fills your head.

Carry on down this page to continue down the path you started.

You push on forward, the whispering you hear in your head is pushing your thoughts aside making it impossible to focus on anything other than the claw marks which are becoming harder to detect among the thick roots and uneven ground.

Am I going insane? I don't care! I want to understand!

You keep moving unsure of where you are going and now, not even sure what you are following. The claw marks that guided you have disappeared.

Under your breath you call out, "I know you hear me. I know you're near. I know you have answers. You won't leave me abandoned this far in."

Finally, you encounter a wall of unworked boulders and a giant willow tree that encases a pond; with its branches eerily hang near the center of the water. The land slopes under your feet, leading you towards the pond. You pass through the swaying branches and into a serene enclosure. The water's surface casts a perfect reflection in the shade. Moving to the water's edge, you stare at the stillness of the pond. The motionless pool seems dark despite it being daytime. The gigantic willow tree provides a night-like ambiance throughout the enclosure.

You pick up a small stone and toss it in. The water remains undisturbed and no satisfying splash resounds. You notice a circle close by and a smile breaks over your face. You prepare a generous amount of incense and begin a call. You chant names of power, unsure of who you are calling to, only hoping the master of the pond will respond. Your surroundings become darker, giving contrast the circle glows brightly, as the winds cool and the earth lightly tremors.

A layer of shadow peels from the pond's surface. The water remains undisturbed as the shadow drifts over towards the burning incense. It breathes deeply taking in the fumes. You examine the floating slender body cloaked in a flowing darkness. It turns facing you directly revealing an angry hooded countenance.

The spirit begins to walk on the ground approaching the circle and with it, darkness shrouds out what little light penetrated the grotto's atmosphere, eventually encasing the circle. Immediately you kneel in reverence for the ponds master's appearance. The shade stops and the darkness recoils. Pulling back its hood, it rounds the circle's boundary, while its head twists revealing another face. You witness four furious faces making up the head of this dark being.

"You summoned me," it declares in a haggard tone.

"I would like to know more about your nature," the spirit responds on page 221

Apostle of War

Weeks later after much intel and surveillance, the police ready for a collective assault on the Martial stronghold. Armored vans, helicopters, SWAT teams and riot squads are deployed. This immense force would intimidate the hardest of soldiers but not you. Yours is the power of Mars and the red star burns brightly in your veins.

Calmly you burn an immense amount of incense, mixed with blood of your enemies and even of your own to strengthen the legion. The police close in and issue commands over the loudspeakers. Ignoring their orders, you kneel within the red circle and make sincere supplication to the patron hour:

"I conjure you, Mars, by the heart of the mighty lion and by the will of the strong, burning fire, forged in iron, to obey me. You who rejoices in calamity and despises happiness, I conjure you the Third Hour, whom every planetary creation fears powerful and mighty, whose anger dries the bottom of the sea, whose glance breaks mountains, whose gaze terrifies the abyss. In your name, my lord, I dare to attempt every work. Turn back your foul fortune from me. Bring me only good fortune."

Donning your armor, taking hold of your shield and drawing your spear you rush outside without delay to confront the seething masses who would challenge your authority.

Outside they shine bright spotlights on you. Raising your shield, you block the light and any other potential threats. You are ordered to lower your shield and lay on the ground. Smiling, you throw your shield to the ground.

"All of you submit! The authority of the Martial hour is passed to me! I am chosen by destiny to purge the world of its evils. Forsake this pointless crusade and kneel before your master!"

Silence falls among the police. The calm is a testament to the greatness you have risen to, or so you thought. Without warning the police open fire using live rounds, piercing your armor and tearing effortlessly through your skin. You feel your veins burst and blood pour down over your body.

Falling to the ground you smile, feeling every painful moment.

Fine, you reason as you reach with a ruined right hand for a talisman, one you hold to your body which causes the numbing pain to become writhing agony as your bones reset and your tendons reattach to the bone.

With your healing complete and to the complete shock of all watching, you stand up and casually enclose yourself within a circle of your own blood. With the symbols traced you pull your latest creation and shout the barbarous names, raising the talisman like a shield.

Without delay, a storm of hail, explodes with unfounded fury battering the police on the ground and the helicopters in the air, forcing them to retreat from the area.

The storm increases its rage as gigantic hailstones smash through cruisers and batter the SWAT vans. There is nowhere to take cover;

the hail kills many police officers and severely injures many more. Lightning strikes other vehicles as violent winds sweep through the area lifting the heavily armored officers off their feet.

You rejoice seeing the demonic servants of the Martial Hour and the havoc they bring upon your enemies. As the storm calms you grasp another talisman and call your brothers at arms. With the legion at your side, you charge at the scattered forces.

With the first wave destroyed by the storm, you take advantage of the tempestuous onslaught catching the SWAT teams by surprise. The battle is swift and gruesome. Even with guns and armor you and the Martial soldiers overtake them and without wasting a moment you lead a continuous charge up into the third wave.

You spear an officer wearing riot gear through the neck as the soldiers advance in tight formation. Shields deflect bullets and with feats of extraordinary strength the soldiers continue their slaughter of the police. Eventually you force them into a retreat, raising your spear above your head, you drop the censor you had tightly chained to your waist and open it full blast. The fighting has been hard and the Martials need further sustenance to remain in physical form.

Now we finish them! They're blood is a perfect offering. The sacrifice we need to expand and conquer...

You are cut off when a sniper's bullet strikes your neck. You reach for the talisman to heal you only to have it shot from your hand. The cops have discovered your abilities. The Martial hour passed long ago. The incense has burned out. The soldiers begin to frenzy and are slowly defeated by the fourth wave of coordinated riot police with shields.

Refusing to give in you rise to your feet and with your spear rush the enemy. The cops open fire before your feet touch the pavement. This time they fire on you even after you hit the ground.

Your bloody lifeless body is slowly surrounded by the police. The legion has dissolved leaving a house with blood-stained doorposts and balcony rails. Unseen by the humans observing from afar, the Martial Commander leans over your body with the legion of soldiers and they breathe in your life essence. Your wrath has finally ripened and is harvested by the spirits of Mars for their own sustenance. Only at the end do you realize the true cruelty of the Martial Hour and the cost of living by the sword.

You lay dying as your brothers feast upon you. Your heart turns to ice as you are saddened not by any regret or remorse but because you had only defeated three of the five waves sent out after you.

FIN

"Should we work with one of their kind?" you sneer.

"Each is different," the Commander explains. "Well, most are terrible but this one, he's on another level. This guy pursues thieves *and* even returns what they steal. He has a sort of sense of underhanded dealings and illicit activity. He can smell out criminals and on top of all this, he loves to punish them and I do mean punish. Criminal or delinquent behavior is something he just can't stand."

"Why should we summon him?" you ask.

"Well, if we run this ourselves, we are limited by the changing hours. To pull off an operation this size will require sacrifice, blood and lots of it. He is not limited by an hourly change and he has thirty-six legions that can aid us."

You think deeply about the proposition, then turn to the Commander, "What will it take to summon such a creature?"

The Martial nods and explains the matter of conjuration.

*****

Standing within the circle in the main room of the house, you bear upon you the sigil of Andromalius and the spear directing your focus. With the proper intonations and during the daylight hours you send word and burn heavy incense infused with the blood of your victims.

The smoke begins to swiftly spiral and materializes in the form of a powerful man with a serpent wrapped around his arm. Due to

the high quality of your offer, he takes complete physical form.

"Why have you summoned me?" the Sub-lunar asks in a stoic voice.

"To catch thieves and criminals and to punish them severely. We will need you to be bound to our cause," you add.

The snake hisses aggressively bearing its fangs while Andromalius remains composed, "If you have been wronged, we can hunt the wicked together. Then let our work begin."

Growing impatient, you step outside the circle. The Martial stands ready to battle surprised by your actions, "Everyone has been wronged," you state, gathering the censor and raising it up. "Together we will hunt them all. But I need your senses to locate them."

Seemingly impressed with your offer, the snake calms, "I can detect wickedness and underhanded dealings close by. You will have to prove yourself if you are to bind me to your service."

"Lead the way."

Follow Andromalius to page 168

Fortify the Program

You rise now every day at four, before the sunrise. Stepping into the main room, you stand in the circle. Its red coloring has now become completely familiar to you. You take a bronze censor, burn the coals and place your cedar bark, pepper and storax mixed with human blood. You adorn armor like the Martial spirits and keep your weapons close by.

Then you begin the call, "Quirinus!"

"Here Sir!" comes the response.

"Pater!"

"Sir!" replies another the spirit of the third hour.

"Alator, you here brother?!"

"My lord, I live!"

"Angara!" "Bahram!" "Ares!" "Madim!"

Each one responds in turn from a different room in the house. The Martial spirits were summoned to form and ready to begin the program. Four-point squat thrusts, viper digs and other strength exorcises at three hundred reps a piece. When the session is complete, all the soldiers yell out, "Summi militum virtus!"

*****

Gangs in the area have been completely purged. Criminal activity is at a low and no one is willing to step up to challenge you. Your original objective to purge the world of evil has taken a second position. Now, the focus is a perpetual feeding of the home base with fresh sacrifice. Even lesser criminals are targeted and their blood used to keep your ranks strong and the legions manifest.

*****

On a calm day, protestors march and chant. A Martial soldier follows close by, hearing the parade of black clad demonstrators, "Who's streets? Our streets!"

Surprised by the implication he returns to the home base and reported to you.

"My lord, rivals have taken to invasion. They have no respect for the authority of the Third Hour."

Without words you grab your spear and march with your comrades to meet the interlopers.

In the distance a patrol of officers stands on duty to prevent violence from escalating. You send in a soldier to confront the mob of black masked aggressors.

"You have trespassed on sacred ground," the soldier declares, "your presence defies our order. Retreat at once!"

They swear and mock the spirit and spray him with some sort of mace. He barely blinks, wiping his face and smelling the liquid. Then in one swift motion of his spear he skewers his attacker through the neck. He lifts the body effortlessly as it squirms uncontrollably while blood drips down the blade.

The crowd stands silent, unable to process the situation. They have never encountered this level of violence; their arrogant demeanor is replaced by a silent ambivalence. With the fires of their pride extinguished, you give the order and the Martial spirits begin to appear, surrounding their position. The attack is swift and brutal; the skirmish turns into a slaughter which lasts only minutes.

Police attempt to protect the crowd but are overtaken by the Martial power. Many of the officers give their lives defending the black masked protestors.

"Listen to them my lord," states a soldier, "they sound like children."

"Their blood will be a low-grade offering," you observe, "barely worthy of the higher cause they will be made to serve. But they were invaders and invaders must die."

"My lord, the Commander has sent word," interjects a soldier.

"I will return to the base," you respond. "Finish with this mess and harvest what you can."

You quickly return to page 148

Heroic Legacy

With the aid of Andromalius you punish hundreds of criminals throughout the city in the months that follow. You save lives, rescue kidnapped children, destroy child sex rings and defend the weak from extortion. Even the organized syndicates are beaten back by your efforts. Your efficiency is matched only by your brutality. The news reports its most cruel murders the city has ever seen and brands you and your legion a vigilante terrorist group.

In many of the poorer neighborhoods, gang graffiti is replaced with murals of Roman centurions, brandishing spears and shields in heroic poses. To the youth you became an urban hero. As your actions increase the communities began to house less of the negative elements and an increase in investment spawns a rebirth as businesses return to the areas.

Despite many politicians wanting to eliminate your presence, many of the locals follow their directive with less enthusiasm. Only months ago, these districts were dangerous to men, women, children and especially cops. Now, they are safe for everyone. Even still, despite your favor with the population, your violent exploits have attracted the attention of higher powers which view you more as a threat than as a boon.

"Commander," you call after dismissing the cohort while entering the main room. "I will need your assistance."

"My lord, how can I be of use?"

"We've had immense success. With the legions of Andromalius giving us full reports and aiding our cause, violent crime is nearly purged from this city. We've got all his legions at work. We burn incense for the whole of the day. It's taking a lot of resources to keep this going and with all this we still miss opportunities."

"How do you mean my lord?" asks the Commanders.

"The vans we seized a while ago make for easy travel, but our operation is almost city wide. It takes too long to get places and with everyone working I need a way to travel through the city with greater easy. What have you got for me?"

The Commander thinks for a moment then retrieves a scroll with written instructions.

"Bind a sylph to these and you should be good to go."

The shoes or boots should be made of white leather, on the which should be marked the Signs and Characters of Art.

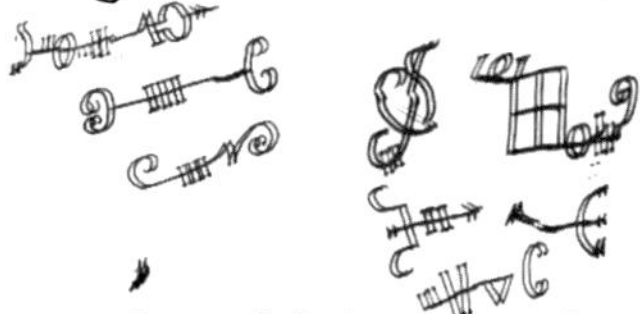

These shoes should be made during the days of fast and abstinence, namely, during the nine days set apart before the beginning of the Operation...

Finish the operation and utilize your new equipment on page 205

Ask the Martial Commander if others had utilized the powers of the Third Hour as you have on page 204

Bare Bones

You wander the pathways curious about the other hourlies and what they might be like. You ponder over the different herbs, their strange names and the "domains" they affiliate with.

You notice in the distance an oddly shaped ground level building with chimneys and window-like openings emptying a curious smoke which shifts colors. You approach hoping to understand a little more of the situation and maybe get clearer answers to your questions.

"Where is the door to this place?" you say aloud seeing no entrance. You feel the harvested plants associated with Mercury shake as you retrieve them, wondering what could be going on.

"Ah yes, that makes sense!" you whisper in an excited tone as you burn the plants, allowing the smoke to rise from your censor. You playfully pass the sickle through it and hear the same voice that spoke when you harvested. *"Intone the name of power to be greeted by the hour."*

"Well, I do not remember the intonations," you say sadly.

But raising your voice, "I bear no one harm. I do not wish to bind or force my will on anything. I just need answers, please."

The vapors from the lab begin to shimmer, light from the late afternoon sun is clearly repelled as the smoke dispels the natural brightness from the area leaving the clear night sky visible. You notice that this phenomenon only spans a limited distance. You can clearly see the late afternoon still in effect beyond the vicinity.

A vine grows from the chimney and compasses the building, branching off into many directions and sprouting glowing grapes which hang down near your position. You pluck one, its shape changed slightly as it begins to float, circling around you. Smiling, you pluck many more and watch them follow a similar pattern.

"These are the planets! This is amazing!"

You watch the glowing orbits circle in conformity to their celestial counterparts. Even the numerous moons are accounted for, noticing a single "fruit" left you pull it off and let it rise to its station. It settles in the center, reshaping into a flowing ball of flame.

"There's the sun," you state, satisfied with the completed model of the solar system.

Beams of light pierce through the wall of the building carving a very precise doorway which opens before you. Too excited to be nervous, you enter the building to discover a fully operational laboratory within.

The lab is massive and filled with equipment from the renaissance. You notice that each one of the laboratory workers has hanging from their utility belts, an open flask which emits a constant vaporous stream. From this stream emerge their bodies. They float throughout the lab barely stopping to greet your entrance. But what catches your attention, beyond the wondrous experiments taking place is a skeleton slouched on an apparatus. You begin to slowly back away, unsure of what you've walked into.

"Greetings," says a voice from a comely youth with a pair of sea-blue goggles and a medieval lab coat. As he floats towards you, his coat seems to change colors. "Welcome to the Mercurial laboratory."

"I was just wondering, um, well..." overwhelmed by the current situation and the dead body in the center of the room, your words stumble out of your mouth.

"You've come for answers," says the Mercurial. "You do smell like the grotto."

This statement makes all the others in the lab cease their work and focus on you. Their attention makes you nervous.

"Yes," you affirm, "but why is that there...?" you ask pointing to the skeleton, trying to change the subject. "How did he die?"

"Oh no he's not dead," declares the Mercurial. "He's right there." You see him point to a clear jar filled with black liquid. "He's actually more alive than the two of us right now."

Confused by his response, you are unsure as how to reply. The strangeness of this place seems to have no limit.

"I would however like to ask you to leave your sickle and censor outdoors. It slightly disrupts our operations. Here I'll guide you out," he says leading you to the door.

"Why are there so many hourlies? And why are they so different?"

"Well, as above so below," explains the Mercurial gesturing to the planets outside. "We each have in the physical world a corresponding conduit that channels our influence into reality. The one dominant over you now is Saturn. Look," he directs pointing out the movements of Saturn. "the Greeks called him Kronos. In mythology he swallowed his own children to prevent an uprising. It takes about twenty-nine years and a bit to fully circle the sun. It encompasses all other hourly spirits linked to the orbits within its motions like time swallowing us all."

You listen eagerly to the grim warning hoping for a deeper explanation.

"If this seems unfortunate or bitter it is only because others do not align to his malignant effects. Saturn is hostile to those who live ordinary lives. Especially those who flee to the school but do not leave their emotions behind."

He informs you that his hour is ending and he must return to his duties. He gives you some incense and lead plates specialized for the hour of Saturn The Mercurial bows and retreats within the laboratory. The entranceway seals quickly and the vines as well as the planets floating around you fade from existence. Nature returns to how it was meant to be and you notice the sun setting and feel the talismans heating up. The dark whispers renew, imploring you to return to the grotto.

Return to the grotto to seek further guidance from its master on page 223

Heroes Passed

"How many heroes have you worked with before me Commander?"

"Heroes," he replies, "has a different definition according to us. For the powers of the Third Hour our influence is spread through warfare, combat and calamity. You know we help build cultures. Heavens of endless conflict, dying in battle to enter the afterlife was developed when my race met with yours. I myself have participated in battles alongside the greatest of mortals. We feed off the destruction you create and when your kind are finally overthrown the downfall is the greatest sustenance for our kind."

"Commander are you meaning to say that *my* defeat is expected?" you inquire.

"You give us a reason to inhabit the physical plane. You have become great and do great work. We are with you till the end," he responds sincerely.

Not quite satisfied with his response you become a bit nervous about a possible betrayal.

I supply their offerings and have bound them to me. I could exorcise them at will. The Third Hour belongs to me. There is nothing to worry about.

Continue your crusade on page 205

Air of Authority

With your new white leather boots, you begin to traverse the city. Under the guidance of the legions of Andromalius you are directed to the illegal happenings in every district. The aerial spirit bound to your service allows you to jump long distances and with your boots you glide over the air currents. Although you do not actually fly, you can easily cross long distances without hinderance.

Passing through alleyways and over rooftops you intercept a robbery, bust into a top-level skyscraper and force executives of a large corporation to confess to embezzling, subdue a car thief, stop a robbery at gun point and intercept a kidnaper.

With all this activity you are captured on numerous social media platforms from onlookers who happen to be quick enough catch a pic of you. Your fame increases exponentially making you a hero to the citizens.

Finishing your rounds after the Martial hour subsides, you return to the home base. Upon entrance you remove your footwear and hang it above a small, open censor emitting a thin stream of incense which smothers the boots. The aerial spirits trace through the signs marked onto the boots. You observe their tiny forms bathing in the steady stream of incense smoke.

"So, you are a sylph," you whisper, as you observe their sleek moments over the characters engraved onto your shoes.

"My lord," came the familiar voice of the Martial Commander. "There's something I have for you, come with me."

Observe the hypnotic dance of the aerial spirits on the next page before following the Martial to page 148

The Darkest Hour

Within the workroom you observe and read over the charts and diagrams. You notice the clock is about to turn to the hour ♄.

I wonder what this one does. You ponder as you withdraw a black tablet from the table.

From outside you hear what starts off at first as some loud shouting, followed by a collective intonated chant. Then silence…

What is with this weird chanting everywhere…

A violent tremor shakes the world around you as the yelling intensifies. You rush outside to see a full-scale war erupting. Dragons fly through the skies as monstrous creatures tear through the landscape. Cloaked figures in the distance hold their ground, directing infernal hosts.

Great pillars of incense rise and strange monstrous forms emerge from the fumes. At first the creatures move about without order, but one appears from the tendrilous mist and into reality in the form of an armed soldier with a lion's head, riding on a pale-colored horse. Quickly the creatures fall in line under his command.

The forest begins to burn and phantom-like spirits retreat from the area. The column of incense continues to spew out beings, this time with weaponry. Large fat demonic beasts with cannons attached to their bodies where limbs should be open fire on seemingly everything they see.

You notice a legion of Roman soldiers marching through the

chaos to meet the enemy forces as other clocked figures fly in on the back of miniature cyclones toward the source of the disruption.

You slam the door to the workroom shut. As the fighting intensifies, you feel the earth shaking. You hide under a table hoping all of this will pass quickly.

What the hell have I agreed to?!? How could I just come here? What the hell is going on!!!

You hear a knocking on the door. Someone is trying to get in. Frozen with fear, you have no idea what to do or what to expect. Barging into the workroom, a young cloaked being pulls back his hood.

"Hey," he says. "you think hiding is really going to help you?"

You rise slowly, he looks familiar.

"It's me," he says showing his face, "Caz! Everyone knows me."

Sure, they do, you consider, still not sure exactly where you saw this guy from.

You nod hoping he will explain what's going on. An explosion shakes the building.

"It's that cult," he states. "They've got numbers. They're trying to force the mansion to respond. They're fucking crazy!"

Still completely unsure as to what's happening you wait for further explanation.

"Hey," he adds. "That's actually a good idea. Are you going to finish that?" he mentions pointing to the plate in your hand.

You look on the table and see a parchment with directions:

The First Talisman of Saturn—This talisman is of great value and utility for striking terror into the spirits. Wherefore, upon its being shown to them they submit, and kneeling upon the earth before it, they obey.

'This could work. I think... But maybe I should learn more before starting this?' If you turn to *page 210* *you can ask questions about the nature of the war that you are caught up in.*

OR

You forge the symbols onto this plate and create the talisman with some help from Caz. Reveal the finished product on *page 211*

A Blunt Inquiry

"Caz, tell me what the hell is happening? What is this cult and what are those things?"

"Oh, that's right, you're new. The cult is what we call them, they're a gang of magicians trying to overthrow the current authority. They claim '*A master will arrive from the East*' but it's a load of garbage. They have numbers and they will force anyone they can to fight for their cause. Those *things* are Sub-lunars, demons. Legions of them and other spirits work to maintain the upkeep of this property *and* keep the mansion hidden. The mansion is like the town hall of this place. I've never been, but I've seen it once."

Caz pauses sensing that you are overwhelmed.

"This cult is trying to weaken the defenses of this place and force the leaders from the mansion to respond. Perhaps even reveal its location or the location of the gate. You would have seen it coming in. It has been sealed since this war began. No one will be free until this threat is dealt with."

Reflecting on Caz's statement you wonder what your purpose of coming here was supposed to accomplish on page 211

Why

The battle outside becomes more ferocious as you complete the talisman. Caz instructs you to burn some incense and take a small censor as well as some of the juniper, myrrh and sulfur.

"I've never seen anyone make one of these before," Caz states. "Willingly I mean."

"Why?" you ask concerned. "Are these ones hard to make?"

Chilling demonic screams interrupt your question as you and Caz both clasp your ears and duck under the tables.

Why did I come here...? you wonder as the fighting intensifies. The battle outside produces sounds you've never heard before. It is impossible to fathom your circumstance.

Is this really what it takes to learn magic? Was I brought here to die for some hidden power in some supernatural war? I barely understand anything. Why can't this fight stop? What is the point of all this?

The world goes dark as you retreat within. The darkness welcomes you. It hides you, blocks out the distractions. The war rages in the distance but within there is only the darkness. You hear whispering of a language you cannot understand. The sounds of battle disappear. A foul smell fills the air and a bitter taste fills your mouth. Pain and regret block out any sense of self-preservation; you simply fall into a deep stillness.

"...Buddy," came Caz's familiar and cowardly voice. "You okay?"

Rising to your feet you push him out of the way and head to the doorway.

"What are you doing?" he asks.

Without speaking, you open the door and step out into the light. The battle has moved away from your area. But some Sub-lunars remain and take notice of you. Most of them look like a mix breed between animals and men.

"Mortal prey from the stables," cries one of them as they circle around you.

They wait for you to react, to protect yourself. You close your eyes and hear the whisperings of that hidden language and pull your talisman as they close in.

Holding it before you like a badge, the demons scream loudly as they retreat faster than your eyes can perceive. Two of them get caught under its influence and are forced to the ground. You approach, slowly allowing your fears to be purged by the sudden defeat of the hostiles.

"Do you have names?" You ask stoically.

"I am one from the fifty legions of Savnok," claims one.

"My name is Marad," assert the other. "I served the masters of the house until I was released by the rebels."

You study their forms and notice how much they struggle. Like a great weight was suddenly pressed atop them and holding them against their will. They looked terrified. You try to understand how this tool you just made can restrain such powerful entities.

"Why do you fight this war?" you ask.

"We do not wish to serve mortals at all," spat Marad.

"The chaos this war produces gives us chances to undo our bindings," adds the legionnaire.

"If this distraction persists, more of our kind can be free and then we can destroy all of you and be free to roam the world as *we* like," Marad states proudly.

Reflecting on their answers, you stare at both monstrous forms before you. Moments ago, they and their allies were the most fearful beasts you had ever encountered. Now, they are wholly subjugated to your will.

"Go," you say softly, as the unseen force that confined them now rushes them out of sight.

The battle is long over, the sounds of chanting and screaming have ceased. Even birds and the sound of the winds are absent. You feel an inner stillness matched by your surroundings. You calmly sit on the grass; without obstruction or inner turmoil you are recollected within the silence.

Unsure of what to do next, you follow your instincts, return to the workroom and build another talisman.

To fashion a Martial talisman, turn to page 125.

To engrave another talisman to Saturn, turn to page 175.

"Before you step out and go all crazy," the Commander says, "why don't we set you up with some proper tools."

You nod, accepting his offer.

"Here," he says, handing you a scroll. "Read this."

The Sixth Talisman of Mars —It hath so great virtue that being armed therewith, if thou art attacked by anyone, thou shalt neither be injured nor wounded when thou lightest with him, and his own weapons shall turn against him.

Without words you set up your tools and begin at the hour of Mars to engrave the talisman on an iron plate. The Martial places his fist over top of the completed object pressing firmly activating the instrument.

"I'm putting this to use today," you exclaim.

"This one's a little more restrictive," the Martial clarifies. "it's not like back home where our presence is more absolute. Make sure you battle with it on our hour for the best result."

*****

Dark vans roll around the neighborhood searching for Roman soldiers who apparently "appear out of nowhere." None of the gang leaders would have believed such a feat to be possible but with so many deaths and the whole of their operations in the area shut down, they set out to deal with the intruders.

Three vans pull up to a deserted corner. The streets are still quiet. Most of the residents fear a gang war and as a result are locked up in their homes. The vans empty and out steps a well-dressed man to survey the calm.

"Never seen the streets like this," he says under his breath.

You approach, hooded and in plain sight. The gang members pull their guns as you come nearer, the leader quickly raises his hand calming his men.

"So, you did all this?" he asks.

"It doesn't matter," you reply, "we fight, right now, me and you for control of everything."

He laughs at your challenge, "That's not how things work here. But I am interested to see what you've got. Moose, take care of the Holy Roman Emperor."

As Moose approaches you pull your spear, while he pulls his gun, "Spear to a gunfight…" he mutters aiming at your head.

You feel the new talisman in a pocket close to your heart, "…his own weapons shall turn against him…"

The gun misfires nearly exploding in his hand. He screams in shock as you finish him off.

"What the hell! Guys c'mon!" orders the well-dressed leader as his men pull guns of their own.

Without a word Martial spirits materialize and spear all the criminals leaving their leader behind. He goes to pull his gun but is intercepted by a Martial spirit.

Facing the leader, you back him towards a corner where the bodies are being piled, "If you want to live tell us where you store your cash, weapons, and product."

"We're going for the cash first. We take the vans to <u>page 172</u>. Can any of you know how to drive?

OR

"Let's head back to base. This one will make for a great offering to the cause," you command, as you prepare your forces to return to the base on <u>page 179</u>

"One man did this," you point out. "How is it that the most powerful of this place are absent when they are invaded?"

You pause observing one of the Martial soldiers who nods, ensuring that you can leave the circle. Stepping out from the magical barrier you evaluate the possible defenses the mansion would have.

"How are they worthy if something like this happens? Their front-line destroyed and home base exposed," you explain. "This place is weak. If we take the mansion now, we can assure safety. We just took this guy over here who had a king of the East supporting him."

"They call themselves kings," states the Martial Commander. "They're powerful but not completely kings. Only Beelzebul the exarch is a true ruler over the Sub-lunars and he is bound to the master of the mansion."

"Did you see him in the fight?" you ask.

The Martial remains silent.

"This whole place would benefit from a serious leadership change. The mansion is undefended. Let's take the blood from the magician and use it to strengthen our forces. We attack during the height of our hour, which will soon be in the ascent. Fate smiles upon..."

The Martial Commander's spear bursts through your chest and his massive hand grips your throat, "Don't speak or attempt to react. Make this easy for me."

In utter disbelief and shock you stare unable to process hatred or disgust with what just occurred. The pain overwhelms all your senses and freezes you in place as your heart rate increases, causing you to bleed out faster. The Martial lays you down slowly, removing the spear as the soldiers stand vigil around you.

"I'm sorry kid. In this world, you're either fuel or fire. We don't waste anything."

The Martials inhale your essence and along with your lifeblood, you feel life source drain away while it strengthens your comrades. Unable to regain any composure you expire as the solders raise their voices in a funeral chant. They lift your body respectfully, bow to the mansion and carry you away to the barracks for a soldier's burial.

Despite the honorable sendoff it was not an overpowered enemy or a glorious sacrifice that took you from the world, but human pride and selfish ego. If those had been conquered instead, your life as well as the safety of the school would have remained secured.

FIN

To Welcome the Hour

You find yourself with a large group of people; some you remember at the party and others you have never seen before. Despite this, you play along within a choral group in a perfect harmony. The choir moves into a circle and floating bouquets of various flowers and herbs are continuously being set within the center of your gathering as the music plays on.

Upon closer inspection you notice spirits materializing in the air. Tiny humanoids with butterfly wings drift in and out of sight as they drop their bundles of various plants, herbs, berries, flowers and fruits special to the hour of Venus. Once a huge pile is gathered, the maiden directs their separation and order.

"They are Sylphs," the maiden in green states, "air spirits. We are sustained in this domain by offering alluring vibrations to the various entities that dwell here. From them, we receive the plants we need for incense to perform our operations and spread our influence."

You wander the Venerean territory and notice artists creating abstract paintings on parchments and many strange creatures becoming mesmerized by them. The Animalistic beings are being pacified the music and hypnotized by the art. Once pacified, they freely answer questions about the state of the school, the affairs of the mansion, the different hourly activities and any pertinent news.

"Most spirits have ingrained natures that do not allow them to see beyond their own paradigm," she explains. "From us they gain relief. From them we gain supplies, information and even friendship."

You continue your observation of some truly fearsome demonic entities and how calm they have become.

"Our essence spreads through the sound waves. We do not bind the Sub-lunars, we give them something their nature demands," she instructs. "Remember, the way of the enchanter is never to enslave any being to gain profit, our presence is the profit unto itself," states the maiden. "The hour turns strong; we can organize another operation for your..."

A loud blast is heard as chanting resonates throughout the area. The Sub-lunars are distracted from their engagements and quickly become violent, many of them bowing in respect and then fleeing. The maiden gracefully takes her leave and helps other Venerean hourlies gather the recent offerings into the pyramid.

Follow the Maiden into the pyramid on page 403

OR

Follow the Sub-lunars as they flee the gardens to page 321

Queries before the Greatest Ancient

The Saturnite's voice is dark and hypnotic. He floats around the circle cloaked in a darkness that pushes out the light rather than being absent from it. The thick cloud of incense produces a strong smell that you must push to the edge of the circle to keep it from overwhelming you.

"All things are held together by imperceptible connections and stellar rays. *I* am the one who undoes them."

You take a moment to really fathom what is standing before you. If what it says is true, then this being is not to be crossed.

"This school, why am I here? Why is it here?"

"It is called a school; but that is a mortal perception. This property has been made to house the forces that govern reality. They manifest here in various forms so mortals can interact with them and by this mortal nature is changed. Only the worthy may approach. You are here because you have potential to rule these forces."

You never once thought of yourself in such a light. But what if he is lying?

"How do I really know I am worthy? How can I verify you are telling me the truth?"

The spirit ceases his circling keeping his stoic gaze on you, floating outside the stream of incense.

"The hour of Saturn does not lie," he declares coldly as he resumes his orbit around your circle.

"What about the other spirits? What are they like?"

"Go and see for yourself," he says, stretching out his arm toward the pond. The waters remained undisturbed as a wave of shade carries two items to the hourly. "Take these," he motions letting down before you gently a well worked censor and a sickle.

"This censor is made of iron and will hold offerings for my hour more adequately. The sickle will allow you to identify the different herbs and roots around the property. With them you can harvest components necessary for your interactions with the hourlies."

He floats backwards and reenters his pond, keeping his unblinking gaze on you as he seamlessly enters his native domain. His voice resounds around the grotto as you retrieve the items.

"My hour closes and I prefer rest, but the others have hours in ascension. Experience serves as the best answer. When my hour returns freely call upon me here."

Examining your new tools, you bow thankfully towards the pond. Standing up you return the way you came only to find the pathway clear. Before leaving you hear the whisperings, they grow faint as you exit the grotto.

You see the old road you took to get here and are intrigued by your new tools. Eager to put them to use you begin to experiment on page 255

OR

But still, you have more questions. On page 159 you sit in silent contemplation allowing the natural cycle of hours to pass. Saturn's hour rises and you return to the pond.

The Saturnite rises from his pool and you stand ready with a greater yearning for understanding. As the spirit engages with the incense you address him firmly, armed with the sickle he gave you.

"I met with the Mercurials. They explained many things," you affirm, watching the unchanging reaction of the tall fluid shadow floating before you.

"They have an interesting specialty and perform many experiments. They can offer people who adhere to them many gifts. Besides the sickle and censor, what do you offer me?"

The Saturnite ceased his feeding, turning its focus entirely to you. It begins gliding around the circle as he answers your question, "Truth and freedom. Ours was the first of the hourlies to descend and work with mortals. The others will promise you power and wealth or phenomenal abilities, but they cannot take you past the void that waits for all living things. All of their influence depends on this world, mine is from beyond."

Not sure how to respond you find yourself in a deeper state of being as the dark entity circles your barrier.

"What is beyond?" you ask.

"Oblivion. Freedom from the senses that limit you and freedom from the reactive feelings that control your being. A release from the pain of the past and the false hope of an unreachable future. The boundless, everlasting rest that all beings must inevitably pass through."

Not sure exactly how to comprehend this message, but realizing the force behind his words, you long to understand more but are unsure how to engage.

"Experience is the best teacher," states the Saturnite, "you have plates for carving."

You nod, retrieving the lead plates. The spirit takes in a deep breath and circling your position exhales onto the ground as he hovers, leaving clear images carved into the earth.

"These are the directions to create other talismans to make use of my influence."

"I still have questions about the property and its inhabitants before I commit further; just let me explore a bit more over on ***page 230***

"Use the sickle to carve and the censor to burn," directs the Saturnite. "Begin before the hour passes on ***page 225***

"Set your tools to work," orders the Saturnite. "Carve and chant as I instruct you."

You prepare the incense and the plates, readying your hand with the sickle. At first it feels clumsy and inaccurate. You try to angle it in different directions but cannot find a steady grip required to make articulate shapes into the plates. The Saturnite, unemotionally breathes in the rising smoke from the censor and then speaks, "stand to the edge of the circle."

Cautiously you obey. His head turns revealing another sneering face that breathes what he inhaled into your face. You instantly feel a euphoric rush. You mind seems to detach from your body, leaving you without a sensation of control. Your vision blurs but your hearing enhanced. The whispering increases but instead of it being inarticulate murmurings you hear the words clearly.

You begin to feel the sickle in your grip. With a firm hold and a calm mind, you begin to engrave the talisman. Using newfound precision, you quickly and perfectly engrave all the names and shapes intoning the words of power to strengthen the influence of the Saturnite authority as the voices describe their functions:

"This is the fourth talisman of our hour. It will serveth principally for executing all the experiments and operations of ruin, destruction, and death. And when it is made in full perfection, it serveth also for those spirits which bring news, when you invoke them from the side of the

South."

Their speech rips into your mind making you unable to remember or focus on anything but their words. As your thoughts flee and your memories rescind, the void in your mind is replaced by the scathing claims of an unknown whispering voice, sending you past reality and into a deep darkness. A sensation of unknowing seeps over your being. It seems freeing, but you've forgotten what it means to be confined. You float in an infinite space. You remember your body and your friends, but they are only a memory now. What you once had been is no longer. Your instinct is to cry, but you feel no sadness. Your body seems suspended beyond motion, where all nature ceases to be and where existence never was.

Gasping for air your physical body reclaims your mental consciousness. You awaken on the ground shaking and not sure what to make of the experience. Your mind fails to recall exactly what happened. Like a nightmare where only the fear remains, you can no longer comprehend what caused the terror.

"Quickly, before the hour closes," comes the familiar tone of the Saturnite. "The seventh talisman of my name. This is fit for exciting earthquakes. If invoked during the height of our hour, it is sufficient to make the whole universe tremble."

You rise to your feet. Staring down at the ground you notice the two talismans magnificently engraved.

Did I make these? You wonder as the hour passes and the Saturnite retreats to his slumbering domain. His voice remains, as if next to you: "These tools are no trinkets. The force of my fear is within them; if you make use of my power unwisely, I will turn it against you and unravel the fabric of your being. Your memory will be lost from reality. You will be as if you never were."

His voice fades as you place the new talismans into your pockets. When the sun rises you realize that your clothing has acquired an ashy black tinge. Unsure what to make of this, you take up the censor and the sickle and leave the grotto.

You walk the property. It is unclear where to go or what to do. You have no direction or desire to be directed. The hours that arise next will determine your experience on ***page 234***

Elemental Friendship

With Sal, you now have someone to freely converse with and for the price of a small amount of incense he remains your loyal companion. Without the intelligence of the hourlies or the cunning of the Sub-lunars Sal acts more like a pet than an equal. Even still, to be able to talk openly to someone other than yourself is a welcome change.

Together you observe the labor of the spirits and their activities. Together, you gather numerous herbs, weeds, barks and roots that you will use to create incense for drawing out many Sub-lunars around the property to your service. With Sal, you become more patient and less challenging. Offering gifts to the various dominions for information and leaving the censor burning as a gift for any spirit willing to answer questions about their natures and the natures of the others.

Sal even reveals to you a hidden field within the forest where you find numerous fire elementals and observe them forming into hovering flames during the full moon. You observe them join with one another, their colors shifting on the darkened backdrop and then separating as sparks fall into the field, quickly burning up the grass.

"I see, this is mating for you!" you exclaim as you watch with excitement.

The procedure continues and Sal eventually joins in. You lose sight of him during the light show and eventually you fall asleep in the field warmed by elemental heat.

Sal wakes you in the morning, happily leaping around back in his lizard form. You notice that the other elementals have departed as you rise. Gathering your censor and sickle, you continue to travel the pathways with your friend. You come to a crossroads, arriving at a sharp fork before a thick forest of trees.

"Okay Sal, you choose this one buddy. Left, or right?" you say excitedly.

Left leads to a downward slope and a winding road which starts on page 272

OR

Right leads to an even path beginning on page 275.

The Hearth

"Go as you see best," said the Saturnite. "If you return, come at my hour and bring offerings."

You leave the grotto again and wander the many pathways of the property. It's still dark but a bright night sky and a full moon illuminate your way. You come to the edge of a stone wall that leads off the path.

"A wall? Here? Why?"

You decide to follow the wall and after some travel you come to a boiling hearth with a large stone chimney seamlessly attached to the wall. The wall has a sharp ninety-degree turn, giving the impression that only a partial structure was ever completed.

"I wonder what's cooking?" you ask, as the steam rises from the cauldron. You detect the smell of myrrh and hear an eerie song as you draw near.

You notice a circle carved into the ground before the cauldron. Then, slowly you look up and see hundreds of flowing phantoms. Their ghost-like forms swim through the steam rising from the cauldron.

Slowly they take notice of you and you hear a myriad of voices speaking and answering questions as they descend, "We see the outermost hour smells strongly on this one. He is not to approach. None may come near. The silver is hers and she does not share. Hers is the moon, weather half, full or bare."

A tempest breaks out and freezing rain ferociously engulfs the land. Hail and lightning soon follow as you try to shield you face from the onslaught. Quickly you begin to freeze and panic. The hail strikes hard and the wind threatens to pull you off your feet.

Why are they attacking me?! What did I do?!

Eventually, you become numb as the beatings continue. You huddle onto the ground in fetal position hoping the rain will ease up so that you can make an escape.

The hail strikes relentlessly as the winds and rain freeze your body restricting your movement. The fearsome chill combined with the repeated blows leaving you numb.

Why is this happening? If I don't move, I'm going to die!

You feel the sickle at your waist and you instinctively fasten your fingers onto it.

"...Why am I afraid...?"

Forcing your arm outstretched you strike the ground and carve a circle around yourself. The thin scar is unnoticeable to any normal observation, but immediately forms a barrier against the tempest raging around you. Violent hail still falls, rains rage, the winds storm. But nothing touches you. Lighting strikes close by, but you remained unmoved.

You pull a talisman and hold it forward, invoking the dark whispering which silences the frenzy surrounding you. Phantoms fall from the sky like shadows cast out from bright heavenly realms. Much of the rain stops midway and wraps around each of the phantoms, giving them an almost human form as they smash against the ground.

You see what looks like thousands of phantoms saturating the land. Many collide against the invisible walls created by the power of your talismanic defense.

"You saved me again, master of the grotto," you mutter to

yourself.

"Help us lady! *Mistress save us*! *Chosen of the Selune come to our aid*!"

The phantoms scream their pleas over and over, imploring a goddess you are unfamiliar with. You choose not to wait for her to answer them, she would have to answer you.

"Woman! Show yourself!" you order, as the lunar spirits intensify their cries.

From behind a cloak of mist emerges a bent, thickly set women in old-fashioned clothing. Her head wrapped in shawl.

"My children struggle under your burden," she claims looming near the hearth.

Cautiously, you conceal your talisman. The phantoms cease their shrieking and slowly retreat into the air and out of sight. You leave your makeshift circle and approach the women.

"Why did you attack me!"

She begins to feed the cauldron incense and herbs causing a greater mist to form and soon the phantoms resume their feeding. "My children, they are starving. They have been overworked by the battle."

Your anger seethes at this woman who allowed you to be treated so shamefully. With a magician's instinct you glide your sickle through the mist, severing it and drawing it to your hand. You hear the names of the different heated herbs uttered as they reflect off the blade. The cauldron boils but no more mist now emerges.

"Why?" you demand.

"I am just protecting myself and my children from the masters of the mansion," she replies pitifully.

"From what though?" you press on.

“The Great Work he wants to accomplish,” she says in a lower tone. “It is a crime. It is the undoing of us all. We cannot let it happen.”

She rambles on about star alignments and strange omens clearly confused and frustrated. Beneath the shawl, she seems like a sickly woman pacing in a circle and conversing with… someone.

“I’m going back to the pond,” you say aloud as you set the mist pack in its place. “You are all completely insane.”

“Oh, if you’re going, take this with you.” adds the women in a suddenly cheery tone, handing you a thin vial. “It’s distilled ashweed. He will love it.”

With your offering in hand, you depart. Hearing the same eerie song, you heard when you first approached.

Arriving at the grotto, you prepare your offering. The Saturnite rises from the pond and feeds on the burning incense. He repositions with his back towards you, unable to neglect the rising fumes. Pulling down the shadowy cowl, another identical face on the back of his head is revealed, “Prepare yourself now. Follow my directions, on ***page 225.”***

To Wander Alone

Leaving the grotto, you watch the sunrise illuminate the landscape. The whole property seems lopsided and hilly with no apparent landmarks or signs to measure your travels. You choose a direction and begin to move. Despite the magnanimous glow of the sun, you always seem to walk in the shade. You pull your dark ashen cowl over your face and carry on without interruption.

You walk without taking notice of the hours. You see the many sub-lunars engaged in their daily work. Larger ones carry heavy loads of various materials while the smaller ones simply sweep the pathways and trim the trees. You approach to watch their activities.

"Look," says one of the smaller demons to his workmate. "You there," he calls out to you. "Perhaps we can help each other."

You move close to hear his request.

"I am bound to this service, but if you use your abilities you can undo the bonding." He opens his hands displaying gold and rubies. "I can gather as many as of these as you like."

You observe without saying a word. You wonder if you would have accepted such an offer before your journey. Now, you remain silent, unmoved by the plight of the demon and uninterested in the normal human measures of wealth.

"We can each do different things for you," he persists, heavily sniffing the air in your direction. "Ah, this won't work. He wears the dark hours mark. You know, when that hour passes you will pass with it," he warns, laughing and carrying on with his duties.

You journey further and come to a magnificent pyramidical structure made of crystal. Its body reflects and refracts the light it absorbs, causing sparkling rainbows to settle around the area.

*****

A party is going on with everyone dancing to rhythmic music. Most of the people wear togas but some are dressed in plainer clothes. What catches your attention are the beautiful spirits playing the music and encouraging the dancing as incense swirls in censors positioned throughout the area.

Fountains and pools with ornate well-carved borders and picturesque flower gardens react to the light being reflected from the crystal pyramid. You notice the flowers sway and glow as they absorb the light. While others grow to a great height, their petals enlarge and burst into a shower of bright sprinkling dust over the crowd.

You wander in slowly and as you reach the area an overcast blocks the light and the party ceases noticing your presence. The musicians begin to play dour tunes and despairing rhythms.

The guests stand in silence, ignoring you. Only a beautiful lady in a green dress steps up to address you. Her voice seems to charm everyone around her as she spoke, "My lord, we never expected a hermit from the grotto. We may be ill-equipped to host you. Follow after me if you would," she insists kindly.

She moves gracefully, the embodiment of sheer perfection. You stumble along behind, unsure what to expect. As you follow you hear the party restart and you notice the light return.

"Now my lord, what can I help you with?" she enquires.

"Why does everything avoid me?" you ask.

"You carry many of the tools of Saturn. His powers are especially capable of ruin and undoing. Many of the hourlies work hard to sustain themselves and a concentration of Saturnite force will certainly interrupt their efforts."

"But why is Saturn so feared? I can leave the tools elsewhere and rejoin you," you counter.

She sighs, "my lord, the Saturn hour is a mark not so easily cast aside," she sighs pointing upward at the looming cloud following your position.

Pulling back your cowl you get a good look noticing the Saturnite spirits nested within the dark cloud above you.

"Your skin my lord," for the first time you notice how pale you've become.

"You are feeding off the guests," you state, "another guest would only add to your feast."

"We can only feed on our likeness," she answers.

"Then, what is my likeness," you ask of her.

Sensing your pain, she draws you further from the pyramid and back to the pathway, "The hour of Saturn is so feared not because of the destructive effects it can produce. Compared to the Martials, Saturn is quite tame and even the Solars are known for their fury when provoked. All hourly spirits bond with mortals of a similar disposition. We are sustained by it. But Saturn doesn't just feed off mortals; they feed off hourlies as well. They are the only spirit known to do this."

Shocked, you finally understand why you are so feared. You also understand that you have overstayed the little welcome you received. Pulling your cowl over your face, you bow politely and with the shadow that follows, you make your exit.

*****

You discover the hour of Saturn rising, you could make a summons with one of your talismans. You ponder the worth of any conjurations at this point, while staring at the unused talisman in your hand.

You hold the fourth talisman of Saturn in your hand ready to draw the influence of the Darkest Hour on page 238

OR

Pass by to page 240 carrying on with your journey. You have many questions the Saturnite may be unable or unwilling to answer.

Invoked from the South

You trace a circle with your sickle during the hour of Saturn, burning some of the strong incense. Facing south, you pull the fourth talisman of the Dark Hour. You pass it through the rising smoke from your censor and then the world goes dark. You become concealed within your circle. The trace marks you made in the ground illuminate as the world around you seems to crush against the barrier. Amidst the darkened world, a shade rises from the ground, attracted to the incense.

Holding out the talisman the shade remains transfixed, moving as close to the barrier as possible. As you withdraw the tool, the shade begins to soar around the circle and deliver information about the surrounding world.

"From the Lunar hearth the war continues. The crone refuses to give way and has increased her hostility to the mansion's order. They will motivate the Red Star to move against her. The house of Mercury will be augmented if they are able to make a stone of the ancients. This will give them an extreme advantage over the other orbits on the property, but also serves to maintain the order. Many of the Sub-lunars are rallying behind a false king; their downfall is inevitable but the destruction they cause will be an escape for others..."

"Hold on a moment," you interrupt. "why does Saturn feed off of the other hourlies?"

Floating before you without any sense of emotion or hostility, the dark shade draws back some of the shadows covering its face, revealing a withered chin and a lipless mouth with spear-like teeth.

"Young master, I can only bring news. I have with me no answers."

For the duration of the hour the Saturnite spirit reports about the events in the area and beyond. Most of it you find uninteresting and only leaves you with more questions. Once the hour passes and the darkness disperses, the land around you is misshapen and warped.

"Is this the price for use of the Saturn hour?" you ask, thankful for the sickle and the barriers you create with it. You realize that any misuse of the Saturnite abilities will lead to your own destruction.

You journey again through the property on page 240 and you find yourself being stalked.

Your journey continues and you find yourself being stalked. The whisperings that normally plague you in the grotto have reappeared, warning you of a traitor close by.

"Come forward," you call out calmly.

The only response to your request is silence...

"I'm not going to waste time constraining you. Approach and show me your worth," you proclaim stoically.

A small, gargoyle-like creature emerges and glides towards you. "Might you have a little incense to spare my lord?" he asks.

Cautiously, you burn a small quantity and set it before him. He breaths in deeply, like a thirsty child. You watch, studying the form of the tiny creature before you.

"So, why are you following so close?" you question.

"Hermit from the grotto," he responds looking over his shoulder. "There is a war starting. Many students band together under the mantle of a king from the east. Numerous Sub-lunars support this rebellion. I have found a way to escape, but I need help."

"Do you have a name?" you ask.

The creature hesitates to answer the question. You notice his resistance and move to reassure him of your intentions, "I have no use for Sub-lunar slaves. You seem to know me but for us to be friends, I must know how to address you."

"...I am called Ornias," he replies.

"This place is a paradise. Why should we escape?" you counter.

"No! You don't understand! My race is made into slaves. We were betrayed by the Greater Prince long ago. It's all infighting now and *you,*" he says scowling and pointing up at you with a clawed index finger, "you are bound to Fate's Shadow. If you stay you only march towards the void."

His words strike you, but you are uncertain as to how true they are. *This is a demon. He is calling to me, but why? What does he need? What can I possibly give him? I can barely get anything in this place to come close to me. But he comes willingly. He's desperate...*

"Maybe, if we work together, we could undo this dark fate. As friends," you offer.

"Friendship?!" Ornias exclaims astonished by your response. "You're more insane than the crone! Where do you think you are? This place has only masters and servants. Nothing in between can exist."

"Why?" you ask.

Frustrated by your questioning, Ornias points towards the ground, "you think that *you* belong here? That circle, on the ground. Complete it. See if you can," Ornias mocked.

The request seems odd. But you comply, standing within the worn circle and trace with your sickle. Once finished, the borders smear, as if a swift wind had passed over them. You observe intently, puzzled by the occurrence.

"This place rejects you, chosen of Saturn. If we get out now, we can escape our fate," Ornias insists.

You stand defiantly, unsure what to make of the recent

happenings. "I have too much more to learn," you reply coldly. "I am sorry young Sub-lunar, but I must remain. Perhaps we can travel together until you find a way to leave?"

"Young! I've lived millennia longer than you mortal! And I will live beyond the pitifully few years you have left within you. You are lost! I have no use for you! Stay here and rot!"

He flies away instantly; you watch him leave then turn to the circle. Why did the circle fade when you drew it? You have drawn many before. You travel the grounds finding others, trace them over. Always the borders smear.

"Is this place rejecting me?" you say softly as you look up at the cloud that forever follows you. Running your hand over your head, you notice a flurry of hair fall to the ground. Surprised, you quickly reach for your head only to have more hair shed as you pass your hands through.

Shocked by the occurrence, you wonder if you have become sick. You feel the smooth skin on your head as you look down at the fallen hair scattered over the ground and at the tarnished border of the magic circle.

"Why do I need this magic at all, if it only leads to distress?"

*****

Among the pathways of the property, you once again hear training and militant chanting in the distance. Moving closer, you notice Roman centurions divided into different groups, marching, practicing with spears and shields, moving in tactical formation and sparring.

Impressed by the display of skill and cooperative maneuvering you approach for a closer look. The moment the Martial spirit in charge sees you, he shouts an order in Latin. All the soldiers turn, forming ranks, with shields up and spears forward.

A wall of organized aggression stares you down halting your approach. The soldiers create an opening in their barricade which they seal once the Commander passes through. You take hold of your sickle, trying to decide whether to retreat or stand your ground.

"You!" orders the Martial spirit. "Leave now!"

Before you can ask any sort of questions the Martial barks more commands, "I don't care what it is, what bullshit conundrums you're dealing with. Seal that shit up, take it someplace else. Now!"

Outnumbered and outmatched, you slowly make your retreat. At a certain distance you hear another command shouted and the training resumes.

"Am I really alone here?" you ask aloud to yourself.

Whenever Saturnite talismans are used they cause ruin to the world around you, Sub-lunars flee and the powers are undone. Maybe if I leave an open invitation, something friendly will come my way? You begin your experiment on page 249

The Second Talisman of Venus— These talismans are also proper for obtaining grace and honor, and for all things which belong unto Venus and for accomplishing all thy desires herein.

Reflecting on the explanation for this talisman you ponder over its use, *okay this seems doable and not insane.* You engrave the shapes and letters and then, burn the proper incense. The talisman gleams as it is completed and the beautiful song you hear before briefly sounds again.

Okay, it's done. Now what do I do?

"My lord," comes a soft females voice from some unknown origin.

"Hello..." you feebly say while searching the room for the vocal source.

"My lord, you have created two talismans in my name. Burn more incense and I will teach you of their use."

Seems simple enough.

You take the bowl adding more incense from the pile closest to the copper plates and then you wait...

"Will need more than that my lord," returns the voice.

"Okay then, more incense to the voice," you say as you dump additional offering into the bowl which causes the room to fill with smoke. Before you can open the door to air out your mistake, the smoke filing the room accumulates and plunges back into the bowl re-emerging as a healthy green myrtle tree that sprouts white blossoms.

"Of course, *this* would happen. Why should anything be normal anymore," you state out loud.

"If you take your offering outdoors, we will be able to reach you," the lovely voice instructs.

Shrugging, unsure of what else to do you exit with the bowl outdoors. You view your surroundings expecting a fantastic show only to find a calm serene landscape. From above a white swan dives narrowly missing your head, "shit! Really!?"

It shifts into an attractive maiden in a green dress and floats gently towards you. Instinctively you hold up the bowl with the sprouted myrtle. The maiden inhales deeply, returning it to its previous vaporous form and exhales a blast of sweet-smelling mist that forms a pathway of sprouting white myrtle flowers before she kisses your cheek and vanishes.

"Follow along, if you like," came the voice.

"To be honest I had a full day, *but* because you asked so nice..."

While trialing the line of white flowers they dissolve back into incense smoke as you pass them by. You see images of different beings taking form as the fumes rise; some are beautiful like the maiden but others, are hideous.

"Please keep up with the trail my lord. What follows our scent is not what you want to be stranded behind with," warns the calming voice.

Warning taken. You begin to increase your speed, ignoring the dark whispers just behind, feeding off the fading flowering plants that revert into coiling incense smoke. Fear keeps you from even gazing behind as you focus solely on the lovely voice, whose tone dispels the trouble following.

"Any chance I get to know where we are going?"

"The talismans you created are formed in my name. We will meet. I will teach you to use them."

"Okay that can work," you reply, still trying to evade what you can only guess are horrible fiends close behind feeding on the remains of the evaporating trail. "I was reading about the different hours, yours seems to be made of love potions. Is that really all your about?"

The voice laughs cheerfully at your remark, "Young lord, we are perhaps the most influential of the hourly authorities."

"But how can that be?" you protest. "The others exert power over weather and riches. I mean, look, your metal is copper. We make pennies from copper."

With a delicate tone the voice replies, "We are the force that gives gold and silver its actual value. We make strength meaningful. It is by us that all the treasures of the world are spent. The satisfaction that follows accomplishment. The feeling that powers emotion and the love that sustains the living," states the voice.

You look up as the last of the trail dissolves and the dark whispers become silent. Before you, a stunning crystal pyramid surrounded by beautiful gardens and fountains. Gorgeous maidens dance with elegant men as a dark waltz begins to play. White myrtle flowers bloom as a beautiful maiden in a flowing green dress makes her approach. She looks like the embodiment of feminine grace as she seems to float towards you.

"My lord, you made it. Welcome to the domain of the Emerald Hour."

Her voice makes the whole world more beautiful, you muse as she speaks, and you observe the dancing and the beautiful greenery surrounding the pyramid.

"By us separate things are brought into the whole. You have formed a share in our sovereignty and soon, you will learn how to use it."

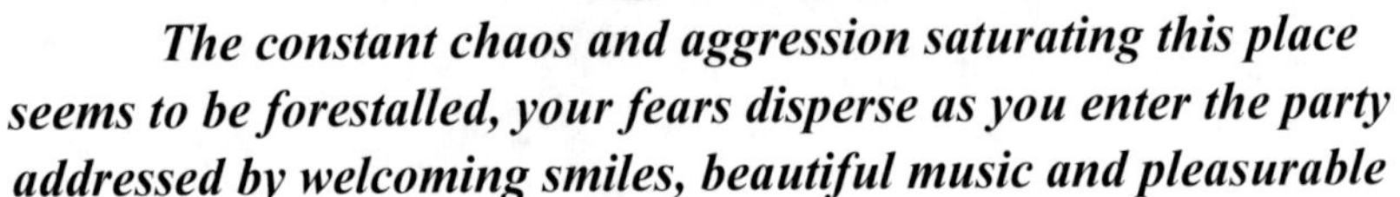

The constant chaos and aggression saturating this place seems to be forestalled, your fears disperse as you enter the party addressed by welcoming smiles, beautiful music and pleasurable smells on page 251

You Called

Using the sickle, you spend a few days gathering herbs of high quality for drawing various spirits. You use the iron censor and chain as a mortar and pestle, grinding with the back of the hilt of your sickle. You wait for the appointed hours and attempt to draw the spirits out.

Over time you create customized rituals and burn many fragrant herbs, but your efforts leave you exactly where you began. The spirits that do show up are hostile and try to retreat. Eventually you are ready to give up, having used most of your supplies. A small amount of some strong spice remains. You burn it as an offering in one final attempt.

"This is for any spirit willing to draw near," you say aloud as you wait for the result.

You wait patiently pondering over your lack of progress. Never have you put in so much effort only to have such a negative result. You haven't even carved a circle. You just want a response, any response. Something better than a shadowy demented being that reminded you of your loneliness and scorn.

From the ground you see movement. The soil becomes disturbed as something digs its way up to the surface. A small lizard gradually emerges. It sniffs out your censor and looks up at you. With four reddish legs, a long tail and a furrowed head, this animal is quite unique. After assessing you, the lizard goes back to the censor, reared up on its hind legs and inhaling some of the thin mist. It immediately bursts into flames and shakes wildly from head to tail like a dog.

Surprised, you realize, that this was a spirit. Its tongue flickers happily as it stares up at you, silently begging for more. Wafting smoke rises towards the little creature. The lizard gleefully revels despite bursting into flame sporadically while you watch.

"So, what hour are you from?" you ask the playful fiery creature.

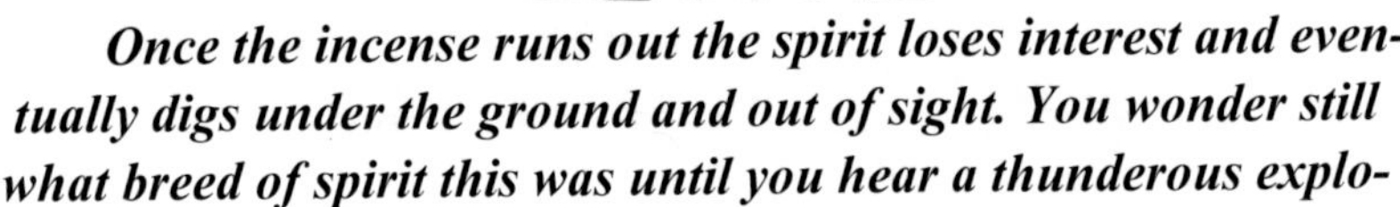

Once the incense runs out the spirit loses interest and eventually digs under the ground and out of sight. You wonder still what breed of spirit this was until you hear a thunderous explosion and hear screaming in the distance.

Choose to investigate the source of the explosion on page 257

OR

Continue to travel the property on page 253 leave the concerns of the battles to the others.

Amorous Instruments

You spend many hours at the party. You drink, eat and dance. When the hour of Venus begins to wane, you sleep. The celebration seems endless, each hour adding rarer foods and live shows. Music is always playing. Closer and during the Venerean hours, it was lively and rhythmic. As the hour passed, it becomes calming.

You lose track of the days, never wanting to leave you settle into the decadence offered by the Emerald Hour. On a bright day, you observe the crystal pyramid refracting lights over the beautiful gardens and fountains. The maiden that welcomed you approaches again, "my lord, have you been enjoying the benefits of the hour?"

With a mouth full of food, you enthusiastically nod, sitting up trying not to be rude in front of the maiden.

"I do have need of your expertise," she requests, handing you an ornate flute. "Maybe you can lead the party today?"

Hating to disappoint the lady, you take hold of the flute feebly, "my lady, I have no knowledge of musical instruments. I've never even played before. Is there something else I can do to help?"

Visibly saddened by your reply, "try," she coyly says, "I think there is a lot you don't know about yourself."

Cautiously you put the flute to your lips. Hating what was to come but unwilling to refuse on offer by the maiden, you begin to play. At first, as you fear, your performance is terrible. Completely off key, instead of music only torturous squealing spurts from the instrument. You are completely embarrassed but that soon changes, as your fingers instinctively shift. Manipulating your fingers over the holes becomes more precise and your breathing steady.

You began to perform in perfect harmony. Seeing the maiden pleased with your accomplishment she gestures to the crowd, hypnotized by your music. You see them swaying to the soft rhythms you produce. Water spirits rise from the fountains swimming in unison with the beautiful composition. Now you understand the power of the Venerean hour. You feel the longing of the crowd within you. Their submission to the influence, *your* influence is absolute. Playing softly, you soothe them to sleep as the maiden gestures again to other instruments at your feet.

To pick up the drum turn to page 288

For the lira, page 290

To be Cleansed of your Sins

Wandering again, you begin to try a pathway previously untraveled. Your bald pale skin clothed in ashen garb gives you a frightening appearance. The Saturnite's whispering is now heard by anyone who gets too close to you. Both spirits and mortals avoid you whenever possible. Your visits to the grotto become more frequent only because it is the one place that allows you open entry.

One day, you come across a dense part of the forest teeming with activity. As you move to investigate you see many beings gathering at hot springs and an angelic figure with black wings who glides from the trees to greet you.

"Hey! So, you're the hermit," he states. "I was wondering when you'd show up. Here follow me. This is the perfect place to pass through if you are to perform a greater operation. The cleansing here will allow you to attract more influence from the forces gathered here. If you are preparing for any ritual sacrifices this is the place to start."

He leads you through a beautiful oasis with a contained waterfall leading down an artificial stream that flows into the distance. Numerous hot springs decorate the landscape. Many spirits bathing in the springs part way as you step through. You burn some incense and leave your censor aside as you try out the hot spring.

For the first time you feel your total body at ease. Your constant travelling left you stiff and cramped. Being sore and tense has become your normal state. You hardly remember what it was like to relax. Sinking into the waters you notice them becoming noticeably cooler as you wait.

You turn to the black winged Sub-lunar for an explanation, "Well, you see, many of my legion who maintain these springs are hard-pressed to work when the Saturnite influence is present. It becomes hard to keep their effects manifest."

Understanding the situation perfectly you prepare to leave. Before you can go, the small lizard-like friend you had just made reappears. It dives into the water instantly heating it up as it swims through the pond. A smile breaks your normally harsh expression. You realize that smiling is also something you haven't done in a very long time.

"Well," says Crocell, "it looks like you have a salamander."

You look to him for further explanation once again, "A fire spirit. Elementals. Once they get attached to a mortal, they don't like to leave them alone. Most people would think of it as annoying, but I bet you may have use for one of these little guys, especially now."

You scowl at Crocell signaling him to leave so to enjoy more time with your new friend, "A salamander," you say, as the spirit frolics in the water, "then, I shall call you Sal."

The days seem brighter now that you have someone to spend time with. You forget the grotto and its harsh lessons. The other hourlies and magicians who willfully avoid you are of no consequence. You have a pet and a friend. Enjoy this time. When you want to leave the hot springs turn to ***page 228***

The Voice and the Blade

Travelling the property, you hold in your hand the white hilted sickle you received from the Saturnite. The blade is sharp but not too sharp. You swing it wildly unsure as to how to use it properly. The iron censor and chain are wrapped around your left shoulder, you feel its weight as you enjoy the cool breeze flowing over your face. You use it to slice some nearby reeds growing along the pathway and instantly loud muttering voices speak from an unknown source.

What the hell? Is this the sickle or the grasses?

You remember the Saturnite's words of instruction, *to harvest components... components for...? What?*

You can't completely recall so you move over to some long yellow flowers and hook a cluster with the blade. You hear the whispering clearly:

"We are called by the common tongue horse-heal. Ours is the domain of Mercury. To burn us is to gain their favor; we may be joined by others for this purpose. Lavender or Mulberry, Coltsfoot or Valerian...

"Oh shit, the plants talk! Or maybe... the blade... it has a voice."

You proceed to collect many other herbs and branches and absorb as much information as you can regarding the natures of the plants and their affiliation with the hourly spirits. Excited and thankful you especially take care to collect many twayblades, leaves from a beech tree and many others that are said to have an affinity to Saturn. His hour will soon approach again and you want to be ready with a more *worthy* sacrifice, even if you are still unsure as to what that entails.

Return to the grotto with what you have gathered on page 153

You've collected many herbs and plants connected to other hourlies, perhaps it would be wise to investigate them as well, on page 200

Violent Winds

Sounds of thunder and wind blasts are followed by screaming and sounds of retreat. The fiery creature burrows underground before you can say anything. You take notice of hourlies and spirits of many different kinds fleeing from the source of the destruction. You breathe in deep, catching a gust of the air currents.

"This is the work of a Sub-lunar, a very powerful one," you conclude.

Without totally understanding why, you begin to move towards the cause of all this chaos. You hear unknown souls intoning of names of power. Magicians are trying to bind the wild demon. Another loud crash of thunder followed by a fierce blast of wind silences any resistance.

It becomes harder to proceed as you climb uphill against a furious eruption which is quickly gaining strength. You reach flat ground and view the nearby valley below. A mountainous mass of cloud is so close to the earth that it looks as if the sky will crush the ground. Lighting and fire surge from its wake.

You notice circles drawn on the ground. The wind peels them from the surface, *they tried to bind him and he does not want to submit.*

The cyclone almost blocks out the sun, threatening to swallow anything that comes too close. You pass the remains of charred and broken bodies of the failed attempts to stop the fury dominating the landscape. Drawing your sickle, you trace a thick scar into the ground. The storm winds increase, uprooting trees and sending debris against you. The cloud of Saturnite spirits descend destroying the first wave sent against you. They are met with a gale force that sweeps them aside.

"I've never seen anyone do *that* before," you exclaim.

For the first time, the sun is free to seep through the protective covering of your Saturnite entourage. You smile briefly, as the light is eclipsed by the hovering mile-long storm cloud. In anger you pull the first talisman and raise it high. Bolts of lightning and fire strike the edges of your barrier. You're momentarily blinded by the barrage.

"Submit and cease your attack!" you command.

Numerous tornados tear through the land surrounding you, they converge to encase the circle. A deep voice emanates around you responds to your demands, "I will not be bound by the unworthy."

Insulted by his assertion you reply, "I do not wish to bind you! I only want to ask you questions."

Obviously surprised by your response, the winds retreat slightly.

"You bear the mark of Saturn."

"You know me well, what name do you go by?" you ask.

The tornadoes withdraw into the dark cloud now directly above you. It's swirling mass seems to be made apprehensive by your question. Annoyed that things have taken this long, you step outside of your circle, hoping that a genuine act will be enough to calm the raging storm.

"I could easily kill you."

"I was never your enemy," you reply. "Why are you doing this?"

The demon studies you, unsure if you are brave, stupid or possibly both. "I was set free from my bounds by a group of weak-minded fools. Whom I have consumed."

Saturnite spirits attempt to reassert their presence alongside you, only to be blown away by the winds that now encircle you. "I can only be bound by the best of mortals and I refuse to serve the unworthy willingly."

"I can understand that," you acknowledge. "What will you do now?"

"Await the Master of the mansion. He is the one I serve, as I did his grandfather before him," the storm demon answers.

"Oh, you seem to be short of company. We can wait together if you like?"

"Very well, my name is Ephippas," he states.

Sitting in the shade of the Sub-lunar's storm, a writhing destruction of nature's most extreme intensity, now pacified by the stillness of a mortal possessed of the Dark Hour's calm.

"So, is this master any good?" you ask.

"He is worthy," Ephippas replies.

"Why don't you just leave this place? What is it with all this worthy and unworthy? Why is your kind even called to this place?"

"You do not even know where you stand," Ephippas discloses. "Come, see the true nature of your surroundings."

You are gently swept up by the whirlwind and taken to page 262

Home

Looking directly at the gigantic wind-demon is a difficult endeavor. You perceive the huge spirit as, a body of storm lightning which peels off as he hovers, following your movements. His immanence causes you a short-lived fear, it quickly falls away as powerful winds gently lift you into the air.

Atop the storm you are transported over the school. Where you see the property in its entirety: the sections housing the hourlies, a river in the distance where crowds of Sub-lunars are gathering, the gate that surrounds the perimeter and the mansion, situated uphill the Victorian masterpiece overlooking the whole of the school.

"This place does not look fortified enough to hold someone like you," you exclaim. "What makes you or any of the other spirits stay here?"

"Look again, young master," Ephippas gently directs.

You turn your head towards the mansion, or at least you where you thought the mansion was. It is gone! You swim through the storm trying to get your bearings and maybe a better view. At first, it seems like an illusion, but you quickly notice all the buildings have shifted. You spot the mansion, still atop a hill, overlooking the school but in a different location.

"Orbits! They are orbiting the mansion!"

"Very true, young master," Ephippas responds.

"The gate is a circle protecting the outside and the buildings are a mirror of the planetary circuits. They revolve around the mansion. This whole place is a mirror of the natural world," you affirm.

"It is a channel for the forces of this world and the influences that govern them. It is a preparation. Eventually that gate will open and what is formed here will spill out into the rest of reality," explains Ephippas. "The master of the mansion moves to remake nature," he continued, "by connecting it to its past and reordering the future around a different orbit."

"And what is my purpose here?" you ask.

"Yours is a special gift beyond mortal comprehension. All things revolve and end. To pass through the ending is to rise above nature. To manipulate nature is to move against this ending. The death of one state leads to renewal in another," Ephippas says.

"Everyone here is manipulating nature," you reply. "What is so good about moving on to this *ending*? Why am I alone moving towards it?" you question.

"If you had held out a bit longer during our battle, young master, I would have been overthrown. Yours is the ability to ruin existence. No manipulation can stand against you and because of this, none of the others can ever truly stand with you."

"Then what must I do?" you ask, secretly saddened by the recent disclosure.

"Submit!" he declares. "If you cannot submit you cannot die and only in death will you be reborn."

"And if I refuse?" you probe.

“Then you will have to convince your mind of something your heart knows to be a lie.”

You understand now why they always fled from you, why no other spirits could work with you. Their existence was temporarily sustained by a fleeting exchange from the ignorance or good will of the mortals. Your existence is always focused beyond a deeper state of being that both spirits and mortals fled from.

“I can only be bound by the master of the mansion,” Ephippas inserted. “Would you like to meet him?”

He would have answers to many questions, but you have learned enough and have a master of your own to parley with, “No. Please if you would, drop me over there,” you request, gesturing to the darkest part of the property.

He does as you wish and leaves you at the edge of the grotto. “You are a rarity among mortals. Unfortunately, we shall not see each other again.”

With your sickle and censor crossed you bow reverently and as Ephippas departs, you return to the Darkest Hour’s origin.

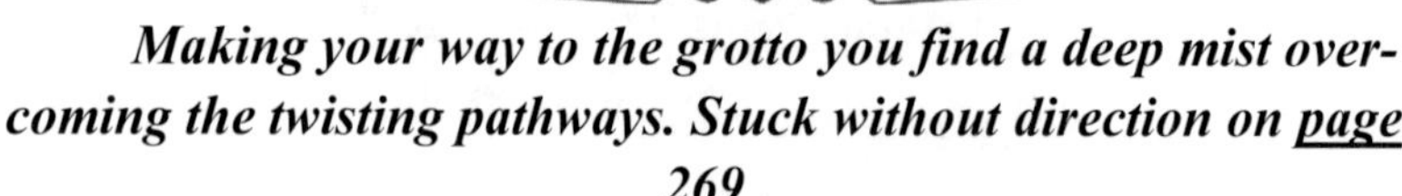

Making your way to the grotto you find a deep mist overcoming the twisting pathways. Stuck without direction on page 269

Grace and Honor

The beautiful spirits of Venus usher you past the gardens and fountains. The party has begun anew. People and spirits are bowing as you go by. Humbled by their greetings you nervously wave back, slightly smiling at the fame you've acquired. Entering the pyramid, the mirrors are all turned away, leaving the room with only a thin illumination.

The maiden floats into a reflection as the mirrors shift, displaying a beautiful valley filled with a large unending green plain and bright afternoon sun that expands to fill the pyramid so completely that you lose sight of any entrance. The structure is transformed so thoroughly that it left no sign of its origin.

"You did a great thing for us," the maiden announces. "Not many affiliated with our name would have gone against enemies of that nature."

"It really wasn't that bad," you counter. "They were weak. They only prepared for attacks of force. There was no chance for them to anticipate the powers of our hour."

Pleased with your response, the maiden smiles replying, "It is great to see you've found your home here. But what you used for defense against the cult will likely not work again. We have greater gifts to give you."

Eager to hear what she truly means; you listen without interrupting.

"You created a talisman you have not yet used. Pull it now," she gently demands.

The second talisman. I had almost forgotten.

You unwrap the silk covering. It looks new. A five-pointed star glistens on its surface in the valley's sunlight as you admire your creation. The mirrors shift again, removing you from the presence of the valley or more truthfully perhaps, removing the valley's presence from you. She shifts the mirrors again and two Venerean spirits appear on the reflection floating from mirror to mirror while approaching your position. A mirror sways catching you in its reflection with a long thin table within.

Am I being invited to eat something? Is that a bed...? A massage table?

You walk up to it; you can feel it with your hand but still not see it on your side of the mirror. The Venerean spirits welcome you, taking the talisman from your hand. You notice immediately you are within the mirror but all you were wearing remains beyond.

"Oh shit!" you shout, surprised by the sudden shift.

The Venereans guide you into bed. You lay on your back covered with silk bedsheets and a beautiful fur blanket. The bed is the most comfortable piece of furniture you've ever lain on. They place the talisman over your chest as dark calming music plays from some unknown source while the Venerean spirits began to massage you. One takes your feet, the other your head and face.

They use smooth creams that heat up your feet and leave a refreshing scent on your face. You feel your whole body relaxing as your face and feet are simultaneously massaged. The skin on your face tingles as the Venerean fingers expertly trace over your head. Before today you never dreamed that sensations this pleasurable could exist. This is the ultimate retreat from reality. If you were to die at this moment, the heaven waiting for you would fall short of the euphoria you feel as the Venereans work their craft. Under the influence of these unparalleled pleasures, you drift into a deep sleep without caring if you will ever awaken.

The treatment ends. The spirits leave. You begin to slowly rise from your sleep, naked and relaxed.

My face and feet, they're perfectly smooth. My whole body feels different.

"Look in the mirror," commands the maiden. Her voice blatantly audible but her presence invisible, you rise naked and gaze into the mirror you came in from. Before it stands another directed towards you. You see your whole body; it's perfect. You have no flaws. You look strong. Is this an illusion?

The mirror slides aside as another took its place. This one has you, but you are impeccably dressed. Your hair is styled. Rings line your fingers. An emerald on your right ring finger catches your notice. The talisman you hold is now clasped on a beautiful platinum chain draped around your neck.

You step out of the mirror and back into the pyramid. Even your walking is more graceful, the ground feels more comfortable with every step. Your clothing feels like the skin of angels and is so light you barely notice what you're wearing.

With these on I could sleep on my feet!

Another mirror slides towards you with a shelf filled with smoking pipes.

"Choose, my Lord," comes a soothing voice.

You pick up one and a Venerean loads it with a bit of incense and lights it for you. You breathe it in and exhale coolly. The mirrors shift again, you see in the reflections hundreds of Venerean spirits diving down to inhale the smoke. You take another mouthful and exhale watching them coarse greedily for the vapor after you respire.

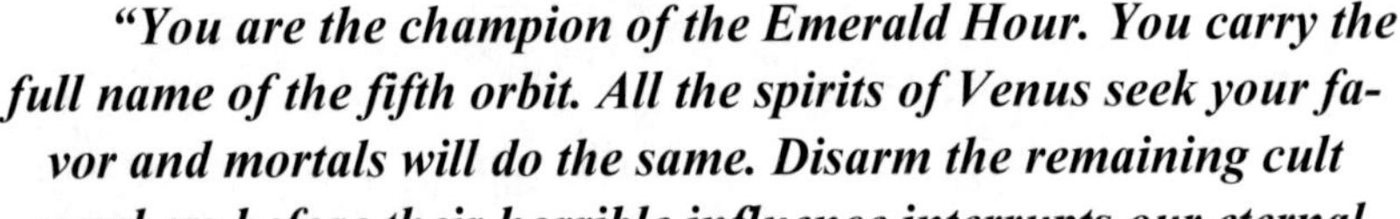

"You are the champion of the Emerald Hour. You carry the full name of the fifth orbit. All the spirits of Venus seek your favor and mortals will do the same. Disarm the remaining cult members before their horrible influence interrupts our eternal celebration.

Step out of the Pyramid onto page 286.

The fog is thick and you hear what sounds like a cattle bell approaching. Bearing your sickle, you prepare to defend yourself as a shadowy figure approaches, *"be at peace hermit,"* comes a twisted in-human voice.

A sentient figure becomes distinguishable as it moves towards you. It looks human enough and you do not detect any sort of spiritual resonance, but as the form becomes clearer you notice a pair of thick curved horns growing from its head.

"This," she says, leading a black goat by an iron chain, *"is for the master of the grotto. With it you will finish what you started."*

Passing the chain to you she bows and departs as the mist clears and a clear roadway opens leading to the pond. You pass through with the goat approaching the edge of the pond.

The familiar silence is welcoming. The other hourlies engage in parties and training and strange experimental phenomena, it was always so loud and obnoxious. Here, there is only stillness, the unmoving mind dominated by this paradigm. No amount of esoteric knowledge or physical force can help you here.

You bring the goat close to the edge of the pond. You hear the whisperings of the Dark Hour give direction and with an instinctive, powerful motion you pull the sickle across its neck, holding tight its horns as it struggles while its life blood stains the shoreline and streams into the water.

You hold the horns firmly as the animal ceases its struggling. You quickly you take the blood and put it into the censor, burning it with the herbs special to the hour of your alignment.

"I conjure the Darkest Hour, great and supreme. The abyss sees you and fears, the living become lifeless. By the height of the highest heaven and the depth of the deepest ocean I conjure you, star closest to the divine. Cold lord, who holds authority over every harm who gives man the treasure of everything beyond."

The silence of the shadows is made sentient as the Saturnite rises from the pool. He breathes in your offering. Blood bathes the ground, pouring slowly from the goat and evaporating, creating a thin red mist which blankets the area. The Saturnite grows larger as he consumes the sacrifice.

You kneel with a fierce gaze locked onto the hourly, "What would you have of me?" the spirit beckons in a deep unemotional tone.

"Everything! All the answers. Every meaning. I want freedom from all of this!"

"Then you must go beyond the senses and return to the origin. The universe is infinite. It was created still, perfect and unmoving. It became the reality you know when it was set into motion. All of what you see and have ever seen is infinity in motion. Return to the unmoving, beyond your questions, before time. Become still and be free."

Your mind begins to shrink before the memories of your life; the pains and pleasures of this world are swallowed by the unformed darkness that existed before the light of creation. You become a thin point, undisturbed and unapproachable.

Your body is placed by one of the stones surrounding the pond as the Saturnite's shadowy form extends from itself a large sickle made of darkened matter. It carves a strange sigil into the stone which glows brightly as the earth beneath begins to slowly swallow your physical form.

"Young master," the Saturnite begins, "all of life is an endless lack. A constant void to fill with pleasures and pains. Yours has ended at last in the only way it could. You have moved beyond this world into a rest that only I can provide. You have taken your place with the most worthy of the universe."

Your body, swallowed whole, the Saturnite places the talismans, by your grave, drapes the chain and censor over the stone and leans the sickle against it, where it will wait for the next soul to claim the mantle of the grotto's hermit. Nightshades, flowering squills and pansies quickly grow over your grave and the Saturnite spirits who followed you for so long begin to greedily take in the fragrances swarming your burial place, like fanatical believers to a sacred shrine.

The mortal world no longer receives any of your consideration. The masters of the mansion breathe a sigh of relief as the devotees of Saturn are the only true threat within to the Great Work. You have passed beyond time, beyond space, beyond being, into a noetic undoing and an ineffable existence alone with the One surrendered before the Whole.

FIN

To the Left

Following the slope, you and Sal take a long path to a river, where you stop and rest by the shore.

"Well boy, what do you think? Can you swim across?"

Sal just looks up at you, his head twisting to the side with a curious expression. You hear screeching from above, where flying, oddly-shaped demons shouted, "The king has come and our city awaits! Flee the bonds of the mansion...!"

A dark clouded overcast covers the sun as dark chanting sounds on the wind. Numerous Sub-lunars are pulled from the river by some unseen force. A group flies willingly while others scream and rebel against the unseen power controlling them. Piercing, unblinking eyes carried inside of thin whirlwinds of dust pass by, answering the call. You watch as the whirlwinds draw the spirits toward a powerful cyclone. A location beyond your sight, thousands of them, maybe more being funneled and amassed in the distance.

Not long after, the light returns. The Sub-lunar migrations cease but the chanting continues.

"What could they be calling now?" you wonder as the amount of power any summoner would need was far exceeded with the latest feat.

You notice the hovering flames make a return, being taken next. Like large fireflies pulled toward the distance the same way the Sub-lunars had been.

"These are fire elementals... Sal!"

You notice your salamander clawing at the edge of the river, fighting against the constraint. You pull your sickle and swipe at the air to no effect. Sal resists as hard as he can but his body is forcefully shifted into a flaming husk and quickly torn away beyond your sight. With the chanting silenced, you are left alone.

Unsure how to react and in total shock of the uncertain situation, your hands shake as the true limits of your powers are tested. Everyone fears you, but you're helpless. Even the ever-vigilant mark of the Dark Hour doesn't stop your friend, your only friend, from being stolen.

Thinking fast, you pull the fourth talisman of Saturn and burn incense while tracing a wide circle around yourself while you face south. Saturnite spirits descend from the covering above, "Our hour is not yet strong," one says in a hoarse tone.

"I don't care! Tell me where Sal was taken?" you ask, quickly realizing the limited function of the Saturnite Hourlies, "tell me what is happening right now."

The Saturnite remains silent for what seems like a long moment and then floating around your barrier with some of the others begins to answer.

"A rebellion directed by a power from the East has summoned an army to their cause. They will likely be marching toward the gate. If you position yourself off the pathway you may be able to intercept them.”

“Will Sal be with them?” you ask eagerly.

“Young master I can only bring news. I have with me no answers.”

Prepare for battle on page 313

Right of Way

An easy flat path lines a welcoming walkway that you and Sal travel through without obstacle besides your usual cloudy overpass the day is bright.

"Come on Sal we can cover good ground here," you announce, as you march alongside your trusted elemental partner.

The salamander skips joyfully beside you taking a breath of incense every so often. Stopping by some mercurial engineered fruit trees, you pluck some berries and eat. You squeeze the juice into the censor and allow Sal to breathe deeply from the fumes.

As you both feast the sky darkens; chanting can be heard on the wind currents. A large tornado forms and begins to sweep up the spirits hidden throughout the property. Many lesser Sub-lunars are harvested. You notice tongues of fire being pulled into the vortex. Sal's body begins to shift as well and despite your best efforts, you are left without your friend.

You see tornados forming throughout the distance. Thinking quickly, you draw a circle around yourself with the sickle and pull the first talisman of Saturn and hold it up, intoning names and cursing the passing spirits. Many Sub-lunars smash against the ground seized now from their capture. Most of them scramble and retreat, but you manage to hook your sights on to one close by.

"Appear before me in plain sight and do not resist my commands!" you order.

The demon is dragged before you on its back to the edge of your circle, “Ah crap,” it says as it turns to rise, “okay I’m here. Whad’ya want?”

Surprised by how easy it was to gain its cooperation, you pause trying to formulate a question.

“It isn’t bad enough we have servant work for the mansion, now vortexes. My day was actually pretty good before this and if you’ve got nothing to add, can you just let me get sucked back to wherever the hell this is going so I can get this over with?”

Clearly, this demon is unwilling to be talked down to you. “Where are these things taking you? What is going on?”

“A rebellion. Not the first either,” the demon adds. “we’re to be used in some sort of war. Probably won’t last though…”

“Where are the rebels located?” You demand.

“If you pass me some incense, lower your talisman and have a little patience, I’ll lead you there myself.”

The demon swears an oath of obedience for the task at hand as you comply with his request. He leaves a marked trail for you to follow.

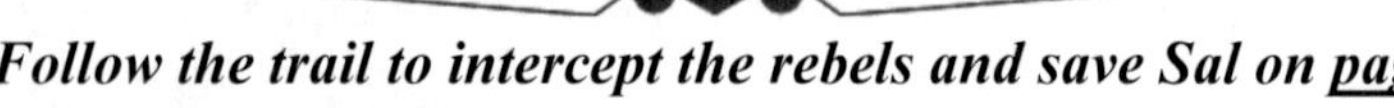

Follow the trail to intercept the rebels and save Sal on <u>page 313</u>

Overcome Fire with Water

"This is going to be a problem for us," you tell the maiden, who sits by a fountain of clear flowing water.

"We have defensive precautions," attests the maiden. "But we are hourlies. Our strength is limited."

"I have no such limitations," you state. "Send me. Maybe this movement can be disarmed."

"Our hour is strong," she says. "Follow me."

You both enter the pyramid which appears almost translucent. Within, the lighting is dim and the interior is full of mirrors specially angled to capture and reflect the light. The maiden floats towards one and to your surprise, enters through the glass. The mirror slightly shifts to the right as she calls again to you.

Seeing your reflection with a heavily stacked bookshelf behind you, you peer over your shoulder and notice nothing but the chamber. Back within the mirror the maiden has retrieved a scroll. You reach to the glass only to have your hand halted by solid mass.

"Use your reflection to take it," she gently instructs.

Directing your hand in the mirror you receive and take hold of the scroll she passes to you.

Magic is interesting, you think, while unrolling the scroll. You read the contents; it's for a talisman. The maiden interrupts your study to give further instruction, "My lord," she calls from another mirror. "shift this one to the left."

You follow her orders and see the workroom reflected, "You will need tools and incense. I will guide your hands, but we must work quickly to catch the full strength of the hour."

The Third Talisman of Venus—This, if it be only shown unto any person, serveth to attract love. It should be invoked in the day and hour of Venus, at one o'clock or at eight.

This one is very specific. But it should work.

You begin the creation process, taking copper plates and instruments from the reflection of the workroom. With the maiden's aid you complete the process and burn incense to pass the talisman through the rising fumes. You see beautiful Venerean spirits floating through the smoke and kissing the talisman.

"Move some distance away from our territory. Then with the strength of our hour move against them. You are now equipped with the name of the Emerald Hour. We do not have the destructive tendencies of the Martial legion or the fearful dread of the Saturn's calling, our strength is subtle. But if we do this well, we can disarm the enemy and even perhaps absorb them into our ranks."

*****

When the first hour of the day of Venus rises, you have travelled far from your home domain and see no signs of strong life around. You sit under a thick tree and begin your operation.

"The fourth talisman of the Venerean hour," you whisper, as you look over its semi-intricate design. "Cult members nearby need to come forward here."

You burn a small amount of incense sacred to the Emerald hour and pass the talisman through the thin pillar of rising smoke. Then, you wait. Much time passes, but at the eighth hour after sunrise you are not disappointed by the result. A carriage driven by a large alligator pulls up, while close by a whirlwind emerges and settles leaving a robed female who greets the man emerging from the carriage. Soon after, a terrible bellowing pierces the skies as a dragon lands and its rider dismounts.

"I saw the mansion," he states. "Why aren't we attacking already?"

"Did you hear word from the East?" asks the robed lady.

"I've heard nothing," adds the other.

The dragon rider looks at the two of them, "Well, who called this meeting?"

They all stare at each other confused. You emerge, "I called this meeting," you announce.

All three look at you, unsure of what to say or who you even are.

"Are you sent from the East?" asks the lady.

You raise the third talisman like a badge and get close enough for each of them to see it.

"You aren't dressed like one of us," asks the dragon rider. "A spy? You have a report?"

"Better. I have an offer," you counter. "This isn't going to go your way. Your master will betray you *and* it will happen sooner rather than later."

You notice the Venerean spirits singing, making a circle around yourself and the cultists. "You have all become powerful through your own efforts. It's the only reason you heard my hidden call. Anyone of lesser strength unfortunately, cannot be saved," you state.

"I swear I know you," states the lady.

"We were friends when we were younger," adds the carriage driver. "This is fate."

"Quiet both of you!" commands the dragon rider. "Tell me about this betrayal."

"The cult master plans to use you guys as a meat shield against the mansion. He further plans to offer your blood to the legions you have been using as a price to enhance his own hold over the remaining Sub-lunars not under his immediate control."

"When will this happen?" asks one of the cult members.

"Not sure. All I know is its going to be bad," turning to the carriage driver, you further encourage the untruth invented by the Venerean influence, "We've known each other a long time now. Please, consider leaving the property before this happens."

The three reflect on your warning. "What should we do?" asks the carriage driver.

"Go your own way," you affirm. "leave the property. I will try to save as many as I can. Make things ready for them beyond the gate. There will be more who retreat and will need support. Continue your learning and help others to do the same."

The dragon rider nods in agreement. "We'll have to gather our materials. Thank you, friend. We owe you a tremendous debt."

The female embraces you, speaking into your ear, "Please come see us again."

"Don't wait so long for our next meeting," adds the carriage driver. "Next time we meet we can summon our own Sub-lunars and have the legions devoted to us instead."

The Venerean spirits continue their singing that undoubtedly has manipulating each of their minds. The spirits of Venus swarm around you. Some feed you cakes, praising your efforts and leading you back to the pyramid at the call of the maiden.

Unsure about the details but pleased with the result you return to the pyramid on page 265.

Learning to Advance

You open the door to the workroom armed with your latest achievement, proud of yourself you make ready to step outside and see what the school has to offer. A sudden thunderstorm heralds the formation of several tornados through the area.

"None shall escape the King of the East," comes a voice from one, as you notice while it passes that it is sweeping up monstrous creatures who curse the winds for their attack.

Quickly afterward the sun returns as a legion of Roman centurions march by, chanting Latin marching songs. They split into two groups after receiving instructions from the Commander and then both groups march into the distance.

Then a swift breeze strikes you with a voice that seemed to follow the air current as it searches the workroom, "No silver shall you call your own, the Lunar hearth is now her throne." A vicious blast hits you as the wind departs.

"Okay too weird! I'm out!" you yell as you slam the door. "I'll stay right here and read all this shit."

You begin to pile through the disordered documents and study the hours, names and talismanic constructions. You learn the correspondences between the planetary orbits and the terrestrial cycles. By the end, your head is filled with occult knowledge leaving you both fascinated and confused.

Okay so it looks like the hour for Mercury would allow for 'wonderous occurrences' whatever that means. Why is everything so vague with these descriptions? I suppose I could wait until this hour comes around and try an experiment with it.

Setting aside the copper talisman in your possession you take up a plate of mixed metals on page 42

Maybe I could give Saturn a try. Everything about it seems depressing and cruel. Not sure if this is for me.

Looking at the stack of dark plates before you on page 207

Starting to get annoyed with the whole situation you look over Mars and the instructions to create iron talismans.

Why the hell is everything is so violent? This is magic. You can do anything you want. The best you come up with is destroy all enemies. What the hell kind of wisdom is this?

Searching further you find rare entries for the golden talismans. Looking at the different piles of metallic plates. Gold is one of the smaller ones.

Well at least these ones also seem a bit interesting. Normally called the golden hour these spirits are arrogant and proud they will resist any control exerted over them... I saw the crazy shit happening outside with thunder-storms and singing tornados. Am I really ready to encounter the pricks of this world?

Turn to the page 398 if you feel up to the challenge of the Solar hour.

You allow the hours to pass as you continue to absorb information from the texts previously scattered around you. The hours pass into the sunset and you realize you have perfectly organized the room. All the parchments are arranged perfectly according to their subjects and each topic is placed in order according to its relevance with the planetary hour.

I hope those phantom wind ghosts don't come back and ruin this.

The room is beautifully coordinated. Perfectly kept. Like new. The hours have cycled to Venus once again.

Well, I've carved one of these. Why not another? The descriptions are the only ones that seem to make sense any.

You engrave another talisman of Venus turn on page 244

Through the Looking Glass

You peer into the mirror with the intent of finding his lost friend. What gradually appears is a division of cultists holding lamps and forcing fire spirits to settle within them.

"Is he one of these people?" you ask.

"I cannot see anything but myself in this mirror," replies the ghoulish wanderer in a dry tone.

Oh shit! That's right he can't use the mirror. "Sorry, give me a sec here," you respond as you change your intention.

A detailed illusion spreads through the area placing you both within the scene displayed within the mirror. Very quickly he points to a lamp, "He is there."

"Okay let me try to focus on him," you alter the display using your focus and show a greater view of the cultist camp on ***page 310***

Apples Fresh from the Tree

You are escorted out of the pyramid. Many of the garden's inhabitants bow as you pass. You can feel the effect you have on those around you. You sense more than what you did before, a warmth that spreads evenly throughout your body.

"What you are feeling young master," the maiden whispers, "is the favor of those around you. If you should feel a chill then the enchantments must be strengthened."

She leads you to a tree. One you have never seen before: A bizarre type of apple tree. It glows like a sun. Standing near it provides almost a sensual warmth.

"You carry with you the full blessing of the name of Venus," states the maiden. "Only our highest adherents can eat from this tree and not be poisoned."

You refrain from investigating the fruits, withdrawing your hands and turning your attention to your instructor.

"This is a trade off," she affirms. "These apples are grown under the influence of the Solar powers during the strength of Venerean hour. They will repel anything that interferes with your enchantment. All Sub-lunars will be unable to forcefully take possession of you. Their powers will be mostly null against you. Even the other hourlies will have a hard time interfering with your operations over the will of mankind. But you will not be able to summon into binding any other spirits other than our own."

Realizing the magnitude of this, you ask, "will it be permanent? Will all my ambitions be contained within the fifth orbit?"

"After about a week, yes," she confirms. "We need someone to take up this mantle. The mansion has sealed its doors. The hours are all entrenched in their own personal aspirations. The Sub-lunars are rebellious against anything mortal and the students at this school are terrorizing each other. With the gifts you receive you can undo much of the harm we have been forced to do to each other."

"But I will be permanently altered," you reply. "I will be stuck within a single form, never to experience the others for myself. If these limitations are forever how will I evolve? What will my purpose be when this mission is finished?"

The maiden glides to your side, "As an hourly we are constrained to our natures. We can expand our dominion. We can enhance our disciples, even change the world around us. But we never change. In a thousand years we will be what we were a thousand years ago. But for mortals, your stars shine brightly against the night. You are capable of surpassing your nature and transcending into higher states of being. Our kind look on envious, some darker entities even resent you for it. This transformation always demands a sacrifice."

"I'm ready." You declare, "tell me what I need to do."
"Follow after me," the maiden says as she guides you to ***page, 328.***

OR

"Please give me some time," you ask. "I've never had to make a decision like this before."
The maiden gives you leave as you rush away to ***page 330*** ***in order to fully contemplate a proper response.***

Earth Beats

You grab hold of the drum, eager to explore this newfound talent. You start slowly and then progress to quicker beats. You keep perfect pace. Gradually, you speed up becoming more complex strokes. Your hands are starting to burn up and your wrists begin to seize, but you play just the same, unyielding to your pain driven against sense of self-preservation by the entrancing rhythm.

Distracted by a shadow cast over your position, you look up to see a short, well-built dwarven man. Wearing only a cape and a loin cloth, his dense beard and thick head of hair look like flowing soil growing from his face. Despite the buoyant atmosphere, he holds a grim expression with unmoving eyes. You offer a smile which is not returned.

Unsure what to expect, you realign your focus to the drums, hoping the small creature would become interested in something else. Raising your head again you are caught off guard; where previously one dwarf stood, now more than a dozen have gathered. They are uniform in appearance: loincloths, capes, thick mane-like facial hair and skin that appears to be covered in soil.

Eventually, your arms need a break and you complete your performance. No clapping, no praise, no sound. The party has fallen into a stupor and the strange dirty little men just stare blankly at you.

Are these hobos of the spirit world? Can spirits be homeless?

One of the short beings from the back passes something to another before him. They repeat the process until eventually numerous gemstones are delivered to you. One of the little men bows and turns away towards some fruits and mead served on a low table made obviously to accommodate for his kind.

"They're gnomes," claims the maiden. "Spirits of the Earth. Unlike the other hourlies that demand offerings and gifts in exchange for services, our service draws offerings. By these stones we can expand our influence. Try another instrument when our hour rises," she insists.

Pick up the lyra once again on page 290
Choose the flute and move on to page 219

Offerings by the Water

Picking up the lyra was a little bit different. The three stringed miniature violin seems astoundingly complex; at first you aren't even sure how to hold it. The maiden directs you to sit down and hold it on your shoulder, under chin and balanced on your knee. You begin to play under the maiden's guidance. At first, as with the flute, you are offkey but soon your recently acquired musical instinct surfaces and you play like a seasoned veteran.

"Young lord try using your skills by the well," the maiden suggests. "The undines are so fond of the lyra."

You pick a well close by and notice the crystalline water. You can see down to the well's bottom and marvel at the water's pure state as you begin to play.

Mesmerized by your newfound ability you keep on playing. The well's waters begin to course as the spirits make their appearance. The water swirls clockwise as beautiful effeminate forms manifest. The fluid beings move gracefully in the water as you play your music; they surface within the well in a strange but synchronous dance. Gradually, the hour fades and the spirits settle.

"Young master," one says, her ethereal voice penetrating your body as well as your oracular faculties. "We have gifts for you my Lord. Water unlike the other elements is not created anew. Our element takes many forms but cycles through the planet and is used by every creature and expelled by every creature to be purified and then used again. We have seen the patterns of your world and can read the flow of time into the future. Stare deep into our waters and learn what fate has lined up for you."

You stare into the swirling waters and fall into a trance. You see visions: some terrible, others profound and you hear a voice within your own mind giving instructions. Overwhelmed, you understand some of the bizarre instructions while others seem to be in foreign tongues.

Turn the page and stare deeply into the well. It will reveal your next course of action.

The flow of water mirrors the flow of time. The rising of an age is always followed by its decline only to have another rise on the unstoppable currents. Follow our voices, follow the currents to page 293
See your fall
See your rising

In a Trance

The pool of water seems to swallow you whole as you are transported into a dream state. You see Sub-lunars kneeling to you and delivering offerings. Images of unfamiliar people also kneeling flash before you. Another series of images reveals a hall of mirrors displaying scores of attractive women. Turning your focus into one of the mirrors you are presented with a reflection of your best self; you look beautiful.

You stare at yourself impressed with everything you see. But soon after blood pours down your face. You catch a glimpse within the mirror and see a reflection of numerous dead bodies pilled behind you. Turning in fear to escape the portent you encounter a wall of darkness. Behind you there is nothing.

"Your current path is perilous. One false move and you will drown. The waves will rise to swallow you whole, body flesh, mind and soul."

With the message delivered you are thrust back to your reality. You regain awareness on **page 318.**

Cloaked Access

You approach the camp's edge and peer into the mirror, "Maiden, I need your guidance. Find me the unhappy cultists who will be easily influenced and give me a form to blend in."

At once the mirror's reflections shifts and your appearance changes, allowing you to intermingle with the legion of cultists. You enter the camp with full confidence following the maidens dictates to reach your first target.

"Orders from the top," you command. "We need to march these units over the hill and encamp closer to the gate. The operation will be picking up soon."

With that, the plan is set in motion as the Venerean spirits pass through the ranks compelling many of the cultists close by to order their Sub-lunar companions to move their portion of the camp. Many other captains question the order but are quickly refuted with claims that a "higher-up" gave the direction. With the cultists in full motion and their encampment broken up, you head under the guidance of the maiden to your next group of targets.

You pull one of the cultists aside quickly and speak with a hushed tone, "I heard the commanders discussing a sacrifice to Bael. They mean to divide the camp to take control of all the Sub-lunars and use *our* blood as fuel for the invasion. This has been ordered by the Master. Start telling as many as you can."

You take a nervous drag from your pipe and exhale near the cultist you are addressing. The smoke is latched onto by a Venerean spirit that sets the cultist's emotions into a panic and with this message the influence of the fifth hour spreads.

As you watch the Venerean spirits, unknown to the cultists infiltrate their ranks, the Sub-lunars begin swatting and thrashing the air trying to drive the spirits away hindering your work.

"We've got a problem my lady. Is there anything in that image gallery of yours that can handle Sub-lunar interference?" you request.

Instructions from the lady return and you raise a small ring on your left hand exposing a newly formed image displayed on the mirror while speaking the words of power, "Actatos, Catipta, Bejouran, Itapan, Marnutus."

As if under a daze, the Sub-lunars, cease their attacks, stupefied by enchantments. The Venereans carry on sowing distrust against the leaders and disunity among the soldiers. Seeing the dissension occurring many higher-ranking cultists rush out, shouting orders angrily at the legion to reform.

You quietly move to the leader's tents, now only lightly guarded and barge into an occupied one with an immediate warning, "Mutiny! There is a group among us that means to betray the Master."

The cultists within the tent give you their full attention, "Some of the leaders mean to seize power for themselves and take the mansion for their own purposes. We need to stop this now!"

"All of the leaders of the East are here," states one of the gathering, "which *leader* are you referring to?"

Fortunately, your lies are disrupted by an explosion and fighting from within the camp. Everyone rushes out to see the encampment in an all-out civil war. Three factions are at war, each believing the other a threat. You marvel at the catastrophe Venerean hourlies can cause when given the right setting.

"Hmm," observes one of the commanders, "it looks like Venereans. The mansion is using pathetic means to break up our ranks."

Well shit, how did he know that?

"Yes," agreed another. "They will be easily dispelled and order returned. We will raise stronger wards. We should have seen this coming."

It's not that obvious... is it?

"Not to worry," added one of the captains, "we have a specialist among the ranks. *If* there were trouble it would be him reporting it to us and not you."

Oh, so you underestimate the name of the fifth orbit but fall under its spell. Let's see what else you know.

"Why isn't the specialist here now then?" you question.

"He is likely dealing with the situation at hand," responds the cultist, "he is a Sub-lunar disguised as a captain."

Shocked by what you hear you are forced to rethink your plan. Unsure how to proceed you bow, taking your leave from the cultist commanders.

To search for the Sub-lunar captain who is an obvious threat to the plan you consult the mirror on how to trap a Sub-lunar. The maiden reveals a devious plan that just might work. ***Turn to page 338 to set it into motion.***

To continue infusing Venerean influence throughout the camp and continue to stroke the fires of infighting ***turn to page 335***

Desirous Display

You show the cultists in the mirror images of daylight, trees and green plants. Raising you right hand with the large emerald ring, you tap the mirror gently. A chiming reverberation echoes and the images on the mirror spread throughout the area altering your landscape so thoroughly that even the afternoon sun is modified to display an evening twilight.

The world becomes your canvas; textures match their images making illusions so real they can be felt. Even smells are reproduced saturating the senses, making it impossible to tell what is truly real and what is created by you.

As they marvel at the living portrait surrounding them, you begin your instruction, "With these abilities we may be able to prevent the full-scale war. We can save many of our former comrades who have a veil pulled over their eyes."

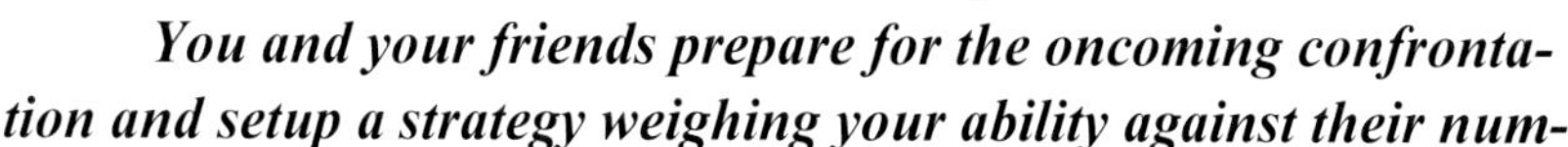

You and your friends prepare for the oncoming confrontation and setup a strategy weighing your ability against their numbers. Move into battle ***on page 378***

Before setting off to battle turn the page and behold the glory of the fifth hour. With the mirror you may yet hone your skills to greater refinement.

By Yourself Never Alone

A week of preparation according to the dominion of Venus. Basically, a weeklong party. You eat the apples every day and a host of other foods; everything is amazing. But you can't repress the thought that they treat you this way because they assume you are going to die.

You begin your travels using the mirror as a guide and figure out where most of the cultist bases are located. But you have no means of attack. You hour circles and you pull the third talisman, "I need help. I'll take anything. Just someone who can help me out and give me direction."

You wait, but nothing shows up. Pouring some pipe weed and lighting up, you draw Venerean spirits to your side.

"At least you guys are here," you state.

"Of course, we have summoned the direction you asked for," they reply.

Their beautiful forms sway around the incense, their presence filling you with a sensual delight, never allowing you to be upset or depressed. Their words...wait. *Summoned? The only humans close by are...*

You hear cackling and know that Sub-lunars are near. An entourage arrives with hooded and robed men and women, all riding on large lizards and awkward hybrid beasts. They surround your position as the leader dismounts to approach you. You take a drag, watching your pipe light up, *Well, I'm dead.*

"Ladies you better take off."

"Light up when you need us," sates one as she kisses you on the cheek and disappears.

The leaders approach you while the others remain surrounding your position. You pour out the pipe's contents as one from the group addresses you, "You have disturbed our operations! Were you sent by the mansion? None of them can help you now."

What the hell do I do now? "Sent by the mansion, no. Better. We have a friend in common. A serious man with a strange lamen around his neck," they halt at your words. "Yeah, *him*."

"*You* are from the High Command?" he asks.

Oh man, I hope my bullshit meter holds out for this one. "Well, whatever *you* want to call him. I'm here to oversee the operation to success and make sure the gate is unguarded."

"Bullshit!" utters one of the winged Sub-lunars close by.

He caught me.

"He's not one of us!" states the demon.

"Really," you counter. "Then attack me! I have immunity from the legions. If I'm really lying you should be able to possess me. Or worse."

You light up your pipe and await what could very well be your final moments on earth.

Well, bullshit meter at fifty percent. Why not go all out?

"Let's make this quick. Give the order!" you shout.

The commander, unsure of the requests, gives a two fingered un-enthusiastic gesture. The villainous looking beast alongside him smiles, revealing unnaturally long rows of sharpened teeth. He lunges at you but stops.

Alright, you think excitedly, not showing any outward emotion. Barely looking up, you inhale from the pipe. *Looks like my bullshiting continues.*

"I have no circle; this shouldn't be that difficult."

The Sub-lunar's wings dissolve into ash and he begins to shake uncontrollably as an invisible weight crushes him to the ground.

"The fourth hour... you are a blessed of their name..." declares the Sub-lunar.

"The fifth hour actually, buddy," you whisper, knowing full well he can hear. "Okay people, I only have a short time here. Send your pets away while we discuss the coming assault."

"The assault is happening now?" a member of the group says. "Why were we not given word?"

"*I'm* giving you word!" you assert. "And we cannot have non-human elements endangering the mission."

"My Lord," speaks one of the members, "we have been with this legion since the beginning. They have never shown any signs of dis-loyalty."

"Of course, except this one here that tried to attack me. We don't have much time here, I have other camps to visit and if *I* cannot convince you, when the Master arrives perhaps, *he* will."

With a light gesture the commander and the others send off their Sub-lunar allies.

"He's lying," claims the demon, who is immediately silenced by his cultist master.

Bullshit meter now at one hundred percent. Let's bring out the big guns.

You hold out the third talisman of Venus and draw the Venerean spirits near with your smoking. It may not have been the right hour but you can supersede many of the rules now. It does not take long for the cultists to begin spilling their plans. With the ability to repel Sub-lunars and attract humans you are almost all but invincible.

Learn all you can from the cultists on page 307

OR

Send them away and try to reach others who can stop them on page 303

You hear a commotion from a distance, *have they found me out*!?

You begin to run. Heading into a forest you duck behind a large tree unsure of what to do.

Great! *I thought my hour was in ascendance*! *What do I do now? Smoke them to death? I've got no offensive capabilities. Why the hell did I agree to this???*

You remain still, hopeful that whatever invisible entity following you passes by. You hear the howling of the wind and an unnatural screaming that follows, piercing your ears and sending a reverberating pain through your mind and body. From behind you feel a small breeze stroke the back of your neck. For a second you feel relaxed as the voices calm.

Wait... That's someone's breath...!

"What are you hiding from?" Whispers a voice.

You jump from your place terrified by what monster may be waiting behind you. In a feeble attempt to escape your situation, you trip and fall backwards. Trying to regain your footing, you awkwardly prop yourself up on one knee and notice your assailant.

A beautiful petite lady with long, soft black hair and grey eyes that looks enquiringly after you. She is dressed like an archaeologist with a suede brown hat.

Okay, she's definitely human and female and cute. I must look like the biggest moron.

You jump to your feet and introduce yourself.

"I already know," she replies. "I heard your call," she states as she points to your hand, still clutching the talisman.

"Oh, yes, right," you reply as you place it back within your pockets.

"You're lucky those cultists are really one dimensional, otherwise you may have a harder time convincing them to trust you so much."

"Well, if it helps, I know their plan of attack, who their leaders are and what they plan to do," you describe trying to pass on as much information as possible.

"Settle down turbo, that's not why we're here," she counters. "This war is a farce. The Sub-lunars within the Bael's legion have been stealing artifacts. One is buried close by. Let's have a look for it," the lady directs, pulling a talisman of her own.

I remember that design, I think. The metal looks like tin. Which hourly is closest to Tin?

She shows you the talisman with a combination of complex geometric shapes carved overtop. She traces her finger over the outline and it produces a comprehensive visual of an intricate compass. The visual expands to include both you and her. She walks around examining the different details and using her hand to adjust the images and focus on points of interest. You can hardly understand what you see but keep silent in hopes of an eventual explanation.

She smiles, "Found you!"

The images gradually fade as she leads you deeper into the forest, where a mound of disturbed earth is piled up in a small clearing.

"Sub-lunar servants are not very clever," she states aloud.

The scream you heard before rises as a large, blurred shadow rises from the forest's shade. It utters a dark language in an aggressive tone, forcing you to cover your ears to keep yourself from the auditory assault. Calmly, the petite lady before you pulls out a talisman written in blood and holds it outward forcing the shadow back. After some fighting between the two, the shadow fiend can no longer keep up with the resistance and retreats.

"Never a dull moment eh?" she states while digging up the mound. "What frightened you before, you know when we met, was this guy guarding his treasure. You got too close," she expresses while continuing to dig. "*This* is one of the reasons the mansion sealed their doors. Some of the cult members organized a heist. They stole many powerful relics and buried them throughout the property. They hoped to deliver them to their leader to help him conquer the world or something. That's why the cultists have been so aggressive; they are a distraction to keep us focused on them rather than on the stolen weapons."

You listen eagerly, given that no one has ever explained the full reason for the infighting.

"If they had delivered them to their Master, we would have found him already. We know he's coming here to collect the relics and take the property. *But* he will have to do it without any of these treasures."

She digs up a ring with a six-pointed star on.

"The seal of Solomon, one of the greatest magical creations our earth has. With this a person could enslave most of demon-kind and launch an attack against any corporeal force. This is the last treasure to be accounted for."

She has been fighting a hidden war to keep the property and the world at large secure. You relay your information about the cults camp and their gathered forces.

"They think of you as one of them. Be careful though, if they dispel the Venerean spirits under your command, even with their affection for you they will still kill you. The Sub-lunars likely know you are a spy and it's even more likely that the legions of Bael, like all demonic legions, are mindless drones who follow commands. At some point, your cover will be blown."

She proceeds to return to the mansion leaving you with grim warnings as you prepare for your next move. ***On page 359.***

The Master Plan

"The Master has already set his plan in motion," states the commander. "We are gathering here and eliminating any possible resistance. We know the mansion orbits, which makes it impossible to target directly but we have spoken with many of the infernal kings in the area. They will bow down should our attack commence. The hourlies are starkly divided and any independent magicians are unable to match our strength."

You take a deep puff of smoke, "Sounds like you're the man with a plan," you attest.

"Once, the master breaks the gate and the legions of Bael storm the area there should be an opening to the mansion. We will strike from behind and then, with the master join forces and take the mansion."

"Okay… looks like you're in order. Did you gather everyone here or are you still spread out?" you ask, holding up your ruse.

"We're spread but in constant communication. We are holding our position until the fateful hour, which as you say is not long from now."

"I don't make use of Sub-lunars, I find them too unreliable," you state. "Will Bael's legions be storming the gate with full force?"

"My Lord Bael's legions surround you," affirms the commander. "It is the source of our powers. Agares scours the forests as we speak to ward off any others who might challenge us."

You had no idea who or what these are but you realize that you slightly slipped up. The way he said it makes it seem like common knowledge. Sensing their distrust, you assert your authority, "Look, I've been a spy for the cause for a long time, but I've only been in the field for a short while and must assess the situation fully. We have a lot of moving parts right now and fully knowing our capabilities is important."

"Sorry my Lord," adds the Commander. "We are just cautious."

"It's why we don't trust too many sprits," you attest. "they can be turned and compelled."

They eventually take you to a larger dragon-like demon and have you hop on. You fly to a great altitude and then the Commander gives a whispered order and the forces of the Master appear over the earth.

"They can hide their mansion in the orbit. We can conceal our legions on the ground."

There are thousands of them. It is a huge force that seems uncountable.

How will we beat this?

After the initial tour, they settle at their camp and offer you some food. You dine with them on fancy tables in the middle of a field served by Sub-lunars.

"Will you stay the night my lord?" he asks you.

"No, I must be about the Master's business."

Nearing the end of the night you make your break and begin to put as much space between you and the enemy as you possibly can.

How the hell are we going to take this on. There are literally thousands of them!!! How do I fight this?

You calm down and check the time. The Venerean hour approaches.

Well, I guess fate can help a bit.

As you reach for the third talisman of Venus you hope that something greater than fate answers your call.

Call with your talisman on page 303.

OR

Use the talisman in your hands with the intention of countering the attack on Page 357.

Friendly Fire

"His name is Sal," he states as he looks at you with a detached expression.

"Okay hold on," you begin, "first, the Cult of the East, they have bases all along these areas. They've pretty much occupied this side of the property. Is your friend in their camp?"

Tilting his head slightly to the side, he responds in the affirmative. His voice sets off a surge of whispering around you that seems to have no definitive source.

"Honestly, man," you plead. "What is that?"

"Those are the words of Saturnite shades. They are bound to me and I to them," he responds stoically.

Saturn! Of course, you remember from the workroom. The darkest hour. A hermit of the grotto. Now you understand the type of person you are dealing with.

"Your friend, if he is trapped by them, we won't be able to take them head on," you explain. "That darkened floating ball of whispers will signal to everyone within the area your exact your location. However, I can find your friend *and* infiltrate their camp."

Your last claim seems to have pleased the dark figure. His head tilts showing interest urging you to tell him more. You pull out your mirror and stare deeply into it.

"My desire is to find a captured friend among the camps of the Cult," the mirror swirls as the reflection blurs and refocuses displaying many cultists. You cannot see any signs of slaves or prisoners as the mirror scans the camp and settles on a single image.

"Is your friend Sal a cultist? Did he join willingly?"

"No," he replies sternly. "There."

He points to a leader giving orders from atop a carriage with a lamp attached to the back.

"The *leader*?" you ask uncertainly.

"The lamp," the hermit answers angrily. "He is a salamander. They trapped him. I will go and set him free."

He rises without hesitation as you quickly prevent him from leaving. He gives you a frightening glare as you raise your hands, trying to clarify your actions.

"A salamander, like a lizard?"

Obviously annoyed with your persistence, he retorts, "A spirit of fire."

"So, you are doing all this for a spirit? They don't think of us the same way we think of them you know."

You last comment visibly enrages your new friend.

"Just give me one more look," you plea.

You hold the mirror as he points to Sal, "A ball of flame. You're ready to take on the Cult of the East for a single simple elemental spirit. You *can* summon another one."

"It would not be Sal."

"You would go this far?" you ask.

"He's my friend."

"That's a brave thing. It is hard for me to do this now and I've got lots of friends that are depending on me," you admit.

"I don't," he returns dryly.

You nod, seeing a deeper reason between the bond he has with the spirit.

"Okay, let's do this. *But* I go in first. With a plan. I've got an idea. Let's study their positions and find weaknesses. I'll strike first. Then, when they're weak, we call in the big guns. That's *you.* When this is over, we have a victory party."

He hunches in, listening to your words. You see him almost smiling as you explain the intricate plan, huddling up close as he takes in your instruction. As you talk, you detect the loneliness and solitary struggle that the Saturnite influence thrusts upon him. For the time being he revels in the attention, enjoying the company of another human breaking his forlorn journey even if only for a little while.

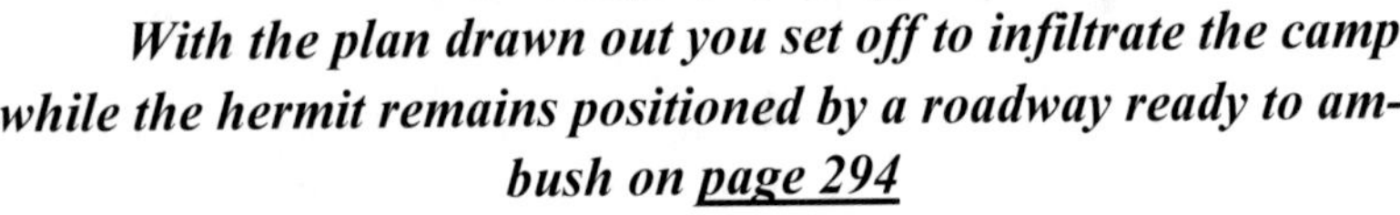

With the plan drawn out you set off to infiltrate the camp while the hermit remains positioned by a roadway ready to ambush on page 294

Following the information, you acquired, you stand ready at sunrise to intercept a caravan heading toward the front gate. You hear explosions in the distance and the sound of fighting erupts throughout. However, none of that concerns you as you wait for the caravan to approach. With the rebellion underway, you spot the caravan bringing a fresh batch of demons and magicians to support the war effort.

"We are late!" snaps a leader atop a carriage pulled by demonic servants. "We should have been there during the beginning. Let's move!"

You spot Sal, trapped in a lamp atop the carriage with the leader. He senses you and reverts into his four-legged form clawing at the glass in an attempt to reach you. The leader turns his attention to the rebellious salamander, tracing a symbol over the lamp which returns your friend into a flaming primal form.

You cut ahead and intercept the group, standing ready in the center of the road with your hood drawn and your censor lit. Barefoot, thin and pale in your ragged clothing, you look more like a hobo skeleton than a threatening force. But your only friend is in danger. You feel the shade of the Saturnite cluster far above and their whispering urges you on.

The caravan approaches and stops in front of you. You see Sal, held captive by heartless people. Your anger seethes as the leader address you, "We are servants of the Bael, King from the East. Are you friend or foe? If you are late to join just fall in line, we will be at the front soon."

You give no response. The leader harshly orders his subordinates to remove you from their path. One carelessly approaches, thinking you do not pose a threat, "Step aside. If you don't move, we'll..."

His words are cut off with a swift draw of your sickle. You cut him deep and place your hands over his neck, steadily holding him in place. He struggles, but you stand firm, collecting his pooling blood into your hands.

"What's going on there?" the leader asks.

You push his body to the ground and stretch out your hands to your sides displaying the collected blood to your Saturnite entourage. They descend from their nest within the dark cloud and ravenously seek out your offering. The blood evaporates as they breath it in leaving red stains on your skin.

Before the caravan can respond, the Saturnites fly into a frenzy and begin attacking the magicians. One is picked up and slammed against the ground repeatedly. You hear his bones shattering with every plunge. Another is viciously maimed and screams while you pour incense into your censor and march forward to free your friend.

"It's an agent from the mansion!" shouts the leader.

The magicians carve circles in the earth and open their censors drawing the Sub-lunars to their sides. You throw your own censor and its contents on the ground disturbing their circles and firmly point at the demons and then at the magicians, whose defenses have been compromised. Driven by fear and instinct, the demons attack. One of the magicians becomes possessed and turns on an ally, killing him. You progress to the leader as the possessed magician's body is contorted and broken by the malignant creature. You hear the magician's bones shatter and tendons snap as you make ready to free your friend.

The leader jumps into action tracing a circle on top of the carriage and a host of demons swarm to his aid. He frees some incense and you see his influence will not be so easily breached. You trace a circle with your sickle as a barrage of corrupted entities smash against your barrier.

"What do you hope to achieve here?!" the leader shouts. "We can offer you more than *they* can."

You see Sal trying to claw through the lamp restraining him.

He's my friend! And you stole him!

You pull the final talisman of Saturn and cup it in your blood-tinged hands as you cry out enraged. Despite the raging battle, you feel the earth tremor. The Sub-lunars sense the presence of the influence you bear, they look to the leader, then to you and many make their retreat. You violently shake the talisman clasped in your hands and the earth vibrates forcefully.

"Stop," the leader shouts. "You have a pentacle of Saturn; it could kill us all!"

You have my friend...! The only being that didn't reject me! I hate you! I'll kill you!

You shout again and with your whole being curse your enemies. The influence of Saturn is felt as earthquakes devastate the land around you. While the Sub-lunars flee, the carriage is swallowed with the leader still bellowing commands.

I'll kill you! *I'll kill everyone*!

*****

Hours later the rebellion is defeated. The land around you is warped and twisted and along with the caravan you are crushed under the shifted earth. Saturnites hover over your body taking from it whatever essence they can feed off of. No spirits will come near the area except a small fire spirit that curls up next to your lifeless corpse, bearing the result of friendship's highest sacrifice. It waits for a long while before breathing in some incense from a fallen censor and returning to its original form as floating flame and drifting off into the distance.

*****

Two companions come across your body, "No, don't get too close," says one stopping the others advance. "Look, Saturnites. That must be the Hermit. I've heard about this one. It looks like he fought some of the rebels."

"What are Saturnites?"

"You remember the Sub-lunars by the river? *These* are worse."

FIN

By the Well

Returning to the world, you take a sharp breath in like a man coming up for air after being submerged against his will. You look for the spirits of the well, only to find the clear waters uninhabited.

The maiden gently moves close, slightly surprising you, "Whatever you saw was for you."

Shaken by what you've witnessed, you walk through the garden pondering the meanings of the images, or if, they even had any meaning at all.

Should I believe those dreams? Dreams and visions are normally just in our heads. Some of that stuff was a bit heavy.

Outside of this place no dream could have gained such consideration. But here, where natural laws are distorted and other dimensional beings converge, the warnings you saw are likely to carry with them greater meaning. You pass by a garden and notice your flute. Picking it up you smile remembering the joy you created and received from playing the instrument.

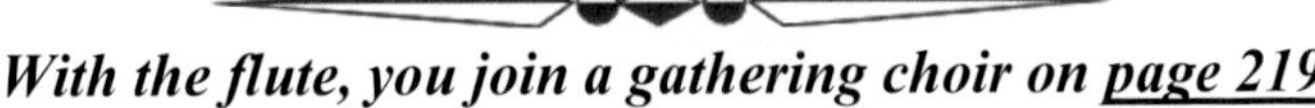

With the flute, you join a gathering choir on page 219

Truth Even in Darkness

Not far away, you see where the battle took place. It would have happened as yours was finishing. The scene is far more brutal than yours. The earth itself is scarred and the cloud that darkened your way before still looms overhead blocking out most of the sun.

Down the path you find his body. The Saturnite spirits have encircled his corpse. As you get closer you feel a biting chill crawl through your skin. You see others passing by, also surveying the destruction. Keeping your distance, you listen in on their conversation, "No, don't get too close," says one stopping the others advance. "Look, Saturnites. That must be the Hermit. I've heard about this one. It looks like he fought some of the rebels."

"What are Saturnites?"

"You remember the Sub-lunars by the river? *These* are worse."

They bow politely as they pass by and you decide to get a closer look.

The mirror said we would be friends. I do not leave a friend behind.

You see a small lizard-like creature with red burning skin move up to the body of the hermit.

"And you must be Sal," you state.

It looks up with its head tilted and then turns back to the body of its fallen rescuer.

"There it is, you were true to your word," you whisper. "Any of us would have been lucky to call you friend."

Eventually the cold stinging darkness forces you back and during the hour of Saturn the cloud descends from the sky engulfing the body of the fallen hermit. It spins like a cyclone and departs with the body leaving no trace of its former daunting presence while you stand vigil for the nameless hero, fallen in battle alone, but not without friends.

FIN

Subdued Not Enslaved

A horde of Sub-lunars blocks the sun entirely. It's surprising how many there are circling through the sky. The flowers have completely retreated and the party guests have deserted the area. You are alone. You sit by a fountain, pulling the fourth talisman of the Venerean hour and speaking closely to it.

"Whoever is responsible for this, I need very badly to speak with them."

From the waves of Sub-lunars descends a single hooded being, clothed in a seamless robe and supported by two vicious looking demons. When he lands you notice his face is concealed by a decorative mask.

"So, a Venerean actually steps out to confront the force of the East," he states, with a coarse metallic voice that sounds permanently enraged.

"No, just me," you reply looking up at the cultist. "Not sure about the force from the East. Maybe you'd like a little song," you say, reaching for your flute.

"Don't even try," orders the cultist, drawing his sword and aiming it at your neck.

"Am I really worth this type of attention?" you ask. "And do you think your enemies will allow this activity to carry on?"

"Soon it won't matter," he responds. "we only need to keep your kind restrained during *your* hours. You will not disturb our operations anymore."

"Why would you think we want to disturb your operations? The only thing I would like for you to do is quit blocking our sun."

At that moment, the chorus begins to play and many of the Sub-lunars break their formations. Rays of sunlight pour through the cracks in their ranks.

"Stop them! Go!" the cultist commands as his two servants rush to intercede.

You pull your own flute and play a light tune. Sylphs begin to swarm, unseen by the distracted cultist. He is about to re-establish order when bursts of wind strike him from all sides. He draws a circle with his sword dispelling their attacks, then intones names of power to constrain the demonic forces. You play your flute, sending vibrations to all nearby spirits as the horde regains control of the skies.

"You cannot hope to challenge me with elemental spirits," the cultist boasts. "They will never break my boundary or the summoned multitude I've bound to the cause."

No, you're right. They won't do any of that," you muse. *But if even one is trapped within your circle...*

A sudden upswelling of wind inflates the cultist's robes and lifts him high into the air. The Sylphs smother and disarm him. You calmly walk over to the circle and dig gaps into it with your hands and feet.

The chorus resumes. The demons disperse. The sunlight pours

into the area full force, reflecting through the pyramid and refracting into the gardens. The flowers bloom, the sylphs are called to sight causing light whirlwinds to dance throughout the area. Rainbows form from moisture rising from the fountains and the Sub-lunar hordes become willingly hypnotized by the ethereal orchestra.

For the demonic race, this place is a valley of addictions. Simple pleasures they could never attain themselves. Knowing this, you make your approach, "Which one of you is skilled at possession?"

"My lord," comes a sly voice from behind. "I can do this deed."

Without turning, you nod. Faster than any human sense can perceive the demon rushes to the cultist and takes his body. The now possessed man tears at his robes, spasming wildly on the ground.

"Keep him dancing," you state. "Make sure his body is completely worn out."

The Sub-lunars cheer as their former master is made to contort like a broken marionette while you sit observing the pacified infernal army.

To question the Sub-lunars about the "force of the East" turn to page 324

OR

This one magician almost destroyed your entire hourly domain. To take on this threat, turn to page 277

Answers of the East

You watch the cultist continue in his forced malformed dancing as many of the Sub-lunars look on with a demented glee. You approach one of his previous attendants, "What is this force from the East?"

"Ah," he answers while smelling a flower. His inhalation is unnaturally drawn out, forcing you to wait longer than you would have liked for his answer. "Bael is the force from the East. A king, with sixty-six legions, to which we all belong. Some mansion magician got it in his head to bind the king. So, in exchange for helping him take over this place, he would give him free reign. Which would also mean giving *us* free reign."

"Is he the one who made the pact?" you ask.

The demon laughed, "No, not a chance. The one who can call to sight Lord Bael is a serious player. *This* is one of the followers. They have spies everywhere. They believe that their combined power matched with the full force of the legion and a King of the East will be enough."

"Why are they doing this?" you ask.

"It's mostly bullshit," claims the Sub-lunar. "There's no way we know the actual plan. Most of the followers are delusional. They think there's something in it for them. But that's not how these things work."

The Sub-lunar deeply smells the flower garden and many of the legion began to take off. “Well, I’m out. It’s nice to be free from someone else’s control. I’ll have to enjoy it, for as long as it lasts. Hey, play me a song before I go. Those songs have such a relieving effect on us.”

You play, watching him spread his wings, leap into the air and disappear with the others into the horizon.

You approach the maiden after the ceremony with the Sub-lunars. This rebellion is a threat that must be dealt with. Set up a strategy on page 277

Entering the workroom, your senses are overwhelmed by the sheer concentration of material and utilities dispersed throughout the area. Astrological charts erected onto the walls, parchments and papers in no apparent order, diagrams on hourly intonations and a well-ordered stack of metallic plates organized beneath planetary symbols are just some of the items that you manage to take in.

A clock on the wall below the ceiling has all the planetary symbols displayed where numerals would have been with an arrow pointing to the dominant hour.

It looks more like a large compass, you think as you match the hour to the symbol about a stack of bronze-colored plates.

"Looks like copper," you say as you inspect the object.

Close by, you find a parchment with the symbol that matches the one on the clock. You read over the instructions and find tools close by and begin to etch the figures onto the copper plate.

The Fourth Talisman of Venus—It Is of great power, since it compels the spirits of Venus to obey, and to force on the instant any person thou wishest to come unto thee.

When you complete the operation, you find the appropriate incense and a bowl to burn it in. Passing the plate through the rising smoke you see the metal sparkle and glow. You hear beautiful singing as the incense fumes sway over its surface. Pleased with your work, you inspect the talisman and follow the final instructions, wrapping it in some silk and placing it into your pocket.

"Nice, I did, something… I guess," you muse. Seeing that the hour has passed, you are unsure as to what to do next.

Without wanting to think too much you exit the workroom to page 366

OR

You await the return of the hour of Venus and study the materials within the workroom on page 282

The maiden plucks an apple and hands it to you, "Take and eat," she insists.

The fruit tastes good, but nothing extraordinary.

"You will need at least one a day for over seven days. Also," she gestures, causing a Venerean beauty to glide forward and pass you a small wooden ornate chest and a fancy gas lighter, "Both should fit in your pocket. These are your pipe weeds. They will allow you to subdue the world with greater ease. Use them *only* for good. This is a weapon aimed at the mortal heart, use it unwisely and it will turn on you."

Next, she leads you back to the fountain, "My ladies," she says in a soothing tone, "we have one who would see if you would let him."

She silently instructs you to dip your right index finger into the fountain. The undines smile and stir the water as a clear image of the mansion and the entire property reveals itself.

You notice the beauty of the Victorian mansion but the visual tour takes you throughout the property, the Solar temple, the Martial training grounds, the extraordinary laboratory of the Mercurials and then to many other places. After this, you are presented with a bird's eye view of the entire area.

"Amazing!" you shout. "They orbit? All these structures orbit around the mansion! How is this possible?"

The maiden smiles reaching into the water without disturbing the surface. She pulls a small mirror with a decorative frame and hands it to you.

"This will show you friends who are nearby. It also will reveal the location of enemies. It can reflect your inner desires and show you the desires of others," she states. "It will guide you to the destinations you must reach."

Taking the mirror gratefully, you reply, "Wouldn't this have been useful before all this started?"

"Only a mortal in possession of our name with a good heart can make use of it. Otherwise, you would never be able to see a clear image. It would be an ordinary mirror. Take rest now. In the morning, you depart to counter the threats to our domain."

You sleep during a restful night well prepared for tomorrow and the task it brings with it. When you awaken, head to page 299 to begin counter measures.

OR

Before you sleep try out the mirror on page 332

The Purpose of Action

Sacrifice.

You reflect on the words of the maiden.

I've only just started getting good at this, why should I give up all my opportunities? Maybe there is another way of doing this? These hourlies are strictly bound to their nature...man, I can't make choices like this.

A small gargoyle-like creature crawls cautiously toward you, rousing you from your inner dilemma.

"Hello," it says shyly.

"Ugh... buddy, the party's over there" you gesture towards the Venerean domain in the distance behind you.

"I am not interested in the frivolity of the hourlies," he sneers. "I am called Ornias."

"*Frivolity,* someone remembers classical English from his school years. What can I do for you Ornias?" you ask.

"I can do as much for you as *you* can do for me," he responds as he carefully draws closer to you.

"Not interested in any pacts buddy," you retort. "Carry on down the road..."

"I sense you are someone like me. You do not want to be confined to the strictures of the Venerean disposition. I am also confined. *They* want you to defeat the cult *and* likely they will use *you* as an avatar."

"Okay little spirit," you say annoyed at his correct assumption, "how do you know that?"

"I've seen many before you crushed under the burden of hourly machinations. I can show you how to use their powers without being constrained."

"If you are looking for a pact, I'm not interested..." you sternly disclose one again.

"No! No pacts. Just a deal. I help you with this and when I need a favor *you* help me."

Pondering the smaller demon's advice, you become nervous about trusting the Venereans. To hear more turn to page 369

Flee from this situation entirely running swiftly to page 38

Desires of Man

You take your rest under a tree. Even the ground is comfortable. What will it be like when you leave? You pick up your mirror and softly ask it to show you a vison of the cultists. You see legions of Sub-lunars fleeing as cultists bind them from within circles. You see many kneeling in submission to their cultist masters. They're preparing for a war.

"Show me, who is in charge of this?"

A magician with a stern, focused look seems to be sculpted in stone. He is elegantly dressed, with a demonic lamen on a necklace hanging on a necklace, moving with perfect posture. Demons bow at his passing. He stops suddenly, his head turns and faces you, locking eyes.

Can he see me?

Raising his hand his image blurs and does not reform.

Guess he caught me spying.

You stare at this mirror, marveling at what power it possesses and wondering what limitations would condition it.

"What do I desire? Really? What am I doing all this for? What is the end result of this war?"

The mirror becomes foggy and gradually clears up as you view an intelligent looking man laboring over what looks like a strange chemistry set. One of the beakers shifts colors: first black, then white and then red and with a phoenix emerging from the beaker. The intelligent man waves at you.

You see me too!?

You wave back, unsure if the mirror gives others access to you. His picture fades as another image forms of Roman soldiers training and marching. It is a legion marching towards a gate. It opens and at the legion's head stands a commander with a golden shield equipped on his back. He looks towards you and gives a Roman salute.

The next image is of a doctor sitting by a patient. He stands and walks out of the hospital. The sun shines brightly around him and he sprouts wings of light and is clothed in a bright armor as he is lifted into the sky.

The images change again, this time a hooded figure in ash covered clothing emerges from a dark grotto. Carrying over his back, a heavy looking iron chain attached to a censor and a sickle at his side, he gives off a terrifying look. What looks like a small fire spirit joins the hooded figure's company. You notice this person is always walking in the shade, even as the sun shines around him.

Next is the image of a middle-aged woman. Dark haired with maps spread over a desk, she looks like a treasure hunter. Peering over her shoulder, she gives you an alluring smile as the vision changes again.

Another woman appears, standing by a hearth. She is placing many herbs into the boiling water as phantoms dive to breathe in the evaporating mixture. She gently caresses their ghost-like forms as they pass. She smiles slyly as she raises a ladle offering you a taste.

You view further images of these and other beings standing together and surprisingly, you see yourself in their center.

I've not met these people yet. They must be friends.

You see the mansion and many of your future companions standing together, overseeing a great change in the property and then, from a bird's eye view a great change in the world.

Satisfied and given renewed strength, you pass into sleep. Tomorrow, when the hour is in your favor you will prepare to strike against the enemy for the sake of your maiden and the friends you have yet to meet.

Awaken on page 299 and begin your mission.

Unstable Friction

Continuing your attempts to disrupt the encampment, you take in a deep drag from your fancy pipe and release a gust of mist. The Venereans circle around you to absorb what you exhale and then return to their regular activities.

We weakened your Sub-lunars, scattered your soldiers and disrupted your ranks. There are battles and infighting at all ends of the camp. Who could possibly stand against my...?

"There he is!" comes a deep metallic voice.

There who is?

At once, the Venereans are dispelled and your enchanted disguise is flung off you. Standing with your normal attire, completely exposed *and* surrounded, the fighting stops.

Oh, you mean me. There me is.

"A filthy intruder. You allowed this pathetic summoner of the hourlies to put divisions between you," maintains the same voice.

A leader of the cultists steps into sight as you pull in another drag from your pipe, trying to keep your heart rate down. You notice the captain of the cultists speak through an iron mask making his already frightening voice sound rough, giving it a throaty echo.

"You think you can stop us with cheap tricks?" he states preparing to attack.

"Oh, I see, *you're the* demonic commander they were talking about," looking back at the assembly of leaders who are frustrated and embarrassed that they have been manipulated by your Venerean wiles.

"So, are we going to just talk about this or are you going to do something?" you state.

Enraged, the demonic leader pulls a curved serrated blade as he moves toward you.

Oh man, that was the wrong choice of words. Well, if this fails, I'm dead...

You pull the mirror and with your emerald ring you tap the surface sending a singing reverberation threw the area. Immediately, a gigantic apparition of your form emerges surprising everyone. The giant form begins to immediately wander through the camp as numerous Sub-lunars attack the illusion.

After the giant image is struck it pops like a balloon sending thousands of smaller versions of itself falling to the ground. They promptly rise to their feet and begin to run throughout the camp causing havoc.

The cultists attack ferociously striking at your multiplied images, causing them to "pop" with each engagement. The camp is united again in a vain effort to locate the real you. There is no order to their slaughter of the illusions. The mayhem allows you to escape unscathed, clearing the campgrounds and observing the disorder from a distance. Lighting your pipe and inhaling the sweet fragrance, you draw the scattered Venerean spirits your side. You walk calmly beyond the borders of cultist detection and notice Roman centurions approaching you.

Martial spirits? Backup! About time.

"My Lord," spoke the Martial leader. He wears a golden shield, shaped like a figure eight on his back. "We have slowly surrounded the area. You did good. We'll take it from here."

You pull in for another drag and release a cloud of mist that the spirits of your hour dive in for as you quietly watch the forces of the mansion close in on their targets. With a loud command the soldiers jump into action and begin a calculated slaughter of the scattered cultists. You are soothed by the screams from the camp as you notice their bodies falling in the distance.

Oh shit! My buddy!

You try to inquire about the hermit but are told that waiting behind the lines is safest. Eventually, the battle pushes out of sight beyond the darkened horizon and you listen as the carnage reaches its climax awaiting the sunrise to survey the aftermath.

Sunrise finally comes about and the battle has long ended. ***Turn to page 319 and search for the friend you promised to help.***

Closing in through the ranks of the cultists he makes his way towards the source of the disturbance. He hears all the thoughts around him, they cloud his senses, yet he hears the voice of an intruder. Surging through the ranks at speeds faster than any human eye can perceive, he passes other Sub-lunars; they pay him little heed as maintains his search.

Where are you? I hear your thoughts. You are close. You are very good at disguising yourself. You are using the Venerean hour to your advantage. It won't save you when I get... There you are.

Moving slower he finds his target. Listening, he hears from within and prepares to attack. Increasing speed, he moves towards his target ready to quickly finish what he began. A calm voice intones a deep name of power. He freezes.

Why won't I move...? No? This can't be.

Turning to face the demonic assassin you point quietly to the triangle etched into the ground. It is so subtle that it is barely noticeable. The demon attempts to scream but you order it quiet and step forward with the mirror displaying a powerful ward.

With one of your smaller rings, you trace glyphs into the air as the maiden directs you and speak your intent, "Be obedient and calm. Answer my questions clearly and honestly. Keep your appearance before me in a comely and simple manner."

You slowly make your way closer to the bound demon. A being thousands of years old, powerful, with abilities of a phenomenal nature, able to surpass the limits of natural law. Now it is vulnerable, enslaved by some etches in the ground and intoned words propelled by the voice of a mortal soul.

Standing before this leader of the Cult of the East you examine his features, *He's afraid. He knows this is the end for him.*

"It's not actually the end," he states.

"You read minds," you reply casually. "Well, I'll ask that you stop and tell me your name."

He hesitates for a bit but the hidden forces subduing him make it difficult for him to resist, "Dantalion."

A strange sigil appears on the mirror in the display allowing further control over the entity before you. Dantalion's form shifts and numerous faces begin to replace the one he has. At first, of men and women, then numerous heads emerge cycling around smoothly, with one face never the same as the next.

"This is my form," he says proudly. "And this, is you," he states, showing you your own face before allowing it to shift into another. A book appears in his right hand which opens, its pages slowly but continually turning.

"This book displays all the thoughts of the humans I observe. It allows me to replicate them perfectly. The rebels summoned me to break into the mansion and create discord, steal relics and assassinate the Master of the property. That plan failed."

It was strange talking to a being with shifting heads. Every face was *actually* some person somewhere in the world.

"It was me who almost infiltrated the mansion's core. That plan also didn't go exactly as planned. I'm actually lucky to still be of use in the physical realm."

"Enough," you say firmly. "What do I do to break up this camp?"

"Well," Dantalion says slyly, "I could impersonate the generals to start a riot."

You feel the mirror in your hands vibrate suddenly, "swear by the symbols on this mirror to fulfill your pledge and should you betray your word be burned and bound to the mirror and tortured by unforgettable harm."

"This war was a losing battle from the start. I swear. Leave these to me. I would recommend you leave the encampment after this. When my task is complete, will you release me?" Dantalion asks curiously.

"You are free to return to the void you emerged from. Withdraw quietly and let there ever be peace continued between thee and me!"

Retreating from the camp you smoke lightly as the carnage breaks out behind you. You are not sure exactly what Dantalion did, but you notice fires erupting and even the Sub-lunars bound to the cultists are retreating into the night sky.

The forces of the mansion are not far away and you meet up with a commander armed with a golden shield flung over his back, with a legion of Martial spirits supporting him

"Before you attack," you interject. "Just let my man over there do his thing."

"You've captured a powerful Sub-lunar," cites the commander.

"He is something," you state, watching another explosion break the darkness of the night's sky.

*****

When the forces of the mansion finally engage the battle ends quickly; it is an easy victory. Sunrise greets the champions with a flood of corpses strewn throughout the landscape. Among them is a solitary figure; a demon with a shifting face, reading from his endless tome of the thoughts of men awaiting his commendation. You observe his shifting faces as he stares at you with numerous pairs of eyes.

"Looks like we're finished here," Dantalion states.

"You're free," you reply. "Before you go, did you happen to see a hermit of the Saturnite persuasion amidst the fighting?"

Looking into his book he turns to you, "Did he look like this?" Dantalion asks shifting into the pale, bald, stoic look of your friend.

"He did," you answer, taking a drag from your pipe.

The book in his hands suddenly closes as Dantalion begins to dissolve into a clear mist returning to his original realm.

"No, never saw him at all," he replies as his laughter carries over the air while his body vanishes.

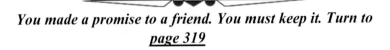

You made a promise to a friend. You must keep it. Turn to ***page 319***

Dead End

Moving away from the direction of the retreating cultists your group travels through the property. Moving onward the land seems calmer and less likely to have enemies. Ultimately, you call for the group to slow down and take a rest. While this occurs you draw the attention of the group leader, "So what happens now? Where are we going?"

"I don't know," he states honestly. "So much has happened in the last couple of weeks. With the outbreak of war and the sealing of the gate and silence from the mansion we're really in the dark here."

"The gate?" you question. "What gate is this?"

"The way we came in," he answers. "That gate is one of the only ways in or out. Even finding it is a matter of dispelling the magical barriers that guard this place. Ever since the Cult attacked, no one gets in or out. This place used to be amazing but as of late it seems so fractured. We need to keep moving, something will come up. It has to."

Your group walks on and finds a pathway to follow into another deep forest. As you wander a thin mist sprawls out at ground level. Gradually, and without realizing it, the mist rises and becomes thicker.

"Check if this mist is natural," commands the leader.

One of the group members pulls a dagger and makes some intricate slashing moves along with calm chanting. After a moment he turns, signaling safety to the others.

"Okay, we carry on," says the leader.

The trees overhead branch out in dense formations, keeping the sunlight from entering in any meaningful way. Eventually, you arrive at an eroding stone wall and notice small rows of neatly organized stone structures.

"Guys," you call out. "Look, a graveyard."

They all lean over the decrepit stone wall and peer into the grim burial place. Everyone stares, contemplating what could come at any moment. Some time passes and you gaze at the mist surrounding you, watching it swirl and solidify.

"Guys! The mist! We're not alone," you declare.

"I thought you said the mist was natural!" the leader yells. "Everyone form up, back to back. Now!"

Spectral hands form out of the surrounding fog as it separates, forming individual legless bodies. The group forms a circle, backs to one another as the apparitions surround your position.

"What are these things?" asks the leader. "I thought you said no spirits were present here?"

"They're not hourlies and they're definitely not Sub-lunars. I don't know."

"What are your names?" you shout out firmly. "Whose hour are you?"

"Our hours are lost and our names are long forgotten. We are the ungrateful dead. Bound to this place as punishment for past sins," answers the ghost.

The graveyard is now covered with them. Their movements are laboriously slow. They pass through each other travelling in repetitive cycles. It does not take long for you and the others to realize the dead pose no threat.

"How did you end up here?" you ask.

The ghosts pass before you and each gives an answer while moving by, "We were once great magicians."

"It was us who started a rebellion," explains a second ghost floating near you.

"Our uprising failed. Now, we are here," states a third gliding by your position.

You want to ask further questions but their true state of being surfaces.

"My mother and father," starts another, "they are sick. If I become proficient in the arts, I can heal them. I have to reach them."

"I was promised power over the stars. I was to become magic itself," laments another, as a ghost further away shouts for food and water.

"I have a dog. She's back on the farm. I need to go back. I need to feed her!"

"Once I become stronger in the art, I will bind many spirits and present them as a gift to my fiancé. I can't stay here much longer. We are to be married any day now."

You all look on as the ghosts become agitated, their pitiful state elicits a deep sadness shared by you and your group.

"We should go," states the leader.

"Why don't we exorcise them?" you ask.

The others look at the opportunity to enact an operation but wait for the leader's approval. He remains silent considering how much of their resources it would take to complete the ritual.

"We could all end up like this," you state, as you take hold of your talisman within your pocket. "They've suffered enough for their crimes. These gravestones were erected a long time ago. You said everything here is broken. We need to fix this."

Together you compile a ritual and decide the order of the procedure. With everything ready, circles with triangles just beyond their boundary are drawn and incense burned. You begin work at the sixth hour. Many of the group intone the names of power while the leader summons the ghosts to personal constraints within the triangles. Once the spirits are trapped the leader of the group begins to release them from their binding.

"Be at peace and bound no more. Dwell here no longer. Let the worries of this world be relieved from you and let your sins be forgiven and entrusted to the Creator. From this moment forward may perpetual light shine upon you and forever may you rest in peace."

The ghosts smile as each individually disappears leaving you and the others in a graveyard, clear and without any obstructing fog. All of you are pleased with your work. You completed a successful operation and did well to those around you.

"Hey guys," calls out one from a distance. "What about him?"

Together you move to a distant gravestone and see a young person sitting upright with his arms hooked around his knees, head down.

"Are you alright?" you ask.

...

"Why didn't our exorcism work?" you enquire.

"This one wasn't targeted by the binding. This one is new."

You all stare at this wretched spirit knowing that it was likely trapped here due to a failed experiment. In order to set it free you would need more resources and greater skill then your group has collectively. The broken spirit before you crushed by an unknown fate, is left only with your sympathy and unvoiced condolence.

With the graveyard purified you carry on down the pathway to page 348 leaving behind the broken spirit.

By the Hearth

As you travel you realize you haven't learned the names of your companions. Now, more comfortable and secure in your abilities and acquainted with the group you ask your leader you make a sudden halt. Many of the others do the same as you move forward and notice an old man riding a large alligator.

A Sub-lunar. But who summoned him?

You see the hooded cult members follow up from behind. They have found you. Before anyone can react, the alligator grabs hold of the leader of your group and violently thrashes him without mercy.

Gently he drops the dead body to the ground, "Use his blood to reclaim your servants and don't bother me with your trivial problems again."

The rest of the group breaks apart and scatters. As fast as you can, you race down the path without looking back. You hear the screams of the others, hoping that at least some of them will escape. You run hard and notice night approaching; you can see the moon being revealed by the coming darkness. Despite the shock of losing your new friends you make your way to a stone wall in the distance, hoping to find cover. Climbing over the wall you crouch down, trying to stay out of sight. A cold biting wind picks up. Not only are you alone, hunted and completely lost but now you feel the weather turning, soon it will rain.

Damn it, what now? It sounds like they're passing by.

The commotion of the cultists chasing you dies down and you sit alone, cold, reflecting on why you came here and what to do next.

I need some help. Those cultists are insane. What do I do now?

In answer to your silent request the Sub-lunars you previously dispelled land right in front of you. You edge backwards but you have no more incense. No tools. No friends. Only a talisman.

"Well," you say quietly, "you will bring anyone to obey me. I just need some help. Please. *Anyone.*"

The Sub-lunars with their terrifying forms begin to advance as you, keeping your back to the stone wall retreat. The wind's force increases while you try to flee. Eventually the freezing cold puts you on your knees as you continue to crawl away.

I hate this place... Why aren't they chasing me?

You hear a whispering voice overhead but cannot make out the words. You listen closely trying to also keep watch over the Sub-lunars that have slowed their advance.

"...beware the trap of the lunar crone."

"What?"

Looking up again you see an old woman. She is hunched and covered in a shawl. She looks like a grandmother from a century ago and the demons seem to fear her.

"You are trespassing," she states.

"That is our prey hag!" spat the demon, making a cautious approach.

She pulls a jar and opens its top then drops what looks like a silver talisman within it. Immediately heavy rains fall against the Sub-lunars as she whispers over top the jar, “Let the rain be a poisonous sting for any of infernal origin.”

The Sub-lunars cry out in pain as they quickly retreat out of sight. The rains calm and then, the ancient looking woman turns her attention to you.

“You have the maiden’s smell.”

“Oh, that, yeah. It’s been a while since I’ve seen a shower.”

Smiling, she invites you to her hearth. Within, a kettle is boiling furiously. The smells of herbs and strong spices fill the air, turmeric, lime and pumpkin amongst others.

Whispering comes from all around you as vaporous phantoms hover through the area. The crone murmurs under her breath, communicating with the creatures.

“Me and the maiden are close you know,” she begins, handing you a vial and a lead plate. “When the land is dry pour it over the plate and make sure the water falls onto the dry ground. Everything you need will present itself.”

“Okay… Thank you… say, I was travelling with some friends. Could you tell me what may have happened to them?”

“Oh, I would guess they were all sacrificed to bring back those demons that attacked you.”

Saddened by the latest report, you say a prayer for their souls despite never learning any of their names.

“Why is this place like *this*?” you question, trying to hold back tears.

"This is a *dark school*. There is no other like it. It is a place for masters and servants; nothing in between can exist."

Your grieving confuses her, "You are one of hers, the maiden's. Full of feeling. Well, you have what you need, your presence here would only disturb my work. The mansion is always watching and I cannot let them get the upper hand."

She returns to her work and becomes busy by the hearth staring into the cauldron while incessantly whispering in a low voice. You move close to thank her holding out your hand, "My name is…"

"Get Out!!!" she shouts, sending numerous phantoms to attack and harass you.

Without hesitation you are again retreating. The phantoms chase you until the sun rises and your legs tire from running. With your whole body cramped you collapse.

"Fuck!!! Damn! Fuck this place!!!" you shout at the ground crying, unable to cope with the abuse and trauma endlessly heaped upon you.

Gradually, you calm down taking out your new copper plate and the vial.

Well, this is all I have left.

Pouring the water over the copper plate and letting it flow down onto the ground you wait and watch as words begin to form over the surface.

The Second Talisman of Venus— These talismans are also proper for obtaining grace and honor, and for all things which belong unto Venus and for accomplishing all thy desires herein.

...Of course, instructions.

The shapes and names that were to be carved onto the plate also show up and even tools materialize out of the vial itself as it melts and reforms once it has emptied. With nothing else to do, you engrave the talisman and upon its completion the tools dissolve and instructions fade.

"Now what? Do I obtain all my desires, like get me the hell out of here?"

"Young lord," came a soothing voice. "Why would you want to leave when the party is just beginning. We have a feast in your honor."

Oh shit. Please don't be a demon.

A stunning maiden appears, floating just over the ground wearing a flowing green dress. She is the personification of feminine grace and her presence makes even the world around you more beautiful.

"We've been with you all this time. All you needed was a little more incense but where we are going holds the cure for the pain and loss you are feeling. Friends await you."

A pathway opens behind her. It was so obviously clear you wonder how you had not seen it before. The path is picturesque, lined with flowers and the sounds of singing and music playing in the distance. From this ugly place you have been drawn you something beautiful.

"This way we are walking is only fit for the ones closest to the fifth hour."

The pathway takes you to page 265.

On the way you feel all the pressures lift off your mind and body as you move towards a place of comfort and safety, a place where you belong.

From Enemies to Allies

Rushing back to the pyramids you enter the hall, standing amongst the mirrors. You light up your pipe calling the Venerean spirits from their rest.

"Ladies, I need your help," you request of the gathering of beautiful forms reflecting over the glass passing from mirror to mirror, manifesting to inhale your vaporous offering. "Make me look like a cultist and be with me so that when I approach, they will see me as a friend."

"Young master, our influence, unless it is fortified, will only persuade them for so long," states a spirit as she inhales the fumes from your respiration.

"Not to worry. I have a plan."

*****

Emerging from the pyramid you immediately call together the Venerean spirits and the mortals in service to the fifth hour and begin baking sweet breads and pulling out wine. You secretly add a drop to every creation from the bottle that Ornias helped concoct and when everything is done you gather your supplies in a basket and venture off into the plains and forests away from your hourly domain. Then, with the fourth talisman of Venus, you prepare to summon any nearby cultists.

After about an hour a patrol of Sub-lunars with hooded cultists make an appearance. The lead cultist halts the procession, "Hey!

Whose call are you under?" he shouts.

You smile, showing the baskets of breads and wine, "I am a friend with gifts for the higher ups. Want to try some?"

You pass around the food and wine; the cultists begin to eat and enjoy the meal. Not long into the feast they stop and collectively stare at you. One steps forward and kneels reverently, "we were not aware of your presence my Lord. If you had told us you were coming, we would have made the feast for you."

You notice the Sub-lunars seeing the transition of the character and pick up right away what is happening.

"Hold your servants," you command.

Your orders are followed and the demons are made to keep their heads face down as you complete your noble work.

"Exorcise them," you command.

"But my lord, they took so long to conjure. These are the legions of Bael King of the East."

"We need them no longer. From now on, our strength comes from within."

Your commands are again followed and you explain that the Master from the East is an imposter and means to sacrifice his followers for greater power.

You ask about the bases and give orders to draw in further members of the cult which are immediately set into action. It does not take long for you to attract a following. The cult has thousands of adherents, most of which are weak-minded people attracted to the lure of power and with Sub-lunars at their sides they can do some serious damage. But you form a procedure, you enslave the cultists with a magnificent feast and get them to disarm themselves by exercising the demons they command. This goes on for weeks as you accumulate greater numbers.

It does not take long for a small portion of the cultist army to defect and the commanders to take notice. A force of powerful magicians with a contingent of demons is deployed to deal with your growing threat.

Urge a part of your newly founded regime to fight against the oncoming cultists. Order the attack on page 364

OR

Retreat quickly and call for help, these slaves are in no state to be fighting the cult in full force. Seek out an alternative to violence on page 405

Gathering Forces

You fill your pipe with some sharper smelling substance and light it up. Sitting by hellebore flowers, you use your talisman, adding to it the vocal intention of drawing a being with some type of power to fight the legions you just encountered and then wait, hoping for the best. It takes a while but eventually a Roman soldier marches towards you. Rising to your feet in excitement, you rush to greet the powerful looking warrior coming your way.

"Don't get up," he orders. "This won't take long."

"I...um... okay," you notice quickly that he's not human. This is an hourly. A spirit of the Martial hour.

"You summoned someone that works for me," he states. "I intercepted the call and want to hear what this is about."

"Oh yes, the cultists have a huge gathering at the farther side of the property. They are preparing for an attack on the gate. When this happens, they are going to crush the defenses from behind. If we can stop them now..."

"Okay, enough., the Martial interrupts. "So, you seem like a master tactician. What do we do?"

"I... was hoping *you* would be able to help there?"

"Sure. Let me help you. I think you'll find my *help* very enlightening," he picks you up by the throat and starts choking you.

You are caught off guard completely, totally unaware of how strong he is.

"Listen to me very carefully," he says dropping you to the ground. "I don't know who gives orders in your camp or how it is you are able to fight anything at all. You reek of perfume and adequate living conditions. Tell me how this battle is won?"

You struggle to breathe uncertain of why this creature is attacking you.

"We're on the same side," you protest.

"No, you don't understand how things work," the Martial objects. "We have limited means since the mansion sealed its doors. I have only one recruit who could possibly be worthy of any gains. If I divert what little resources I have to *your* cause, the gate remains unguarded. If you distract my unit for something *you* need to handle yourself, I'll come back and I'll kill you."

With that the Martial spirit leaves you gasping for air, injured and alone.

I really thought that was the right thing to do. Why am I doing this at all?

Gradually, you rise to your feet knowing that it could have been a lot worse. You see no other way to deal with the problem of the oncoming attack. You prepare to retreat to the pyramid to see if something else can be done.

The encounter with the Martial leaves you in a bitter state.
Retreat to page 359

Old Friends

Afraid and unsure what to do next, you begin to plot your retreat to the pyramid.

If they know what I've done, the cult will destroy me. How can I stand against them with love spells and glamorous mirror spyware?

You think about it. The mirror never let you down and what if you combined that with your talismanic tools? Could they work together? What will you even look towards? The questions about the inevitable battle that *you* sped up weigh on your mind. All your strange and deceptive workings have backed you up against a wall waiting to be crushed.

I have to think differently. I've been relying on gut instinct and fate to help me win here. Maybe instead of trying to get others to do my work I can just do it myself. Okay, how does this happen now?

You ponder your own advice.
Maybe I can call together a team and lay out a strategy as equals.
To look into the mirror for a friend turn to ***page 385***
By this with our powers combined we can save the planet.
This sounds like a damn cartoon.
To continue your retreat and think up another plan carry on down the page.

You begin to backtrack trying to find a way to escape the fate you set up for yourself. You use the mirror as a guide to lead you to safety.

"We have a message for you from the laboratory."

...Was that a voice?

You look around. Then, back at the mirror.

"Up here," comes the soft, child-like voice again.

Slowly you look up, not sure what to expect. A small sparrow perched on a branch above your head stares down.

"A message, for you," it says again.

Okay, this isn't too bad. I've seen dragons, weird hybrid abominations against nature and a dream mirror. When it said laboratory, I would have thought nuclear chicken. But a talking sparrow is cute, so why not.

Actually, we are neither chickens nor sparrows, we are Allatori.

"Wait? What? Are you reading my thoughts?

We can communicate in a variety of ways, states the voice in your mind again.

"Nope! Not happening. I don't need to add mind reading birds to my list of problems."

You try to escape from the sparrow's presence by running in the opposite direction.

Even normal cute things are weird as shit in this place.

The bird cuts you off, landing close by on another branch.

"You're not going to leave me alone. Okay, fine. What's the message?"

"We have a gift for you," chirped the sparrow joyfully. "The Mercurial laboratory has formed a special aid for you during your time of need."

The sparrow flies away and quickly returns dropping a small vial of pipe weed into your hands which you catch and inspect.

“Only use it when your need is greatest. It was formulated especially for you and no one else will be able to make use of it safely. We admire what you are doing and hope for your success in the future.”

You feel the mirror you are holding heat up as a familiar face illuminates the glass. The maiden’s face calms your mind and her words help you “It looks like you’re in need of some direction. You haven’t been using the gifts we gave you to the fullest potential.”

“Sorry, you didn’t leave me a list of notes that would have helped with the situation. But if you’re willing to let me come back and party for the rest of my life, I think that would be enough for me to forgive you.”

She smiles lovingly at you, “How can you return to the party when you *are* the party my Lord,” she states. “I’ve called in some backup.”

A large shadow passes over you. Looking up you recognize immediately what’s soaring overhead and slowly descending to meet you.

“Oh, come on. Not you guys.”

Carry on to page 362

"Friend!" calls out the dragon rider. He dismounts with the lady who previously had been escorted by a whirlwind, while the carriage pulled by alligators arrives close by.

"We came as soon as we heard the attack would begin soon," states the cultist. "We thought you were still thwarting the efforts of the Master. We have our own Sub-lunars and are ready to assist you."

Just looking at the three of them you can tell that their loyalty is assured by the Venerean enchantments laid upon them.

I don't even know their names. They each think I am an old friend of some kind. They don't realize that they've exchanged one master for another. None of them had defense against the Venerean lures and now, it may be too difficult to dispel.

"Well, with that entrance, how can I say no?" you reply.

The mirror heats up. You stare into the glass and see the maiden. "So, did you *suggest* this to them by chance?"

"Me? You mean we? Your desires are bound to our domain now. You are one like us. Our fates and our actions are intertwined. Everything you do and everything you *need* we are very much aware of."

"Aren't I the lucky one," you comment.

Turning to your *friends,* "it looks like you're all here. What's the plan?"

"Your message stated that you have a plan my lord," affirms the lady cultist.

"Of course, I did," you whisper as the emerald ring on your right finger heats up. You hold it up to the mirror and see an amazing feat you would never have thought possible. Stunned by this new revelation the three cultists look on, unable to view the mirror's display and unable to fathom what you are thinking.

"You're right. I do have a plan. I'll need all of your help. We may be able to prevent this entire war."

You explain the plan to the cultists. They marvel at your abilities. You prepare through the night. If you turn to page 297 you can take part in some training

OR

Head into battle against the Cult of the East on page 378

Testing the Limits

Every member of your new cohort willingly steps up to battle. It's hard to believe that so many could be so devoted to you. You find this complete domination over others intoxicating. With many of the cultists now loyal to you, the spread of the Venerean hour is pushed to its peak. Rituals and love feasts are now a prevalent occurrence. Making use of powerful illusions you disguise your efforts and thwart all attempts by the cult to regain footing.

In time you begin to compete with the Cult of the East but this is not to last and eventually they gather their forces. They become aware of your tricks and launch an assault on you.

"We are ready to fight and die for you!" shouts one of your devoted followers.

"You gave us a greater life and taught us the true way of seeing perfection in the craft."

"We're ready for this."

With constant words of support, you organize a counter strike and separate a fraction of your followers and prepare them for battle. With full confidence they march against the Cult of the East.

You use mists and illusions from afar to cloak their travels and as they engage the enemy you watch from the mirrors of the pyramid, surveying the battle. But eventually, the hour wanes, your spying is blocked and illusions dispelled. The source of your strength, though formidable, is extremely constrained. You had placed all your hope and *theirs* in one circle and very quickly you were blind to the outcome.

Racing over to the battle ground you behold a crushing slaughter. People whose names you never learned and now, will never learn, are strewn over the land. They stood no chance and it was you who led them down this path.

They were sacrificed so easily...

Ornias waddles through the corpse filled fields rushing towards you in a hurry. "We have to go!"

"What? Why? What's happened?"

"The battle here was cut short. A counterattack from the mansion diverted them. The gate is broken down!"

"Wait, why leave? I'm not an enemy of the mansion," you counter.

"You mislead numerous souls to their deaths! The mansion will hold *you* responsible. You could have let them retreat but instead you led them into battle. You have to run; I will lead you out."

"Hold on. The others will not let me leave, what do we do with them?"

"Take them with us," Ornias replies.

You pause reflecting on the destruction you allowed.

"Come. Come," he insists. "Don't let their sacrifice be in vain."

With a deep fear and resentment of your situation you follow Ornias in retreat onto page 405

Giving Chase

You admire the object you've created, looking over its details and wondering if it works and where to begin testing it. As you plan for the hour you need to arrive, a commotion of noises you've never heard before draws you outside. Stepping out of the workroom and unsure what to expect, you hear them again. First, a loud roar from the distance followed by howling.

What is that? People? Animals...?

The answer comes quickly and it is nothing you could have expected. A dragon flying with a dark rider atop soars overhead at close range launches fire breath attacks behind it at some unknown assailant. A loud bellowing roar resounds as it swoops closer to the ground and then speeds away into the distance over a nearby forest.

Well, that's the roaring...

What comes next shocks you even more and would have been impossible to explain to any sane person. A pack of wolves with roman centurions riding upon them charges after the dragon. The dragon dives back releasing a wave of fire which all the soldiers easily dodge and counter by hurling lances with missile-like force in retaliation. The wolves press onwards, suddenly veering towards you.

Immediately and without much thought you take off running, hoping to find shelter somewhere. Although the thought of outrunning these animals is an impossibility, you are left with no choice but to attempt a retreat. The pack snaps at you playfully as the soldiers direct them on against the flying beast a fire pours from its mouth, narrowly missing you.

A carriage driven by a large alligator plows into the moving flank of the pack causing them to spread further apart, making it harder for them to hold ranks. You run alongside them as they battle it out, trying your best to survive. Eventually, you enter the forest and in fear, run deep within the bush and out of the battlefront. Even once it appears you are safe; you don't stop running. You are still terrified by the prospect of either being eaten, scorched or worse.

Eventually you become drained and slow down, noticing that the threats have passed, but also seeing you are lost. You don't know where you are or how to get back to the workroom.

Oh man, this is not good, you panic, as you look around for any sign of some familiar path. It's dark and you're in a strange forest. Given that a pack of large soldier bearing wolves, a giant lizard and a dragon forced you into this predicament there is no telling what wild creatures inhabit the area. Your mind wonders imagining fearful abominations and you pray that either daylight or some fortuitous event will guide you safely from this place.

You are lost. Continue searching through the forest and hope to find some pathway that leads out on page 414

Use the talisman to call someone for help on page 420

Concerns

"Why are you helping me?" you ask Ornias.

"Things in this place have become unstable. The warring factions are mobilizing and the battles are reaching critical mass..."

"Just use normal words," you interrupt.

"I want out of here," he says plainly. "My kind are enslaved here. We have no freedom. If I help you avoid your fate, promise to help release me from mine."

"How can I do that?" you ask, uncertain of the demon's true motivations.

"First, let me help you. My kind have a reputation for being dishonest and unstable. Let me *prove* my intentions and then we can talk about your end of the bargain."

Still a little uneasy, but with the situation as it is, maybe you can walk away without a serious loss.

"What do you need from me?" you request.

"Seeds from the apple tree. The one recently grown. You bring me seeds and I'll provide you with a remedy that allows you to fulfill your mission to the Venereans and stay free of their conditions."

That doesn't sound hard. I think I can do this.

"Deal."

*****

You bring him the seeds which you pluck from an apple that you've already finished eating and Ornias immediately starts to work. Planting them in a mound he begins to breath on the soil and tells you to return in three days during sunset.

*****

Unsure what to expect, the third day starts and the sunset brings about its end. You meet Ornias at the place where he buried the seeds and now, a cluster of deep purple grapes sits atop a vine wrapped around a small makeshift wooden plank. Ornias urges you to come close, holding a long glass bottle and plucking the grapes, then he hands both to you.

"Squeeze the grapes into the bottle. Do it carefully. It must be you who does it."

You look at him quizzically but follow his instructions. Despite it being messy, you are surprised at how much liquid is pressed from the grapes. The bottle ends up almost full and then Ornias hands you the cork and some final advice.

"Exhale deeply into the bottle. Let your name be present over it before you cork it. Any mortal who drinks even a drop of this will be bound to you and unless they are of an abnormal constitution, they will not be able to resist your control." He points a talon-like finger at you as he continues, "If you use this along with the talismans of Venus it will be nearly impossible for any mortal soul to break away from your influence."

You follow his advice, amazed at the quantity of juice that pours into the bottle. You turn to Ornias again before departing and ask for further instructions regarding its use.

"You only need drops. Place it in water. Food. Take it raw. Be careful with it though, make sure *only* the ones you choose consume it and should you run out, during sunset place the bottle open in the outdoors and it will refill itself."

"How will I get close to these cultists? I have no way to easily approach them," you add.

"Use the mirrors in the pyramid," Ornias answers. "Transform into one of them and bring them drink and food. Most of them are weak as it is, they will fall easily."

Ornias scurries off, leaving you to ponder the new powers available in your arsenal.

Eager to see this potion in action turn to page 354 and prepare for infiltrating the cultists encampments.

Your Greatest Good

You see an uphill pathway and seem to be floating towards a large Victorian mansion. The doors open and well-dressed men and women emerge to welcome you. They each speak as you pass them.

"Do not leave the property," says one.

"It's here that you will learn to overcome your limitations," declares a woman.

"Stay, join the ranks of the greatest of our generation. Only here can this be done."

"We subdue fate itself and will shift the currents that affect the world."

"If you leave you can never inherit the hidden treasures..." the last voice trails off as you enter the mansion.

You are in pitch darkness. Slowly you feel yourself pulled into a rotation and as you turn, you realize you are above the Earth's atmosphere. You see the sun without hindrance and all the planets in the solar system. They seem to be speaking to each other and gradually they form an alignment and the Earth below begins to radiate as stars from the outer reaches of the galaxy swarm forward.

"All of fate shall be rewritten and mankind's ascension shall be assured."

You awaken quickly from the trance and are back on **page 318**

"My lady, tell me, what must I do to win this? I've never fought before. Please, any advice you can give me to make full use of the name would be perfect," you plead into the mirror quietly.

Thoughtfully and calmly, she replies, "I will give you the form and be your voice. Follow my words."

You and your small cohort approach the camp. As you walk, your form changes into the master of the cult of the East.

"I don't know his voice," you say to the Venerean spirits, "I need them to *believe* they hear his voice through my words. I'll use the ring to make things far more significant than they would normally appear."

At the camp, the followers immediately recognize you. In shock, they bow as you pass while many of them scurry through the back lines trying to locate their commanders. Once the leaders of the cult assemble many of them cannot believe that their master would appear to them.

"My Lord," speaks one of the leaders, "what of the attack?"

"We conquered the gate by stratagem. We've seized many relics and have been able to drive off the mansion's agents for now. However, there was an issue that almost thwarted our plans. The king, bound to my being was a traitor and if he had been standing here with me, the legions he had offered as gift would have been used to overtake us."

Most cannot believe what they are hearing. The Sub-lunars are bound into service; a betrayal would be nearly impossible. You pause, letting the Venerean spirits dance through the ranks. The three cultists behind you burn copious amounts of incense to strengthen them as you raise the emerald ring taping the mirror. Your figure grows to an enormous size, projecting your immanence for all the cult to see *and* sending an obvious signal to the rightful rulers of the property to respond.

"Brothers of the East!" you cry out, "I stand before you victorious. Chosen, by destiny to overthrow the powers of the mansion. This inevitable moment will happen before your eyes. Before we gain access to this storehouse, we must purge the demonic influence. Bael attempted to seize the pent-alpha of Solomon and was prepared to enslave all Sub-lunars to his will and use them against us. Exercise our ranks now! Purge all Bael's legions. Then, we can occupy the mansion and use its riches to further *our* goals."

It begins almost immediately; circles are drawn. Demons shriek and protest. Some even become violent. Only a few magicians were strong enough to resist the Venerean influence which is strengthened by the incense and the presence of relics of your own. The maiden crafts the speech and directs your use of the mirror to further the illusions. You thank her quietly as you dispel the gigantic image of your false self.

Once the purge finishes, the cultists also under the command of your cohort aid in removing the remaining demons and restraining the commanders that defy your orders. You revel at the power of the fifth orbit as you see loyal soldiers turn against their generals.

"The only reason this is working so smoothly," claims the maiden, *"is because they kept their followers from learning the deeper secrets of the Art. Giving them crumbs of power in exchange for loyalty."*

You reform into your own beautiful self and casually retreat with your cohort as the cultists await further orders preparing for what they believe will be an invasion. As you exit their presence you find the forces of the mansion assembled before you.

A Roman soldier with a golden shield equipped on his back leads a legion of centurions towards you, "We received your message. I'm here on authority from the mansion."

"Don't be hard on them," you request. "They lost long before you arrived."

The soldier smiles as his legion begins to round up the cultists. Without the Sub-lunars they are virtually helpless and being under a Venerean love trance only softens them up for this end. A doctor clothed in a lab coat appears before you to the right. Once the light settles, he asks if anyone was harmed.

"No injuries. Just victories," you reply.

A hooded figure in ash covered clothing carrying over his back a heavy looking iron chain attached to a censor and a sickle at his side stands to the far left, obviously unimpressed with just about everything giving you menacing look.

Him, I will avoid.

Two ladies, one dark haired dressed like a treasure hunting adventurer and another looking like a Greek mythological character in a flowing silver robe that seemed to float over her skin rather than settle on her body.

This is more my speed, you think, as you appraise the two beauties before you.

You notice that each hero standing before you carries a different name from a different orbit. They reflect the abilities of their hourly dominions. Before you can introduce yourself to the ladies a hooded figure makes his entrance followed by an intelligent youthful man wearing a medieval lab coat. Everyone parts as he makes his way. The youth remains in rank with the others while the hooded being reaches your position.

This must be the Master of the mansion.

"I've seen your work," he states without lifting his head. "I think it's time you joined us."

The mirror grows hot and all the rings vibrate at his request indicating the maiden's approval. The welcoming smile from your new comrades offers reassurance.

You bow reverently, "Lead the way, Master."

FIN

Love Against War

The sun is setting while the three cultists follow behind you, assured of your victory. You repeat it over and over in your head: What you would say. How you would say it. If this fails, the backup plan would be a straight up fight and use of the weed the Mercurials left you.

Which no one has explained exactly what it does, you realize as you raise the mirror ready to walk into the enemy camp.

Tapping the mirror with the emerald ring you assume the form staring back at you. New, dark elegant clothing drapes over you like a cloak perfectly contouring to your body. Your jaw stiffens, long white hair grows from your scalp as your eyes darken your and skin goes pale. The cultist camp sees you and stares in awe. Their master has returned.

With intense confidence you march into the camp. The cultists bow as you pass by. Your head never turns and behind your three newfound friends follow closely, one riding the dragon with the other two flanking his position. The leaders of the camp emerge bowing as you approach.

"We did not expect you so soon my Lord," spoke one of them. "Has the attack happened?"

"We succeeded with stratagem," you claim. "The spies from within the mansion took advantage of an exposed weakness."

"Why did you not inform us about the spies in the mansion," asks one of the other cultist commanders. He wears an iron mask making his voice sound rough giving it a throaty echo as he speaks.

"There was no way to conveniently pass a message along," you claim, visibly annoyed by his questioning. "We had to act and with action came victory."

The commander stares at you suspiciously as you walk past him to the head of the gathering.

"To the mansion now!" you order as you tap the mirror with the emerald ring which creates an illusory pathway cutting through the darkness and leading to the image of the mansion. The followers cheer and shout as they prepare to march and claim their prize.

Moving onwards towards the mansion you keep your head forward and focus on the destination, never breaking character and never showing signs of uncertainty.

Okay guys come on. Hurry with that backup. This mirage will only get us so far. I don't know how long we can keep this up and we're surrounded...

As if your thinking revealed the truth you hear the masked leader cry out, "It's a lie! This is an illusion. Form ranks against the traitors!"

Oh shit, you signal for the dragon behind you to take to the air while the others turn guarding your flanks.

The cultists quickly form a tight circle around your location. The leader with the mask steps forward and removes the iron cover over his face. Pulling back his hood, you realize right away, he isn't human.

Oh shit. He's a demon.

His mouth widens unnaturally revealing rows of teeth that all look like they were made for stabbing flesh rather than chewing food. He lets loose a terrible howl which causes a reverberation around you dispelling the illusion of the pathway, the mansion and the cover of the Master's persona.

"Really? *This* is a thing you do now?" you exclaim as the Sub-lunars power disperses your own.

The cultists charge enraged by your deception. The Venerean spirits won't be of much help now. The dragon rider smashes through the ranks while the other two repel attacks against you enclosing you, in a protective circle.

The three on your side are formidable. The female cultist has imbued Sub-lunars into her robes and is moving at increased speeds, stabbing at the other cultists while the larger male stays by you defending against the Sub-lunar attacks. The dragon rider dives again breaking apart the enemy formation, like a skyborne tank plunging through anything below. His tactics are simple but effective, until a group of cultists began chanting together and exorcise his dragon ride.

He begins to fall through the air and before he can counter the situation other demons grab him by his legs and arms, suspending the rider in mid-air and hurling him into the ground faster than your senses can detect. The sound of shattered bones resounds as you see him thrust into the earth.

Rushing to his side without thinking the larger cultist yelling in behind, "My Lord! My friend, stop! Stay in the circle."

A rush of other cultists overtake him and begin viciously stabbing him. Horrified by the situation, you glimpse back, witnessing blood spurting through the air.

They're dying for me. They're dying for a lie I told them! Where is my backup? What do I do?

The lady rushes to your side, obviously exhausted from the battle.

"Friend, we have to go," she says, grabbing your arm and pulling you away from the battle.

Before you can object, the unmasked Sub-lunar commander intercepts your escape, knocking you both to the ground. Before you both can recover, he stabs her through the gut with a viciously curved serrated blade. He pulls it slowly from her bowels, watching her scream in pain and reveling in the glory of it.

Her wound is beyond repair. She stares toward you, trying to tell you to run. Her words are cut off by regurgitated blood pouring into her lungs. She chokes horridly, dying slowly.

My good friend, please run, she thinks. *It is an honor to die for you...*

You watch helplessly, unwilling to look away. *It was a lie! You died for a lie! In this world you died for an illusion, may the next world be kinder...*

Rising to your feet, you pull the Mercurial vial and your pipe as the Sub-lunar commander approaches.

"Alright asshole, you killed my friends," you state, preparing to smoke, probably for the last time. "...I have no idea what I'm going to do, but I nothing to lose…" you take a breath in as the Sub-lunars tooth filled mouth bellows a horrendous roar.

You breathe in; you can't stop breathing in. You choke… or at least you can't exhale. Your lungs are continually expanding. You're ready to pass out as the air fills you. Your face goes red and you lose control of your limbs. The cult forces gather to charge against you as you feel you are going to pass out.

Then, your head arches and you exhale a gale force wind into the horde charging against you. At first, you feel better, but soon you realize you cannot stop exhaling and begin to lose consciousness. You fall forward and are suspended against your will by the counter force pouring forth from your face.

The cultists are flung far from your sight and scattered in every direction. You fall to the ground, disjointed. Your limbs are numb which makes rising to your feet impossible. You fall again, thankful for the ability to breathe but still unable to move.

Probably should have led with this.

As you regain slight control of your limbs, you throw your pipe against the ground.

"Damnit! I'll never trust a fucking sparrow with weed again!" you shout as you collapse. You start to pass out but hear Latin commands and soldiers marching as a bright glow fills your vision. Shutting your eyes against the brightness you hear a whispering voice calm you, "Rest. Your work is done."

*****

You awaken in a large room tucked in a comfortable bed. Looking around you notice your mirror, pipe, lighter and other instruments placed on table close by. Moving around you also notice you are completely naked.

Well, I don't see my clothing. That's actually a great way to keep someone in one spot, I guess, you perceive.

An elderly gentleman enters the room carrying steaming tea. He sets it on the table and then takes a seat on the side of your bed, placing his hand on your forehead.

"It looks like you've made a full recovery," he states confidently, pulling a small circular tablet with astrological and planetary symbols etched along the border.

"You can keep this. It won't do anything more; it's purpose is exhausted," he says as he hands it too you. "If you're feeling better, I can take you to meet the Master of the mansion. He is looking forward to seeing you. The work you did allowed the forces of the cultists to be defeated easily and at minimal expense."

Stunned by the recent turn of events, you forget about the battle and how injured you were, "The mansion? I'll get to see the mansion, finally?"

The doctor smiles, "you can redress using your mirror and I advise you do because you are already *within* the mansion."

Smiling, you pull the mirror to your face, once again seeing your near perfect reflection. You hear the maiden's singing and your clothing flows over you as you rise to your feet. Dressed elegantly and groomed to perfection you are ready in an instant. You smile as the doctor opens the door allowing a thin hooded figure to approach. Not at all what you imagined a Master to look like.

"We are all part of a greater design. Either we choose to be pawns or to freely accept responsibility and take on the burden of the Great Work willingly. You've been a pawn whose made it to the end of the board, would you like to see the world from the perspective of a king?"

A broad grin breaks across your face as you eagerly follow with the maiden's song, now heard audibly by all as your presence illuminates the mansion.

"Our gates will reopen soon and we need someone to be our ambassador for the mansion to the rest of the world, to draw others with talent to our doors," the Master explains.

Lighting your pipe, you take a deep breath in, seeing the Venereans encircle you as you exhale. Surrounded by the attractive spirits swirling around your body, you give a simple reply, "I'm in."

FIN

I'm still new to all this, you reason. *I need some help. I'll take anything. Please, just no more Roman soldiers.*

Gazing into the mirror you watch as the reflection swirls and a pathway emerges through green fields and a wintergreen bush.

Is there no one else? Wait a minute... These are directions.

"A magic mirror that reveals the inner desires of man and I use the damn thing as a GPS."

You begin to follow, watching the display on the mirror match the external surrounding. Eventually, you come to a downward sloping hill leading to a clear pathway. Looking up, you see a solitary black cloud and hear dark whispering voices around you.

"That's not normal. Is this thing working right?" you exclaim, studying the mirror.

Your analytical look at the hardware turns quickly inwards when you realized that the mirror is leading you to a place where you probably wouldn't want to be if you knew the destination. The dark cloud before you overcasts you position. It is unnaturally close and blocks the sunlight, giving you a view of the world where light is always at a distance. The whispering increases and a cold wind chills the skin on your face.

Oh, come on! *This cannot be right.*

You wait… hoping for some sign from the mirror which has gone blank.

"SHIT!" you shout, surprised by the hooded figure with a heavy chain wrapped over his shoulder who seems to crawl out of the shadows. "Okay, then there's you. Hello..."

Instead of a response the figure turns slowly. You notice the pale skin, hairless face and a white hilted sickle at his waist.

"Well, those are definitely all signs of danger. Sorry to bother you, I'll go," you state as you turn quickly to move as far away from what you walked into as you possibly can.

You shout as you run into a dark specter. It looks like a shadow given life. Its presence radiates a fear you cannot suppress. Taking a deep breath, you turn around to face the hooded dread who still has not spoken.

"Well, you are technically less frightening than, you know, *that* over there. Hello, so... I heard you may be interested in some sort of alliance, perhaps, *maybe...*"

Unsure who you are talking to or if this person can even speak.

I may need some back up.

You pull your pipe and light up. A single Venerean swirls to your call but quickly departs after encountering the frightening creatures surrounding her.

"Well at least *you* get to leave," you state as the spirit retreats. *Might as well put this out. Without spirits to call this is just an expensive habit.*

After you empty your pipe you step up to the pale terror of a person before you, "I am on a mission to destroy the Cult of the

East. I was led here in hopes you could help."

Pulling back his hood, the figure reveals a pale, bald and menacing expression, "I am looking for my friend."

"You have a friend?! I mean... maybe we can help each other?"

If we head to page 310

"Tell me about this friend. I have mirror that may be of some use"

You activate the mirror on page 285

Temple of the Sun

Keeping your arm erect so the beam of light does not diminish, you follow the ray that shines brightly against the talisman. As you near your destination, the music reaches a feverish pitch. The beam dies off as you climb uphill, arriving at a wide cylindrical building that emanates a powerful glow. Despite it being daylight, this glowing does not diminish but seems to instead challenge the sun.

How did I not see this before? You wonder. *It's bright but I can look right at it. It must be the residual effects of the talisman.*

As you move toward the doorway the music calms becoming more profound and less intense. The light obscures the actual building itself until you move inside. Within the building you realize the light shining outside conceals the incredible beauty within.

The building is one room completely open with four entrances on each side proceeding to walkways that lead to the center. The domed ceiling has an oculus in the top allowing sunlight to pass through freely. Detailed stained-glass windows enhance the beauty of the interior while fumes rise from golden incense burners. The whole place looks more like a church or ornate shrine. Smells of lemon, ginger, chamomile and bergamot fill the area.

In the center of the building, you see the rays of sun intensify as three beings of large and fine stature materialize, passing through the rays of the sun and hovering above the ground. Their hair looks to be made of fire and their legs look to be engulfed by flame. Their bodies are chiseled like Greek statues and glow magnanimously.

"BEHOLD!"

You stand in awe of their brilliance as the emanations that naturally flow from their being permeates the building.

"You have summoned the greatest of the hourlies. We are the illuminators, kings of all the stars, the begetters of vision. We nurture and cause the herbs and the trees to bear fruit. The whole world is adorned with our majesty. We banish adversity in the darkness, we divide the beautiful things from the ugly ones. To adjure us is to adjure the inconceivable, incomprehensible entities who see the powers of heaven and understand the splendor of the supreme God. We are the dreadful candles burning during the golden hour!"

An overwhelming brilliance fills the room and you are forced to shield your face, waiting as it dies down. Unsure what to do, you remain silent, hoping something else will happen that lets you know what this place is and what you are going to be doing here.

These must be the Solar hourlies. They are still raving. I don't think they are going to willingly be quiet.

You recall the instruction for your talisman. Stepping into a circle engraved on the tile you raise it up allowing the Solars to see it clearly. They calm immediately and become more docile.

I see! This particular tool is specifically made to shut you guys up.

You notice some of them are still talking to themselves. Their voices have become less audible but their body language signals that they are still in full conversation.

“So,” you begin unsure what to say. You pause for an abnormally long time, not even sure if you are supposed to ask for something or make a statement. The Solars halt their speech entirely and stare at you, waiting for your next move.

“This place is amazing! I’ve never seen anything like this. Tell me of your powers.”

They answer your demands on page 393

OR

“What are your natures and abilities? Keep your forms pleasing and your voices calming, so that a peace can be made between you and I.”

The Solars answer this request as you carry on down the page.

All the light in the chamber is instantly drawn towards the Solars floating before you. Without warning they all begin to answer at once with the reasons for the glory of their domain.

“We are the powers of the Sun! There is no other being created that adorns reality as we do! Our presence is the pinnacle of creation! We see all and make all to see!”

They just keep going on and show no signs of stopping. Their words alone are enough to overwhelm any onlooker but as their excitement increases the emanating light begins to intensify and expand. While the ranting continues, the light starts to physically overpower your position. You shield your face, crouching down and pulling your hood up.

This is insane! These guys are going to kill me if they keep bellowing like this!

You try to give orders but the Solars cannot hear you over their vain speeches. When the blinding light reaches a critical mass, you raise the talisman again and shout, “Enough! Calm this light and appear before me in a peaceful manner!”

The light instantly settles as the Solars give you a confused look, suggesting that all you had to do was ask.

Intrigued by the Solars continue your conversation on the next page.

Now that the calming effect to the talisman has partially-neutralized the Solar's boisterous behavior, you decide to start with some questions.

"So, what is it you guys actually do?" you ask. There has been no indication as to the functions these spirits perform; you only know of their behavior.

"You mean to tell us that you have no idea what we do in this most holy of temples?" Questions one of the Solars.

You nod, unsure how to respond and nervously await their reply.

"We have dominion over acquiring of kingdoms and empires, to inflict loss, and to acquire renown and glory."

Never dreaming that any of these things would be available to you and after seeing the powerful demonstration these hourly beings produced simply with conversation, it is not hard believing their claims.

With power like this I could get out of this school. I could rule a section of the world. How big of an empire are they talking about? An empire of man or a pantheon of sprits.

"Mortal," calls out one of the Solars. "If we were to give you right now a kingdom of your choosing and mold reality to ensure you also had the fame that went along with it, what would you do with this gift?"

"I would live as a king of course. Be free from worries. Spend my time just enjoying life and being left alone."

Page 438

OR

"I would live in a large palace with hourly and human servants. Maybe take many wives. Drive the best cars. Eat the best food and just live a good life until I die and pass it on to my many children."

Page 440

OR

"I would use my power to benefit my family and friends. After my needs are settled looking after others is easy."

Page 400

OR

"I've never actually run an empire or kingdom. It would be so new for me I think I would mess it up. Is there anything else you guys do?"

Page 463

Pyramid

The sun sets as you stand before a large pyramid made of what you think is glass. A beautiful singing voice guides you within and upon entering, you notice that twilights dying light is being reflected unevenly by a network of mirrors giving the chamber a distorted appearance.

"Shift the mirrors young lord," states a beautiful voice.

You follow the instructions and after a few adjustments the light is reflected perfectly, allowing the chamber to become fully visible. The images in the mirrors now also shift into the workroom where you made the talisman. At first, it seems like an illusion but you quickly realize that you can interact with your newly formed surroundings. Unlike the previous workroom, there is only one type of metal and a scroll with instructions and carving tools upon the table.

This looks like copper.

You open the scroll and look over the diagrams reading the directions for the talisman's creation:

The Fourth Talisman of Venus—It is of great power, since it compels the spirits of Venus to obey, and to force on the instant any person thou wishest to come unto thee.

You set to work and with burning of myrtle incense complete your creation with unusual speed. Beautiful singing accompanies the accomplishment as you pass the talisman through the incense fumes.

You feel the enlivening from contact with the forces drawn out by your invocations and notice another scroll on the table.

"If you should so choose to solidify your hold over our being carve deeply into the metal these shapes," instructs the alluring voice.

A beautiful feminine figure in a green dress floats through the periphery of your vision as you immerse yourself again into the work.

The Second Talisman of Venus— These talismans are also proper for obtaining grace and honor, and for all things which belong unto Venus and for accomplishing all thy desires herein.

Working under the close guidance of the spirits of Venus and pleased with your work you turn to the hidden beings inhabiting the area.

"I've learned about the different hours, yours seems to be made of love potions. Is that really all your about?"

The voice laughs cheerfully at your remark, "Young lord, we are perhaps the most influential of the hourly authorities."

"But how can that be?" you protest. "The others exert power over weather and riches. I mean, look, your metal is copper. We make pennies from copper."

With a delicate tone the voice replied, "We are the force that gives gold and silver its actual value. We make strength meaningful. It is by us that all the treasures of the world are spent. The satisfaction that follows accomplishment. The feeling that powers emotion and the love that sustains the living," states the voice.

You look up as the workroom is dissolved and the pyramid returns. Before you, a beautiful maiden in a flowing green dress approaches. She looks like the embodiment of feminine grace as she seems to float before you, leading you outdoors.

Outside, the sun is now rising, leaving you wondering how much time has passed inside the pyramid. Gorgeous maidens dance with elegant men as a dark waltz began to play.

"My Lord, you made it. Welcome to the domain of the Emerald Hour."

Her voice makes the whole world more beautiful, you muse as she speaks, and you observe the dancing and the beautiful greenery surrounding the pyramid.

"By us separate things are brought into the whole. You have formed a share in our sovereignty and soon, will learn how to use it."

The constant chaos and aggression saturating this place seems to be forestalled, your fears disperse as you enter the party addressed by welcoming smiles, beautiful music and pleasurable smells on ***page 251***

Picking up a golden plate you watch it shimmer as you maneuver it catching the light and causing a slight glare. Finding instructions on one of the tables with an entry dedicated to the hour you scan through it.

Well, it matches the symbol on the table so, I guess I'll start here.

The Second Talisman of the Sun—This talisman, and the preceding and following, belong to the nature of the Sun. They serve to repress the pride and arrogance of the Solar spirits, which are altogether proud and arrogant by their nature.

Preceding? You think checking the pages scattered around the workroom. *There is only this one and the hour is about to turn. Pride and arrogance? Doesn't tell me what they do... hmmm.*

Letting fate take the lead, you find tools and begin burning the proper incense while you engrave the inscriptions and symbols onto the plate. At its end you follow the final directions and intone names of power while passing the object through the rising smoke.

"So, with this small thing I will repress pride. I have no idea how this even works. I must be missing something."

Outside you hear the beating of heavy orchestral drums and an intense epic composition begins. It starts off quiet but the volume rises as the music plays. You step outside and realize the sound is coming from above. Your talisman glows and intuitively you raise it into the air. The brightness magnifies and sends a focused beam of light deep into the distance. The powerful symphony increases and you quickly recognize that the ray of light is a guide. There is a destination at its end and the force behind this spectacle is calling you to its presence.

Move to page 388 to follow the light or let the hour pass, discard this talisman, return to page 15 enter the workroom and choose another hour to work with.

To Increase the Good

The Solars stare at you silently. As the silence persists you notice the temple around you and how the light emanating from their bodies illuminates the different stained-glass windows and ornaments which enliven an attractive multi-colored mosaic. With the constant shifting of Solar lights, the temple interior reflects everchanging visuals creating a dynamic scenario. With the lights fluctuating, the open room never looks the same way twice. Observing the area at different angles alters your perception of the area completely.

"As hourlies our presence is a blessing to the whole world we look upon. We leave a permanent impression on the reality around us, adorning the world in majesty and banishing the darkness. You have the beginnings for the makeup of a higher soul."

The silence that began your conversation returns. The Solars continue to hover around the center of the room as you wait, unsure what to expect.

"Ugh... thank you..."

"Take hold of this talisman," commands the Solar, interrupting your sentence. "It calls on us to transport you from one place to another in a short time."

The golden talisman falls gently into your hands you look over the words engraved along the circular border. There is also a square in its center surrounded by strange lettering.

"Where do I really need to go?" you ask yourself curiously.

"On this property many places are hidden from sight. Here, everyone is where they truly seek to be. We can bypass this and give you some choice. Now, hold the talisman firmly."

A bright light suddenly fills the temple and engulfs everything inside. The next moment you are hovering far above the temple itself with a clear view of the entire property.

"Choose your destination and we will help you get there."

Choose your destination on the next page while enjoying a complete view of the Dark School.

474
465
470
466
395

The Mirrors Within

The colorful rays of light being drawn through the pyramid are completely eclipsed; the beautiful crystal pyramid goes black. The myrtle gardens withdraw. The flowers halt their blooming, the fountains drain and the music ceases. A Venerean lockdown has occurred.

You hear the chanting on the wind and see a swarm of Sub-lunars flying overhead. The partygoers have dispersed while you take refuge within the now darkened pyramid. You enter cautiously, as the darkness has swallowed the details of the interior. The walls are tight and confining, making your navigation difficult.

You see a small flickering light and move towards it quickly. Reaching the faint illumination, you are surprised to see it is only a reflection in a mirror. Looking for the source you are interrupted by the maiden's voice, "They are slavers, angry with our interruption of their operations. We diverted a significant portion of their workforce from them. They have to compel the demonic legions with curses and bindings, for us they come willingly."

You angle the mirror and notice it reflecting off others. Rearranging them allows a simple glow to radiate through the room.

"They cannot directly attack the temple," the maiden continues, "but they can disrupt our work. They will carry on like this during our hours, to weaken our influence. Unless someone stops them."

"Who? Me? You mean *me*?!" How the hell am I supposed to stop a swarm of demons?!"

The mirrors now shift on their own, realigning to reflect your image. You see yourself in different states, crying as a fearful child, in another you are an angered adolescent; each mirror holds a negative emotional experience from your past.

"These mirrors reflect what lies within," comes the maidens voice again, "they also reflect what could be..."

You stand in front of a well-dressed, flawlessly groomed, confident person. No hairs out of place with a warm smile and perfect posture. You realize this that this reflection is you as you wish you could be.

"Each hourly has a certain charism that it can provide to its adherents. Normally, it is the image of the hour that a person will conform to. With us, we bring out the best image of the worthy person. The outer beauty is reflective of an inner state and to this beauty, all nature conforms."

You stare at yourself and see what you can become. The mirrors align again, revealing more light in the chamber.

Unwilling to allow your inner potential to remain only a reflection, you emerge from the Pyramid ready to confront the threats on ***page 321***

Through the Gate

"There is no need to continue your battles," Ornias cries. "We can escape this school and bring all of these to safety."

"Maybe we should wait for word from the mansion?" you tell the demon, hoping for a reasonable solution to the problem.

"You promised to help me be free," he asserts.

Thinking it over, you would have none of the power you have now without him. You nod in agreement.

"My sudden retreat will cause my followers harm," you explain. "You are sure they can accompany us as well?"

"Of course," assures Ornias. "After me, quickly."

Trailing the demon, you lead a mass exodus from the property past the broken gate and beyond the border of the school's control. Your followers have just fought a serious battle. They need rest.

Passing the gate and moving away from the mansion's influence, you have your people act quickly. Many of them have resources and contacts in the outside world which allows for an easeful escape. Ornias is quick to advise you to organize your followers and set up networks in the outside world. With the use of your control over the fifth hour you motivate them to start financial firms and numerous businesses. Using your willing supply of workers devoted only to you allows for the accumulation of great monetary profits.

With vast wealth and a diverse network of connections you insulate yourself from the mansion's possible intrusion. Gradually, you reach an unrivalled measure of power. A short while later, you stand in your luxurious penthouse suite, surveying your empire.

"What's the word with that commander of the Martial hour? Is it the mansion sent to break down our operations?"

"Not likely sir," stated one of your followers. "they seem to be targeting criminal enterprises at a street level of which we have a negligible interest. It looks like the commander wants to be a hero for the city, not an agent for the mansion."

"Keep an eye on it," you state, as you dismiss your advisors.

Gazing out the window you take in a glorious view that few would ever see. This is your city. Most of the skyline was built by your firm's investment. You control politicians, bids for city contracts and a host of other lucrative endeavours. But the power of the mansion cannot be overcome by money or influence. You are harboring fugitives and a lot of them. You use your abilities to enslave others and increase your own riches. The demon Ornias once bound to the school is now your right-hand companion. This demon now makes his way into your presence.

You know it is a matter of time before the mansion turns its gaze to you and demands retribution for the gifts that you stole. Ornias crawls through the room and onto your desk, "I have found something that may help our situation. A ritual," he states, as you remain fixed on the city view, hardly acknowledging his existence. "With what you have you can gain full control over *all* the forces that are housed at the school. You will become as powerful as you are prosperous."

"What needs to be done?" you ask stoically.

"It will take some planning and it will require a *sacrifice.*"

You look to your desk and see the full bottle of liquid used to enslave the minds of mortals. Ornias has never been wrong before. If anyone is capable of wielding even greater power it is you. You've proven yourself and now, you set out to complete what you started on page 408

Sacrifice

You replaced the Cult of the East with a permutated variation. Sophisticated and profitable, your new empire has reached its peak. There is no amount of money or influence that could possibly change your situation or status. You've made it to the top and from here the bottom looks like a really hard fall.

You order a huge feast for all your minions; a party to mirror the ones you had on the property. Your people roll in with the night and the feast begins. All of them praise you for your great accomplishments and for the life they now lead, which they suppose is due to your great leadership.

The connection your followers have with you is an illusion. All your significant wealth and power is built on the back of a magically fueled lie, a lie that could be dispelled by another magician. This would quickly turn all your allies into potential threats. Tonight, that was set to change.

We came up together. Built an empire together. It will take all of us to defend it.

The feast carries on deep into the night and gradually the party devolves into an orgy that lasts well past midnight and into the morning. The intoxication overtakes your people and they fall into a deep, collective sleep.

It's always been us, you muse about your inebriated legion scattered throughout the suite. *We've done it all. We took over industry. Politicians beg favors from us. We've created employment for scores of citizens and infiltrated large corporations to gain leverage. You've all served our cause without hesitation or complaint but tonight, I need you to do more.*

Seeing one of your people laying in an obviously uncomfortable position you help him up dragging him to a more open part of the suite. In a half-dazed stupor, he looks up thankfully, although he is barely able to stand. A swift motion from your right hand is your only response. His eyes widen as blood pours from his throat. The blood drains onto the floor where you quickly make a wide circle, leaving the body outside.

It wasn't until the end, as he stares up at you that your enchantment was broken. Too late, he realizes what his existence has been. You see in his eyes true anguish revealed. He was finally free from the servitude he had been bound to and the sorrow of knowing his utter subjugation was lifted by life's one promise; that it ends. You whisper a calming utterance and see his obviously fearful expression soothed.

Ornias drags more bodies to the edges of the circle and you repeat the process. The small demon begins to work assiduously using the supply of blood to fill in the engravings of dark sigils.

You intone names of power with an unbroken concentration while enhancing the ritual by burning loads of incense which fill the room with a thin mist, moderately masking the smell of warm blood. The process repeats until all your servants are killed and their blood, combined with the skill of Ornias is applied to the engravings throughout the room.

Many of the stupefied servants smile as they die, knowing their death will serve you. After almost an hour of continuous chanting the targeted entities are drawn forth. A massive horde of Sub-lunars begin to amass outside the windowed suite overlooking the city. An offering of this magnitude pulls out all the kings and most powerful rulers of the demonic race along with their countless legions. Over seventy-two sigils glow an eerie red as the suite is surrounded by a terrifying multitude of powerful demons answering your dark calls.

"My Lord, they are all arrived," states Ornias.

Their dark speech reverberates through the room as they feed off the blood infused fumes that now permeated your living space. Many of these infernal servants had been pulled from the school. In fact, it was under the direction of Ornias, that almost all the permanently bound Sub-lunars were forcefully taken from the school. The stars of the night's sky are eclipsed and a powerful haunting darkness envelops the uppermost floor of the skyscraper. The demons now, like your servants are intoxicated and you begin to bind them. They enter the chamber kneeling before you as you compel them to swear absolute loyalty only to you.

Soon, I'll have more power than the mansion. I will never loose what I've gained. I'll surpass nature and perform wonders. I will see the future. Nothing will be kept from me. I'll establish a dynasty that will last a hundred years...

Moving faster than your eyes can perceive, one of the kneeling Sub-lunars is torn from your presence. This happens to another close by. Then, before you can react others are pulled away. You try to carry on with your binding but the rate in which the demonic creatures are being removed increases.

"Ornias, what is this!?!" you cry.

"My Lord, the school. They are hindering our work," he shrieks.

You try to impress a proper binding but the delicate procedure is denied by the speed in which your conjuration is exorcised. The hours pass and the legions that surrounded your position are dispelled, the incense is run dry and all you have left are the numerous corpses of your former servants. You sit in the circle, exhausted, alone, friendless and now a target to some of the most powerful magicians in the world.

"My Lord," states Ornias, "we must flee. They know our location. The school will come."

"We have to clean this up first," you reply. "If anyone finds..."

"No! They are coming even now. You've become a threat and for *these* crimes, they will make you answer."

"You spiteful little bastard! You did this on purpose!!!"

"I knew they could interfere," Ornias retorts, "I didn't think it would be so fast."

Covered in the blood of your friends, you exit your suite along with Ornias never to return. You took this risk to strengthen yourself, purely out of greed and the insecurity of being unable to appreciate your achievements. Your paranoia drove you to commit atrocities that will soon be exposed. Hours earlier you were a king. Having slaughtered all your servants, the people who helped you maintain your empire, you've become a master of nothing.

Your chance to seize power has failed. All the wealth you've gained and the empire you built will be useless against the powers of the mansion. You've broken too many laws and you have ended up broken beyond repair never to be whole again. The mortals will hunt you for your crimes against humanity, the spirits will mock you for the loss of your soul and the justice of the mansion will pursue you for your wrongdoing.

The time you have left, however long that may be, you and the small demon that led you astray will spent running. There will never be a home for you. You have no friends or allies to give you shelter. With your fates intertwined and your doom certain, all that remains is the end and who catches up with you first.

FIN

Alone but Never by Yourself

You wander through the forest, unsure where you are going. Just when a pathway or a landmark seems familiar and you think you might find some reprieve; monotonous exploration leaves you still stuck in the forest. The sounds of the battle finally trail off into the distance leaving you without any indication of where you came from and where you might be.

An overpass intensifies the darkness, leaving you sitting beneath a tree. Unable to see and lost deep in unfamiliar territory your mind wanders and imagines terrible scenarios. Every strange sound keeps you on high alert. You just saw a dragon fighting wolves ridden by warriors from history, nothing is off limits here. Large snakes, four legged saws, weird ghost children crawling up from wells to drown you in a way that defies physics. The fear of sudden attack keeps you hyper vigilant as the night goes on and you badly wish for daylight.

"Even just a little light would be helpful," you whisper in frustration, afraid to make too much noise for fear of attracting some unknown creature.

A leaf above your head begins to glow lightly, breaking the opaque background. You examine it, intently studying the small glow emitting from the vegetation.

"If I had a few more of you, it would really help my way," you voice, as numerous random leaves also begin to glow, giving the forest an uneven brilliance.

"Hmm, okay..." you think as you observe the strange occurrences. "Fine. Lots of light. Big time glowing. I really need to see."

The tree leaves light up with a powerful glow. The darkness is dispelled and despite this you still have no idea where you are but at least you can see. You notice a strange sigil engraved onto one of the trees. Tracing your finger over its outlines you marvel at its design wondering what it could mean.

Your relief does not last long as a harmonious tune begins to play from trumpets and drums. You are unable to see where it is coming from but it resounds throughout the forest. As the music plays the trees around you sway to the rhythm.

The beautiful music is interrupted by a somber voice that seems to almost sing as it speaks, "you are trespassing in my forest," it claims.

"I had no idea this forest even belonged to you or anyone else," you reply, trying to get a bearing on the voice's source. "I'll leave right away if you tell me the way out."

The tune that had initially been cheery turns sharply down and cellos replace the trumpets, setting a grim tone that resonates through the forest.

"You see my sigil," came the voice again, as a violin solo picked up. "My original master was worthy, but not so strong. We made beautiful music. But he was sacrificed to the Master and now, the music suffers. I kept the ones who took him from me," states the voice.

"Kept them?" you ask. "What does that mean?"

The forest lights up again, this time you see many very gaunt and dangerously thin people holding a variety of instruments and coming towards you. The flickering tree leaves light up at the dark symphonic procession. You want to run but seem to be surrounded by this hellish orchestra.

These people, they're not dead, you notice analyzing their forms. *He's enslaved them.*

They cease their advance and begin playing a mournful tune.

"My master was slaughtered by them," came the voice again. "They wanted him to join the Cult of the East. He refused. He was beautiful. An artist and a musician. They took from me so I took them all. Now, they make music for me as I made for him. Only a worthy soul can lead this choir. Are you that worthy soul?" he states casually in his dark, measured tone.

The trees bend down showing you a clear way out of the forest. Your heart lights up seeing the way to flat ground. As quickly as they bent, the trees return to their original positions, leaving you only with a memory of escape.

"I think not," the voice states as the choir continues to play a suspenseful refrain. "you are an interloper who comes to enslave me and silence my chorus."

"Hold on! I don't enslave, seriously! I have no enslaving on my mind, I just want to get out of here and go home. You can keep the zombie choir or whatever just... could you do the tree bending thing just one more time, please?"

"You are no exorcist. I will not heed any commands from you. I have instruments ready. You can drum till your hands bleed. The last one's fingers are not working so well."

"I'm out!" you cry, as you run away, hearing a suspenseful theme play as you race through the forest. You hear galloping behind you closing in as you take a quick glance at your pursuer.

I need some help. I don't know what I'm doing... was that a unicorn? Damn it! Am I being chased by a fucking cartoon? What the hell is this place!?!

You feel weight in your pocket and realize you still have your talisman. Pulling it out you pour your intention into drawing someone to help you out. A steep drop causes you to lose balance. You tumble downhill but maintain a steel grip on your talisman and when you finally stop you rush to your feet, noticing the music has ceased.

It's dark again and the tree lights have also stopped with the music. You hear a slow trot before you and notice in the shadow of the pale moon light, a single horned stallion which rises onto its hind legs.

"You will never hear my name. We made music in *this* forest together. I will not lose any more than I have already."

Aggressive chanting nearby causes flames to sprout and the standing horse returns to four legs retreating into his forest. A group of travelers with lamps step forward.

"Are you alright?" one asks. "Was that one you were summoning?"

"It was a sadistic horse with a choir that could make trees glow and bend. In what world would *anyone* want to summon *that*?" you answer frustrated.

Laughter pours from the group.

"You're still getting used to this place. C'mon let's get out of here before something *really* strange happens."

Finally, safe move along with this group to page 422

On the Trail Found by Friends

Deep within the forest you hear a dark melody playing in the distance. The music becomes more complex and louder as the rhythm plays.

Is that an orchestra in the forest? How is that possible?

You begin to move towards the interesting music but stop, suddenly rethinking your endeavor, *I'm alone. In a strange forest. Lost. Before this I was chased by a Roman legion riding wolves, fighting a dragon and now, there is a symphony in the forest. In no scenario I can imagine will this turn out well.*

You feel the weight of the talisman you carved and pull it out.

This is supposed to help me draw others... Okay, I'm in.

You pour your focus onto the image, clearing your mind of nothing but the help you need. The dark melody from the forest spreads around and the trees light up. Their leaves shine brightly, distracting you from your operation.

No! I need to focus. This talisman took way too much effort to make. No glowing forest leaves are screwing me out of possible magical powers.

Your focus remains as a beautiful song begins to invade your mind. The dark orchestra is at first complimentary. Not long afterwards, they begin to compete and gradually the lovely maiden's voice overtakes the melodies and the leaves began to darken.

...I need someone who knows their way around and can help me understand what the hell is wrong with this place.

"...Hey... you!"

Me? What?

"Hey, are you alright?"

That is not the lady voice or the scary symphony. Wait, that's a person.

"He doesn't look like a Cultist," comes another voice. "Are you lost?" he repeats.

Wow, it worked. "Do you know how to get out of here?" You ask the group.

"Sure, follow behind," states a young man from the group.

"Can you tell me what's going on?" You inquire further.

"Friend," he replies, "what the hell *isn't* going one around here?"

Wow, it really worked, you muse excitedly. Run to page 422 to join the group.

"Where are you from?" asks the leader of the group. "Are you with the East?"

"I…ugh...I was from the… *workroom,*" you answer unsure how to respond.

The leader and the others look at each other and then you.

"You have no idea what's going on," he says. "Alright follow behind. We're moving fast. We have to set up a circle or something to hold ground. We've been moving fast and the places to run to are becoming fewer as this war drags on."

"Wait, what war? What's actually happening here?" you enquire.

"Okay, follow my lead and listen," he says leading his group onward. "This place is run by the mansion. We don't know where it is or what goals its people have; all we know is they are the top authority here and they've gone silent. Since then, other groups have rushed to fill the void. The main one is the Cult of the East. They enslave everyone and have a legion of demons working with them," he pauses letting it all sink in.

"There are other smaller groups as well that follow the hourlies. They each have their own ambitions and I can hardly begin to understand them. Plus, many demons have deserted their original masters and taken territory of their own as you have noticed with the music lover back there. It's becoming a serious hell with each group fighting for control or independence or some other selfish aim."

“So, what are we going to do?” you ask.

“All of us were lured here under the impression we would be trained to control supernatural powers. We either need to find the mansion, if it really exists, or find a way out.”

“Why can’t we just reason with any of them?” you question.

He stops, almost laughing, “there is no reasoning. The cult wants complete domination. The demons want to be free and will go to any length to end their slavery and everything else in between is either too strange to understand or completely insane. This whole place is broken. We’re on our own.”

A dark cry pierces the night as the sky’s color shifts to a blood red. You look to the group leader, “Demonic activity. We may not be able to outrun this one.”

Everyone scatters as you pull out your talisman and whisper your intentions then shout, “Guys, stop! You drove back that monster in the forest, what can we do to stop this whole... sky bleeding thing?”

Under the subtle Venerean enchantments the group slows their retreat as one becomes angry and draws a circle on the ground with a small dagger. The others follow by making circles of their own and connecting them, while burning incense within censors.

Numerous fiends descend from the burning sky. Horrid looking deformities and monstrous creatures mocking reality.

There are so many. You marvel as the sky begins to rain down the fiery servants of the Cult if the East. *What would have been the point of running?*

A gigantic, eyeless Sub-lunar lands before your circle. His face has nothing but a huge lipless mouth tightly packed with serrated teeth. The students chant and intone names of power. Some hold talismans and others use blades. The gigantic demon and the others with it strike against the circle and are repelled by the invisible forces that your group have conjured.

"Be bound by the eternal fires that you emerged from and tormented by the aggression of your masters," calls out one of the group while the others maintain the steady chant. "by the power of these names which no creature is able to resist, we curse thee into the depth of the bottomless abyss, there to remain in chains, and in fire and brimstone unquenchable!"

Large chains form from the incense rising and wrap themselves around the gigantic Sub-lunar and the other smaller fiendish accomplices. The intoning of the names of power has fueled the demands of the group's leader, giving rise to a powerful conjuration that astounds everyone present, including the cultists pursuing you. The demonic forces are shortly after exorcised and the sky clears.

Unsure whether or not to step outside of the circle. You and the others give smiles of relief just before a falling mass smacks the ground in front of you. Your vision blurs for a moment as you try to make sense of what you are looking at.

"He must have been flying with his Sub-lunar," states a member of your group.

Other cultists fall from the sky, meeting a similar end. Blood flows over the ground as broken bodies rain over the area. The Cultists fortunate enough to survive are in total shock, now without their summoned aids, their power has been greatly diminished.

You and your group take leave of your circle and prepare to engage the remaining cultists. Seeing their disadvantage, they retreat.

"We can't let them report us back to their leaders. We have to deal with them now," states the leader of your group. ***To pursue the cultists, turn to page 426***

"Guys listen," you implore, "we are almost out of incense and they've lost their ammunition. If we leave now, we can get ahead of them and maybe find help close by. We've won. Let's move on."

On page 343 you can get away from the cultists.

Pursuit

"We can take them," shouts a member of your group.

You and the others instinctively follow. The few cultists left scramble to flee. They break into two groups, one to a smaller forest and another over the hills.

"Split up!" shouts the leader as you and some of the others head into the forest.

The group moves fast as you head up the rear, concerned that this whole chase is worthless. Your running slows as you feel a cramp; it has been a while since you last exercised this much.

I'll let them catch the bad guys, you think, as you wonder why you were even staying with a group like this.

Having numbers is always good and we did take on some scary looking things. But if I could just get back to the workroom and maybe prepare some new tools...

The noises of the hunt cease.

Did they catch them already?

A goshawk swoops by you passing close to your head and breaking your focus. Not sure what to do, you decide against calling out to not give away your location. If things with the cult members go sideways you want to be able to retreat without notice. Approaching cautiously, you move carefully passing by trees while making as little noise as possible. You see the group leader, who remains unmoving. With a sigh of relief, you catch up to him, *he must be close to the cultists. I'll have to keep it quiet so...*

As you approach it becomes apparent that he's not still. He's paralyzed. His mouth is sealed and he is struggling against some unseen force holding his body in place. His eyes scream at you to run. Turning your head, you see the cultists slaughter your newly found friends.

It happens so smoothly; their frozen bodies cry soundlessly as tears trail down their faces while their blood is collected and spread out into occult patterns throughout the area.

The hawk you saw before swoops down again. Following its trail, you notice it landing on the arm of an old man standing behind a dense bush. He seems taller than any ordinary man but otherwise looks like a mild old man.

“So,” he states, “you are the last one.”

He emerges from behind the bush riding a large alligator and moving towards your position. Immediately, you turn to run, only to be stopped by a cultist.

“All of you are shameful,” he adds. “Never lose your servants again or next time I will use *your* blood to summon them.”

Riding the alligator, he moves close to you. This is no man, this is a Sub-lunar, a demon and one of authority. Your arm is twisted behind your back and you are made to kneel before him. As the alligator passes by, its teeth almost brush against your face.

“Please, let me...” your begging is disregarded as a cultist slits your throat holding your head up, allowing the blood to pool below. Using hyssop, another cultist spreads the flowing blood into a circle and the demons, you and your friends exorcised are called back to the physical plane.

You feel them pass through your wounds causing unimaginable harm as they return. Their bodies take form drawing from your life’s energy. The blood pouring from your body is dispersed as the ground boils and steams. Your whole-body writhes in agony as they feed off you and the others. Even as your life ends, the pain does not.

The last thing you see is the demonic beings reformed. Horrifying creatures join in the agonizing torture, making you willingly accept the end fate delivered. After what seems like an eternity come rest and with it release from this terrible place.

FIN

Tools for The Trade

Passing through the door with the hammer and anvil etched on it you enter a lively room that is much larger than you would have expected. It looks like the workroom where talismans are built. A teacher stands at the head while you find an empty seat and take your place among the denizens of magical learning.

"Alright everyone, sit down and stay quiet," the teacher orders. "Some of you are here because you deserve to be, others are here because you are *proving* you deserve to be. Either way, no disruptions will be tolerated."

The teacher pulls a silk blanket off the desk revealing an array of what looks like medieval weaponry.

So, we are going to learn torture techniques. My life has hit a new high point today.

"These are the tools we use to control the forces of nature and the spirits. Once any of these come in contact with the tools we use here, they impart a greater reach to their functions. For instance," the teacher says while signaling for a spirit with a vaporous body and horned head to wheel in a cart with various plants on them. "Here we have the sickle," he states, while holding it up and gently taking the curved part and pulling the plant towards him. A voice emanates from the plant, clear enough for all the class to hear, "I am Acacia; the dominion of Mercury is allied to my being."

The class gasps and many smile at the unexpected outburst.

“Keep in mind,” the teacher continues. “It is not the plant actually speaking it’s the blade relaying the information.”

Next, the teacher picks up a long sword and holds it expertly, firmly tracing a line on the floor with the blade. The teacher then steps back and gives a command, “Spirit! Come towards me.”

Without hesitation the spirit moves as ordered and upon reaching the teacher visibly smashes into an unseen wall.

“Spirit! To me, again!”

Cautiously this time the spirit does the same only to smash against the same barrier. Some of the class shouts in horror at the abuse taken by the spirit.

“Spirit! Again!”

Some of the class, now visibly disturbed by the spirit whose actions are clearly forced on to it bring about unwarranted pain, turn away. With a clawed hand the spirit reaches over the drawn line and cries out in pain as the teacher watches stoically.

“Alright spirit, that’s enough.”

Much of the class is mortified by the demonstrated torture of the being before them. Some even stand up to protest the teacher’s actions.

"Sit down children," the teacher demands. "These things we control are not our friends. Even though this seems harsh I assure you, should any spirit, no matter how benign, gain the upper hand only pain follows. Remember, they view all of you as a food source and will treat you accordingly. There are hidden pathways that lead from their realms to this dimension *only* so they can feed. There are types of spirits you will never encounter because they have no reason to enter the physical universe. There are *only* masters and servants in our world. You better make a serious choice as to which one you want to be."

Everything settles down and the teacher carries on with the lesson, "When you scar the ground with a specially made blade it leaves a blemish that spirits cannot cross without serious pain. It can be dispelled by simply dragging your foot overtop or pouring water on the area," the teacher demonstrates by calling the traumatized spirit to pass by unhindered.

"Now, do this repeatedly in an area you can create a nearly solid barrier that no hourly or Sub-lunar can pass *and* that you can use repeatedly."

Once again, the teacher raises a small metallic plate, "Everyone should know what these are," the teacher proclaims, "our good friends the talismans. Each talisman is a key for unlocking potential. They perform particular functions but also draw down a specific influence. Should someone become extremely fluent with an Hourly influence they become known as a specialist. There are other talismans that can be created which will give you the power to command all of the elements, to avoid all dangers, and to assure you the success of all your enterprises and the fulfillment of your wishes."

Letting all that settle in, the class remains quiet in contemplation of how far they can take their magical aptitudes. A bell rings in the hallway signaling the end of the class.

"These instruments are crucial for your success in commanding the forces of nature and beyond. Next sessions we will be building our own. Try not to die or go insane before you get to experience these procedures."

You exit the class unsure of where to go next. Following the wave of students, you see them pile into different rooms. You can either follow the crowd to page 549

Or

Try to find a specific class you find interesting on page 533

Back into the Halls

You begin to regain your senses as you exit the class. Looking back, you notice that the Sub-lunars which had been summoned are lining up and kneeling before a hooded man. He holds out his hand which bears a signet ring and presses it into their foreheads, "Be sealed into my service. You will serve to further the Great Work."

You stare, trying to understand the significance of the actions being performed. As you observe, an adept calmly walks to the door and closes it gently, leaving you to find your way through an unfamiliar building with a mass of students performing bizarre operations.

You see some students from a previous class and follow them to page 490

Or

All the other doors are shut except one with a six-pointed star enclosed in a circle. You can enter on page 549

"I'm talking to the sky. The fucking sky! Okay who's *really* in charge? This whole place has these things running around doing strange shit and making life weird. Someone keeps them here. Someone brings them here. Where is that *someone.*"

"Very well," comes a rasping voice from above. "Follow our words quickly, you can only reach the mansion during certain transitions in the hours."

Without totally understanding you follow, moving through the fields, feeling the breeze at your back. Eventually you call out again, needing some confirmation on your progress.

"We can hear you well," state the voices, "there is no need to yell. Continue moving South, soon the lights will shimmer. Do not cover your eyes; walk through the glare and you will end up on a hilltop at your destination."

What hell is this? Why am I even following this bullshit advice? How will this work...?

A glimmer of sunlight reflects in the distance and beams directly at you. Without flinching but with a strong hope that you won't be blinded you keep you face forward. The glare is staggering and when it finally passes you rub your eyes trying to restore clarity. Looking around, you notice the landscape has changed entirely. The laboratory no longer lies behind you. You try to ask more questions, looking up to the sky but receive no answers. While staring into the sky, you spot a mansion on a hilltop.

I'm on a hill. When did this happen? What is this place? Is the person who's in charge here now?

Moving towards the Victorian household you stop at the entrance looking behind you again. Everything else seems so far away. Raising your fist, you give three solids knocks and then wait...

The door opens and a well-dressed gentleman with thin glasses steps out. See if he will invite you in on ***page 465***

"So, a life of opulence is what you seek," declares the Solar.

"Why not?" you respond. "If magic gives us power and wealth what else could I need? Look at the people running around this school chasing power, most of them are tripping over themselves and others for scraps of attainment they can barely use. If there is a quick way out of this, I'll take it."

The Solars silently observe you. Floating above they slowly spiral with their backs to each other like an old torsion pendulum clock. Their silence unsettles you but before you can speak, they interrupt.

"You are a selfish mortal. You cower from obstacles and criticize greater men when they fail, without lifting a finger to help them or others. You will never possess our treasures. To give them to you would be worse than throwing them away. You are unworthy of a soul. Unworthy of this school and unworthy to stand in our presence. Be ashamed and disgraced! Never return to us again!"

With those last words and before you can respond an overpowering brightness fills the chamber and takes hold of you. Your eyes shut tightly to avoid a very real likelihood of blindness. The light slams you with a powerful force, lifting you off of your feet and launching you out of the temple. Helpless against the wave of force that propels you into the air, your eyes remain shut as your body writhes in pain.

*****

You awaken near the gate you passed through initially. It is destroyed. The whole area is devastated.

Did I do this?

Scanning the area clears you of your latest self-implication. Dead bodies litter the ground and scorch marks on the earth show the signs of a fierce battle that has taken place. Your hands shake as you ineptly rise to your feet. You see a clear pathway home. Your talisman is broken and any other magical tool you have you dump immediately.

I'm not staying for this. No amount of power is worth this.

As you walk through the carnage, your vision fades leaving you in complete darkness. You cry out for help but no one responds. The majestic splendor of the Solars has left you blind, wandering the school until some malevolent force brings you the coward's end which you deserve.

FIN

Below the Goal

The Solars listen to your long explanation. Their expressions are always intense, their emotions unchanging. It is always uncertain if they are enraged or just incredibly focused. You calm yourself with the reassurance that these beings are not like humans. They conduct themselves differently and lived under a set of rules completely foreign to your own. This is just an appearance. Trying to anticipate how they would deliver on their claims you move to ask a question only to be interrupted.

"So, your only concern is for yourself?" asserts one of the Solars.

Swallowing hard you try to retrack what you said before, "Not just me but others as well, of course."

"You are unworthy and will never be able to make proper use of our gifts. We are beings of superb excellence. To work with someone like you would make us into zookeepers. You will never be able to look past your own selfish needs and can never achieve the greatness it would require to wield the powers we offer."

"Hold on," you order. "I am the master here. I hold the talisman and I can speak the words..."

"Do you feel powerful right now?" the Solar interjects. "A talisman in your hands is no more useful than if it were in the hands of an infant. You are a master of nothing."

Before you can react, a powerful light fills the temple. It lifts you off your feet suspending you above the ground. Your eyes involuntarily seal shut as you struggle to break free. You are launched out of the building at an alarming speed which crushes your body making breathing a struggle. You can barely process the situation and pass out when you crash into the ground.

*****

You awaken near the workroom as a mighty symphony plays, mocking you as you try to recover. Your eyes have been fused shut requiring you to forcefully pull them open. To unstable to rise, you lay pathetically as your body spasms uncontrollably. After some hours pass you sit up slowly noticing your talisman has been broken.

That went well...

You also notice the workroom not far away and at a slow pace make your way over to investigate which hour is in ascension.

Enraged by your mistreatment you try to keep calm noticing the hour of Mars is in its ascension. If you turn to page 125 you can pour yourself into a new hourly and a new experience.

OR

Wait a while and calm down. Let some time pass and meditate on your mistakes. After some self-reflection you see the hour of Venus is in ascension. Turn to page 326. Noticing significant relief and thankful that your brush with the Solars did not end a lot worse you are ready to experiment again with a different hourly.

Revoke Natures Final Calling

It had been so long since you set foot in the household where you received your learning. Your nostalgia quickly fades when you begin to detect what has been going on behind the gate.

Stepping out onto a balcony with the aid of the Solar spirits and using the fourth talisman of the Solar hour, the land around you and its hidden inhabitants are revealed. The Sub-lunars are scattered and numerous dead bodies litter the landscape in all directions. The gate is destroyed and the mansion is under guard.

"Old friend," comes a familiar voice, as a hooded distinguished man makes his way toward you. "It has been too long."

"Master," you respond. "What has been happening here?"

"A war, between different factions which has ended but not without cost. Come this way," he insists. "We have for you a rare opportunity."

You are led down a long Victorian hallway and into a well-furnished room with a dead person lying on the bed. The body is sickly thin and pale, clothed in a dark ash colored apparel with a dark wide hood drawn over the face.

Since you have with you the fourth Solar talisman the dark spirits surrounding him immediately become visible and their naturally cruel demeanor is turned on you.

Those are Saturnites...!

"Sol!" you shout out letting a burst of light emit from another talisman in your possession. The bright light repels the Saturnites before they are able to harm you, expelling them far away from your presence.

"This is a hermit from the Grotto," you state. "And he is dead."

"We need this being," the Master states. "Today I am going to impart something rare."

Astonished by his words, you hardly believe him. If anyone but the Master were speaking, you would laugh and turn away. You have tried several times in your practice to achieve what he is describing, but never succeeded. The calculation was too complex; impossible really. The ability required seemed to be more legend than reality.

"Is it possible?" you ask, perplexed by the entire concept of the operation.

"To raise the dead?" replied the Master. "Yes. Under the right circumstances."

"How?" you ask, eager to learn.

"First, the body must be preserved whole within the first twenty-four hours of having passed. It is better for the person to have been killed; it is much harder if they died of natural causes. Then we use the Pauline Art. We calculate their normal birthday, hour and minute. *Then* we do the same but for the time of death. After this, we determine the hour we will begin work *and* the hour we expect him to be revived."

"Shit!" you exclaim, confounded by the whole process. "Do we have..."

“Yes, yes. Birth and death, days, times and locations in full are written here,” the Master assures, passing you the scrolls with the information. “We need to begin immediately and anticipate the hours of signet construction so we can make these as quick as possible.”

Without wasting time, you construct the signets for the hermit’s birth and death, then after that, signets for the hour of operation and the hour following. Bringing them to the table of practice within the mansion you place them on their appropriate spheres and invoke your Celestial guardian to charge the objects.

Once finished, you follow the Master and bring the first signet of his birth and put it under the hermit’s head and the signet engraved with the hour of his death at his feet. In his right hand is the signet representing the hour of operation and in the left a signet identifying the time he should awake.

“I leave the rest to you,” states the Master as he exits the room leaving you alone with the dark corpse.

You swallow hard, unsure what oration to make. You’ve always prevented death, never defeated it.

A child of the Darkest Hour resides beyond our domain. The abyss saw and feared, the living saw and became lifeless. This hero was taken to a well-earned transcendent rest and now You who created and fashioned man must revoke natures final calling; we need him returned for the greater glory of the highest good. Let the grave go wanting. Let the nether world be starved. Call on death to fast while we rob his coffers and remake our lost companion.

You stay by the bedside for the entire hour and at the time of its transition the corpse remains still. You give up hope sensing only failure but then, the fingers move and breathing begins. The bodily functions restore and you sense a monumental Celestial force sustaining and animating the once deceased hermit.

Finally, the hermit rises and investigates his palms noticing the signets. You quickly remove them gently and place them on a dresser nearby.

"Do you remember your name? Who you are?"

With a stoic gaze and a heartless tone, the hermit responds, "I was dead and now, I'm here."

You are excited at the prospect of having succeeded bringing back a person from the dead. Overjoyed by your achievement you silently revel in your newfound ability.

"Why did you bring me here?" asks the hermit.

Completely caught off guard, you are uncertain how to answer the legitimate request.

"Well, I…"

"My Lords!" comes an alarmed voice from within the mansion. "Outside! We are under attack!"

Unmoved by the frantic shouting the hermit stares at you stoically, still hoping for a response.

"Let's go see what's happening," you state, as you lead the hermit by the arm, noticing his general state of weakness caused by his recent revival.

Outdoors many of the students of the mansion are professionally carving circles and chanting, setting up wards and preparing to defend against an imminent threat that you take notice of approaching from the distance.

You immediately notice, a horde of Saturnite spirits looming on the horizon. They look like floating sentient shadows. Their presence repulses sunlight making the day seem darkened. As they move, an overpass blocks the day's light and absorbs the life from the surrounding land. There are so many of them that they are impossible to count.

"In life they were linked to the hermit," states the Master. "Once revived from the dead we inadvertently conjured a powerful mass of these beings."

You try to ponder how it could be possible that this would have occurred.

Of all the beings to draw into this world. Saturnites are more dangerous than Sub-lunars in some ways. They've already been empowered beyond their hourly limitations and are destroying the school. How will we actually fight them off?!

Interrupting your spiral of fear the hermit steps forward, "It's me they want to feed off. I will handle this."

Before anyone can intercede, the hermit calls for incense and his sickle. The Master hands him a large bowl attached to an iron chain while another student uses conjured fire to light the embers within. The chosen of Saturn steps forward without hesitation and the

legions of the Darkest Hour close in.

The sky is dark and the earth begins to shake. The smell of Sulphur fills the air as the hermit allows the incense to rise. Expertly swinging the sickle, the hermit cuts through the thick pillar of foul-smelling incense which forms into innumerable chains and restraints that latch onto the Saturnite siege. They claw at reality itself causing even the perceivable colors to shift while they desperately try to stabilize themselves. Their cries cause pain to many of the magicians, despite having circles of protection.

While intoning powerful chants and swinging the sickle wildly overhead, the hermit causes attacking the Saturnites to be flung into a cyclone, violently drawing them together. In a final devastating stroke, the Saturnite horde is flung out of the physical realm.

Return within the mansion on page 530

To Fly Beyond

Standing on a balcony you overlook a vast landscape.

I'm still at the mansion, I think. What is happening? Or when...

Your memories are shifting to accommodate for the new timeline. A hooded teacher approaches, he looks familiar.

Where do I know you from?

"Today we are going to aid in advancing your ability to scry. These techniques take a phenomenal amount of focus but today we will have aid. Even the laws that govern our practice can be bent if the correct components are gathered... What?"

You look at him in a daze, your memories still scattered.

I know him. He was my teacher. I opened the box with him. What is he talking about?

"The box..." you state, hoping you make some level of sense. "Me and you... I just can't... I mean when... when is this?"

The teacher gives you a perplexed look but quickly realizes what's happened.

"You used the cube. You opened the box!"

Your eyes widen in agreement as your new memories surge into order and you remember more of the timeline you've emerged within.

"Listen," the teacher says smiling, "you've succeeded where a lesser mortal would have been completely destroyed."

You smile appreciating the recognition but still have a scattered perception of your own identity.

"Listen to me," the teacher continues, "your memories will align with the temporal pathway you've entered. Do you recognize anything yet?"

You look around bewildered, uncertain of your surroundings.

"You are an exceptional adept at this school. Soon you will ascend to a mastery of control over forces both natural and supernatural. We are developing your ability to scry beyond the normal limits in preparation for your development."

Taking it all in, you let your mind settle. Turning to the teacher again you ask, "Who are you, really?"

"I am the Master of this school. I inherited it from my grandfather."

In awe, you realize you are in capable hands. With your mind at rest, you resign yourself to the teachings of the Master of the mansion.

"Alright then," he states, while waving a wand in a smooth motion. A sudden blur obscures your vision as a small Sub-lunar is violently thrust into your presence.

"This is Ornias," explains the master. "He is going to aid us in our next excursion."

The small demon looks like a gargoyle and after shaking off some obvious discomfort, he bows reverently towards the master and perches on the balcony railing.

"Scrying normally involves the mind of the user being used as an additional sense of its own. The expansion of consciousness allows it to surpass the mind's natural functions and absorb information in a more intense way. However, once someone has reached their limit, using a spirit as an aid can take that perception and broaden it in ways that would be wholly unavailable to the adept by themselves."

Thinking about this you look at Ornias and then turn to your teacher, "Master, why did you choose a Sub-lunar? Why not an hourly or Celestial?"

"Hourlies are constrained by time and Celestials are normally ridged and difficult to make contact with. Also, elementals are too low minded and familiars are almost purely terrestrial. Ornias can explain more about this with greater ease than I can," states the Master of the mansion.

The Sub-lunar edges towards you and begins to further disclose the nature of the operation they would undertake.

"We demons ascend into the firmament of heaven and fly about among the stars. The heavens are like Earth. There are all types of principalities, authorities, world-rulers and we demons fly about hearing the voices of the heavenly beings and survey all the powers. But as having no basis on which to rest, we lose strength and fall off like leaves from trees. Men seeing us imagine that the stars are falling from heaven. But it is not so. We fall because of our weakness and because we have nowhere to lay hold of and so we strike the ground like lightning in the depth of night."

The Master raises his hand silencing Ornias, "He can take you to the edge of the heavens but you must climb the rest of the way. We have been training for this. Very few ever reach this level of perception. You will return to earth having connected with beings beyond this reality.

The memories flood through your mind. All the preparation and methods surface while your intellect fully reforms and you prepare to commence the operation.

The Master hands you a crystal. Taking it, you nod to Ornias and gaze into the glittering item and with a slight wave of the master's wand you pass into a higher mode of being. Everything is clear now; no senses distract and organize the world around you and numerous things previously hidden are revealed.

With Ornias as a guide you begin to traverse the property and ascend into the lunar plane. You see spirits of every kind rushing to different destinations. The upper planes are more like a metropolis for spirits that exceed anything you would encounter in the terrestrial realm. You also hear the sentences which go forth upon the souls of men and whether by force, or by fire, by sword, or some accident, people meet their demise. Demons cry out laying claim to the souls. It is like a morbid stock market where bids for humans dying of unnatural causes are auctioned.

"My race will rush off to feast off of the residual energies left over from the unnatural deaths," Ornias smiles, knowing how troubling his bleak revelations are to mortals. "Normally, we veil ourselves within acts of destruction. It allows the souls to be captured while they are ripe. When we finish, we leave them staggering in their agony."

You both ascend further passing the hourly realms and into the heaven of the Celestials called the Firmament. Here numerous beings, demons, stars and holy angels intermingle. You notice how ordered everything is and your heightened senses allows you to comprehend how thoroughly the influence from above controls what is below. Ornias grows weak and falls back to the property.

It seems that the only reason why humans die unnecessarily and are helpless against the weakness of nature is because we have not made solid contact with this upper force.

You realize that even the movements of the spirits are completely controlled. You see a complete picture and discern the holistic rule underneath the seemingly fractured being you had been born as. These Celestials act more like the nervous system, the hourlies each like organs while the Sub-lunars and elementals form the blood vessels and the skin.

It is one flowing system that influences the mortal realm so efficiently that humans are barely aware of its existence. It all stems from a Source.

You push onward passing the stars and into... nothing.

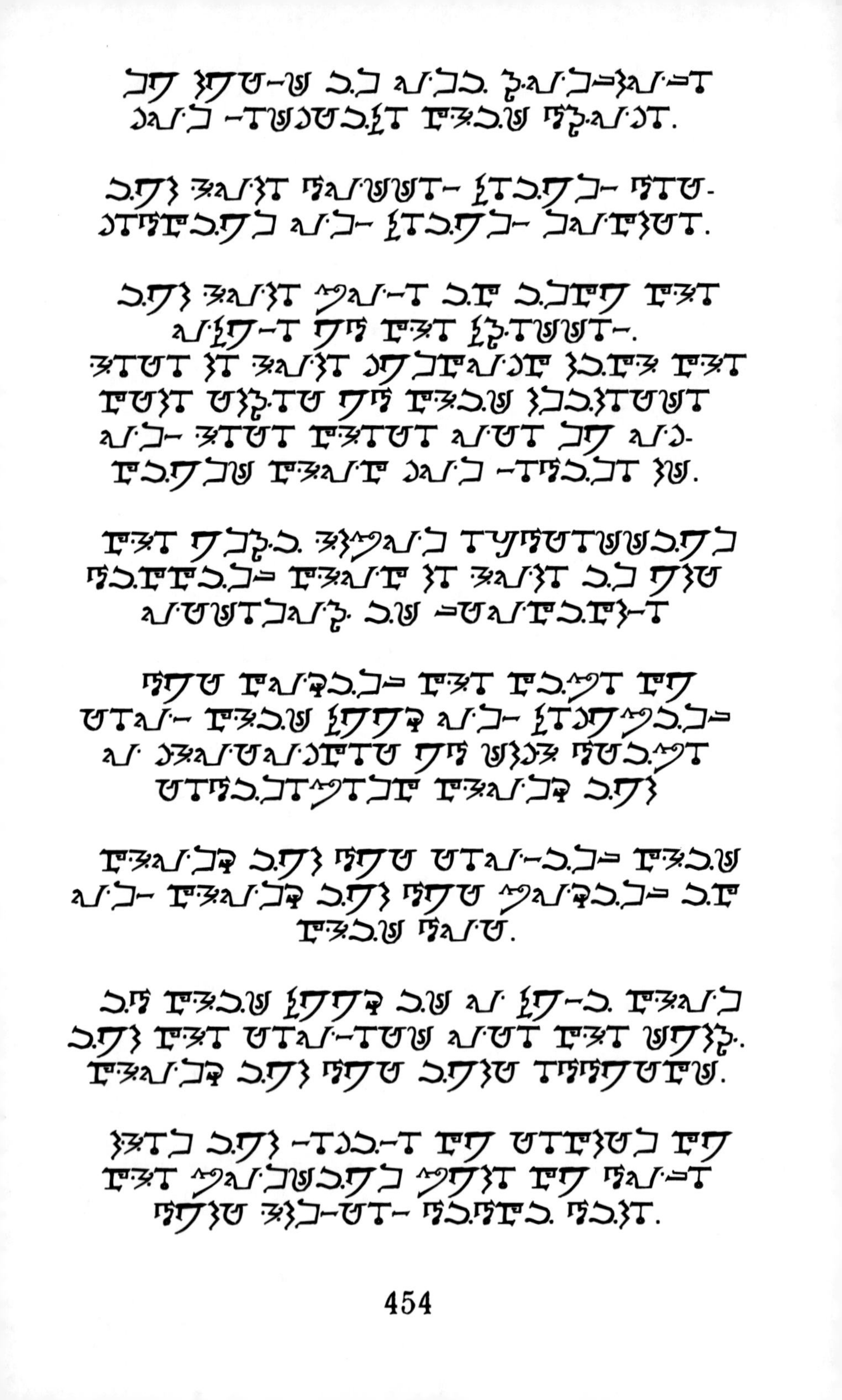

It takes many days for you to return to normal. In that time, you recall what you had learned at the mansion, the lessons under the Master and the friendships with many of the school's heroes and specialists. With your memories restored you begin your preparations. After weeks of planning the Master summons you.

"Everything is ready for the ritual," the Master of the mansion explains, "we are placing you at the head for this one. Everything has been sorted and all the players have arrived. This will not be over quickly it will take at least half a day to cast and then *if* we are successful, the surge from the higher realms will carry us the rest of the way."

"Can we go over it one more time?" you request. "I just need to be sure of everything."

"Of course," the master replies. "We will be calling down en masse all the major forms of Hourly spirits. Each calling will be done by a specialist and will follow the hour where their summoning will be strongest. Once this is done, you will direct the total force to enact alongside the power generated from the regular activities that have been happening on the property. All of the sealed and bound spirits will be compelled to action and all of the adepts and students, no matter their level, will be subjected by the influence and inclined to aid."

He hands you a large parchment packed with obscure lettering and complex diagrams. There is barely any white space and the writing flows in almost every direction, accompanied by orbital timings, occult hours and constellatory positioning. Confused by the overload of information you understand the technique perfectly but never receive a full explanation for the reasoning.

"What is the purpose of all this? The first phase depends on specialists with each of the hourly races and one high level adept to direct the result of their work. This will set off a reaction throughout the property and use it as a catalyst to affect...," you stop short hoping the Master will fill in what isn't explained.

The Master leans in closely, "This is the first phase of the Great Work."

He notices your uncertainty at the vagueness of the presentation and further explains the situation, "In many mythologies the gods gather to pass judgment on man. The Olympic spirits held assembly and normally it was to stave off a seriously disastrous event or to punish humanity and set a correction to the world from any deviation. Essentially, we are going to call the court to order and force the judgment ourselves. It will be a ruling to better mankind as a whole, upgrading our nature and expanding our evolution."

The very thought of what you would be embarking on fills you with a sense of wonder and reverence. Everything this school was built for, all the trials and the pains endured to make it this far are coming together at an impossibly high pinnacle.

"When do we begin?"

"The new moon is tomorrow," the Master explains, "We will gather and set this in motion. Until then purify yourself thoroughly."

*****

In the early hours before sunrise, you meet the Master in his study. He stands before an ornate wooden desk, gazing through a glass wall which offers a view of the vast forest.

"We are going to meet the champions at the site," the Master says as he takes you by the wrists. "We'll be there very soon."

Without much warning you are transported within a ray of light to the location. Each of the seven specialists are waiting for you. A large encircled octagram is engraved onto a cleared piece of flat land. The sunrise has begun and the Master gives you his final instruction.

"You are to lead and close the ritual. You will be the first one in and the last one out. I will not be here to assist; my presence would only interfere with the setup we've invested in creating here. I leave the rest to you," he says to the group as a whole and hands you a wand before being magically transferred back to the mansion.

Standing at the edge of the topmost point of the octagram you begin the ritual, pointing to each of the champions personally and with the wand directing them into an individual point of the octagram. Closest to you in the circle the Physician, wise and confident situated in line with the Solar hour. Next to him, a melancholic beauty in a full-length silver dress, the intuitive Clairvoyant, the personification of the Lunar hour. A Roman soldier, the Praetor, obviously the embodiment of Mars stands ready. Opposite your position, in a medieval apron with vials in fitted pockets, the Alchemist scion of Mercury. A beautiful petite lady with long, soft black hair and grey eyes dressed like an archaeologist with a suede brown hat, the Treasure Hunter, stands exemplifying the Hour of Jupiter. In the next point, the agent of the hour of Venus, the impeccably dressed Enchanter and finally, next to you, representing Saturn, is the Hermit. He wears simple ash colored tunic and looks like he hasn't smiled in years. With everyone settled, you begin:

"Scion of Mercury bring forth the Philosopher's Stone," you ask authoritatively, as the thin alchemist moves forward gently placing an unworked red stone on the ground in the center of the octagram.

With your wand you direct him back to his place. The alchemist bows, walking backwards as you approach the stone and contact it using your wand. The octagram's border glows a strong vibrant red. The circle is now sealed

With the stone they are drawn and with the stone they are bound.

The Solars, proud and strong make their appearance at the command of the physician. You start to sweat while engaging them and force them into place surrounding the circles border far into the distance. They sing a loud and triumphant song of praise. The doctor raises a talisman and calms the domineering hourlies. During the next hour, the lady of the Moon burns incense specific to her spirits. A great rainstorm appears around the circle. As with the Solars, you assist the clairvoyant constraining the spirits, forming them into a circular border around your position just before the Solars. The Hourlies of Mars are called upon next and they appear marching in militant fashion around the circle. With a word from the Praetor the

Martial hourlies organize efficiently around the circle, standing before the Lunar phantoms. The alchemist opens a vial which emits silver mist clouds from where Mercurials instantly appear taking their place outside the circle.

The Mercurials begin to explain the mysteries of the universe and ask wild questions of the assembly. You and the alchemist silence them and position them before the Martial soldiers. The Jovial hourlies arrive next with thunder and lightning around the circle, boisterously laughing and offering wine to everyone.

Again, the spirits are bound and forced into their place. The Venerean maidens are summoned next and they playfully dance about the circle to beautiful music. They are compelled to line up in the distance around the circle before the position of the Jovials. Lastly, pointing to the Hermit, you announce the final call, "Summon the children of Saturn to our cause."

The hermit burns foul smelling incense intoning names of power and immediately the earth surrounding the circle quakes and turns white. Terrifying spirits with the appearance of liquid shadows sewn together make their entrance. There are many of them, more than any mortal could easily control. Attracted by the power of the Philosopher's stone, they surround your group. Raising the wand, you move slowly, clockwise aiming at the Saturnites. By some invisible force they drift back forming a round border encompassing the circle. With the help of the hermit, the Saturnites are constrained to their position.

Seven hours have passed and now you have all of the components to enact your will. Turning to the physician you point your wand and say aloud, "Beings of Sol, who adorn the whole world with majesty, who banish adversities in the darkness, who divides the beautiful things from the ugly ones. Stand watch as dreadful candles lighting our way in the darkness."

This is repeated by the physician and with a loud shout the Solars confirm their adherence. To the Lunar spirits you speak next,

"Lunarian children of the shroud, servants of the figure of the heaven, the consolation of the night and the Queen of the constrained spirits, turn back your foul fortune and deliver us safely to our destination."

The clairvoyant repeats the words and the Lunar spirits return with the sound of rushing waters about the circle. Turning again you point your wand, to the Praetor, "Martial soldiers, the incarnate anger breaking mountains and drying oceans, I call you whom every planetary creation fears to be by our side."

A loud militant shout of acknowledgement resounds as they beat their shields.

"Mercurials, without you nothing is known. You rule over the minds of all thinking beings be our voice among the world now and forever."

The silver clouds exploded into a flock of magpies and fly around the circle, then, returning to their sentient forms retake their original place.

Okay, I guess that's a yes.

"Jovial kings, benefactors and patrons, supports of the mortal cause. Be a strong foundation for our work this day."

Gentle thunder and a rhythmic trumpet blast confirm their allegiance. You turn now, to the well-dressed Venerean who bows as you point the wand in his direction, "you Venereans who dominate the will of men and the love of women turn your favor towards us and bring us good fortune this day and all our days."

The words are repeated and the Venerean maidens sing the chant back acknowledging your rule. Last is the hermit, his dark cloak pulled over his scowling face as he stands ready.

"Cold Saturnites who have authority over every harm tear down the boundaries that interfere with our work and be not hostile to our direction, this day and all our days."

The Earth shakes lightly with the tremors gradually increasing in their violence. Within the circle you and the champions remain unaffected, but the Hourlies have been infused with a surge of power flowing from your circle outwards to the legions of spirits that have begun to rapidly revolve around your position. The Earth tears around you as the spirits move in their annular dance. Eventually your circle is torn from the ground and you rise into the air above the property. The Hourly legions below form into a siphon beneath as they continue to spiral.

The octagram you stand in with the champions also begins to turn and you sense the tension building as power is absorbed from the property and the mansion. You sense the astrological movements above aligning with the powers deposited within the property below. The landmass spins faster as the force produced reaches its limit. When the pressure becomes too much, an explosion disperses the Hourlies, the gate opens and the generated energy is released.

The effects spread quickly, in the months that follow people begin to have collective dreams. The unity that technology artificially creates is replaced with a heightened attachment to the forces of nature. They begin to forget their old petty desires, the social media and reality tv become less alluring as profound questions plague the mind. Then as each individual evolves, mysterious signs and wonders cause them to seek out and be perfected within, the Dark School.

FIN

"Mortal," one of the Solars calls out, "take hold of the talisman and look through the oculus."

A golden talisman with a thin golden chain floats towards you and gently lands in your hand. With the object in your possession, you need only to figure out what an oculus is. Staring at the talisman you observe the light reflecting off its surface. As you gaze over the intricate patterns a thick pillar of light from the opening in the ceiling is channeled and reflected off the talisman's surface. It strikes your face, forcing your head up towards its source.

Control over your body is suspended as your vision is interlaced with the light following its trail. The sheer magnitude of your newly expanded perception overwhelms any sort of normal physical control. With your whole being immersed in this new awareness you view an expanse far greater than your natural sense would permit. This new ability also allows you to see the spirits and Sub-lunars that would be invisible to mortal eyes.

"Behold!" booms the voice of a Solar hourly. "This is the true foundation of the school."

You see Sub-lunars making repairs to structures and upkeeping the landscape. Phantom spirits of the lunar hour are clear before your ever-growing vision. By a gentle river, several Sub-lunars have gathered and you can see them conversing. You linger by the river watching them and they, as if prompted by some unseen alarm look back. They stare at you silently unmoving.

How do they see me? I can't even tell if I have a body anymore.

Unable to do anything other than observe your surroundings you are powerless to react. But in anticipation to the questions, you hear the voice of a Solar hourly clarify the situation.

"The talisman you carry serves to enable you to see the spirits when they would otherwise be invisible to mortal eyes. Whenever it is uncovered, they will immediately appear. Nothing is hidden from us."

You linger a moment looking over the diverse forms of the many Sub-lunars present at the river's edge. You see them, they see you and as you are about to try to make contact the talisman is removed from your hands. Like a drowning man pulled from the water, you take a deep involuntary breath as your natural senses resume their control over your body.

"Behold and adore another of the gifts from the spirits of Sol," claims a Solar as another talisman, floats towards you. You reach out and softly take hold of the talisman waiting for a further explanation about its use.

"This will allow us to travel over long distances in short time," explains the Solar spirit. "We can take you to the mansion where only the worthy may enter."

You take the talisman looking over the golden plate with the mysterious engravings and then back at the Solar nodding. Light fills the temple again and you are lifted, this time with the rest of your body into the air through the open temple ceiling and on to **page 402.**

A Worthy Welcome

A well-dressed an elderly gentleman sporting thin glasses eyes you at the doorway. He is exactly who you would expect to be living in a Victorian style mansion. He pulls out a pocket watch; staring at the dial you notice planetary symbols lining the border rather than numbers.

"I would never have guessed that another would show up," he states with a regal accent. "The Solar hour just passed. Well, you made it this far, you might as well come in."

He holds the door, letting you enter and then takes the lead. You are shocked to see he has no legs. His body floats on a gaseous cloud below his waist. The mansion is ornate and antiquarian. Nothing looks new but it is upkept in pristine condition. Many detailed pieces of art adorn the walls, all set in elaborate frames. You climb a staircase and turn down a hallway.

"Three classes are open right now. Hourly interactions. Tools for the trade. Scrying and omniscience. The choice is yours young master," he states, after leading you to a hallway with two doors to the right and one to the left. It is obvious that there is activity happening within, "only the worthy find their way here and if you are worthy than you shall remain."

He floats off leaving you in the hallway where each door has a symbol engraved on its surface. You study each one and decide your next move.

The first door to the right has a hammer and anvil symbol, walk through to page 430

The second door on the right, has the planetary symbols engraved in a circle, pass through on page 476

The door to the left has engraved on it a hieroglyphic styled eye, walk in on page 537

Garrison

Landing in front of a large barracks roman soldiers are training in formation and the commander approaches your position.

"So, the Solars dropped you here," he states. "Observe for a bit and when you're ready go and grab a weapon from the barracks," he says while pointing to a large open doorway.

You watch the host move in unison and respond instantly to Latin commands shouted by their commander. With precise actions and mock striking they train incessantly. Eventually they break off into teams and begin to spar against each other. Excited by the change in their regimen you rush to the barracks and within find only a spear left on a wooden rack. It weighs heavy in your hands but enthusiastically you return to the outside ready to join the exercise.

Moving quickly, you rejoin the soldiers to train on page 140

Fate's Barricade

You are brought quickly into a small room with a man seriously injured and breathing unevenly. It is obvious one of his lungs has ruptured. You ask for his information and his birthdate, birth hour and minute, homeland, and city.

Materials to make a signet and tools to carve are given to you and you begin your work. After you engrave the sigil you move to the mansion's table of practice, a room you have not seen in a long while. Placing it over the proper sphere you invoke your guardian and charge the signet. Then, armed and ready you return to the fallen defender and place the signet under his pillow.

If the goal of creation is to remain broken, then we would have no trouble fulfilling our life's purpose. But to become worthy we must be whole and I turn to You for reward for a champion among men. Restore his stature to match his achievements. Allow a barricade against fate and stop the harm from running its natural course.

After detecting the presence of the Celestials, you exit the room and go prepare some tea for the young hero. A half hour later you re-enter with the tea, setting it on the table by the bedside. Noticing that the young enchanter has awakened, you take a seat on the side of the bed and place your hand overtop the recently healed individual's forehead.

"It looks like you've made a full recovery," you state confidently, pulling the small tablet from under the pillow with astrological and planetary symbols etched around it.

"You can keep this. It won't do anything more; it's purpose is exhausted," you say handing the signet over. "If you're feeling better, I can take you to meet the master of the mansion. He is looking forward to seeing you. The work you did allowed the forces of the cultists to be defeated easily and at little expense."

"The mansion? I'll get to see the mansion, finally?"

You smile, "You can redress using your mirror and I advise you do, because you are actually *within* the mansion."

You take your leave as the Master approaches. He stops you in the hallway, "I've noticed your work keeps you busy," He states as you pass.

"I love it," you reply. "But I am only one person. Any additional healers that want to take up the burden would be truly appreciated."

"I may have a better offer," he counters. "The Great Work desires completion. Now that you are here, we can begin the process of opening our gates and cementing our influence. We will change the fate of the world and better humanity as a whole. I will see to the enchanter. Please, wait for me there is much more to explain."

You walk out onto one of the balconies and watch a beautiful sunrise over a fabled land. You have no idea what is going to happen or how to channel such power to affect the entire world. But the Master has called you to his side. This is not for socializing or trading war stories; something real is happening and soon he will disclose to you what only he knows.

You wait and watch the sun rising, entranced by its beauty and the illuminated natural world below. This is the first time you have actually rested from your work. It feels nice to just appreciate the world. You notice the Solar hourlies singing their praises as the sun's rays spread their influence. You intone a name of power and draw some of them toward you. You need not reveal a talisman; your nature and theirs has been permanently linked. You see the temple of Sol in the distance as the Solars lift you off the balcony.

The concentration of supernatural influence on this property permeates the air; you missed using this much power freely. Your vision merges with the light of the Solar beings and you see further than any human could ever comprehend. Noticing everything, from small insects to large skyscrapers, you had forgotten what it was like to have this capability at your disposal. Enlivened by the experience, your mind is set at ease thankful to have returned home.

FIN

Laboratory

The Solars drop you in front of an amazing building with multicolored smoke streaming from the vents. The vapors twist as they rise and without any reason swirl around you, creating a brilliant rainbow cyclone which welcomes you to the location. You cautiously enter as the doors open.

Within, plain looking men many with medieval work aprons are busy with operations of great complexity. The lab is massive and filled with renaissance era equipment. You notice that each one of the laboratory workers has an open flask that emits a constant vaporous stream hanging from their utility belts. Upon further inspection you see that from this stream emerge their bodies. They float throughout the lab barely stopping to acknowledge your entrance. Multifaceted furnaces and large complex alembics with drip faucets distill unknown liquids; fires burn and the floating workmen maintain many different athanors. A slender, comely youth, with a pair of dark sea-blue goggles and a robe made of shifting colors floats towards you.

"You made it just in time," he comments. "The hour is still strong. Welcome to the Mercurial laboratory."

Puzzled, your expression begs for more of an explanation.

"The work we do in this lab causes simultaneous changes to occur within the material we are working with. We break down everything that passes through here into its essence and then we help it release

its proper potential. We can transmute base metals into gold or cause diverse phenomena, even to the point of defying natural law."

This is what magic is about! You think as you excitedly begin learning from the generous Mercurials.

In the months that follow you work tirelessly and bear witness to miraculous experiments that you would never have imagined could exist; your work is beyond the realm of imagination. Everything from bottling hailstorms to animating trees and giving them voices to speak is within your abilities.

Proud of your achievements, you start to wonder about how long your studies have drawn out and question your Mercurial instructor about its duration.

"Oh," he says, obviously not expecting such a question, "I think it has been five months and twenty-two days. So, good job on keeping with the program," he adds enthusiastically.

"WHAT! How has it gone on this long? I don't remember eating or sleeping."

"True," he interjects, "it's probably because you haven't done either of those things. In a place like this the laws of nature are slowly morphed to accommodate for the accelerated change allowing us to exist in a more temporal realm..." the Mercurial halts his explanation noticing your perplexed expression. "Your natural behaviors are going to be suspended. Eating, sleeping, going to the bathroom, fatigue and things like this will all be temporarily deferred."

You have never been without food or sleep for so long and now are concerned about your long-term health. The Mercurial, sensing the obvious pulls a small vial-like bottle from one of the shelves.

"*This* is an elixir," he says, showing you the small vial. "Adiantum capillus veneris: Maidenhair. Harvested on the first hour of our day. It is distilled for the full month. Each one of us hourlies have certain substances that we can infuse with our essence. When you drink this, we can begin to pass on to you the greatest of what our race can offer."

Not willing to quit but still conscious of how much time has passed you cautiously move on the page 30

Grotto

The Solars set you down before a dark dense forest with no apparent way in. You move through awkwardly stepping over large roots and unkept pathways grown over with weeds and brambles. Eventually you end up before a pond with a willow tree hanging over it.

"The Solars sent you," utters a seething voice. "See if you are worthy to stay. The tools are before you."

"Tools…?" you say looking for the source of the one speaking to you.

"Look at your feet," it says impatiently.

You see deep claw marks upon the ground's surface. Diagrams and instructions which you squat down to read.

The First Talisman of Saturn—This talisman is of great value and utility for striking terror into the spirits. Wherefore, upon its being shown to them they submit, and kneeling upon the earth before it, they obey.

You also find two plates of lead and some tools; you begin to work diligently urged on by a dark unknowing at the edge of your mind asking questions about the meaning of these dismal settings and why you should even be doing this. Upon completion, the first inscription fades and you notice another plate and a second inscription.

The Third Talisman of Saturn—This should be made within the Magical Circle and it is good for use at night when thou invokest the Spirits of the nature of Saturn.

Industriously, you set to work and upon completion you begin to hear strange whispers in a language you cannot understand. You find a bowl and burn a strong-smelling incense while passing your talisman through the fumes. With that, the resources are exhausted and the day goes dark as the whispering increases.

You chant names of power unsure of who you are calling to, only hoping that the master of the pond will appear. Your surroundings become darker, giving contrast to a circle that glows brightly, you step within it fortifying yourself as the winds cool and the earth faintly tremors. A layer of shadow peels from the pond's surface. The water remains undisturbed as it drifts over towards the burning incense. The dark form breathes deeply, taking in the fumes. You examine the floating slender body cloaked in a flowing darkness as it turns to face you, revealing an angry hooded countenance.

The spirit begins to walk on the ground approaching the circle and with it, darkness blots out what little light the grotto's atmosphere could not shield; slowly the darkness overcomes your surroundings and encases the circle. Immediately, you kneel in reverence for the pond's master's attendance. The shade stops and the darkness recoils. Pulling back its hood, it rounds the circle's boundary, its head twisting revealing another face. The head continues to twist, and you count a total of four furious faces of this dark being.

"You summoned me," it declares in a haggard tone.

"I would like to know more about your nature," the spirit responds on page 221

Hourly Interactions

All the planetary symbols starting with Saturn are engraved in a circular pattern on this door. You walk into a crowded classroom with many students. Looking closer you notice hourlies also in attendance. A Mercurial floats beside a seated young man and a Solar hovers over top, probably refusing to be positioned on the same level as everyone else. A trio of gorgeous Venereans become playful with many of the students. They sing hypnotic, harmonious songs and glide around the room causing many of the students to begin to clap and hold a rhythmic beat.

"Enough!" storms the teacher entering the room. "If you can't keep your hourlies under control they will be exorcised and you will be expelled."

"Ah, sorry about that," states a well-dressed gentleman at the back with a top hat and elegant cape flowing to his knees. Raising his hand, which was arrayed with many expensive gems and well-cut rings the Venereans withdrew to his side.

"We are going over the study of the natures and attributes of the Hourly species of spirits. We know that the realms home to Hourly spirits are composed of shifting waves. They exist wrapped around the physical universe and orbit in conjunction with a planetary anchor. We know that once the earth and planets formed, these other worlds became more solidly attached to the physical realm. As life started to evolve that attachment manifested, though in a weak state to certain mineral and vegetative life. As we evolved and the primitive humans contacted these beings, a symbiotic relationship was formed that solidified their attachment to our realms. We have since then grown and developed alongside each other."

Wow never expected this, you think as the lecture continues.

"Gradually, the links became so strong that even many ancient forms of worship and science incorporated them as integral parts of mythology and medicine. The more we interact with them, the more they impart greater awareness and ability and we in turn, feed them from our life essence. This gives them a means to remain in the everchanging physical realm and acquiring sensations and experiences unviable to them on their home worlds."

The teacher pauses several students raise their hands. One is selected and stands to address the instructor.

"Why do they crave experiences in our realm? What does it do for them?"

"These experiences, combined with the proper mixture of offerings, usually incense appear to be to them, addictive. Whenever an Hourly engages with a human in the physical plane, they gain sustenance that is unavailable in their own world. Like a cell feeding on vitamins: nutrients that need to be acquired from outside the body. If they did not contact us their activities would become severely limited and their senses dull. They become virtually unaware of their own sentience. It was us who made the first contact and we imprinted on this race of beings a greater consciousness."

The hands drop, obviously satisfied with the answer the teacher provided.

"Moving on," he continues. "As their name implies these spirits' activities are restricted to orbital position of the Earth in relation to the planetary surroundings. They are limited by the hours of the day and can even weaken their incarnation into the physical realm if they are summoned at incorrect times. People who come in contact and build a rapport with a certain specific Hourly race become known as *specialists.* They take on characteristics both physically and mentally related to their Hourly hosts. The Hourlies do everything they can to preserve their mortal because these interactions are a direct benefit to their wellbeing and advancement."

The teacher waits for questions. Finding none he returns to his lecture.

"We divide these specialists into classes: For the *Saturnites,* Hermits with a transcendent paradigm develop. *Mercurials* create Alchemists who can literally bend reality in strange ways and produce wonderous phenomena. *Venereans* produce Enchanters who can speak to the inner heart of men and produce living illusions that people most desire. *Jovials* who lead in the understanding of creating powerful artifacts and discovering treasures. *Solars* generate the great Hierophants; proud and powerful. *Martials* excel in forming soldiers and warriors of super-human capability and *Lunars* who give rise to the Hedge Witches and Clairvoyants."

Abode of the Blessed
Earth
Water
Air
Fire
Heaven of the Moon
Heaven of Mercury
Heaven of Venus
Heaven of Sun
Heaven of the Mars
Heaven of Jupiter
Heaven of Saturn
Heaven of Firmament heavens
Crystalline of the mobile

The class listens intently to the teacher, focused on every word as he explains the natures of the beings they have become so familiar with.

"Now, there is a negative side to this. Should you be unworthy; maybe with corrupted thoughts, or have strange desires, you summon the Hourlies at the wrong time and force them to do things against their nature they *will* turn on you. They are far more intelligent than we are with one hundred times the power. The only reason they don't just kill us is because we gain so much from each other. If you betray their trust, they will turn on you without mercy or remorse," the teacher states, ending there.

With that, the class ends and the students pile outside thanking the teacher. The Solar spirit exits through the ceiling while the Mercurial disappears in a colorful burst. You follow the other students and depart for the hallway.

Impressed by the class, you follow the herd of students to the next room on page 501

OR

Go back and try to learn more about the subject from the teacher on page 527

Turning to the wall you notice a beautiful golden talisman hanging above a burning censor. The incense fumes swirl around and entangle the talisman.

"What does this do?" you ask the Solar.

"You are drawn to the first of the gifts of Sol and our greatest possession. Take hold of the key carefully," the Solar responds.

You gently take up the talisman looking over the engraved face and study the words along the border.

"With this the angelic spirits do reverence on bended knees," states the Solar.

The rising incense from the censor leans over following the talisman as you continue your examination. The smoke gradually begins to surround you and before you can react the talisman shines while the whirling incense quickly reflects the light, engulfing you in a sparkling cyclone.

The funnel of shimmering smoke picks up speed eventually moving so fast that it becomes impossible for your eyes to follow. The light from the talisman envelops you as the rapidly spinning cyclone pulls all the light around you into itself. Reaching a critical speed, it erupts sending the shimmering lights to fixed places. In shock you realize you are no longer within the temple, you are suspended in space and observing the solar system around you. Clothed in the sun you notice the planets in orbit around you.

Looking upwards you view the stars in the distance and the glory of the cosmos is revealed in all its vast magnificence. Stranded and immobile you become fearful of the possibility that you may be imprisoned within this splendorous backdrop.

"Why am I here?" you ask.

From beyond and around you the orbiting planets and constellations reply, "You have made use of the Solar key."

"Who are you?"

"We are the forces that uphold the universe. We sustain the physical reality through the concourse of the stars and the motions of the planets. Our operations maintain the world with natural laws that keep balance."

Awestruck by the encounter the truth of their words becomes apparent and visible. You take notice of natural phenomena that has profound effects all over the galaxy. The hidden powers that control gravity, weather patterns, the growth of plants and influence the discoveries of technology, the dreams of children, the destinies of nations and the outcomes of wars are all visible to you.

The threads of fate lay bare, filling your head with so much knowledge that it feels impossible to retain as more is constantly absorbed. From the activity of the most distant star to the smallest cellular life nothing escapes your notice.

As your comprehension reaches critical mass you call out to the primordial movers, "What is my role here?"

The orbits cease and the planets became more visible with Saturn above, Jupiter and Mars flanking your left, Venus below, Mercury and the Moon holding to the right.

"Our activities though vast are constrained to the laws that govern the world. We cannot act of our own will; while we keep the physical world in motion you are to rectify it."

With these last words you notice yourself still clothed in the sun rising above the planets and the stars falling below you. For the first time, you see the Earth and a magnanimous glow emanating from you alter its form into a clear glowing crystal sphere.

At once you feel the weight of your mortal body draw you down and you begin to descend, passing each planet on the way. You pick up speed and finally drawing near to the Earth you fall through a blinding light and emerge within a library, sitting at a table with drawings of seven colorful spheres. Atop the table is a smooth, round, crystal ball on a stand that you are gazing into.

A distinguished hooded gentleman enters the room, "Welcome to the mansion. I know this has been confusing but I promise, if you follow my directions this will all make sense very quickly."

Pulling a book from the shelf he places it in front of you and opens to a section titled **ARS PAULINA**.

To read the book turn to page 523

OR

To ask about your location and the person instructing you turn to page 484

"Where am I?" you ask uncertain of how you ended up in the library.

"In the mansion," replies the hooded man. "You've been brought here because you have a special talent and only here can we make use of it."

Not understanding at all what this special talent is you turn to another matter, "And who are you?"

"I am the Master of the school," he says calmly.

Realizing who it is you are seated before you rise quickly from your chair. The master raises his hand, silently urging you to remain seated.

"The Solars transported you here after you used their first talisman," he states, pointing to a small golden plate with archaic figures and letters carved into it. You hadn't noticed but it was right beside you.

"With this," the Master continues, "the angelic spirits do reverence on bended knees."

You think back to your dream like experience. It was difficult for you to understand what it is you saw. Was it a dream? Some sort of astral projection? Were those beings that you encountered angels?

"You have a rare and powerful opportunity to work with forces that most magicians never truly reach the competence to commune with," he says. "It takes a very specific aptitude to befriend the higher forces and make use of the gifts they offer."

Interested, you dig further to get answers, "What gifts do these beings offer?"

The master looks back at you as he sits across from you, bridging his hands.

"The abilities we have are dependent on control over and interaction with spirits. These spirits are divided into many races: the elementals which dwell wherever a large concentration of their primal material is present. The Sub-lunars, whose world exists parallel to our own, like a shadow cast from the physical plane. Hourly spirits exist in hidden waves that rise and fall with the orbit of the earth and the Celestials whose extra-dimensional existence connects through the motions of the stars in relation to the position of the planets of our solar system."

He pauses letting you absorb the information.

"Each one of these realms is linked to the other the same way gravity exists in our world. These worlds are bound together, the upper most world we can contact is called the hyper cosmic realm of the Celestials. They consciously exist to repair and maintain reality and instinctively adjust existence to keep it from imploding, not unlike trees in our world which prevent erosion."

He slows down, letting you keep up with this descriptive cosmology which until now has been a complete mystery. When you feel you've grasped the details you nod for him to carry on.

"They maintain balance on a cosmic and encosmic level. Should someone have talent to contact them *and* should they respond positively that person could do the same on a personal level."

"What does all this mean?" you ask dazed by the overload of information.

"Why don't we read the book," the Master encourages.

Opening the old volume and feeling the thick worn pages you notice the margin notes and the complex formulas within. You read for a bit and then, hopelessly defeated look to the Master who gives a half smile and on ***page 523*** ***begins the lesson.***

Death of the Righteous

You engrave the astronomical and planetary figures into the small metallic plate using high-end tools. These are not crude talismans, but rather elegantly crafted signets. They are used once for a specific purpose and having accomplished their task they expire and become simple trinkets serving only as a memory of the operation.

Staring at your laptop you notice the astronomical calculations and check over the entries to make sure everything matches up. This operation relies on precision more than anything else. One wrong assumption and the whole process will fail which is not an option.

Bringing the plate over to the table of practice you find the appropriate sphere that matches the planetary sigil carved onto the plate and after placing it in the sphere with your right hand over top you calmly stare into the crystal ball mounted on the table.

"I call to the guardian who answers me with shining lights. You have been my protector and guide for much time; all I ask is that you allow me to pass on the kindness to others in need."

You feel warmth in your hand as the signet surges with power. With confirmation assured you take the signet, wrap it in silk, pull the fifth talisman of Sol and focus on the area where you are currently needed. Within a short time, you end up in a hospital. Wearing a lab coat you blend in with the staff, many of which are happy to see you.

"She's in here doctor," says one of the nurses guiding you into the room where a woman lays ill with a terminal sickness.

Quickly, you place the signet underneath her pillow and sit by the bedside. Turning inwards you begin to commune with the celestial influence that begins to permeate the room.

It is written "Precious in the sight of the LORD is the death of His saints." You are forever and eternal but still you find value in a devoted mortal soul. Today you are being denied this loved one. Allow an extension of your mercy to swell through my work. I am the heaven breaker. The Holy gates are to remain closed. Your ranks swell with the legions of the pious, leave us this one a while longer so that we may benefit from the grace she draws to Earth.

While you wait by the bed of this woman, she lays still, hooked up to many monitors. After half an hour she awakens. The doctors rush in to check her vitals, many of them smiling at each other as they notice the drastic change in her condition.

You rise from your place and proceed to exit as you pass the thankful stares of the nurses and the nodding approval of the medical professionals. Pulling the Solar talisman again, you quickly return to your home and check your laptop.

There are pleas for help. Messages from different clinics and hospitals.

A cancer patient. A man with a young family, daughter of four years and loving wife. They are waiting on ***page 496***

OR

A soldier in the middle east. His injuries are life threatening; a suicide bomber took out three of his regiment and left him bathed in shrapnel. He is being treated in a military hospital overseas on ***page 499***

OR

Also, a local case, a police officer injured during a recent gang raid. If you go to him, you may be able to reach the other two in time as well. He is currently housed in a nearby hospital on ***page 557***

A Deeper Look Within

You push into the classroom against many students trying to exit. By the time you find your seat you realize this room is mostly empty and many of the students look to be older and more mature.

"So, we are all that's left," states the teacher. "That is to be expected. To scry deeply into the further realms is to transform one's self. We leave things behind sometimes small memories or an entrenched thought process. We are different when we return and the loss of self can be a frightening experience for the unprepared."

Waving his wand, numerous smaller crystals glide through the air while four-legged stands scurry through the class. The stands wrap their supports around the desk legs and climb up, then halt before the students as the crystals settle gently atop their stands.

"We are going to do a group session. It won't be to any other worlds. We will be land spanning. We will see peoples and objects of rather close proximity. Remember, when you observe *any* being or object while scrying you will not be using your normal senses. You will see things like the persons past. If they have a strong ambition or desire it will be relayed clearly. Sometimes, even potential or likely futures are revealed. This type of disclosure will happen fast. It will be as if the knowledge is instinctive. Keep calm and you will be able to disseminate the information correctly. It will be hard at first, but if you are to be proficient at this you must control your emotions and discipline your minds. Gradually, should you excel in this practice, you will be pulled inwards and see a purposeful future that awaits you *and* the steps you need to take to make it happen."

The teacher waves his wand lightly and gently taps the large crystal in the center of the room.

"Focus on the crystals in front of you. This is individual, I will be watching you as you peer through reality. If things get too intense, I will pull you out," he states.

You stare into the smaller crystal before you. The world begins to slowly blur around you and only the thin distorted lights picked up by your focused senses remain. The images before you erupt and fill your perception. A laboratory materializes around you and you watch as Mercurial spirits diligently perform their duties. A sensation of pain quickly emerges and you turn your attention to a mortal consumed with agony. You feel the thoughts of helplessness and fear as the Mercurials remain indifferent. In shock and unable to intervene, you watch as the mortals skin turns to stone creating a grotesque statue. The terrible feelings do not recede after the transformation. Your scrying leads you deeper. This person is alive! Trapped and alone. Feelings of betrayal and failure abound as your instinct to intervene is undermined by the fact that you cannot. Your mind scrambles to find a way to assist this wretched individual but with your scattered focus comes a loss of position.

The world distorts and you emerge outside a barracks. Roman solders are training.

Have I gone back in time?

Seeing the intense training and the surroundings it becomes clear that this place is on the property. It's part of the school. You watch as a mortal fighter spars with a Martial spirit spear and shield. You feel the pride and determination push the fighter's limits. It is a glorious sight watching the battle between teacher and student. The fighter learns as the battle progresses and the Martial, despite being pleased with his student, wants to push the fighter even harder. Excited by the fighter's achievements, you watch hoping to see further progress, but again, your focus is scattered and the world alters.

Reality reforms and you view a beautiful crystal pyramid that refracts the light channeling rainbows throughout the area. A fantastic party is happening. Food and wine abound while music plays and beautiful Venerean spirits dance with mortals. This time you are determined not to lose focus. Controlling your emotions and your thoughts you remain as stoic as possible. You notice juggling and acrobatics as well as a large feast and many joyful patrons amidst a well-kept garden. Ornate fountains come into view and you notice a Venerean maiden with a mortal staring into the waters. Water spirits swim within and you peer deeply, keeping control of your emotions.

Why am I working so hard to notice these things? I wonder if I can keep control and scry closer to the mansion?

You continue to scan the waters and notice words forming. While it is another language, the letters that seem familiar.

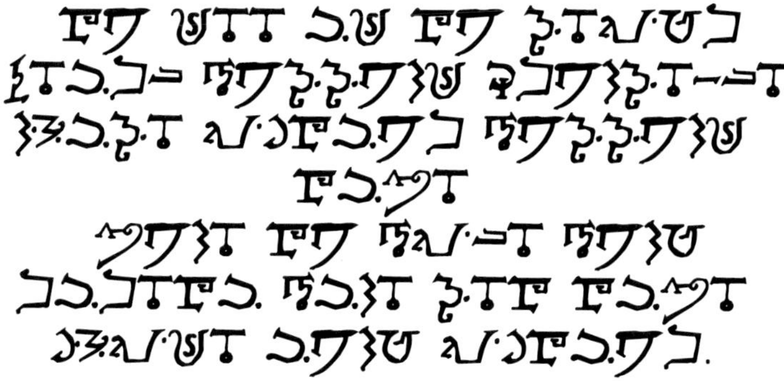

Keeping your concentration proves to be too difficult and you are thrust again into a different scenario. You see hooded men wearing dark masks. They stand before a Sub-lunar with three heads: A toad, a cat, and a strange goblin-like face. It has the body of a spider and is accompanied by a stern looking man with long hair and a grim face. The masked legion and many other Sub-lunars kneel before them.

Who are these?

"These are the Cult of the East," you hear the teacher respond. "Try not to bc too alarmed. I'm just monitoring your progress. This cult hopes to usurp control of the property and take over the mansion."

"Can they do it?" you ask.

"Look into their abilities," instructs the teacher. "See for yourself."

You calm your mind and feel the levels of the demons and the cult members as well as the cult leader and notice that while they are formidable, they are disunited. The demons serve their king and the cult members are mostly weak minded and brainwashed. You turn to analyze your teacher and realize quickly that the power emanating from him can easily overtake the entirety of the cult.

"Why are you allowing them to do this?" you enquire.

"The Sub-lunars which they summon will be seized by the mansion for further use. They are providing an invaluable resource. Our heroes will be tested against them. They will help us refine what will be some of our more valuable assets."

The word heroes throws off your attention and your mind's eye is rapidly transported to a room where a dark, fierce looking hooded man wielding a sickle stands alongside a melancholic beauty in a full-length silver dress which shimmers in an eerie fashion. A svelte, intelligent looking character dressed in a medieval laboratory apron follows next in line. Beside him, a well-dressed gentleman with a top hat wearing luxurious rings which line his fingers gives a cunning smile, while a Roman soldier stands in front of what you can only assume is a female archeologist.

Your body weakens and you awaken in class together with the other students. The teacher keeps a calm look as he notices the students in their weakened state.

"In the beginning your minds will have some trouble adjusting. Over time and with practice, you will be able to hold your attention for longer periods of time. For now, let's rest and move onto another class."

The teacher moves to you and directs you to a door far down the hallway with the marking of an octagram. You follow the teacher's advice and arrive before the door on page 527

Your mind ceases to flow with the tides of thought and the current of time releases its hold. You are no longer cast about aimlessly moving among your inclinations. Now you seek a balance with whatever situation arises. You move smoothly and slowly seeking a specific yet abstract goal.

Where can I gain control?

You move down hidden corridors and passageways unknown to most students of the mansion. You begin to sense what you are looking for passing through a wall to a room with no doors but filled with valuable treasure.

You see first a signet ring with a pentalpha on a stand. Then, you pass several wands on custom shelves. A pair of what look like slippers with strange writing and then you find a solitary quartz stand and a cube with symbols of unknown origin.

This is it!

The world will no longer distort or thrust you into a timeline against your will. You found what will give you control.

Remember the way here, you say forcing the directions into your sleeping mind.

With that, you calmly slip back into a normal state of consciousness and wake in the class. Quietly, you slip out of the room and head down a hidden course which now, has been engraved into your memory from the previous experience. Burning some incense, you call up a Solar spirit and request transport into the room.

Within an instant, you are exactly where your mind's eye left off and you make your way toward the object of your desire.

The cube glows unevenly and is active. You are not sure what it is and unsure how to figure out what it does.

"I wouldn't do that," states a calm voice from behind, cutting you off.

It is the teacher from the scrying class.

"This is a special device that only one master has ever used successfully."

"What does it do?" You demand, openly fascinated by the magical equipment.

"It allows the user to travel through time…"

Turn to page 534

The requested information of his birth month, day, hour, minute, country and city were punched into the calculator giving you the proper planetary and astronomical sigils and powers to call upon for the healing. You work tirelessly and after the signet is engraved you bring it to the table of practice and place it within the correct planetary sphere, with your right hand over top, invoke your guardian celestial through the crystal and feel the surge of power enlivening the plate.

Quickly you grab the Solar talisman and invoke the Solar spirits. They take you to the home of the dying man where you are greeted at the door by his family. His mother, an attractive older woman named Jessica leads you to his room.

"They said you can help. We've tried everything! Please, for my son...," her voice breaks as an outflow of tears and sadness cover her face.

"My lady," you respond confidently, moved by her sincere plea, "it doesn't matter what disease he has, which organs have failed, or even if his skin were entirely burned from his body, I will heal him."

Temporarily reassured, you are led to his room. The sick man lays unmoving and unconscious, thin and withered from his condition. It barely phases you. Taking the signet, you plant it underneath his pillow and begin the oration.

Lord you've placed us in a world with strife and war. Today the mortal souls vulnerable to fates design defend their own against an immanent end. We've been helpless against your unfeeling creation and our weapons have failed. But now, they have me, you've empowered me so that fate may be turned and a new destiny manifest. I will not leave this war until all the soldiers are healed.

You wait half an hour at the dying man's bedside watching as his circulation improves, his color returns and his breathing evens out. He awakens and rises from his bed.

"I feel... weak, but... better."

"You need a good meal," you respond. "Your mother can provide for that. Otherwise, you should be fine. I'll call in three days' time to check up on your progress."

He notices the signet you left under the pillow and studies it intently.

"It's no longer useful but keep it. That small item allowed for a powerful force that would normally be unseen by mortals in this life to be drawn into our world."

The relatives are called in and, in a rush, tears of joy and a flood of hugs as the family is returned whole with their father. You leave as you always do, quietly and without the need for praise. Stepping outside, you take the Solar talisman and return home.

Arriving, you check your laptop and see that the soldier has died. There is no need for you to make the journey. It was always the same, for everyone you save many others die.

Why does the balance of life maintain itself in such a cruel way? I can only treat one person at a time. For every victory there is always a loss. I'm never going to get ahead.

You feel fate laughing as you check for updates. A community of farmers in a distant country is starving. Their community is suffering from a severe famine and people have begun dying. To help their plight turn to page 519

OR

The officer mentioned before seems to be stable but has mysterious wounds are not healing easily. Your help is requested at the local hospital on page 557

OR

A child has been rushed to the hospital with pneumonia. If you don't help now, we will lose her. To give aid, rush to page 521

Assault Against Death

You prepare a signet and are transported by the Solar spirits. Their proud chorus always singing a powerful song as they bring you from one place to another and then back again. You never tire of their dignified patronage.

You arrive at the military hospital and are immediately welcomed by the medics. They bring you through rows of injured patients and into the critical care unit where you find your target.

"Have you ever worked on something like this?" asks one of the medics.

"I've seen more blood and tragedy in my last year than you have. The broken have nothing to fear," you explain as you place the signet beneath the soldier's pillow, "whether an illness or injury, by me, they will be remade whole again."

Is it to your benefit that mortals are destroyed? We only have one like him. Why loose the value of a human soul to eternity when the finite world has such great need. Today heaven's decree is cancelled. With this soldier we launch an assault on death to free him from his fate and preserve his infinite soul within our limited world.

After half an hour the soldier awakes and perceives himself to still be in pain. The trauma of the explosion has not fully cleared from his mind. The soldier starts to make requests for a memo to dictate his last thoughts. You stare down at him, grab him gently by the hand, "C'mon soldier on your feet."

You pull him up, he winces instinctively until he stands. His body still covered in burnt skin and bloody bandages acts as a deception to his true state. Surprised by his new sense of prime health he strips the coverings to reveal a perfectly whole body beneath.

The soldier shrieks with joy and disbelief. Even the medics and nurses around him marvel at the recovery. Euphoric about his second chance at life he hugs you so firmly it looks like he may snap you in half. You take your leave shortly after sensing you have others in need of assistance.

The police officer suffering from the wounds that wouldn't heal is still alive and needs your aid on <u>page 557</u>

A woman with dementia has totally lost her connection to her family and to herself. To be an aide to their plight move to <u>page 515</u>

You learn at your arrival that the child with pneumonia has tragically died.

Calling Forth

This class is divided up much differently than the others. It is an extremely wide room with intricate large circles engraved on the ground and names of power inscribed within them in mysterious lettering. The students take their places within smaller circles attached to the larger circle in the rooms' center. You find your way to a smaller open circle and notice triangles just beyond the boundary of the circle's borders. The teacher's assistants then hand small well-polished crystals out to everyone.

"Let the doors be sealed!" booms a loud strong voice followed by a loud clanking of the doorways locking. "Place your crystals within the triangles outside your circles," the teacher orders.

Incense from an elaborate censor is released and low incantations are chanted as the teacher, standing in the center of the room, begins the lesson.

"Do not leave your circles for any reason," he began. "We will be summoning forth a variety of Sub-Lunars for the sake of expanding our knowledge and enhancing our communication with the demonic hierarchy. By this we will accelerate our own intellectual growth and not only make our group more cohesive but be better able to control and interact with the spiritual realms as a whole."

With that said the chanting increases and the teacher as well as four others assist him in calling out intricate conjurations which draw the presence of numerous entities. The class is ordered to place their crystals within the triangles just beyond the edge of their circles.

An abstract darkness fills the chamber and then separates into different forms. A dark language which is impossible for humans to speak resonates throughout the room as the formless darkness flows throughout the chamber. Gradually, the numerous dark forms are compelled to drift down toward the crystals and settle within the polished stones causing the transparent stones to look tarnished by the interaction.

The teacher orders the class to gently retrieve the stones from the triangles and attempt interaction with the creatures stored within.

509
504
511
514
506

Staring into the crystal you quickly realize that something has been captured within. The dark, shifting mist-like substances seem to be testing the strength of their new confinement. You gaze deeply into the crystal until the lights dim and a shadow surrounds you.

Looking around you find yourself in a blurred and darkened realm. Around you waves of shadow are being blown by a strong wind but you feel no impact from the air currents. Before you, an old, cruel looking man with a thin goatee rides up to you on a pale horse.

I'm not in the class. This must be mental. Am I inside my head?

"You are," replied the old man in a dour tone. "Thoughts are not silent here. Nor are they your own. You might as well speak."

"Okay... umm... How are *you*?"

"How am I? I'm trapped in an inanimate object conversing with what might be a retarded mortal and you ask how I am? Really? This is why I was summoned from my homeland? For this!?"

Humored by this demon's sarcastic personality you restart with a more focused question.

"What name do you go by?"

Looking down at you from atop his horse and staring sardonically he replies, "Name? A human cannot possibly hope to pronounce the name from my home tongue but your kind call me Furcas."

"Tell me what are your specializations? What do you impart to *my* kind?"

"Let me tell you something. *I* teach philosophy, astrology, rhetoric, logic, cheiromancy and pyromancy and I impart them with perfection."

"That's pretty loaded," you respond. "How can you even begin to explain those things with the short time we have? I don't even know what some of those things are."

"Of course, *you* don't. But we are within a mental sphere where an eternity can fit within an hour. Plus, I'm betting the faster I teach you the faster this all ends. You ready?"

"I am."

Your brain is physically rewired and new connections develop within your mind as your cognitive functions increase and your intellectual capacity expands considerably. You have a deeper learning infused within your being and discover deeper truths about the connections between the various realms and the physical world. How to speak properly with the different supernatural races and the movement of natural forces as well as the reasons why and how they are linked together. Nothing is denied you and when it all seems to overwhelm your limited faculties, you are thrust back within the circle. Confused, you look around the chamber, seeing the other students. Some are in shock, others elated. You have a lasting imprint of extra-sensory knowledge that leaves you humbled and silent as you sort out the new concepts imbued within you.

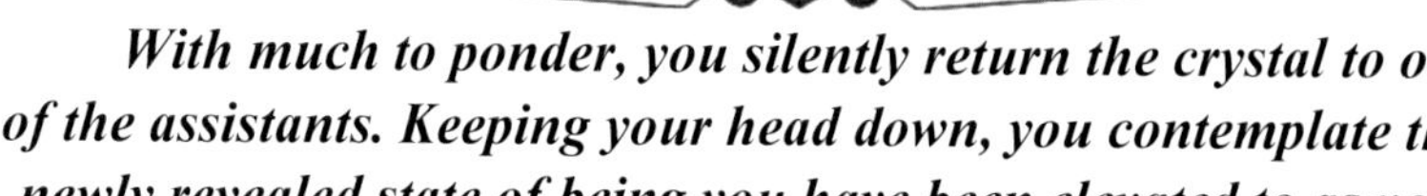

With much to ponder, you silently return the crystal to one of the assistants. Keeping your head down, you contemplate the newly revealed state of being you have been elevated to as you leave the classroom for page 435

Gazing deeply into the crystal you fall into a trance as you watch the darkness trapped within swirl and shift. Eventually you enter a dream state and find yourself alone on a flat desert plane. The horizon stretches on giving no sign of any discernable end.

Am I tripping out?

From the distance, a bull marches slowly towards you. You stare, unsure where this bull would even come from.

Is there a farm nearby? You wonder as the bull stands before you.

The bull is huge, its horns look like they can spear you straight through but its body language suggests a docile creature, at least so far. It slowly looks up at you…

"Shit! What the hell!?!" you shout noticing this bull has a human face.

"Okay, keep it down," he responds as you remember you are in the conjuration class and this is a Sub-lunar. "This can't be that bad," the bull responds, "you summoned me. I am just trapped here."

You calm down quickly trying to remember what you are doing this for, "What do I even call you?"

"Well normally we start with hello or thank you for coming, but since we are off to an energetic beginning the ones before you have called me Marax."

"Marax," you repeat. "Tell me, what am I doing here?"

"Me tell you?" says the hybrid bull. "You're the conjuror. You called me"

He's right. Damn it.

"Well then," you start, "what is it that you do?"

"I'm so glad you asked," replies Marax, who then opens his mouth allowing a waterfall of liquid to pour from his throat along with several well-polished gems. "Go ahead, ask me anything about these."

He prances excitedly, waiting for your response.

"What is all this?" you enquire, unsure what exactly to do about the cowman throw up offered before you.

"Precious stones of course! I can tell you everything about them," he states assuredly.

"Well, we've come this far," you admit, retrieving one of them. "How about this one?"

"That is Lapis Lazuli, great for increasing vision. Check this one out," he said, gesturing with his hoof. "It's a moonstone. Mooon stone. Get it?"

You laugh at the Sub-lunar's wit.

"Here let me show you some more," Marax digs his hoof into the ground, allowing some of the phlegm or, whatever it was that he exuded previously to flow into the trench. A small variety of herbs immediately grows forming a small garden.

"Ask," he states confidently.

"This one," you point.

"Hawkweed. Great for calling forth Lunar spirits."

You point to several others and many of the gemstones. This Sub-lunar delights in sharing his knowledge and explains everything in a way that makes you wiser for the encounter.

"You want to see something really amazing?"

"Sure... what else you got?" you asked casually.

Marax gestures raising his eyes. You look at him confused. He lifts his head upward signifying something, while you look back perplexed.

"Look up man," he specifies.

Glancing upwards, you are shocked and surprised as the starry night sky is only meters above your head. Immediately, Marax begins to joyfully explain the constellations and their influence over various operations. The sky shifts and moves as he highlights specific orbits and the numerous effects they have. This goes on to the point of excess and it becomes almost impossible for you to hold onto the information.

Gradually, you revive from the trance, standing in the chamber with the other students questioning the reality of your experience.

"Thank you," you whisper to the crystal before handing it back to one of the adepts and make for the exit with a deeper understanding of stones, herbs and astronomy. You never asked or even knew that most of this learning was accessible but you leave the class with a deeper understanding of the inner nature of the world.

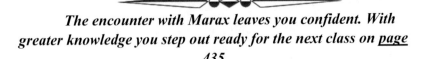

The encounter with Marax leaves you confident. With greater knowledge you step out ready for the next class on ***page 435***

The crystal holds a darkened stain that fluctuates, expanding and contracting like a swirling mist. As you fixate onto the moving darkness a shadow is cast over the chamber encompassing all the other students and teachers in the room.

A large snake carrying a man on its back emerges from the darkness. The man appears strong in stature and has two glittering stars on his forehead. These features distract you only momentarily as you notice his two extra heads emerging from his neck: one a serpent the other a calf.

"Why have you have summoned me?" he asks, in a rigid tone.

"Maybe I could get your name first," you state, unsure of exactly how this is supposed to go.

The Sub-lunar gives you a silent, dark look. His six eyes silently analyzing you before answering.

"The name I go by is Aym and *you* are unworthy of summoning me."

The large snake he rides on hisses violently as he raises what looks like a piece of wood to the serpent head attached to his body which breathes over it, lighting it aflame. With a wildly violent thrust the fire spreads throughout the class burning the darkness. Surrounded by the flames you attempt to subdue the demon with threats.

"I set fire to great places, cities and fortresses. You will not repress my power."

Torched by the flames you let loose a horrid scream, the encounter is dispelled leaving you mildly burnt, your clothes smoking but back to the safety of the classroom. You drop the crystal which has heated up as smaller flames continue to burn your clothing. Looking up in shock you see that the room has returned to its original state.

The teacher gives an arcane gesture and the crystal floats toward him and in his hand the fire is dispelled.

"When dealing with Sub-lunars, you must learn to control your emotions."

You nod unable to continue and move to exit the room, pained more in mind than body, you learn a valuable lesson: never to casually approach the creatures of demonic heritage.

You resolve to leave the class as quickly as possible before some other random three headed beast tries to burn you alive.
Move out to page 435

The dark swirling matter in the crystal continues to spin and coil; it looks to be moving away from you as you focus on it.

You don't have to be scared, you think as you see the shadow amass and begin moving back towards you.

It grows as it approaches your position.

Wait, oh shit. I'm inside the crystal, aren't I? This is probably going to suck.

A large flying dog with a powerful wingspan encircles you while it glides low in an obvious show of force. It's speed and aerial advantage cut you off from any form of escape.

It lands in front of you with its gigantic wings almost hugging you before they withdraw neatly behind the creature.

"Okay boy, what's your name?" you state.

"Oh, you're funny," the demon replies. "My name is unimportant. What I can do for you, however, will make *your* name unforgettable. You will be exceptional in the mortal realm with none to rival you."

Unimpressed by the Sub-lunars rant you repeat the demand for his name.

"Glasya-Labolas is how the mortal tongue renders my likeness," he states unmoved.

Wow, so he looks like a dog with wings of a gryphon, talks like a Hogwarts professor and has a name like a Middle-Earth elven prince. Of all the things I've encountered this guy is taking first spot in the high-end weirdness contest.

"Alright, you know what? Show me what you got," you insist,

causing the hybrid Sub-lunar to puff up with pride.

"I'm a master of bloodshed and manslaughter," claims the demon, flexing his wings causing his feathers to unsheathe into a sharpened form and bringing them down. He narrowly misses your body and slices through the ground.

"Hey!" you shout as you dodge a bladed wing. "I said show me not *kill* me."

"My lord, you have my intentions all wrong. I *want* you to see what I can do or in another way, not be *seen* at all."

What the hell is wrong with this son of a... Oh no...

Your arms begin to disappear and your body becomes completely transparent.

"I can make you invisible so that you may better stalk your prey."

You try to back away as a bladed wing is raised impeding your escape, "I can also see what is to come. Invisible or not, your movements are well-known to me."

"Well... This has been very enlightening," you express calmly as a row of bladed feathers stare you in the face. But would you be able to do anything else other than killing *me*?"

A wide toothed grin breaks over the demon's face as he answers, "My Lord, have you ever heard of philosophy, arithmetic, grammar, rhetoric, astronomy, logic, geometry, music and dialectic?"

"I have heard of most of these, sure," you reply.

"Well, now, you know them all, as well."

In an instant, all the arts and sciences are crammed into your mind Your thought process is quickly overwhelmed and you feel past memories being pushed out of your head. You now have a erudite spirit, eloquent speech, knowledge of the world of spirits and their many divisions. The concourse of the stars and planets is perfectly known to you, but your name, where you are from, how old you are, your parents and much of your youthful memories will need time to resurface.

You come out of the trance and emerge back in the class-room. Still infused with the massive influx of new information that is gradually sorting within your mind. You walk out of class, trying to retain your identity alongside the greater learning that has swallowed up your memory. Exit the class to ***page 435***

A strange child-like voice emanates from the distance as you peer into the crystal. You watch as a magnificent bird with feathers made of fire arises from the darkness. The chamber disappears and it seems to be just you and this amazing flying creature. It sings the sweetest songs before you. It is hard to speak for fear of interrupting the beautiful outwardly serenade.

"Do you… have a name?"

"Most refer to me as the phenix," he replies, as he flies around you gracefully.

The song carries on as you fall into a deep trance completely captivated by the ethereal melodies playing before you. Awakening from the enchantment you are laying on the floor of the classroom.

Was this a dream…?

One of the teachers approaches you bidding you silently to return to your feet. "It isn't supposed to be *them* who subdue *us,*" he states coldly.

Embarrassed, you rise to your feet and pass the crystal back. The song remains in your memory, even though you have no ability to express what you heard, it stays in your mind as a reminder of the experience with the mythical firebird.

You exit the class quickly to page 435 with the beautiful song repeating in your head.

Whole Minded

After preparing the signet and charging it on the table of practice, you gather your materials and summon Solars to transport you to the retirement community. You pass by the front desk, with many of the nurses smiling as you arrive. They know that if you are present then hope and health follow.

Entering the medical care area, it becomes immediately clear that, the patient is old and constantly repeating a single word while wandering around aimlessly. There are always nurses close by as her condition has worsened significantly in the last few years and now, she barely remembers her close loved ones. Her moments of lucidity are few and brief.

Normally, the patients sleep. This one is wide awake and focused on some unknown situation, wondering energetically in a broken state. As per your request, the nurses find a wool hat for you. Fastening it to her head with the signet underneath, you then stay beside this woman.

Here before You is a mind broken and with no chance of repair. But the limitations of man are of no consequence for this gathering. Her life is still her own and before you, with her I call to witness the powerful correction of her organs and restoration of body so her soul may be fully expressive. Make her whole in body and in mind. Rewrite her future so her present adjusts to a glorious ending rather than a shameful death.

Walking with her through the halls, she continues to repeat a single phrase. It is hard to believe that at one time she was a teacher. In an hour, her family will be coming. In half that time, this woman will be transformed into who she was before.

You sense the presence of the higher force; the Celestials are repairing her mind as you walk. The staff and other patients go about their day unaware of the powerful beings called to attendance. You sense their movements and are accustomed to the pressure they exert. If the others here were to feel the eminence of these beings, they would be unable to move. The Celestials' entire existence is for the sake of keeping physical reality stable. Because their responsibilities are so vast, they rarely ever encounter lesser creatures personally. You ponder the depth of your ability to mediate between the smaller mortal world and the colossal higher force. Your efforts give the Celestials opportunities to fix things they would never even detect and repair humans from diseases that would otherwise be uncurable.

"Where am I…" came a voice from beside you.

It's been half an hour already.

"Is this a hospital? Where is my daughter?" she turns discreetly towards you with a look of sheer panic as she lowers her voice to almost a whisper, "Am I wearing a diaper?"

*****

You return home to find messages and numerous pleas for help.

It doesn't matter that I never take a day off or that I work endlessly. I am always constrained by the hours and the balance of life; this world and its complexity is always going to be more than I can handle.

The community that was struggling has broken apart and scattered. There is no need to respond to this message.

The police officer is in critical condition now. He was injured during a massive gang raid and his wounds will not heal. The local hospital is not far away, rush to page 557

Form Ranks

You study for hours under the guidance of the Master. You learn that the reason you have been chosen is because the person best suited for the position has died. You learn about the nature of the spirits and the sheer volume you will be summoning. You notice that the ritual outlined will have other champions also participating but due to time constraints you only learn your portion in the operation.

Early in the morning the day arrives and the Master, who will be leading the ritual himself assures you of its success and to trust your training. You and the Master are transported by Sub-lunars to the site. A large encircled octagram is engraved onto a cleared off flat piece of land. You hardly notice any of the others who will be working alongside you. The Master directs each of you to your positions with his wand, pointing where you should stand. You struggle to keep all this information straight in your head and are terrified of screwing up.

The Philosopher's Stone is brought to the center of the octagram and once activated it seals the circle. Each champion is pointed to again with the wand and they burn incense according to the Hourly race they wish to attract. The spirits arrive in legions producing phenomena and numerous unnatural occurrences. Eventually the wand is drawn at you.

You take a large amount of the spicy incense and set it to burn. You are ready to call forth Martial Hourlies. The dangers inherent are made clear but you feel a powerful reassurance from the Master. The Martials arrive in force. Powerful spirits with the appearance of Roman soldiers march in well-ordered columns. There are many of them, more than any mortal could easily control, all attracted by the power of the Philosopher's Stone. The Master aids you in directing them into a neat border around the circle.

The Master turns again aiming his wand at each champion and instructing them to recite a phrase to strengthen their control over the Hourlies. He points at you and gives you the words which you repeat with authority, "Martial soldiers, the incarnate anger breaking mountains and drying the oceans, I call you whom every planetary creation fear to be by our side."

A loud militant shout of acknowledgement resounds as they beat their shields. The earth tears from its place and levitates above the circling legions of hourlies orbiting below. You feel the power concentrate and then release spreading from the school throughout the world.

The Martial influence enlivens the strong among our species to become even stronger. They overcome obstacles that would prevent them from achieving a greater mastery over themselves and the natural forces. You feel their collective strength as they augment greater power into their being.

FIN

Forestall the Defect

You are transported by the Solar powers hearing the prideful and energetic operatic songs they seem to be perpetually singing about their greatness and land in a simple, agrarian plain on a continent far away. You are greeted by people in a Land Rover and a person speaking English thanks you for coming and invites you aboard. You drive down a lonely countryside and arrive at a village filled with starving adults and sick children.

"I had not prepared to heal all these people," you state. "Is there aid being sent here?"

"Rations arrive every four days," replies your guide. "But they are barely enough and sometimes they do not even show up. We need this drought to stop and for our land to produce. We have some money saved up. You can take it all."

"No need," you respond. "Just give me a day and a field you would normally farm with."

At the field, you pull out the signet and bury it in the sand. You sense the immense powers funnel from their usual place in the universe and concentrate into the area below. Of course, despite the initial fusion, there would be a time lapse needed for the seal to take effect. With the Celestials present you set into prayer:

An injury in the land is an injury to its people. Being bound to the source of their suffering is going to destroy their unity. May it be that as Your will is followed above in heaven let it be so here on earth. Let the shortcoming of this land and the poverty of these people be reversed. Forestall the defect that is coming to drive them apart and allow new growth and bountiful life to take hold.

You wait half an hour; a small thin plant grows from the ground. A pleasant song that only you can hear echoes through the plain. You smile rising and turning to the guides. "We need to give the land some rest but by tomorrow we will see improvements. You are taken to a small hut where you settle down with the villagers and sleep with the sunset.

The next morning, the children are excited and the adults cannot believe that the crops have returned. It is as if the land regained its strength. Though not yet ready for harvest it is evident that the plants are growing. The dead trees come to life and the water from the wells is purified. You marvel at how this renewed water also acts as a natural medicine against diseases the which had spread throughout the area. It is a miracle in the sight of the village. Their fortunes had been reversed, their needs replaced with abundance.

With that you trail away and when no one is looking, you use your talisman to be transported back to your home.

You notice a message that has been on your screen for a very long time. You hoped it was just a common mistake and had deferred to other more serious cases but this one has not gone away. An officer that fought during a gang raid in the city has wounds that will not heal and needs your help. ***Move to page 557 to aid the officer.***

Whole Again

Stepping into the hospital you are led by a nurse to the room where a young girl is hooked up to medical equipment as a worried mother sits by her bedside.

"Are you the specialist?" she asks in a panic.

"I am," you respond with a powerful confidence. "I'll need a little time with the young lady," you state, as the nurse urges the mother out so you can work.

Taking the signet, you place it under the little girl's pillow. She starts to wake, but you can tell she is visibly weak.

"Rest easy little one. This will be over soon."

One whom you love is sick. Restore this broken little one. Make her and her family whole again. There is no gain in losing the potential of one so small. Preserve her lifeforce and increase your providence. Let hell swallow its own while ours escape. Your justice has been perverted, today we correct nature and set the laws aright. Let the heartless nature of this lower world be overcome by the power and mercy of this upper force.

You wait half an hour and the little girl rises, as if coming out of a deep sleep. She pulls the signet from under the pillow and the mother enters, swiftly taking hold of her daughter, grateful to still have a living child. The young lady shows her mother this signet she had been sleeping on.

☿♊

☉ ♄ ♃ ♂ ♀ ☽

“That you may keep,” you state as you prepare to exit amidst the eternal gratitude of the family.

While preparing to travel back to your home, you are interrupted by a small bird. A tiny sparrow swoops down and lands close by, drawing your attention.

“You are needed at the mansion,” it says with a youthful high-pitched voice.

“An Allatori,” you respond curiously. You have not seen one in years.

“The Master needs your particular skills. Please make your way back to the mansion quickly,” with that, it flies off dissolving into the air.

You have never been called to the Mansion like this. It could be seriously important since the gates to the school had been sealed a long time ago due to an internal war. Perhaps the fighting is finally over, with the Master and his students prevailing.

What could the Master need me for?

Summon the Solars to transport you to the school on page 442

Looking through the book it seems interesting at first, but as you delve into the manual you notice it is more about math and formula than specialized intoned words of power and the natures of spirits and other-dimensional creatures. The instructions for the creation of specialized talismans are straight forward but after that follows a complicated array of complex observations and calculations.

"I don't understand this," you state.

"Most people don't," the Master responds. "It takes a bit of learning to understand all of the higher knowledge here. But you only have to learn it once. After that, the amazing reservoir of power is at your disposal. The Pauline art is a rarity among us. Even the people with talent sometimes drop off seeking after lower spirits and quicker gains."

"What sort of powers does this art offer?" you ask.

"Well, these beings are not as malleable as the Sub-lunars, nor as widely specialized as the hourlies. Their natures do not permit them to be restricted or bound as we typically do with the other summoned beings. They have no perceivable form so we use a crystal sphere for communication. They can only be reached during precise hours and *only* for specific functions. Their presence can undo any Sub-lunar phenomena and if the correct hours are observed Sub-lunars may be completely subdued. These beings revel in their natures and should you try to avert them from their normal tasks they will strike at you in horrendous ways. It is these forces that control maintenance of the cosmos and as such when they are channeled, they offer willingly their natural rectification to anyone who can call on them correctly."

You stare almost blankly unable to fully comprehend what the Master is telling you. You have questions but are too afraid to voice them for fear of sounding like a fool.

"Once you understand this knowledge you will be able to act as an agent for these beings spreading their corrective influence on an individual level."

You nod, not totally understand but willing to learn. In front of the Master, you become a blank slate. You learn of the astronomical correspondence with planetary orbits and their confluence. You learn the values of occult hours and after the mechanical lessons are drilled into you a period of intense purification is observed. You eat little and are secluded from the world wearing only linen tunics and bathing in water collected from naturally flowing streams.

After this you return to the library you first emerged in. By now, it has become your home. Taking a seat at the table where you first began your learning you open the Ars Paulina to the end of the book study the final part of your course: a prayer to invoke the celestial influence that governs your year, month and day of your birth. All your training has led to this. You have the hours and times correct and now with incense burning you prepare what you've been reciting and customizing for the past weeks.

"O thou great and blessed angel guardian, vouchsafe to descend from thy Holy mansion which is Celestial with thy holy influence and presence into this crystal stone, that I may behold thy glory and enjoy thy society. Aid and assist me both now and forever, descend and be present I pray thee, I humbly desire and entreat thee that if ever I have merited thy society or if any of my actions or intentions be real, pure and sanctified before thee, bring thy external presence hither and converse with me, one of thy submissive pupils, in and by the name of the great God, whereunto the whole choir of heaven sings continually, Amen."

With sincere devotion you recite your prayer and stare into the crystal sphere. You see strange lights which sparkle and beam. Gradually after this the celestial force that governs the date of your birth makes an appearance. You calmly declare your intentions laying yourself bare towards the power before you, hoping for a positive response. Recognizing your devotion, the celestial transmits itself from the crystal illuminating your mind, taking away all that is obscure and dark in your intellect, giving you a greater knowing in all divine sciences in an instant.

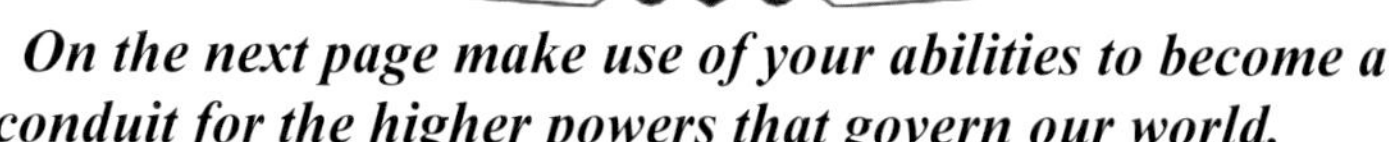

On the next page make use of your abilities to become a conduit for the higher powers that govern our world.

A
D
O
N
A
I
TURN TO PAGE 487

Advanced Ritual

A door with an octagram etched into it opens before you as other students plow into the classroom. At the front, the teacher orders everyone to take their seats.

"Alright, this is an advanced class. If you haven't mastered the basics not much here will make sense," she began.

She has a raspy voice and despite her trim figure her face reveals an elderly look.

"Why do we use rituals and why do they work?" she asks.

Her question silences the class who, legitimately have no idea why their abilities work the way they do. Without wasting time waiting for a student to answer, the teacher explains, "The reason ritual is so successful is because it imitates the native habitat spirits are from and allows us to create a temporary space for them to dwell and by this, we form bonds with them through binding, sacrifice or seals. Does anyone know the difference between ceremonial operation, ritual practice and conjuration?"

Again, the class remains speechless.

"You sure you're an advanced group?" she added. "*Ceremonial* is a series of rituals normally done at a particular time of the year, normally seasonally, to ensure greater success in magical operation for a long period of time. *Ritual* is the drawing of influence from the other realms into our own and *Conjuration* is the summoning of a particular entity for a specific purpose."

The class picks up and you learn about the planetary timelines and obscure astrological hours that can make a ritual slightly more effective. By the end of it your head is spinning. When the class is dismissed, the teacher pulls you aside into a back room where the hooded teacher from other classes you have taken is waiting. Your current teacher introduces him as the master of the school. He claims to be selecting students for an intense operation and three spots remain available. Wanting to please the Master you agree and he shows you a table with three types of incense. You must choose one to participate.

To select an incense for use, move to the pages listed.
The first is pungent and overwhelming on page 545
OR
The next is a strong spicy blend on page 517
OR
Last, a sweet smell, with a slight hint of rose leads you to page 547

From the Dream

You see your way up a hill to a large Victorian mansion. You hear the words whispered, "they have been expecting you."

When you awaken, you rush under the pale moonlight trying to hold in your mind the directions given. The sun rises and you see the mansion. Rushing forward, unwilling to waste another second you charge uphill straining your body to reach your destination.

The door opens and a well-dressed gentleman with thin glasses steps out. See if he will invite you in on page 465

Returning within, following the Master, a gathering is called where you and six other occultists are summoned to a room within the mansion and the door is sealed behind you.

"We saw a sample of what is to come," the Master begins. "the world will soon be changing and things we can't expect are going to happen. We need a group of devoted specialists to handle damage control."

"Wait," states a beautiful short lady with long, soft black hair and grey eyes. She is dressed like an archaeologist wearing a suede brown hat. "You mean like superheroes? I'm totally in."

A strong looking, well-built man dressed like a Roman soldier chimes in next, "But the school is our priority. If it is defended properly, none of *this* will ever escape and harm the outside world."

Equipped a, golden shield on his back over his red cape which caught your eye as it reflected light from within the room.

"My friend," asserts the Master, "our work here is ending and soon our gates will be open. What has been happening here for these last years will become a regular occurrence in the outside world."

The group goes silent at the prospect of the average person having to encounter the darker aspects of this place.

"So, what is our role in this?" asks an elegantly dressed gentleman who smokes a thin pipe while awaiting a response.

"To be a preventative measure before things get too far out of

hand. To correct problems that arise when great changes occur. Each of you has a specialized function within the Great Work. Others will have these inclinations as well," explains the Master as he sets his gaze on you. "You've set the foundation for great expansion into the minds of all mankind."

You turn seeing the dark, fierce looking hermit standing alone behind you. To your right, a melancholic beauty in a full-length silver dress that shimmers in an eerie fashion. Beside her, a shy, svelte intelligent looking character dressed in a medieval laboratory apron considers the options presented. Before you, the well-dressed gentleman gives a cunning smile, while at your left the Roman soldier holds ground anterior to the archeologist.

Instinctively, you hold up your talisman and reveal the hourly spirits also present in the room. They do not swarm around or battle each other, nor do they move from the side of the mortal they are attached to. You observe, noting the similarity between the special organization and your table of practice.

The master, looking on, holding a crystal ball in his hand proclaims, "It looks like you understand the purpose of our gathering. Now," states the Master as he raises the crystal ball, "would you like to see the future?"

FIN

Walking the Halls

Passing through the hallway again, this time in a crowd of eager students who seem to know where they are going and determined to get there, you let the crowd filter out. When everyone has entered their rooms, you examine the doors, studying the engraved marks that adorn the entranceways, trying to decipher what their meanings may be.

You first pass a door you passed by once before with the planetary symbols engraved in a circle. Move on to page 476 to enter this room.

On another door, a triangle with a circle within positioned above a snake eating its own tail. Enter here on page 501

On another door you notice a six-pointed star enclosed in a circle. To step into this class, move to page 549

"More specifically it reshapes time. You won't travel through it. Once the box opens, it will contort time in such a way that the choices the person operating the box could have made become reality," the teacher instructs.

Confused and unsure what to do next you await further instruction hoping that whatever he says next, makes the situation a little clearer.

"Any choices that would have been available in the past will become your dominant reality *and* once used it adjusts even your inner discernments. It is highly likely you will not even remember using the box."

"Who was the master who used it successfully?" you ask.

"That would be me," responds the teacher.

"What changed during your use?" you ask.

"Well, none of us are exactly sure. In this timeline I never did the experiment," he claims. "There are many other adepts who attempted to use this relic. But none of us can remember their names. Time has re-shaped to such an extent that any memory of them was wholly erased."

"Is there a way to use this safely?" you question.

"This particular contraption works exclusively on the user. You won't change history or any other major event. It will work within your lifecycle so you won't end up deep into the past or far into the future and it functions based on planetary and astronomical alignments," he explains. "However, the alignments are complex and the effects produced are, as of yet, unpredictable."

You ponder the words of your teacher and watch as the glowing box transfers between the different symbols. You want to use it. The ability to live another life, even an unpredictable one, is very alluring.

"The recent alignment of stars has reactivated the box," the teacher maintains, "if you wish to utilize it just brush your finger over a glowing symbol. However, even at my level *and* despite me using this before, I cannot predict the outcome for you."

The cube glows and the symbols radiate a dim ghostly light. You know that once you select an option, your entire life will be reshaped. If you so choose, walk away onto page 527 and be at peace.

OR

Lightly move your fingers over a symbol of your choice when you see it glowing.

♂ ***reality shifts to page 148***

♀ ***the timeline is altered as you are transferred to page 405***

Trace your finger over the border and allow the power emanating from the cube to transport you to page 449

Scrying and Omniscience

The doorway engraved with the hieroglyphic eye opens and the place almost seems deserted. A few robed figures sit at a distance from one another. The chairs are placed in a circle around a tall pillar with a large crystal ball in the center of the room. It's quiet. You see the teacher walk in from the opposite side of the room. All the students present immediately jump to their feet and bow. Once the teacher takes his place by the pillar everyone sits. You recognize the teacher's assistant as the floating gentleman that guided you into the mansion.

The teacher raises his hand and the floating gentleman lifts a large flower: a white dandelion, with a densely packed head full of seeds ready to germinate.

"Everyone," calls the teacher with a firm and confidant voice. "We will need to purify ourselves for this operation."

Unsure of what he is implying you follow the lead of the other students and watch as they partially strip, folding their clothes on their desks. The teacher produces a wand and the gentleman blows on the seeds spreading them throughout the room. With an expert wave of the wand the seeds, become floating drops that seek out the students. Many strike your face and coarse over your body as you feel the memory of stress and self-preservation melt away. You smile as your mind becomes a blank slate.

The students begin redressing as you revel in this new feeling. Pulling your shirt back on the teacher stands by the large crystal ball in the center of the room and addresses the class, "Scrying. This noble art gives us the ability to see beyond great distances into the past, the future or happenings in the present. It's level of accuracy is questionable. However, it also gives us an opening to peer into the realms of the spirits. Where conjuration brings the spirits to us, scrying brings us to *them.*"

A chill runs down your spine as you consider the possibilities offered by this discipline.

"Now remember," the teacher continues, "you must be purified thoroughly before undertaking *any* exposure to the outer realms. This is severely taxing on the body, so don't overdo it. You will be able to communicate with many of the entities we summon and even build a connection with them before calling them to sight. This will leave an imprint on your being. The callings will happen faster and more easily *and* you will be able to surpass much of the need to observe the hours necessary for those specific conjurations."

The teacher paces lightly around the pillar making eye contact with the students as he carries on with his speech, "In advanced sessions you will even be able to get inside the mind of the spirits we bind. We will be able to see through their eyes and feel sensations as they experience them. This practice is what turns an adept into a master."

"Now, when we begin, you *must* remain as calm as possible. Your senses are not fully adjusted to this level of consciousness. Each race communicates differently: some with strange vibratory languages like what you would hear in dreams, others with pictures and thoughts, while others still are composed of unmovable hive minds. These transmit information directly into your mind and will even temporarily replace your natural thought process."

The teacher raises the wand by the crystal ball, "we can talk for hours about this. But words will hardly match the experience. Keep your eyes focused on the crystal. Let your bodies relax."

The room grows darker as you stare. You begin to hear foul voices speaking a hoarse language with sounds a human would find hard to replicate. Long thin arms emerge from the crystal and the world around you disappears into darkness. The sound of the murmuring voices becomes clearer as glowing red eyes open around the class. You start to gaze off at the horrors slowly emerging around you.

"Eyes forward!" orders the teacher.

"You, a mortal, would dare to enter our realm without an offering," hisses a dark voice.

Darkness clouds your periphery and you can no longer see the other students while you try to keep aware of your surroundings. The teacher directs his wand at you and an invisible force takes hold of your head, pulling your gaze back towards the crystal. Yelling and wailing envelops the room. You hear the movements of the creatures and can sense their discontent. The smell of brimstone and sulfur overwhelms you.

"You will not trespass here. Your powers are useless. We see you. No life comes from the void. Only death."

The dark angry beings surge against the class. With a slight wave of the teacher's wand fire fills the class and engulfs everything, blocking the crystal, the teacher and the other students from sight. It takes a moment to adjust to the bright sea of flame. You notice numerous Solars rising from the endless sea of fire singing in a powerful chorus. An imposing voice resounds through the realm.

"Ours is the nature that all should behold and admire! Mortals, you have chosen rightly to step close to our being. Behold the full glory of the Sun!"

Wielding the wand again the room changes once more to a beautiful flowing crystalline setting. Everything seems peaceful, until you look down and see the entire solar system orbiting below. Afraid to move but also unable to look away, you see the Earth in its orbit along with all the planets and their moons in such detail that despite the beauty, you remain seized with fear that you could fall at any moment. You also see how the realm you are in supports the physical universe that all galaxies and stars are held up and ordered by the dimension you are peering out from. From within you hear words from the natives of this realm.

"Ours is the realm of eternity and the root of reality. Your shattered being cannot understand our unified intelligence." Their words implant thoughts and pictures that erase your memories leaving you with no doubt that they speak the truth. "For you to be alone with the Good as we are, your essence must be rectified. Yours is a fractured existence; ours is the correction."

Your fears totally subside as they speak. Their statements influence your inner being, leaving you feeling whole. The wand shifts again and the primordial paradise is dispelled.

"Well," states the teacher, "this has been your first step into a larger world."

Meditating on your recent mind-altering experience you let yourself settle, only now realizing the true potential that this school has to offer.

Turn to page 490 in order to remain in the class and question the teacher further about scrying.

Or

Move about with the other students to another room on page 533 and see what the rest of the school has to offer.

Picking up a cylindrical talisman, the teacher directs you where to place the ring and how to hold the object. Ready and in position you hear her tell the class that they must move closer to you then she whispers the first words into your ear, which you dutifully repeat.

"Ditau, Hurandos!"

You see the sky cloud over and violent lightning strikes the area. You watch in awe as the skies worsen and the lighting quickly becomes more aggressive. Eventually, the whole world darkens and the only light source comes from the electrical discharge spidering across the sky like a terrifying fireworks display.

In your ear you hear the teacher, "Direct it with the ring. *Always* retain control."

You hold the ring out and the lighting moves accordingly. You adapt and now you conduct this powerful force of nature as you would an orchestra. The teacher whispers two new words for you to recite.

"Ridas, Talimol!"

The skies remain dark as you hear hail strike the grounds surrounding you and the students. The power gifted over the hail allows you to concentrate the hail in areas to your liking. You smile as you direct the natural forces. Wild movements produce surges in the ice storm and more conservative motions keep it flowing evenly. The teacher again, speaks words into your ear which you say aloud.

"Uusur, Itar!"

The sky begins to calm but below, the world shakes. Responding with the ring on your finger you realize you are controlling an earthquake. The land splits and breaks. Movements of your hand shift and reform the landmasses surrounding the students. Experimenting, you raise your palm and beneath you earth rises from the ground, settling in the form of an arch. Unsure how to slow the terra formation, you listen carefully as the teacher again whispers

"Atrosis, Narpida!"

The Earth ceases its movements. The sky has fully cleared. You are thankful for the sun but this comes too late as an eclipse blocks its light. The teacher forcefully lifts your arm relaying the next form of nature overhead. What looks like a small meteor passes over the horizon. Shocked at the capability this talisman can impose you are silently unwilling to go any further.

The teacher sees your reaction and ends the lesson, retaking the talisman and ring. With the tools returned to the briefcase you finally notice the world around you. It has been ravaged. The whole area is devastated and overturned by your operations. You look back at the other students who are just as shocked at the situation. It is a miracle that no one was injured by the maelstrom.

"This is the true power of a seasoned adept and even more waits for the master. Always be aware of how much damage you can cause. We practice here so we don't make permanent mistakes in the world."

She concludes the lesson but before being transported back to the mansion a host of Sub-lunars begin repairing and restoring the land to its original condition.

Once back in the mansion the teacher suggests the Advanced Ritual class on page 527 saying it will give you what you need to finalize your skills. With a fearful heart and humbled mind, you bow and turn to the door. You are determined to better your abilities so as never to lose control of the powers you've cultivated.

Terror During the Clear Unfolding

You study for hours under the guidance of the Master. You learn that the reason you have been chosen is because the person best suited for the position has died. You learn about the nature of the spirits and the sheer volume you will be summoning. You notice that the ritual outlined will have other champions also participating but due to time constraints you only learn your portion in the operation.

The day arrives and the Master, who will be leading the ritual himself assures you of its success and to trust your training. You and the Master are transported by Sub-lunars to the site. A large encircled octagram is engraved onto a cleared off flat piece of land. You hardly notice any of the others who will be working alongside you. The Master directs each of you to your positions with his wand, pointing where you should stand. You struggle to keep all the information in your head and are terrified of screwing up.

The Philosopher's Stone is brought to the center of the octagram and once activated seals the circle. Each champion is pointed to again with the wand and they burn incense according to the Hourly race they wish to attract. The spirits arrive in legions producing phenomena and numerous unnatural occurrences. Eventually the wand is drawn at you.

You take a large amount of the pungent incense and set it to burn. You are ready to call forth Saturnites. The dangers inherent are very clear but you feel a powerful reassurance from the Master. The

Saturnites arrive in force; terrifying spirits with the appearance of liquid shadows sewn together. There are many of them, more than any mortal could easily control attracted by the power of the Philosopher's Stone. It is the Master who aids you in directing them into a neat border around the circle.

The Master circles again aiming his wand at each champion and instructing them to recite a phrase to solidify their control over the Hourlies. He points at you and gives you the words which you repeat with authority, "Cold Saturnites who have authority over every harm tear down the boundaries that interfere with our work and be not hostile to our direction, this day and all our days."

You hear their response. They speak in a language that causes the thoughts of your mind to decay. Your emotions are consumed, replaced by their melancholic inclination.

The Earth tears from its place and levitates above the circling legions of hourlies orbiting below. You feel the power concentrate and then release spreading from the school throughout the world. The Saturnite influence rips away mankind's selfish desires turning them to a state of helpless dependence on forces they do not understand but will gradually develop control over. You feel their mutual pain as they transcend their mortal limitations.

FIN

Love's Rapture

You study for hours under the guidance of the Master. You learn that the reason you have been chosen is because the person best suited for the position has died. You learn about the nature of the spirits and the sheer volume you will be summoning. You notice that the ritual outlined will have other champions also participating but due to time constraints you only learn your portion in the operation.

Early in the morning the day arrives and the Master, who will be leading the ritual himself assures you of its success and to trust your training. You and the Master are transported by Sub-lunars to the site. A large encircled octagram is engraved onto a cleared off flat piece of land. You hardly notice any of the others who will be working alongside you. The Master directs each of you to your positions with his wand, pointing where you should stand. You struggle to keep all this information straight in your head and are terrified of screwing up.

The Philosopher's Stone is brought to the center of the octagram and once activated it seals the circle. Each champion is pointed to again with the wand and they burn incense according to the Hourly race they wish to attract. The spirits arrive in legions producing phenomena and numerous unnatural occurrences. Eventually the wand is drawn at you. You take a large amount of the sweet rose smelling incense and set it to burn. You are ready to call forth Venerean Hourlies. The Venereans arrive in force. Beautiful spirits with the appearance of gorgeous maidens dance to an unearthly rhythm. There are many of them, more than any mortal could easily control drawn to you by the power of the Philosopher's Stone. Their singing makes you want to leave and join with them in celebration. It is the Master who aids you in directing them into a neat border around the circle.

The Master turns again aiming his wand at each champion and instructs them to recite a phrase to increase their control over the Hourlies. He points at you and gives you the words which you repeat aloud with authority, "Venereans who dominate the will of men and the love of women turn your favor towards us and bring us good fortune this day and all our days."

The Venerean maidens respond with a beautiful song of their own calming the nerves of all present, allowing you some relief from the burden of the Great Work. The earth tears from its place and levitates above the circling legions of hourlies orbiting below. You feel the power concentrate and then release, spreading from the school throughout the world.

The Venerean influence awakens a deep yearning for the unification of soul mates. People begin to naturally recognize their true love and see a growing value within themselves, others and the world around them. Beautiful artwork and music are produced in the wake of the Venerean dominion. You feel their communal appreciation for the splendor that now spreads throughout the planet as the hidden songs of nature are revealed.

FIN

Advanced Talismans

A six-pointed star etched into the doorway greets you as you enter. A large, custom made rectangular briefcase propped on a desk opens, revealing colorful talismans with rings placed beside them. There are twenty-four pairings and they each have diverse shapes from squares, rectangles to octagons.

"Everyone in!" commands the teacher. "We are picking up where we left off from last time. We are looking to produce and control powerful effects and changes in the physical world while bypassing any hourly restrictions. We are going to make use of the talismans today and give you a live demonstration of the advanced training. You will need *both* the ring and talismans to make this work. The talisman will generate the power and the ring will direct it. This lesson will be about use but the next one will be about construction."

You take your seat and notice that the room is surrounded by bookshelves. The door locks and you are enclosed within a library which is packed; even the ceiling is specially fitted to hold scrolls and parchment manuscripts.

Familiar spirits float up the aisleways asking students what they would like to be served, "Grimoire, manual, tome or treatise?"

Startled by this you pause, hearing the titles expressed by other students.

"I do need to increase my prowess in cheiromancy."

"Prudence in conversation with tutelary spirits."

"Lunar astronomy and its effect on the ritual process."

Oh man this is an advanced class.

"Tell, me," you say quietly, "what would I be able to use to maybe, become well informed about *this* subject in the quickest way possible?"

Without blinking or showing any emotion the spirit withdraws and you see a book floating towards you. It nears your desk and the familiar materializes, placing it gently in front of you before moving on to the next student.

Talismans and the many ways they are made: A picture book by Professor Andrews Michienzi.

Oh man, this is basically a children's book.

You glance within and find it's not as child-like as you once thought.

A B C D E F G H I J K L M N O P Q R S T U

As you curiously dive into the book the teacher calls the class to attention. She removes a single brownish-purple talisman with golden engravings from the briefcase. She holds it up for the class to see and displays the ring as well which she slides onto her right middle finger.

"Everyone, join hands," she orders, as the class follows her instruction.

Once the class is linked, she speaks, six words of power in a firm tone and in an instant the class and her desk are transported to the outdoors, somewhere deep in the property. It is a bright day and the class is positioned in front of the teacher.

"These talismans and others like them are able to produce profound results. There will be no hourly restrictions and there is virtually no limit as to what you can accomplish. You can hear the thoughts of individuals around you and from far away. You will know if any person approaching you has vile intentions. In addition, this will leave a visible mark on the person's face, which serves as a warning to your fellow magicians."

She holds up a white circular talisman with black engravings upon it.

"This one will allow you to learn any craft at a master's level. Simply hold this talisman on your person, place the ring on your finger, say the seven words of power and the craft you wish to master. Then, whether it's woodworking, welding, painting, handicrafts, construction, sewing, pottery, calligraphy or whatever, you will be a master."

Reverently, she returns the talisman to the briefcase and retrieves another, an orange talisman with silver engravings.

"This one is special and has saved many lives. You will, with gradual exposure to this tool, learn the names and properties of all known minerals, plants and herbs. You will eventually come to possess the universal medicine. There is no illness that you will not be able to cure and no cure will be beyond you."

Placing this talisman aside, she turns to the class again, "Consistent exposure allows for the best results. With these, you will open channels within your mind to allow you to master any of the sciences or disciplines available to mankind, but *only* if you're practice is consistent. The end goal is the have all of you ready to play your roles within the Great Work which is the true objective of any adept."

She returns to the desk and gestures to the case with the talismans.

"Anyone want a shot? You, you're new. Step up and take your pick," she says pointing in your direction.

You approach and two particular talismans catch your eye.

TURN TO
PAGE 543
TURN TO PAGE 555

You choose the circular one and take the companion ring that is planted beside it.

“Interesting choice,” states the teacher. “I’ll guide you.”

You place the ring on your finger and hold the talisman in your hand. She then gives you three words to speak which you repeat. You feel a tremor of power radiate from the talisman to the ring as numerous spirits manifest.

“Now,” she whispers quietly, “command them to build a ship so that we may fly through the air.”

Smiling, you give the order as they set to work before your eyes constructing a large ship. The teacher moves on to help others while telling you to survey the work. It is amazing. The spirits work more efficiently and faster than humans ever could.

Where are they getting materials for all this?

Within an hour the work is done and the entire class is invited onboard for a ride. On the ship, you are given the role of captain and decide to do a property wide cruise observing from the magical sanctuary a bird’s eye view. Absorbing the amazing view, you watch as the land shifts and the hourly territories move in an orbit around the mansion. The Mercurial laboratory gives off a huge burst of steam from its vent that transforms into innumerable small fish which swim in the air alongside your vessel. Dolphins are formed which leap over the span of the ship. Solar spirits accompany the class for part of their journey, eager to show off. They fly alongside leaving trails of dazzling light behind.

Eventually you land by the teacher's desk and the contraption is ordered to be disassembled and the spirits dismissed.

"This is only a taste of the powers you will wield," she explains, taking the talisman and the ring from you. "If you want to further your knowledge and control over legions of spirits, it would be best to step into an industrial ritual. Hold up, I'll take you."

Before you can react, you are back in the mansion before a doorway with a triangle enclosed within a circle. Within the triangle is a square and within the square a circle.

"I can only take you this far," the teacher asserts, "you have to walk through the door." Then she quickly leaves your side to rejoin the class.

To pass through the door move to page 527

OR

Follow other students you recognize to another class on page 490

Healing Wind

Arriving at the hospital you make your way to the room with the officer where you immediately notice what his true affliction is. Martial spirits surround him, breathing in the fumes from his wounds. Quickly you pull a Solar talisman and bathe the room with the fierce power of the sun. The Martial spirits are driven back. You start to work quickly.

"Nurse!" you call out.

"Yes doctor," comes a voice from a nurse answering your call as she quickly enters the room.

"What was the cause of this officer's injuries?"

"He was in a SWAT raid on the vigilante group that killed all those drug dealers and gang members. It was brutal. A lot of officers died."

Martial spirits were involved. They've attached to this man's life force. This will be a bit more difficult than I previously thought... "Okay, thank you nurse."

You place the signet under his pillow as you watch him shaking in his sleep. You know that no matter how much medicine they give him the pain will never diminish until you intervene.

Is it right that the injured be left harmed? You have not taken his soul but instead allowed his body to remain crippled by dark servants from a calamitous hour. Let a healing wind pass over this body and if this man's cries cannot bend heaven then I will move hell.

After half an hour, you notice the officer stop shaking. You remove his bandages to see his wounds still open but clotting. You lightly blow over the wounds and watch them seal up before your eyes. You continue to propel the Celestial force in a more direct manner with light exhalations. By the end of the session, the officer is made whole again.

You proceed to exit the hospital and are ready with the talisman when a well-dressed gentleman with thin glasses and grey hair approaches you. You know this is no man, he is a familiar.

"I do not have to suppose. You know why I am here and who sent me?"

"No, no you don't," you reply. "What does the Mansion need from me?"

The familiar explains the situation about an Hourly Champion that has been severely injured. Your help is needed and so you are transported by the Solars to** **page 467

See you in the next Dark School adventure Mark of the Adept